EVE OF FYRE

THE FIRES OF QAF: BOOK FOUR

KYRO DEAN & LAYA V SMITH

EIGHT MOONS PUBLISHING, LLC

This book is dedicated to unconventional families. The ones we choose instead of the ones we're given, though they can be (and often are) the same. Blood isn't the strongest bond. That comes from choosing each other every day. I'm choosing to make my family in the happiest, healthiest way possible, even if it looks different than I first imagined. Izkander and Mirri did it. And if you haven't, I encourage you to, too.

—Kyro Dean

For anyone who has ever felt suffocated by who they are supposed to be. And to those who have found the courage to reach for something more.

—Laya V Smith

BAHAMUT SEA
SHAMAAL SEA
Kurrun Muhamad
AHMAR
The City of Pearls
Al-Midina
JASRAIB
SHIHALA
ORKESH
VESPAR
Jurdan
MUTHALATH SEA
Muthalath Al'Ard
IZRAK
Gerib
Ashkab
Kufala
ELMARAN SEA
The Glass Plains
GHALUMA
ZABRIYA
EYRE
Wadi
GHARB SEA
SHARQ SEA
EASTERN ELM
WESTERN ELM
Bahamut
Shamaal
Gharb
Sharq
Janu'ub
JANU'UB SEA
The Nine Kingdoms of Qaf

The Royal House of Shihala

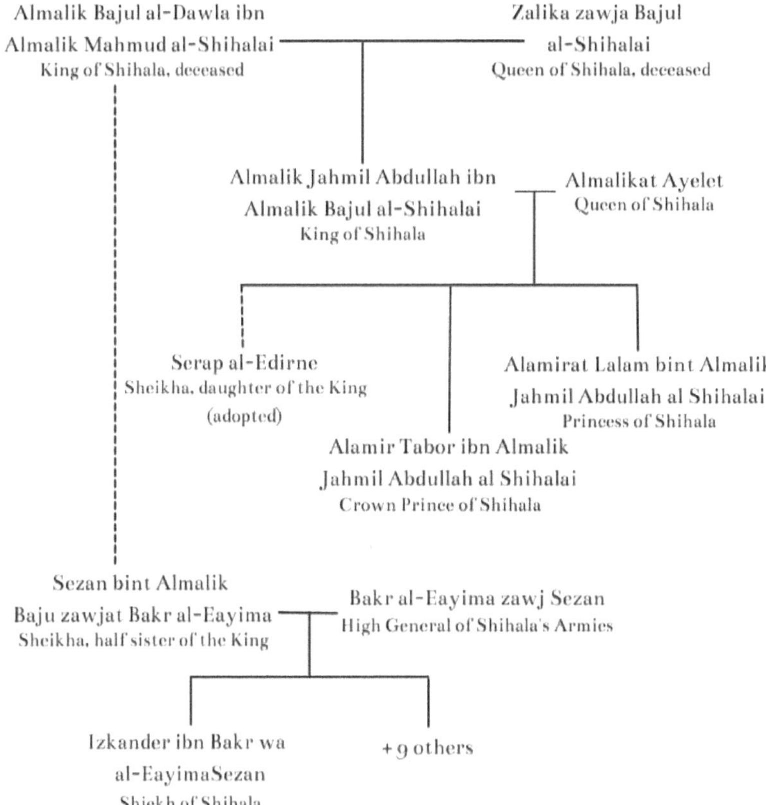

The Righship of Fyre

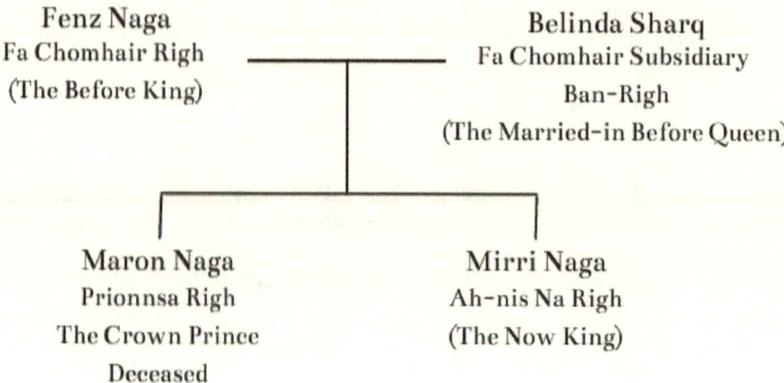

CHAPTER ONE

IZKANDER

IZKANDER WATCHED THEIR REFLECTION in the shine of the glass hutch on the other side of the dining room. By Heaven, what a beautiful sight. Flawless bronze skin glowing with a kiss of sweat, a figure made to be immortalized in marble, eyes that glowed like sunlight filtering through a verdant forest.

And she didn't look half-bad either.

They lay together on the dining table at the center of the room like an opulent banquet put on display. A domed ceiling of golden glass amplified the light from the four full moons shining in the sky above and cast it down upon them.

"Your skylight makes my abs look amazing." Izkander grinned as he tilted them back and forth, playing with shadows as he flexed and relaxed his muscles.

"You're an idiot." She giggled and slapped his stomach.

He smiled, but there was a pit in his stomach. He was doing it again, distracting himself. It was the reason he'd come here today, the reason he'd stayed. And now he was distracting himself from his distraction.

It was all he ever did, and none of it mattered.

Izkander tried to refocus himself on the moment by looking at the Ahmaran djinn's purple skin flushed with lilac and pale pink, her hip-length yellow hair so ratted with sex it barely hung past her shoulders.

He cooed and coiled his naked body tightly around hers. "You're so beautiful, Shayla."

Her muscles seized, and her head snapped up. "Did you just call me Shayla?"

"What?" All the air was sucked from the room, and he froze. He forced a chuckle. "You're crazy, Ya'el. I'd never call you that."

Her face twisted like she was chewing on a wasp, but with those swollen lips, bedroom eyes, and wild hair, she couldn't quite pull it off. "Get off of me."

"Okay." Izkander pushed himself up on his hands and rolled off the table. "Listen, I'm sorry about that. Honest mistake."

She came to her feet on the other side, one arm clenched to her chest to cover her breasts. "Are you still seeing her?"

"No." It was the truth, though there was a part of him that wished it wasn't. "Though I fail to see how that's any of your business."

Her bright green eyes widened and flashed white hot, but the blush of passion was still coloring her lovely lavender skin.

"You two happen to have very similar backsides."

"Excuse me?"

"Hear me out. You're both Ahmaran courtiers, right? So it's safe to assume you're probably some kind of cousins, right?"

Her upper lip twitched as lightning storms of fury brewed in his eyes. "Fourth."

"I knew it." Izkander snapped. "See, it's not my fault. It's in your blood. They're the same shape, the same size, they move the same way. It's uncanny."

Izkander chuckled at his own unintentional brilliance. "Get it?" He leaned in close and poked her with his elbow. "Un-*can*-ny? Do you get it?"

"Yes, I get it." She limply swatted him back.

"Good." He grinned and wiggled his brows. "Now, get that beautiful, purple doppelgänger of a backside back over here."

She stomped across the dining room and snatched her dress from the floor. He'd known it was a long shot.

"You're a real son of a snake, you know that?"

"I'm sorry. You look very similar from certain angles."

"You are never going to see any of my angles again!"

"Come on, Shayla. Don't be that way."

"Did you just call me Shayla again?" she shrieked.

Izkander bit his lip and groaned. Once was an honest mistake. Saying her name twice forced him to admit the very thing he'd been trying to avoid by coming to see Ya'el in the first place.

He *was* thinking about Shayla. And he'd been thinking about Shayla 4 degrees ago when he really, really should have been thinking about Ya'el.

He'd finally managed to get her out of his life, and now he couldn't get her out of his head.

"You filthy cheat." Ya'el cursed under her breath as she struggled to pull the laces tight on the back of her dress.

"Woah, woah, woah." He scoffed a few times as he waited for words to come. "Woah. I *can't* cheat on you, Ya'el. We're *not* together. We never have been."

Her eyes tightened with quick flares of black, orange, yellow, and blue light.

"Oh, man." Izkander squirmed under the weight of her stare. "What am I supposed to do with that?"

"With what?"

Izkander shielded his eyes and pointed. "That."

"My face?"

"No. Your eyes." He moved closer, squinting to survey the colors that moved like liquid over the backlights of her eyes. "I don't know where to start sifting through this emotional cocktail. We've got misery, humiliation, disgust, hope..."

The orange brightened. "Get out of my apartment."

"That, I understand." He snatched his pants off the floor and yanked them on, tying up the laces on the front.

Ya'el had always had a bad temper. Another thing she and Shayla had in common. Bad tempers, big hair, and beautiful backsides.

Izkander shook his head, snatching his shirt off the floor. "If it will make you feel better, I'll call Shayla by your name next time I see her."

Ya'el folded her arms across her chest. Long trails of sparkly green sleeves brushed the floor. "You mean the next time you sleep with her?"

"I don't sleep with her anymore."

"Really?" She glanced over her shoulder. "So you're offering to casually, off-handedly call her by my name in court? In front of people?"

He nodded and yanked his shirt over his head. It would serve Shayla right for the way she acted—flirting with everyone in court, letting every djinn with a pedigree take her for walks around the Royal Gardens. Worst of all were her constant hints—that she loved him, that she wanted to be more with him—only to run for the hills the moment he moved closer.

He was done trying to move closer to her, done chasing her. Never again would he allow any woman to make him look like a jealous fool.

Izkander heaved a sigh. His eye slid back to Ya'el. He hadn't understood why she was so upset, but that was the nature of jealousy. It didn't have to be attached to any actual feelings. It was all about ego.

That's what Aleamu Jahmil always said and he was a pretty put-together guy. King of Shihala and all that.

"I have committed a slight against you," Izkander said, doing an impersonation of his oh-so-formal uncle, "and I shall find a way to make amends."

The twist in her puffy lips and the new sparkle of gold in her eyes said she didn't hate the idea. "If you think that will make me forgive you, Izkander..."

"Ya'el, Ya'el... I will scream it from my loins like a pagan warlord greeting a red dawn." He curved his spine and threw his head back, fists clenched at his sides. "Ya'el!"

"Stop it." She turned away and shut her eyes, but not before he'd seen a smolder of deep red coated with sparkles of pink and yellow. The look that told him she still wanted him, even if she was just a little disgusted with herself. And he wanted her too, mostly because he didn't think he could stand being left alone with nothing but a head full of Shayla.

He stepped closer and tilted his head to gaze into her brilliant eyes. "Ya'el, I beg your forgiveness."

"Don't make that cute face at me."

Izkander got down on his knees before her, took her hand in his, and brought it to his lips. Then he lifted his eyes to hers and his cheeks dimpled.

Her shoulders shivered, and she moaned. "*Al'ama!* Why can't I stay mad at you?"

Smiling brightly, he leapt to his feet. She grabbed him and wrapped a leg around his waist, shoving her mouth hard against his.

The sound of the front door banged through the apartment.

Her fingers tightened on his hair. "My husband…"

"Your what now?"

"Oops."

Izkander stood frozen for a moment, then carefully unentangled himself from her and took a step back. His stomach hurt like he'd swallowed blue cheese that wasn't supposed to be blue.

"You have to leave right now."

"Yeah. That sounds right to me."

He scoffed and shook his head, then swept his belt off the floor and secured it around his waist. A steel sword hung over one hip—a long, thin scimitar from the Mamluk empire on Ard. He secured a strap attached to his belt around the opposite upper thigh that held the holster for an Izrakian matchlock pistol and kept it from bumping around too much so the powder didn't lose its pack.

He twirled a chair out from the table and sat down to pull on his boots, and Ya'el combed her fingers furiously through the tangled nest of her hair. "Go ahead. Take your time. No reason in Jahannam to *hurry.*"

He looked into her eyes and fastened the buckles of his boots at the same pace he always did, then stood and headed towards the door. He paused as a painful bubble rolled through his intestines. "I never agreed to help you cheat on your husband."

"Izkander, you can't—" Her eyes darted, and she snatched his upper arm. "He'll kill you."

Izkander put a hand on his hips and laughed. "Oh, I don't think so."

"I don't want you killing him, then."

Another twinge hit his stomach, each one harder and more nauseating than the last. Izkander set a hand on his abs and squeezed a fistful of his gray cambric shirt. "I'm not okay with this."

"Izkander, please. If he finds you here, he will divorce me. Think about my children."

"Gah!" The noise jumped from his throat, loud and uninvited. He twisted his fist harder against his trembling stomach. "You've got kids?"

"He's coming." She grabbed his arm, knees going weak. "Please."

Izkander glanced at the door, then back to her eyes, the taste of bile in the back of his throat. "How old are you?"

"Does that really matter right now?"

"You said you were nineteen. You know, a year younger than me? But you've got kids and a husband, and this is Ahmar where people don't get married when they're twelve. It's illegal."

She looked over her shoulder, back at him. Twice. Then she mumbled, "I'm fifty-six, okay?"

"Gah!"

She covered the top of her head with her hands and looked down. "I know."

"But you said… and I'm… you're fifty-six? You're already a quarter through your life." Izkander sighed and let his shoulders drop. "I'll go out the window."

"Wait. That window doesn't open."

"I'll slip to Ard, then."

"You can't. There are firewalls all around the building."

"Turn them off."

"I can't do that. It's security for the entire building."

"Then how exactly am I supposed to leave?"

The sound of footsteps drew steadily closer. Her eyes darted all around the room as she shuffled her feet. "You have to hide."

"Izkander ibn Bakr does not hide."

"Please." She grabbed his hands and pulled them to her chest. "Do this for me and I'll forget all about Shayla."

"This is way past Shayla."

Her eyes flashed, and that wasp-marked look returned with a vengeance. "My being married does not give you the right to call me by another woman's name after we've just had sex."

"My calling you by another woman's name after we just had sex does not give you the right to be married."

"What?"

Izkander folded his arms. "Doesn't feel so good, does it?"

Her eyes widened, and swirling in the bright green irises among all the other colors, he saw the beginnings of black terror. Without his permission, the thin shell he'd managed to build around his heart cracked open. He wanted to be angry and righteous and cold, but when she looked at him like that, all he wanted was to help her.

His gaze swept the room. As far as hiding places went, it was slim pickings. A low table made from a solid circular chunk of Sardar wood, pillows scattered around it, and a hutch against one wall large enough to hide in, but made of transparent glass so a moot point. He followed the line of some sheer curtains up to the dome of the ceiling.

With one hand, Izkander swung himself up onto the hutch, then he jumped and caught the ledge of some crisscross glass tiles with the tips of his fingers. Years of rock climbing with his old man had made his grip like iron and his hands rougher than raw stone. Dangling by one arm, he swung his legs back and forth for momentum. When his feet touched the tile, Izkander spread himself out like a star, pressing hard into the sides of the dome to hold himself up, and looked down at Ya'el with a wide grin.

Her eyes sparkled with blue. Then, the door flew open, and a big, burly, purple man wearing a Shihalan bastard sword made of obsidian stepped in. He was starting to bald from this angle. The years hadn't treated him as well as his fifty-six-year-old wife. She looked nineteen. But never could tell with djinn. He'd met djinn in their early hundreds who were still spry as kittens.

Izkander closed his eyes, willing himself not to listen to the conversation because it was none of his business. This was none of his business. What he doing here? Why had he come here?

Ya'el hurried her husband from the room. Izkander waited a few breaths, then hopped down gently, landing on one foot before the other. He took a step towards the back door to check for certain that the window didn't open. Ya'el didn't seem the type to know too much about her own windows.

"I'm just going to grab a drink," a man's voice said.

On the other side of the door, Ya'el protested. Izkander barely had time to do a double take before the door was thrown open and he was standing face-to-face with the man of the house. The djinn's eyes widened and flashed with enough anger to summon a crack of thunder.

"Ahmed, wait!" Ya'el screamed, rushing in behind him.

"What in Jahannam is going on?" her husband demanded, turning on her. Then he windmilled his arm back to Izkander. "Who is this *ibn el sharmouta*?"

Izkander's back tightened, and a light dusting of orange fire flared from his fingertips. He set them on the pommel of his sword and popped his neck. "What did you say about my mother?"

Ya'el inserted herself between them, facing her husband with her arms spread wide. The laces on the back of her dress were messy, and what this morning had been a braided coiffure was now hanging to one side and frizzy. Because he'd taken his time to get dressed, Izkander looked better, though the stinging in his lips warned him they were swollen. Worst of all, the room had that fleshy, moist smell that's only ever pleasant if it's your own. Their lovemaking had ranged all over the apartment, so the smell was faint but omnipresent.

Ahmed's eyes blazed like communal bonfires on the Moonless Night, as did his fists.

"*Alkalba*," he cursed and turned on his wife. "How could you? In the house we share?"

Izkander kept his hand on the handle of his sword, tapping his fingers in slow succession on the finger guard. Ya'el's plea for him not to kill her husband was sharp in his ears, though entirely unnecessary. He didn't go around murdering guys who were mad at him for sleeping with their wives. The situation had never come up.

On the other hand....

"Nobody calls my mother a *sharmouta.*" Izkander ripped the sword from its scabbard and lifted it in an open guard. "*Alhadhar.*"

"You're a dead man!"

"Stop! Please!" Ya'el cried.

"I will deal with you later, *waqiha*" He shoved his wife back hard enough that she stumbled and unsheathed his own sword. Then he advanced on Izkander with all the precision of a wounded heart, that is, none at all.

Izkander twisted to one side, avoiding the spear by an inch. As Ahmed stumbled forward, Izkander slapped his ass with the flat of his blade.

The djinn reeled back from the sting of metal on his sensitive skin. The hit wasn't enough to cause damage through his clothes, but it was enough to smart. Then he came in with another suicide strike. Izkander caught the obsidian blade with his steel in one hand. Sparks flew as rock gave way to superior metal.

The fight ranged around the room. Izkander had drawn his sword first, but never went on the offensive. Every parry, dodge, and foot shuffle made his stomach lurch. Soon enough, he forgot the sting of the insult and was left with nothing but shame and confusion.

There was no honor in this fight. He was the transgressor here. He was the villain. Besides, what was he fighting for? To steal away a woman he did not love away from her husband?

"Wait." Izkander put up his hand, but Ya'el's cuckolded husband was out for blood. He went for a decapitation swipe. Izkander narrowly ducked.

Ya'el screamed, "Ahmed, please! Don't hurt him!"

"You filthy cow! I can't believe you would do this to me again!" Ahmed howled like a bial'dabaye and turned on his wife, his sword raised. "I'll have your head!"

Ya'el cowered, and the horror of what was about to happen flashed before Izkander's eyes.

Without hesitating, he sliced his blade across the djinn's back, cutting through his leather jacket to draw a thin line of blood. The djinn's flesh fizzled under his steel blade. Ahmed howled in pain.

There was no honor in this fight and no way to win it. All he could hope to do now was protect Ya'el. And the best way to do that is to embrace being the bad guy.

"I don't care what she says or what you do!" Izkander cried and executed a convincing feint, leaving enough room for Ahmed to roll away. "Your woman will be mine!"

Ahmed slashed down with the heavy sword. Izkander avoided as easily as a namur jumps a fence.

He gave the djinn another slap with the flat of his sword to push him back, then reached a hand towards Ya'el dramatically. "I warned you, didn't I? I warned you I would not be stopped by locks or threats. And certainly not by your fidelity to this man, this joke of a man."

Ya'el pressed her hand to her chest. "I... what?"

"My passion for you will not be bridled by any means of djinn or heaven." Izkander opened his eyes wide, asking—begging—for her to understand. "I will take you by force if I must and declare to all of Ahmar that you are mine!"

"What are you saying?" Ahmed turned on his wife. "What is he saying?"

They both stared at Ya'el, waiting for her to say something. Izkander begged her with eyes to understand.

She chewed her bottom lip. "I... don't know."

"Gah!" Izkander clawed at his hair in frustration. "I broke in here to steal her, you tiny fool."

"Ahmed, forgive me!" Ya'el cried and flung herself to the floor before her husband. Izkander breathed a sigh of relief. "This man has been pursuing me, even though I keep telling him I'm married. Oh, Allah's mercy. Why won't he just leave me alone?"

Ahmed's eyes flashed brighter than ever, and his gaze turned slowly to Izkander, who fought to put on his most menacing smile.

"Lecher!" the djinn screamed and attacked.

Izkander slowed his movements, barely parrying each coming thrust, letting Ahmed drive him back towards the window. Then he hopped up on the sill and kicked the man in the chest, knocking him to the flat of his back on the floor.

Izkander sheathed his sword and threw his head back in a laugh. "You cannot be with her all the time. I will be back, and then this Ahmaran Maximiliana will be mine!"

Ahmed struggled to his feet and lunged, but Izkander turned and leapt at the window. The glass shattered. He tucked his head under his arms to protect himself, then straightened as he plummeted from the forty-fifth-story window. He closed his eyes, smiling as the wind rushed over him and apparated. The towering skyline of Al Madinat faded into nothingness as tingles swept over his body.

He tried, as he always did, to hold himself in the space between worlds—the Nameless Place, as his father called it. He was only a quarter lilu, so he didn't know if it was even possible for him to linger in that ephemeral place—like the fuzzy moment between sleep and awake. But he always tried, and like always, he plummeted to the other side like a stone through wet paper.

He knew from experience that trying to land on solid ground when you teleported while falling was incredibly painful. He materialized on Ard a thousand feet up. They shined brilliantly in the sky above, winking off the great sprawling blue ocean below.

"Squirt!" Izkander put his fingers to his lips and whistled so loudly it cracked the sky. "Come here, boy!"

CHAPTER TWO

MIRRI

MIRRI GAZED OUT OF her window, lost for a moment in the majesty of Fyre's Founding Festival. Green and gold banners draped every towering wall that lined the streets, and a lantern lit by the Eternal Flame filled every narrow home's window in the gray, stone city.

Her city, wrapped snugly by impenetrable mountains and wailing snow storms on all sides.

Her nation, warmed and kept green by the Origin's hot lava despite the white backdrop, its volcanic rivulets running all over Qaf.

Her kingdom to rule.

Or it would be by the end of the festival. She knew the woven fractals in the glass window were to blame for some of the romantic glow and stretch of colors playing out before her eyes, but not all. Not all. Despite her best efforts, Mirri still felt a childlike giddiness that she could never quite snuff out. It made her fingers want to tap the window sill and her toes to dance upon the stone floor.

Giddiness—and nerves, which her father found even less becoming.

"Child," he chastised, turning his broad shoulders away from the window to face her. "Your toes are curling."

She looked down at her bare feet, the bottoms of which held the mark of the true descendants of Marduk and connected her to the will of the Flame. While in the castle, she was required to always keep them bare..

"I am sorry, father. I will hold steady."

He said nothing, sweeping a skeptical eye over the armored golden plates that embraced her hips and protected her chest, that studded her shoulders before coiling down her bare arms, reminding everyone in Qaf she and her people were not djinn and not friendly toward them either. His gaze lingered on her drakonte-skinned gloves and under-armor made from Nafak 'The Coiled' who bore the first Righ. They had been passed down through every generation of kings and morphed to her skin in a way that was suffocatingly tight.

Mirri's cheeks warmed. Whether because she worried he found her lacking or the Eternal Flame did, she wasn't quite sure. Either way, her gut tightened.

Her father grunted at her adequacy. "Now that you have consumed the blood of the Origin and proven your legitimacy as the next true heir, you will no longer call me father, nor will the kingdom call me Righ. I will assume my role as Fa Chomhair Righ and be content."

Fa Chomhair Righ: the Before King. A concise way of deferring to the old ruler while bringing in the new.

Though, her brother, Maron, was supposed to have been the new ruler, not her.

"And I shall be Ah-nis Na Righ. The Now." She dipped her head, letting a sheet of fire-orange hair slip over her shoulder. "And I will be content."

"As it should be."

Her father faced the window, his back as stiff as his armor and his eyes as sharp as the fire-forged blade that hung from his waist. The thick tendon that pulsed in his neck softened the way it always did when his rigid thoughts became centered on one thing.

"I am sad for you about Maron." Mirri kept her eyes on a pair of deep-blue drakonte outside the window.

They flew lazily around the flag-hung arena down in the city square outside the palace gates. The snakes carried the first riders trickling in for the festivities from the outskirts of Fyre. Both were gilded in bronze and wore tasseled saddles adorned in family colors. The men on their backs beamed with pride.

"I am sad for Mother, also," Mirri said, "And myself."

"From the first day your mother held your brother in her arms, I knew he would be a great righ. *The* Great Righ that legends speak of. The one to raise our people up and let the Eternal Flame burn freely." His glowing eyes grew distant, like a small fire touched by rising light. "It is a humbling day when knowledge degrades into the delusional thoughts of a beleaguered father."

Mirri's throat tightened. Her father certainly did not think that about her. He also hadn't spent nineteen years raising her up to be the righ. All his training, attention, and love had been in Maron, who had never wanted to be righ in the first place.

No, that wasn't true. He *had* wanted to rule. He just hadn't been content with how. And the Eternal Flame could feel it. The second he broke the vow of upholding tradition, it had eaten him up.

In a strange and awful way, that gave Mirri hope. For all the things she did worry over—protecting her people, being an adequate righ, breeding the drakonte and keeping their bloodlines clean, and controlling the immortal beast that snatched children from Fyre's villages—keeping tradition was something she did extremely well. Hence why she was alive and Maron was not. Why she was alone. And why she would work to be the most reliable righ she could be.

Marduk have mercy on my errant soul, she breathed to herself. She missed her brother's smile.

Her father dragged his gaze away from the window and looked at her once more, not so distant a shine in his red snake eyes this time, almost warm. "But we are not to speak of the Fallen Ones. Contentment and a serious mind..."

"Preserve our ways and people," she continued the oath she had learned to speak before *mama* and *athair*. "May the Eternal Flame keep our minds sharp, obedient, and willing, so Fyre may persist."

The softness in his gaze lingered a moment longer, sending that same strange heat up her neck before the hard look of duty whisked it away once more.

He clapped a hand to his chest and bowed. "So let it be."

"So let it be," she returned. "And may Fyre be stronger for it."

He grunted again, and the gilded door to the observatory swung open. Mirri's mother floated into the room dressed in the soft gray Jerboa furs allowed to the role of Subsidiary Righ and Drakonte Progenitor. She carried an air of grace far more feminine and delicate than Mirri's had ever been allowed to be, and was a legendary dancer, though Mirri had never seen it.

"Mirri." Her mother gave a flowing curtsy. Her bright silver-blonde hair was kept up and back in a tight braid, and her slippered feet glazed over the glass floor, unaware of the Origin pulsing through the palace walls and tickling Mirri's feet.

"Mother," Mirri returned with a shallow nod.

There were no skirts for her to pull out, not since Maron died, but it made no matter. She was Ah-nis Na Righ now. She would never bow lower than her shoulders and never curtsy to anyone in her kingdom again.

She straightened her shoulders under the weight of her war gear. Her festival gear. Her courtly gear. The only time she didn't wear her armor was for state dinners and diplomatic affairs, and the chance for her skin to breathe was the only tolerable thing about those.

"Are you ready for today's race?" her mother asked, face and voice neutral.

"I am content with my preparations."

"And what of the probabilities?"

"I ascertain a high chance of success based on traditions and the histories kept by our people but will be content if the Flame sees fit to change it."

"As it should be." Her mother curtsied again.

Her father nodded his approval, kissed her mother on the forehead, and left the room with a click of boots. As soon as the door shut behind him, her mother's shoulders sloped.

"Your father means well." She placed a hand on the bit of exposed skin between the golden buckles on Mirri's back.

Mirri suppressed a flinch at her mother's touch, always unexpected no matter how often it occurred. She wanted to pull away like she had been burned, but also wanted to soak in the warmth.

"As our Righ, he means well for us all."

"Yes." Her mother's lips puckered. She pulled her hand away, settling it instead on the light gray furs that encompassed her neck. A garment Mirri would never need, not with Marduk's blood coursing with fiery heat through her veins. She could stand in a blizzard and feel as warm as Ard's sun was rumored to be.

"But sometimes he can be cold the way he goes about it. I know he's all you've known, but there are many men in the kingdom who know how to smile."

Mirri cast a sideways glance at her, never sure what to do when her mother slipped into informalities. "What are you saying?"

"Oh, you know," her mother niggled. "I'm sure there have been some men smiling at you. What with the upcoming race and the festival. I'm sure a good half of eligible males are hoping if they catch your fancy, you'll slow down just a little during the contest and let them hop a ride."

"*Mother!*" Mirri's cheeks grew hot. "You speak of such things too boldly."

"Of smiles?" her mother scoffed—a very undignified response—and stepped closer. "I wish someone had spoken to me about a lot more than that before my Eve of Fire."

"*Cuidich mi,* Marduk." Mirri cinched her eyes shut, trying to force back the weakness she knew bloomed easily on her pale cheeks. "No descendant and heir to the throne has ever found their Fire Mate and been subject to the Eternal Union before their twenty-fifth birthday. This quarter century's Founding Festival and my first is merely for practice. Show."

"Though you are ready to content yourself if that changes?"

Mirri's nose itched, but she refused to scratch it. The tickle on her skin was imagined, and she had control of her mind. Just as she had control of her thoughts. And the thought of a man's hands on her skin or his breath on her neck was not welcome. It made her feel too out of control. Too unsteady. And an unsteady mind could lead to discontentment, breaking of traditions, and being burned from the inside out by the Eternal Flame. Thoughts of intimacy also made her feel hot—from blushing, she was sure... except the hint of heat in her cheeks always made her worry she had crossed a final line and would be meeting Maron in the fiery depths of the Origin soon enough.

Her toes curled again, and she forced them flat. "It is highly unlikely, but I will do the Flame's will."

Her mother frowned. "You could be more excited about it. I've seen the way the general's sentry, Urramach, looks at you. The way his pupils dilate. He's like a young drakonte in heat when you're around. He's been eying you since you were the annoying little snake that followed him and your brother as a pudgy-cheeked little girl. What if he overcomes?"

"Propriety, mother!"

Mirri spun away and marched — with slow and dignified steps — toward the door. The itch grew more persistent, and the heat in her cheeks reached boiling. Would she die? Was this it for her?

She swallowed hard and allowed a little glare. "You speak as if you're in the bed chambers with me on my Eve of Fire. It's... It's..."

"Untraditional?" her mother asked, eyebrows raised.

"To say the least."

Mirri reached the door, the gold latch in her hand. Then hesitated. She did not want to talk of this anymore with her mother, the one who put all those deadly ideas in Maron's head. But she also didn't want her subjects to see her weak and flustered. Which is exactly the impression they'd get if she ventured out into the hallway now.

She dropped her hand.

"You know," her mother said, stepping up behind her, "not all our traditions are tied to the Eternal Flame. Some of them our ancestors just made up."

"The records say nothing about such indeterminate discretions," Mirri said with a steadying breath. "And I'd prefer to live more than to test your theory."

Her mother sighed, heavy and breathy and indecorous. "So let it be. But there's nothing about smiling in the traditional laws. In any of the laws, actually." She slipped to Mirri's side and tapped her chin. "You might feel better if you tried it. I think that is your father's problem. He needs to smile more."

Mirri dipped her head and stayed that way, hands clasped and hair like a cascade of lava between her and her mother. "I will keep that in mind."

"Very good." Her mother opened the door to leave but turned at the last second. "Good luck on the Drakonte Ride today. Whether you wind up bound for your Eve of Fire or get to sally forth as a single righ for the next quarter, I will be content either way. Give Havu my best wishes. I know she'll be mortified if she's caught."

Mirri almost smirked. "Havu is the fastest drakonte in Fyre, born of the hatchling fires in the Origin's Eternal Flame and connected to me in thought. If tradition and history didn't already disfavor the odds of me acquiring a Fire Mate, her speed will do the rest. No one will ride her with me today."

Her mother smiled. "We shall see. But as a former triumphant Fire Mate who caught your father, some things are not so hot and cold. Especially if you... throw the race? Hm? Give Urramach a leg up? He's very handsome."

It was all Mirri could do not to shove her mother out the door as the itch on her nose became unbearable. "Tradition requires me and Havu to ride with all our might. There is no *throwing* anything. If he catches me after the bone horn blares, The Origin decrees he be my husband and Subsidiary Righ in your place, and if he doesn't—which will be the case today—he can be content to train for another twenty-five years and try again next time."

"And yet, the kingdom must be perpetuated somehow. The Drakonte Ride is meant for bringing people together in a union, not for playing hard-to-get. The race just makes the courtship more exciting." Her mother's normally demure smile widened under sparkling eyes. "Especially when the kingdom is facing a hard many years as we are now. A Righ union would be just the thing to bring our people hope. To give them confidence in the Origin's new heart. And who better to help you lead the people into peace than Urramach? He's stately and charismatic and dutifully informed."

"Because I do not inspire enough confidence on my own?" Mirri had to restrain the sting in her voice. Her muscles tensed, and she counted in multiples of four-point-seven as quickly as she could to quell any surfacing discontent. Then, she cleared her throat. "I believe, despite Father training Maron for the Righship instead of me, that I am qualified to handle the kingdom. I am certainly more obedient."

"I do not doubt it, Ah-nis."

"Besides, it is my first Founding, Mother," Mirri said through increasingly tight lips. "I will not be bound."

"All the more exciting the possibilities of today's events. I'll make sure to wish Urramach luck as well. He's been training for years and only has eyes for you." Her mother winked and disappeared into the hallway, her reflection bright on the polished obsidian floor.

Mirri shut the door. Took a breath. Then rubbed her nose furiously to get rid of the horrible itch.

Improper. Scandalous. Inappropriate.

Not to mention embarrassing. Her mother had definitely been Maron's downfall.

Although, in that giddy, unbridled part of herself that was always at risk of catching aflame the thought of having a Fire Mate—of being bound to someone, of having her Eve of Fire filled with a man's touch and yearning and kisses—didn't sound all that bad, even if it made her insides squirm. Intimacy like that wasn't against tradition. It was honored by it. The Eternal Union earned by any man who caught her in a Founding Festival race was only made official once the physical bond had taken place.

And Urramach *was* very handsome. From a good bloodline. Dutifully informed, as her mother so pointedly stated. And he smiled at her. *A lot.* Even in very public forums like strategy councils and state dinners. He had all but declared his intentions for her to every man in Fyre. And she didn't hate the thought so much. If she did, she wouldn't be meeting him in the secret passageway behind the tapestry of Marduk before the ride. To hear his breath. To catch that look in her eye that left her strangely invigorated and at a complete loss. It was a dangerous game. But one she couldn't help but play. Besides, her mother was correct. Urramach would be a stately match that would appease her persnickety councilmen.

Heat once more roused in her cheeks. Her thoughts were getting away from her. She closed her eyes and breathed slowly, assessing each piece of her body to make sure she wasn't really on fire.

She was meeting with Urramach to wish him luck. A righ offering encouragement to her leading sentry. Nothing more. The Origin may condone intimacy as a seal of marriage, but tradition forbade unions before the Eve of Fire for those of the royal bloodline. Havu would keep her strong. Her drakonte was far more fierce than Mirri about her independence and refused to be bred to any male, no matter how shiny their scales or svelte their frames. Besides, she and Havu had hundreds of years left in their lives. There was no reason to settle now. To be bred. Not when she had a kingdom to rule, which she could do on her own.

No. She would not be caught by anyone. She would show the kingdom she could rule competently and well as righ all on her own.

She clenched her jaw in resolve and tilted her chin higher as she stepped out into the hallway and marched across the obsidian tiles.

She didn't care who entered the race that day. No one would get close enough to see the red in her eyes.

CHAPTER THREE

Izkander

Izkander's aching stomach flipped as he catapulted towards the sparkling ocean, the wind buzzing his ears. Everything he'd just been through and all possible implications fell out of his brain as more immediate concerns took over. He wasn't exactly plummeting to his death, but there would be a lot of pain and broken bones of his trusty steed didn't get off his big fat *radfan* and get moving.

"Squirt!" Izkander whistled loud enough to hurt his own ears. "Here boy!"

He turned his body to face the floating island—Eayima, the only home he had ever known. As big as the palace complex of Karzusan, it hung impossibly in the sky, drifting slightly with natural currents. Stalactites the size of an *eimlaq's* arm hunt from the bottom, as if the rock were about to drip into the sea. Which was getting closer with every passing moment.

"Squirt!"

A wavy line of pale gray rose from the surface of the island like a stream of smoke, then sharpened and dove towards him. The sun winked on the massive drakonte's four wings, white and golden feathers shimmering like breaths of heaven. Squirt's body twisted and slithered in the air, a good one hundred cubits long and still growing. Cream-colored scales shone on his belly, and silver, downy feathers covered his back all the way down to his surprisingly fluffy tale.

The wind bit Izkander's skin and ripped at his hair as he plummeted. "Squirt!"

The drakonte opened its mouth and let out an ear-splitting screech. Always a show off.

Then Squirt finally got serious. He pounded the air with both sets of wings to catch up. When he was near, he bopped Izkander with his fluffy tail from the side to slow his speed, then curled back in a wide c-shape and slipped his massive body under him.

Izkander landed with a hard thump, the air knocked from his lungs. On instinct, he snatched great handfuls of fur-like feathers and tightened his grip on the scales with his thighs. Then he pulled back for momentum and hurled his body forward to land just behind the drakonte's huge triangular head.

Squirt flipped upside down and took a great arc up into the clouds. Izkander snatched his horns, which were like crooked silver jousting lances sticking straight back from the snake's head. They sailed through the roll, then steadied over the flattop of a bright white cumulus.

"You cut it a little close this time, *thuebani.*"

Squirt barked out a laugh, which from his snakey mouth sounded like hot water being forced through metal pipes. Izkander had never heard another drakonte make such a noise.

He leaned far forward to pat the top of Squirt's head. "Take us home."

The snake let loose a cry that landed on the ear like a barrage of explosions. Izkander tightened his grip. His friend was feeling frisky after being left alone for almost a week, and Squirt didn't have a drop of patience in all one-hundred and fifty tons of his body.

Izkander stifled a heavy sigh. He wasn't in the mood to play. Now that the fight was over and all the truth had been laid out on the proverbial table, Izkander felt sick with himself. What was his umi going to think? He didn't want to tell her what had happened, but he had to. He didn't know how not to. Everything had gone wrong and he felt sick with himself. And the only way to feel better was to talk to his umi.

"I'm sorry, buddy." Izkander patted Squirt's side. "I'm not in the mood."

Squirt looped back towards Eayima. When they were near enough to come in for a landing however, Squirt took a sudden nose dive for the dripping stalactites underneath. Drawn all along the bottom and sides in bright red paint were tiny targets, simple dots with circles around them. Squirt twisted his body into a hard s-shape and then let all four of his massive wings go limp so he was falling towards the ocean on his side—his dead-possum pose which he only ever used to force Izkander into action.

If you can't fight them, you have to join them.

Izkander as his stomach twirled in a completely different way. He found his feet on the rolling body then leapt off, his arms pointed straight and his back taut. The wind rushed over him, kissing his skin with sunlight and lifting in his lungs. Maybe a quick game of catching fire was exactly what he needed.

Izkander summoned pure orange flames to his hands, then shot off six quick fireballs towards the targets. Then he leapt off of Squirt's back.

The drakonte screamed in delight and darted after the fire. The game was for him to catch the balls in his mouth before they hit the targets, then come back to catch Izkander before he hit the water. If Izkander hit more targets than Squirt caught fireballs, he won. And if Squirt failed to catch him before he hit the water, everyone lost.

Using his own body as a stop clock—flying high enough to feel a touch of ice on his skin, then plummeting towards the sprawling ocean—was what made the game exciting. And it was because of this game Izkander knew what happened when he hit the water from so high up. Six broken ribs, a fractured tibia, and burns and bruises all over his chest and thighs from the impact.

Now Squirt knew that if it was a choice between catching the fireballs and catching Izkander, he'd better let the fire go.

They played together for some forty rounds and ended with a score of twenty-eight targets to thirty-one fires caught, and no broken Izkander. So, Squirt won. Squirt always won because once he got ahead he didn't want to play anymore.

With a low-pitched howl of victory, Squirt snatched Izkander in the coils of his tail and threw him up high, then dove under so he landed just behind his head in his spot. With both of them dizzy and breathing hard, they flew up to the surface of Eayima. The legendary, eternal, and unreachable resting ground of the Seal of Sulayman, the most powerful magical artifact in two worlds. But Izkander had lived there all his life. He was born inside the temple and spent his childhood playing in the high grass with his brothers and sisters. It was the only place on Earth or Qaf that had ever felt completely normal to him. The world below was a playground; the sky was the only thing that was real.

As Squirt came in to land, Izkander saw his old man standing near the fence that enclosed the perimeter. He propped one knee propped on a rock, his bright green eyes and even brighter white smile catching the sun.

Squirt passed by him overhead. Once, twice. A silent question.

Izkander sighed. He really was in a mood if he didn't even want to attack his old man, standing there all smug and asking for it.

No. He wasn't going to let Ya'el keep such a hold on him. It wasn't his fault she'd lied to him. And he hadn't lied to her, not once. So why did he feel so dirty?

He shook it off and slowly rose to his feet on Squirt's back. When they made another pass on his baba, Izkander leapt at him headfirst, his arm extended for the clothesline.

But his old man was as quick as he'd ever been. He caught Izkander with one arm, twirled him around, and slammed his back into the ground. Then, as he tried to get his bearings, a dusty boot landed on Izkander's chest.

"Keeping trying, *habibi*." His old man boomed between loud coughs of laughter. "Maybe someday you'll beat me. But not today."

Izaknder snarled, grabbed the boot, and twisted. His old man giggled as he fell to the dirt. Izkander wrapped his hands tightly around his father's waist, locking his wrists. Then threw all his strength into heaving his body up—lifting his baba over his head before slamming him hard on the dirt.

His baba gasped and grunted.

Breathing so hard he thought his lungs might burn out, Izkander tried to re-compose, but the moment he stole was one moment too many. His baba swung his head back, conking Izkander in the nose. Then he spun out of his grip, rolled over Izkander's back to get behind him, and wrapped an arm around his neck.

They struggled together in the dirt until his baba got a firm enough grip. He shoved Izkander's face into his armpit, then spanked his ass several times with a sharp flat palm. "What... did... I... tell... you... boy?"

"Get off me!" Izkander kicked like a donkey.

His old man let go and rolled onto his back. Then he put his hands on his stomach and laughed, harsh and breathy.

Izkander sat back on his heels, then wiped his cuff over his lips to see if they were bleeding. Just a bit.

"You dirty son of a snake," he huffed and rubbed his bruised backside. "I'll get you for that."

"Maybe someday." Grinning, his baba breathed out a heavy sigh. "But not today."

Izkander pressed his lips together. The sinking feeling in his gut was worse now than ever. He was home, but in his heart he was still back in Al Madinat wondering where he'd gone so wrong.

He was the first half-djinn, quarter-human, quarter-lilu baby ever born, so anything that might be said about his nature was pure conjecture. From his djinn mother he'd gotten internal fire, eyes that showed his emotions as a rainbow of flickering colors, the ability to apparate between worlds with nothing but a thought. And from his half-human, half-lilu dad he had gotten... brown skin and the ability to touch metal. Though it still gave him a rash.

"What's the matter with you?" His baba hopped to his feet, then walked to his side and offered a hand up.

Izkander turned a cold shoulder and got up on his own. His old man smirked.

He called him old, but Izkander's father still looked about twenty-five and would for the rest of his long, arguably eternal, life. He had no djinn blood and looked entirely human, though above average in every way. Taller, stronger, more handsome, more durable, more athletic.

Everybody always took him and Izkander for brothers.

Izkander's baba was half human, half *lilu*—a mysterious, rare, and painfully beautiful race. Long-lived and all but indestructible, with magical abilities that put even the greatest djinn spiders, witches, and menna to shame. They and their female counterparts—the *lilith*—dwelled in the space between worlds and created their own realities, which they could then inflict on others.

Generally, *lilith* and *lilu* were thought to be irretrievably evil. Capricious, obsessed with sex, manipulative, and sadistic. That had turned out to not be entirely true, not once the blood was mixed with human in any case. Though sometimes Izkander couldn't help but wonder if it was his *lilu* side that got him into so much trouble with women.

"Wasn't expecting you back so soon." His baba slapped him hard across the shoulder blades. "Your mother will be thrilled."

Izkander's eyes swept out over the edge of the island. The sun was beginning to set, lighting the water below like canary diamonds spread across a mirror. "Where is Umi?"

"Somewhere around here. Probably. I hope." His old man shrugged. "The triplets have been driving her up a wall. She's been threatening to quit."

"Quit? Quit what?"

"Everything."

"Umi would never leave you."

"If I ever let myself believe that she would leave me."

Izkander wrinkled his nose in confusion. "What?"

"Marriage, son. It's constant work."

"But you two are so happy."

"Yes, we're happy. Because we choose to be. If I hadn't met your umi, I doubt I ever would have gotten married." His baba turned his gaze to the sunset. "Your umi and I were a freak occurrence. A flash of fire. She's the other half of my soul."

Izkander smiled softly. It always wrapped his heart in warm, fuzzy ropes whenever his parents accidentally talked romantically about each other. When they weren't arguing, or stomping around and cursing each other's names, or worst of all, getting along really well and being disturbingly amorous in public. When they just said simple things about each other that nobody who wasn't insanely in love would ever even think to say.

Izkander had never felt about anyone the way his baba and his umi felt about each other. He wondered if he ever could.

A rustling from behind and Izkander turned to see his mother walking closer in her lavish purple silks. He smiled and her sunshine colored eyes brightened with gold, turquoise skin shimmering almost as much as the sparkles in her black hair that showed under her loose hijab. The dusting of starlight in Izkander's own black hair came from her.

The pain he was feeling in his gut was soothed just by looking at her.

"Umi." He rushed closer and wrapped his arms around her. He lifted her off the ground and squeezed, then set her down and leaned in so she could kiss his cheek like she always did.

"My *eayan almuhit*." She beamed and pressed her hands against his face, then smoothed the front of his shirt. "Why do you stay away so long? Don't you know how it makes me worry?"

"I'm sorry, umi." He frowned and lifted his eyebrows high in the center. Then he reached into a pouch hanging from his belt and took out a little wooden box and held it out to her. "I got you some new playing cards. Hand-painted in Alexandria."

She took them in her delicate fingers and lifted the lid. Every muscle in his body tightened, praying she would like the pattern he chose. When her eyes softened, it was like a breath of spring.

"Thinking of me while you were away..." She swatted his shoulder. "Do you see, Bakr? Do you see how thoughtful a man our Skander is turning out to be?"

His old man ruffled his hair. "He's a regular apple-polish."

"Oh, hush you." She made a face at his baba, then turned eyes warm as sunlit honey back to Izkander. "Just ignore him. He's jealous of the way I dote on you. But how could I not? I don't want you slipping away to make some other woman happy and not coming back."

He closed his eyes and shook his head. "That could never happen. If by some weird twist of fate I ever met the other half of my soul..." He shot a quick glance at his old man. "...she'd be just as concerned with keeping you happy as I am."

His umi pressed her hands to her chest and sighed. "I raised you right. Especially because you don't have any women in your life, right? Even if your other half knows better than to take you away, I'd prefer not to share you in the first place."

"I'll just make myself scarce, shall I?" His old man grumbled as he walked away, but not before slapping his umi's butt. She yelped and glared at him, all the while smiling.

Izakander sighed and leaned over the short perimeter fence made of unfinished lumber. The sun had almost finished going down, just a haze of purple glimmering on the infinite horizon.

"What's wrong, *habibi*? Why do you sigh so when you're home?"

His umi could always tell when something was bothering him, even in pitch blackness when she couldn't see the colors in his eyes. Once again, his stomach flipped. He didn't want to tell her the truth. He didn't want it to *be* the truth.

"I think I really hurt somebody today."

She leaned on the fence next to him and rubbed his back with one hand. "I'm going to assume unintentionally because I know you. But my next question is, doing something stupid?"

"It didn't seem stupid at the time." He shrugged, then his shoulders slipped further. "I've been seeing this Ahmaran woman. It's not serious, just fun, I guess..." Even admitting that to his mother was like an iron stiletto to his intestines. "Today I found out that she's married. And she has kids. And then right away her husband found out about me."

She smacked the back of his head. "So yes, something a bit stupid."

Izkander shrank into his shoulders and pouted. "I know. I'm sorry. I didn't mean any harm. I was just..."

She sighed with a heavy shake of her head. "She's the one who lied. Not you. And while I do not share your father's enthusiasm for the ways you often spend your time, it takes two to... you know." She clenched her teeth, looking up at the sky. "Did you learn anything?"

He bit his lip and tapped his fingers on the wood. "If a girl's apartment is really big, that's suspicious."

His umi groaned and gave him a tight smile. "I guess that's better than nothing. But now that you've helped a woman cheat on her spouse, unwittingly or not, and felt how awful that is, the next time counts. And I'll slap you more than once."

"Okay." He rubbed his hands together and looked down. "I'll make sure I ask. Every girl I like, I'll ask her outright if she's married or whatever. And I'll ask her friends, too. Just in case she lies. That's good enough. Right? Maybe?"

Her tight smile widened, and she blinked a few times. "You tell me."

"I don't get it." He slumped again so his head hung below his shoulders. "I thought if I was just honest with people. Tell the truth about how I feel and what I want, then nobody could get hurt. I don't understand why everyone goes around lying all the time."

She cleared her throat and straightened, taking on the formal look she got when she was about to lecture. "Speaking as a reformed liar, I will tell you it is driven in large part out of fear. The other part out of desire. And often a mixture of both. Not everyone has the foundation you do. Your father and I will love you no matter how stupid a thing you do, unintentionally or not. So you see no reason to lie. But others... "She tilted her head side to side. "Not so much. You can't fix other people's foundations. But, if you care about them like your father and I do each other, you can help create a new one higher up, above all the damage down below."

"I don't think I'm ever going to meet somebody like you, umi." He shook his head slowly, then pulled himself to a stand and showed her a bright smile. "But that's okay. I'm already higher up."

"Yes, you are, baby," she cooed and pinched his cheeks. "And bless any woman who dares to try to reach your heights."

He turned at the high-pitched sound of little girls screaming and looked out across a field of low grass that waved in the wind before the temple of their house. His three youngest sisters—the triplets—were all rolling together on the ground, cursing and pulling each other's hair. The eleven-year-olds looked like they were fighting over some object, but he couldn't tell what it was. They were always fighting about something and no one of them understood the first thing about the other two. Basically, they were the worst triplets ever.

"Here we go again," Izkander said.

"Indeed." His umi kissed him once more on the forehead. "You'll figure it out. I believe in you." Then she slid under a triangular angle of the fence and disappeared, reappearing with a puff between the girls. She grabbed two by the arms, holding the third back with her hip. "Come on, you rugrats. Inside. I want to hear all about it."

"You need any help, umi?" Izkander called. "I can huck them over the fence for you."

"So sweet," she said with a drip of sarcasm. "But I have your father for that." She corralled his bickering sisters up the steps and into the temple, a lecture for them already on her tongue.

He watched them until they'd disappeared through the doors then turned back to the spray of brilliant white stars that had come out to keep him company. He felt tired and restless all at once. If he went inside, smoked some hash, and ate up the leftovers of whatever delicious things his mom had thrown together in the last few days since he'd been away, he knew he would pass out right away.

He was hungry...

But the call of the stars and the night air was stronger, chilly high winds licking at his skin and playing with his hair. Always the wind, whispering to him, summoning him. Seducing him with her eager, transitory touch. Unchanging, yet never failing to bring a promise of something new. If he had ever been in love with any lady, it was the icy kiss of the north wind.

He hopped up on the short wooden fence, walking heel-to-toe to keep his balance as he made his way around the circumference of the island towards the stables. Fajar's sunlight dawned over him as he peeked around the edge of the house. The massive Rukh bird was on her perch, her wings wrapped around her and her head buried in her own breast feathers. Shimmers like embers licked up and down her body, highlighting her soft glow. As he passed, Izkander laid a hand on her feathers. She cooed and lifted her head. When she saw him, she shoved at him with her beak, chattering deep in her throat. Izkander laughed and fell against her chest, hugging her close and letting her radiant love enfold him and wash away the dregs of the day.

His umi was right: he needed to make sure nothing like this ever happened again. And he oughtn't feel sad about it. He had so much—a loving family, a beautiful home, a face and body that many people would commit murder for. He ought to just be grateful for what he had.

Yet all he could think about was how meaningless it all felt. He spent his days mostly looking for ways not to be bored. It had gotten him into trouble a thousand times before, but he couldn't remember a time when he'd ever really hurt somebody. Not the way he'd hurt Ahmed.

It would be one thing if he loved Ya'el, but he didn't. He liked her. He wished only the best for her. And it did make him feel fuzzy to know that she liked him too. But that wasn't love.

And even what he'd felt for Shayla didn't compare to what he knew real love was supposed to be like. A flash of fire when meeting the other half of his soul.

He pulled back from Fajar and a few feathers came away in his hands. She was molting again, dusting the entire island with her magical feathers which to anybody else in both worlds were more precious than diamonds. Izkander used them all the time, as disposable as pistachio shells.

He jogged to where Squirt rested on his big warm rock, enchanted by Izkander's own orange fire so the drakonte had something to cuddle with whenever he was away. The head of feral scales and razor-sharp horns lifted, sharp red eyes opening to peer at him with a flash of fire. Squirt opened his mouth, great fangs shimmering in the moonlight as he showed his wide, snakey grin and flicked his long black tongue.

Izkander patted the side of his face and slung himself up onto his back just behind his skull, which alone was five times the size of any djinn or human. "Come on, buddy," he said, stroking his whiskers. "You want to go for a flight in Qaf? I could use some fresh air."

Squirt shivered with excitement and from behind him Fajar gave a disapproving squawk.

Izkander turned to her with a smile. "You want to come, sweetie? I'll take you to the mountains."

The feathers around her neck puffed up, and she stretched her wings. Then with a loud cry, she dove off her perch into the air. Squirt slid over the edge and spread both sets of wings, putting everything he had into catching up with Fajar. Izkander laughed, gripping the drakonte with his thighs so his arms could hang loose at his sides.

He wasn't going to think about Ya'el or her husband anymore that night. But there was truth to what his umi had said. These circumstances could be forgiven once, but if it happened to him again, he was accountable. And there was really no way to make sure it never happened again, not until he stopped dating around and settled down. But how could he ever do that? In two worlds and infinite heavens, where did a man who lived on a floating island go to find love?

CHAPTER FOUR

MIRRI

THE WALK DOWN THE main hallway filled Mirri with more trepidation than it should have. The way her toes kept trying to curl and the itch she was getting on her neck and arms were indecorous. She wasn't breaking any laws. Any rules. Maybe some conventions, but those *were* the product of the whims of her ancestors. She could meet a man behind a tapestry to wish him luck in his endeavors. There was nothing death-inducing about that.

She licked her lips, assessing and reassessing the heat levels in her limbs until she arrived at the woven mural in which Marduk, the Great Snake god, towered over her purely human ancestors. Her people had been cursed by an Ardish witch of the Nezen Coven to travel the space between worlds. After a constant, horrific state of limbo, they fell into Qaf through a circle of ancient ruins that existed in Ard, Fyre, and the white nothing in between. Magicless and frail in the frozen mountains of a world filled with magic, they nearly perished. That was, until the red-eyed snake god, Marduk, came to them after days of pleading and pouring sacrifice into the only source of warmth in all the Zabriyan mountains—a gurgling lava pit that connected to the Origin.

At the front of the procession, head pressed to the ground, knelt a woman with white flowing hair. *An Te.* The One who had charmed the god and married him to save her people. A sacrifice. A martyr for the greater cause. Though that is not how the legends describe it.

The Mother of All had been blessed.

Had she fretted over her Eve of Fire with such a magnificent god?

Mirri grabbed the woven edge of Marduk's tail and checked the hallway for onlookers. She closed her eyes and ignored the itchiness crawling over her skin with little pricks. Her melting nerves were rivaled only by a strange twist in her stomach at the thought of Urramach and his golden eyes and ribboned hair. He had been growing bolder, letting his fingers slip through strands of her hair when they had last met.

You're not breaking any traditions, she assured herself one last time with a thick swallow, still remembering the heat on her skin when he had been so close. She had not lit on fire. Just felt like it. Mirri pulled the tapestry back and slipped into the nook.

Urramach already waited for her, standing at attention. His copper-brown hair was tied neatly in the back with a green ribbon, and his broad shoulders wore well Fyre's military uniform. Sharp lines of gold cut the form-fitting jacket and pants, the S-shaped drakonte seal emblazoned in silver on the front. Such a symbol of propriety and fortitude in such a dark, little place. Had he stood like that the whole time, or snapped straight when she tugged the tapestry?

"Mirri." His voice was formal and crisp with just a hint of unnerving breathlessness. He took a step closer in the space that could be walked in three. "I worried you would not come."

She rolled her shoulders back to make them as straight as possible. "I agreed I would, and I keep my word. But after today you must not speak to me so informally."

He smiled, eyes creased in the corners. "Our noble leader." He pressed a hand to his chest and bowed, managing to come up even closer to her.

"I mean it, Urramach." She refused to be pressed into the wall like a scared little hatchling, even if she could smell the heather of Fyre's hills on his skin. "I will be the Ah-Nis Na Righ after the Festival. And you will be —"

"Your Fire Mate. Which means I may call you as I please and be happy all the while." His smile widened beneath golden human eyes, too bright for hiding.

"You speak boldly."

"If I may."

She swallowed and looked up at him. "Maybe you may not."

"May I do something else, then?" He leaned forward, placing his hand on the wall above her head.

Mirri's heart raced. She had met Urramach several times before in little crevices around the castle to steal a word, but he had never been so forward before. "It depends on what it is. There are rules, traditions to follow."

"All of which I know your life depends on." His gaze lingered on her face, the smile falling into a straight line.

"Well?" she asked in a mortifying squeak that sent heat spiraling across her chest.

"I've done the research. Hours pouring over books in the library."

His words tickled her ear. "A noble pursuit." She bit her lip.

"It was. And I found that it used to be normal, even customary and expected, for a woman and a man to give each other a token of luck before the Drakonte Ride in an effort to please the Flame and increase their odds of a happy coupling."

"Oh?" she whispered, eyes scanning the square line of his jaw, too weak to look him in the eyes.

"May I give you my token?"

She slipped her nervous fingers behind her back and tilted her chin up, drawing strength from her ancestors to be bold in this moment. "Are you hoping for a happy coupling?"

"I am." His gold eyes warmed with the Flame. "Are you?"

"I—" She stumbled, an itch seizing her side, demanding to be scratched. "I am not yet sure."

"Then take my token now, and I will get mine from you later."

He moved closer. She raised a brow and parted her lips to reply. Their noses touched. She held her breath. And his lips brushed hers. A kiss. Firm and quick. Heat spiraled throughout her. And then it was over.

"I'll see you during the Ride, Mirri. I'll be looking only for you." Urramach's gold eyes rested on her once more before vanishing behind the curtain. "Good luck," he said, his voice fading away.

She exhaled and closed one eye, shoulders tight, waiting for her death. After several minutes, her muscles relaxed one at a time. She looked down at her body and patted her legs and waist. Then her chest. Nothing melting. So... what in the pits of the Eternal Flame had just happened? And why had it affected her so? It wasn't the feeling her mother had once described to her as she begged her to stop talking. That cinching of the lungs and burning of her netheryea, as the poetry they brought from Ard called it. It was more like a drakonte nest of nerves, all tangled up and pulsing with a movement that set her on edge.

She sighed. He had done his research right, after all. And with his diligence had rewarded himself with a kiss, calling it a gift. To her.

But intimacy before one's Eve of Fire was strictly forbidden by the Eternal Flame, which she had always believed more than covered kissing. Though, apparently, if it was given as such a token under specific circumstances... She *was* still alive. Her breath quickened in short little bursts. But what if she *had* died? What if he did his research wrong, and she had keeled over right then, hand falling out from under the tapestry as the fire in her veins consumed her like it had her brother? She would have lit the whole castle on fire as he walked away.

The thought chased away any lingering shock and tightened her lungs with something spicier. How dare Urramach risk her life like that? His ruler? His Ah-nis Na Righ? And now he expected her to let him Ride? To be her Fire Mate and *call her as he pleases.*

Mirri barely remembered to calm her shaking limbs with a deep inhale before yanking the tapestry back and heading up toward the gates. She even allowed herself a brisk walk — the only dignified sign she could think of to warn everyone else to stay the rains from her. The guards at the castle gates hastened to fling them open wide for her. She stepped out onto the ramparts and breathed deeply the whip of cold wind that barraged her skin, feeling no more than the vague sensation she associated with ice. The guards who watched the landings were bundled up in various furs and wools, the noses of those with light-gold eyes red and dripping, while those with deeper gold eyes remained unbothered by the frozen winds. The dilution of Marduk's blood affected their physical beings but not their loyalties. Each guard who managed her ramparts had been vetted by the Origin and found worthy, however much human lived in their blood.

The closest guard, an older gentleman with snow-white hair and deeply golden eyes, bowed and handed her a long brass whistle. She touched his wrist in thanks, his color brightening to a rosier hue. Then she stepped to the ledge and blew. A trill of seven high notes in quick succession cut through the turbulent gale. Hair whipped her face, fire-red against the snowy white. And in the distance, a dusky blue dot appeared against the backdrop of high mountains.

Havu.

She gazed below at the verdant farmland and corrals of drakonte tucked away near steaming springs surrounded by flowers. The Valley of Fyre. The majority of her kingdom, sequestered in the arms of the earth itself with the Eternal Flame keeping them warm. Giving them life. It smelled heady like earth and crisp like snow, all backed by the scent of smoked hickory that rose from the grass above the Flame. And it was hers to rule. *Marduk beannaich i.* She spied a particularly lovely patch of flowers down below and took aim. Then she gathered a running start and leapt.

Havu shot to her side, spinning toward the earth with Mirri in a tight double helix. She slipped her feet into the stirrups and grabbed the reins. And just when she could count each individual petal, Havu arched in a deep circle and slingshotted herself back up the way they came. Mirri gripped hard the splash of orange ridges that rose from Havu's shimmering blue scales. Her wings pressed against the air with deep *thwicks* of creamy feathers that matched the drakonte's underbelly and turned to a sunset orange at their longest points.

"We need to make a quick round to make sure the defenses against the beast are in place," Mirri called over the rushing wind. "Too many children will be out on the fields, we can't let the *Buklak* near enough to dive and grab one."

Havu nodded and broke a hard left, heading toward the farthest mountain range. Mirri scanned the edges. All their defenses were directed toward the Ghaluman peaks, hoping to keep the battish beast from terrorizing the festival. At each point, a swoop of soldiers and their drakonte hovered at the ready, lazy, feathered wings beating the air as they kept sentry in slow circles. All looked right. All looked safe.

The festival could continue with her people safe. She took one last scan of the shining groups of green-clad soldiers guarding their janu'ub borders, then nodded.

Sure the festival was safe, she clicked at Havu. Her drakonte's scales shivered the whole length of her body, then they shot off, high and fast.

When they finally broke above the clouds and into the crystalline air, Mirri slumped against Havu's neck with a groan. Every muscle she kept taut during the day, every worry she carried in her heart dissipated when she was up here.

Havu hissed and chomped twice. *Long day?*

"Can I say yes when it has barely started?"

Yes.

"Then, yes." Mirri plucked at a burnished scale, running its edge underneath her fingernail. "Urramach kissed me."

Havu dipped precariously, shifting Mirri in the saddle that nestled over the drakonte's ridged spine. *And you're alive?*

"Clearly." Her shoulders tensed. "He called it a token and said tradition allows him to give one to me in hopes we will have a *successful coupling*."

There is no way I'm letting that man ride me. Not if all the rains came and extinguished the Eternal Flame.

"I wasn't particularly content with him risking my life either, but he isn't *that* bad."

Havu snapped her jaw.

"If I don't let him ride today, he won't get another chance for a quarter of a century. It is a long time for him to wait." Mirri realized the truth in her words as they flew from her mouth. It *was* a long time to wait.

And? Havu cut through her thoughts. *You'll be waiting, too. Why does he deserve pity for it?*

"You forget. He is not a true descendant. He may couple when he sees fit. The games are a chance for the citizens to have fun and maybe catch a righ. But it is not a sentence to a life of loneliness if they should fail. Not for them."

What? Havu snapped the fans of dark blue skin around her face. *Are you worried he will not wait? He is a shallow mate indeed if he cannot hold himself for a chance at coupling with the bearer of the Eternal Flame.*

"And yet..." Mirri sighed.

Oh, I see. Havu clicked in her throat with an accusatory laugh. You *aren't sure you want to wait.*

Mirri plunked her head against the cool scales of Havu's glistening back with a groan. "Is that pathetic?"

Only because the man you're considering is Urramach. Even with the gift of mind-speak, Mirri could hear the sarcasm coating Havu's voice.

"He is a member of the high council. Only ten years older than I, and has proven his devotion to me for years. He's also... easy on the eyes." She blushed, rubbing the itch on her cheek. "As far as Fire Mates of the descendants go, he's a real catch. Do you remember Roimhe Seo-Na Righ's bonded partner? People say that woman was a psychopath. A terror to be around with an eye that never quite sat right in her face. But she got to be Subsidiary and have children of the Flame because she simply was fast enough. Poor Roimhe never saw it coming."

All I'm hearing is that you descended from a crazy person.

"Ach, Havu," she scolded with a hiss of her own. "I'm saying Urramach is not the worst. In fact... I think I kind of like him. He's easy on the eyes and smells like home."

Havu growled. *Even if he's not crazy and even if you do like him, you shouldn't settle. Not when you have a drakonte who's smart enough not to let someone drop in from above. Amateur move. And have you seen his drakonte? A wisp of a thing. There is no way he can handle the gift that is me.* Havu's scales rippled beneath Mirri's touch.

Mirri laughed, knowing the winds would whisk it away before anyone heard. "Urramach's Ian is an *astar nathair.* Those drakonte are supposed to be small and fast." Her laugh died down, and she pursed her lips. "Ian is very fast."

Havu snorted. *Not fast enough. And not good enough. Neither is Urramach. You could rule Fyre without him. You should.*

"I know." Mirri sighed. "I need to. It's the only way my father will see me as capable of it. He misses Maron too much, and I am not him."

A speck of silver caught light in the distant sea of clouds. Mirri narrowed her eyes, grateful for the distraction. Very few drakonte could fly as high as Havu, and she knew of none that were silver. She clicked her tongue, ready to give chase, when a deep bellow cracked the silence above the world.

Mirri expelled a breath in a puff of steamy air and pushed herself upright. "Well, now's your chance to prove your speed."

The Drakonte Ride? Havu sniffled and rasped with anticipation.

"The Drakonte Ride."

And we are in agreement.

"Are we?"

Havu snapped her head back, red eyes mirroring her own. *Mirri...*

Mirri jutted her chin up, determined not to be won over by stolen kisses and secret meetings. She was the Righ now, she had enough to manage without adding a man to that list. And she could only prove herself a capable leader without one. At least for the next twenty-five years.

"Okay." She released one last exhale. "We are in agreement. No one rides."

No one rides.

She barely had a chance to grab hold of the reins as Havu raced toward the earth like lightning, eager to show off. The chase would last until the Third Moon rose or the Ah-nis Na Righ was caught, which meant she and Havu would have to go all day, missing most of the festivities just so she wouldn't have to couple some stranger. Or Urramach. Already she could smell roasted *yupkick* legs and hear the tinkling of music in the streets below. Crowds of people laughed as children dressed in bright colors scurried between their feet. The field just outside Fyre's walls was littered with blankets and the already happily married, ready to route on their favorites and cringe when they saw someone fall.

Mirri scanned the revelry and the smiling faces her mother had assured her existed. Her heart pinched. Oh, to be one of the people and do as she pleased.

She stifled the thought and turned her face toward the icy wind. She should not be so discontent. Not if she wished to live.

Below the line of clouds, a sea of writhing drakonte filled the arena. So many in past Rides had been caught in the beginning because their drakonte got lost in the fray. Unintended couplings had even occurred as one oaf or another fell off their ride and landed on someone else's. There was no choice. No way to correct it. During the Drakonte Ride, once two people joined on a drakonte's back, a seal of union wrapped around their wrists in bright flame, drawing them closer to each other until they married.

She shook her head, circling high near the top of the flags as drakonte bone horns announced her arrival. Several of her generals and a few of the wiser and bolder citizens were up in the reaches of the allowed starting field. A few men with burly beards, a woman with flowing white hair tied with an inordinate amount of ribbons, and a kid who had to be even younger than she. And Urramach, of course. He flew languidly by, posture perfect and smile radiant. He didn't seem so bad....

Havu jostled her with a snap, reading her thoughts. *No one rides.*

"No one rides," Mirri mumbled, biting her lip.

The trumpets gave three short bursts to ready the riders. Havu tensed and coiled beneath her, ready to jolt to the farthest reaches of the city to keep anyone from touching them. Mirri wrapped the reins in her hand and licked her lips. They were a team. Two sets of eyes. Two minds. Two iron wills. Which combined, made them one.

The announcer blew a single note that reverberated in the nearby mountains. They were off.

CHAPTER FIVE

Izkander

It was easy enough for Izkander to pull his own body through from Ard to Qaf or vice versa using nothing but the fire in his djinn blood, but bringing Squirt along was a different matter. Luckily, Fajar had her own passage back and forth and all it took to ride on her coattails was a feather.

The great flaming bird cut the air with her cry as they materialized in the skies over the Zabriyan Mountains. The huge bird did loops and corkscrews, the snow melting the moment it touched her flaming feathers. These mountains were a home away from home for her, and she always got excited whenever she returned, relishing in the cold, the freedom, the expansive beauty of the largest mountain range in both worlds.

Izkander knew he didn't need to keep track of her. She would fly off and do her own thing, probably hunting herds of her favorite golden-fleeced goats and stuffing herself with their flesh until she was almost too fat to fly. And when he was ready to leave, all he had to do was call for her and she would be at his side within minutes, provided she wasn't too busy rolling around on the side of a mountain to make the largest, most terrifying snow angel anybody ever saw.

Izkander did nothing to try to guide Squirt, just letting him fly wherever he pleased and happy to go along for the ride. They always either ended up where they needed to be or somewhere equally interesting. He'd given up trying to control the impetuous creature a long time ago, and vice versa. They were both beings of wind, ready to spread their wings and trust in destiny. It had never once steered them wrong.

Squirt let out a loud purring sort of sound, and Izkander started, his eyes creaking open. He'd never heard him make such a noise. Deep, guttural, and deceptively quiet, brimmed with hunger and excitement.

"What in Jahannam are you on about?" Izkander scanned the wispy white clouds, narrowing his eyes through the drifts of snow as they tore into the heavy fog. Purple fire glimmered on Squirt's nose and the tips of his horns — the same fire that sailors sometimes spoke of coming to alight on the masts and bows of their ships like a divine lantern. It came most often when they flew through storms, the electricity of the clouds attaching to them, guiding them. Bolts of drakonte-made lighting shimmered down Squirt's back and rested on Izkander's hands.

It was a good sign. Something amazing was about to happen. The divine lantern had come to shine a light on the moment to be sure he wouldn't miss it.

Izkander pressed the soles of his boots against the armored plates that covered Squirt's neck like ready-made stirrups and pushed himself to a stand. Unlike so many drakonte—say Bubbles, or Thueban, or his sister's little Cesar—Squirt refused to wear a harness. Not a saddle, or a bridle, not even a little rope around his neck. Izkander had to hold on to nothing and trust that his bronco would not buck.

He trusted him implicitly.

A flash of turquoise and pink arrested his attention, and Izkander's grip tightened on Squirt's feathers. The drakonte angled his front wings in that direction, too, its powerful back wings driving them forward at full tilt. That aggressive purr shook through Squirt's body again, and his scales shivered with the sound.

Izkander looked down at him. "What is it, buddy? What do you see?"

The haze of purple fire spread slowly to cover both their bodies as Squirt increased his speed. Flashes of white lightning crackled around them and snapped at Squirt's tail, announcing their approach. Another glimmer of coral light flashed through the clouds, like a fan waving in the sky, and then the snap of a turquoise whip moved the wake, slipping in and out of fog to keep from being seen.

It was a creature, there could be no doubt about that, but it was only allowing tiny glimpses of itself to be seen. And the longer he watched it move through the clouds — one moment far to the left, then gone, only to reappear almost at his back —

Izkander started to wonder if it was doing it on purpose. Hiding just enough to be seen, never showing enough of itself to be known.

But why?

Izkander was seized with a sudden, passionate desire to see the creature — plain and simple and in all its glory. Because from what few glances he had caught, he knew glorious would be a word worth employing.

Squirt had a fire in his belly, too—as bright as any Izkander had ever seen from him. Without waiting for any instruction, he barreled into the clouds where the creature hid, announcing his approach with a cacophonous roar that had a queer conversational quality about it.

Flakes of ice clung to Izkander's skin like foil, enshrouding and biting him. Misty whiteness coated his lashes, and he closed his eyes against it, trusting in Squirt to pull them through. His vision was no good in such heavy cover, anyway. Better to trust in his body, to focus on sensing the movement of the wind, and to listen for any tiny sound that made it through the relentless gale.

And then he heard it — the unmistakable shriek of a drakonte. But it wasn't Squirt, not that guttural, ear-splitting roar. This was higher-pitched, an almost musical caterwauling that scraped down his spine like a finely hewn dagger.

Izkander laughed as they broke through the other side of the cloud into a wide, clear area. Dozens of drakonte moved about in the lower sky, twisting in formations around and over each other. Some chasing, some running, some just moving together in lazy circles. He'd never seen anything like it. He expected Squirt to veer down to join the fun, but a quick stab of vertigo hit his brain as they angled upward, arching back into the sky. Higher, faster.

Izkander tightened his grip with his knees and flattened his back. Whatever was happening down below, he didn't see a turquoise and coral-colored body anywhere in the mix. And Squirt was as stubborn and single-minded as he was lively and gregarious. They had their quarry, and there was no turning back.

Squirt straightened, heading upwards at a ninety-degree angle and spinning madly to increase his speed. Izkander held his breath, white-knuckles on armored plates. When Squirt broke from the climb and bowed backward, a laugh tore from Izkander's chest that was as much relief as it was pure, adrenaline-fueled elation. And it was then, upside-down and screaming with raucous cackles that he finally saw her.

Allahallah, she was beautiful.

Her wings shone like an orange dawn against the gray and white storm at her back. An underbelly of smooth creamy scales. A thin turquoise body with a scintillating line of orange points down her back, licking her like fire and coming to form fronds on her long tail. The pretty drakonte paused in the air, her head turning to look at Squirt as she drew back her full wings and twisted her body with a little shimmy. The two ridges on either side of her face shivered, and Squirt made that noise again — that full-bodied murmur that raced down his scales like a warm chill.

"You dog," said Izkander, then Squirt bolted after the beautiful lady drakonte.

Izkander whooped and laughed as they whipped around clouds, purple fire crackling in the sky behind them, signaling where they had been but never where they were going. The lady drakonte was fast and agile, taking hard twists with admirable elegance that sometimes left Squirt reeling in the wrong direction for a second before he righted himself and got back on the chase. On a straightaway, Squirt and his four wings were faster, clawing steadily closer as he threw everything he had into the pursuit, but she twisted through the air like smoke.

Izkander narrowed his eyes against the sting of clouds. A flash of red whipped about on the lady drakonte's back. Almost like an extension of the fire points that ran down her spine, and yet not quite the same color. Brighter, almost as bright as Fajar's feathers.

It was becoming clear that Squirt wasn't going to be able to catch her on his own, no matter how hard and fast he pounded his wild white wings. He made a disappointed, frustrated, and almost sad sound—like nails scraping on porcelain.

Alone the lady drakonte may have bested Squirt, but together there was nothing he and Izkander couldn't do. He lifted up onto his feet and leaned forward towards Squirt's earhole. "Throw me at her! I'll ask her if she wants to dance."

A halting roar tore from Squirt's throat — laughter. Izkander crouched down and leapt into the air in front of Squirt's nose. The drakonte angled back and caught Izkander's body in the tip of his thin, fuzzy tail. He flapped his wings with all his might, angling his body down to get under the turquoise drakonte. Then he turned himself around so his belly was facing up and snapped his tail, catapulting Izkander high into the air.

Izkander snatched onto two long fronds at the end of the lady drakonte's tail and yanked his body in closer. He hugged himself around the thin fronds, then using the tips of his fingers, clamped onto the smooth scales and pulled himself up onto the creature's back. He focused on his hands and feet, moving one foot at a time as the body wriggled and twisted under him. When he was near the wings, he snapped his head up to see how much further he had to go.

His heart stumbled over a beat, and his jaw dropped in a wide smile. The beautiful lady drakonte was not some wild specimen flying free through a snowstorm. She was tamed and saddled. And riding on her back, staring at him with bright-red eyes that shimmered with the same delicate fractals as her drakonte, was a magnificent woman in golden riding gear. She was tall and lean with skin the color of a summer peach and hair as bright as the sixth moon in a blood year, and she wore a silver circlet around her forehead that gleamed like starlight.

Izkander forgot to breathe. His fingers clung to the scales as the icy wind lifted and tousled her hair. Squirt's eager roar cut into his thoughts, shaking him out of his haze enough to draw a quick inhale. Still, he found his mind stumbling to name the shade of pink that colored the woman's lips.

His smile widened, and he shouted over the roar of the wind, "Salam!"

CHAPTER SIX

Mirri

Mirri stared, mouth agape, at the man who had chased her and Havu relentlessly through the clouds and then spoken at her in Arabic, the tongue of the djinn. He had stayed beat for beat beneath or just behind her drakonte's practiced maneuvers, never quite catching up. Her mind couldn't make sense of it. He was below. She saw him. And then she had readjusted her stirrups, and he wasn't. And his drakonte: she knew for a fact the blocky beast wasn't from Fyre. But then, where did it come from? And why today and now? Why... any of what just happened?

A rush of dread filled her up as she processed the situation. She flipped in her saddle and threw up her hands. "*Thig dheth! Thig dheth!*" She shooed him frantically.

He raised a brow and shrugged, his face a mask of confusion.

Echoes of his greeting filtered into her ear. He looked human, not Fyrish, but he spoke like a djinn. Not that there was time to linger on the strange novelty of the peculiar man.

She switched to the Arabic she had been taught to negotiate with the other nations in Qaf.

"*Ainzil! Ainzil! Get off!*"

The stranger's smile brightened, green eyes shimmering with flecks of gold. "Sorry! I didn't realize anybody was up here."

"Why are you smiling?" she asked, still in Arabic, her eyes wide and heart racing.

And why did his smile make her want to smile, too? What was the matter with her? It didn't matter. The bands of fire had not yet formed on her wrist. Maybe they were too high up. Maybe this strange man didn't count because he wasn't from Fyre. Whatever the reason, the Origin had yet to declare their meeting an Eternal Union, and she would do anything to keep that from happening.

"Get off. Get off!" She stood on Havu's steady back, wind pushing against her to help keep her up, and stepped closer, waving him away. "Off!"

"Hang on a second." He turned and whistled loudly, then cupped a hand to the side of his face. "Squirt!" He turned back to her, his smile undimmed. "My drakonte thinks yours is really cute."

A shiver rippled beneath Mirri's feet. "Havu," she snapped, casting a look over her shoulder at her drakonte. "You did this?"

No. Havu replied with a bite. *Did you not see me put up the chase?*

"Then why are you shivering? I know that shiver. That's a mating shiver. Shame on you, Havu."

"Did you hear that, Squirt?" the man called out to the four-winged silver drakonte who was making long twists in the air in front of them. "A mating shiver! She likes you."

Mirri snapped her eyes back to the man. She was getting sidetracked by Havu's betrayal. She dropped to her knees to crawl the rest of the way to him as the drakonte's back narrowed toward the tail. When she reached him, she pressed her hands together and looked up into his unsettlingly green eyes, ready to beg and glad none of her subjects could see.

"Please, get off."

The silver drakonte let out an ear-splitting roar and puffed himself up in the air in front of Havu, dipping and twisting like a shameless peacock.

"My boy is a little distracted," said the green-eyed man, laughing. "He might let me fall to my death if I let go now."

She pressed her face into her hands, then ran one over and down her hair, pulling it to one side as the wind whipped through it. "Then control him. He's your drakonte, isn't he? You can't stay here."

"It's hard enough to control any guy out on the prowl, let alone a drakonte." He chuckled and shook his head. "You're pretty. My name's Izkander."

With another shiver from Havu, Mirri lost the last of her contentment, frayed already by Urramach earlier and this exhausting chase. Only a miracle had kept the bond of Eternal Union from forming on their wrists yet. And miracles only come once. She had to do something. Anything.

She scratched the itch on her arm and scooted closer. If she pushed him off, she and Havu could break his fall before he hit the ground. Grab him in Havu's mouth and spit him out in a hay bale or something, she was certain of it, he just couldn't sit here anymore. If she wasn't going to be caught by the likes of a respectable man like Urramach, then she definitely wasn't settling for this violating stranger. With a big breath, she jutted her hands forward and tried to pry his fingers from off Havu's scales.

"Please, get off. I'll give you... I don't know. Something. We can talk about it later. Just get off."

Squeezing Havu with his legs, he sat back and set his hands on his knees. "No problem."

He whistled again, lifting his eyes to his own drakonte, who was now flying right beside Havu and tickling her neck with his long black tongue.

"Squirt! It's a negative. We've got to go, buddy."

Mirri winced at the sight. At Havu's suspicious silence since this Izkander had arrived.

She snapped at her drakonte. "The man is right, Havu. If you keep playing, the boy isn't going to listen."

Hmm?

"Havu!"

She clenched her fists, heat spreading from her cheeks down and across her clavicles at the sheer embarrassment of her drakonte's disobedience. At her lack of decorum. She held them in front of her and forced each one to open when a string of fire began to bloom in the air around her wrist.

"The Eternal Flame." Her eyes widened, and she tried to shake it loose. To tamp it out against her pants. "No. No, no no no no no."

"What's happening?" the man asked, lifting his own wrists in front of his face as identical strings of fire wrapped around them. He pushed himself up to his feet, widening his stance to keep from falling. Shrugging, he dropped his hands and glanced to the side at his own misbehaving drakonte. "Sorry for dropping in on you like this. Have a nice day!"

He gave her a lazy salute, then jumped off.

"Oh, no, he doesn't."

Mirri stood, twisting herself toward his drakonte and clambering up Havu's back. There was no way she was going to let some stranger drop himself on her drakonte, bind her to him for eternity, and then saunter off so the Eternal Flame could melt her flesh. She bit her lip, judged the distance, then leapt. Just missing the second wing of the impressive drakonte, she landed with a thud on his soft back. Dazed and out of breath, she wanted nothing more than to examine the traits of the specimen for breeding. But her senses came back in a rush of pain.

"You!" she called. Then she twisted her lips trying to remember his odd name. "Izkander of the green eyes. You can't leave."

He craned his head over his shoulder to look at her, then deftly flipped himself around on the drakonte's back to face her. "Hi, again!" Smiling, he shook his head slowly. "You have got to tell me your name."

She climbed forward until she found a decent spot between one of the drakonte's vertebrae. Havu slid beside them, a sheepish look on her backstabbing face. Mirri turned away from her and focused on the green. Pulling her shoulders back, she stretched her neck long and lifted her chin in the way a righ should when meeting someone of respect. Whoever he was, he had to be that at least, didn't he? If he was going to rule Fyre with her? The thought made her want to roll off the drakonte and fall to the earth, but she held steady.

"I am Mirri Naga, Ah-nis Na Righ of Fyre, and..." She swallowed hard. "Your Fire Mate. As you are mine. Dictated by the Eternal Flame and the prize of this contest."

He drew his eyebrows together and closed his lips, though they quickly tipped up in a lopsided smirk. "Okay."

She dropped her chin. "Okay?"

"I've met some pretty liberal girls, but nobody has ever called me their fire mate within five seconds of meeting me before." His bright, toothy smile returned, and he wiggled his eyebrows. "I'm down."

"You're... down?" Mirri shook her head. She couldn't have heard that word correctly. Then again, her Arabic, while impeccable, was a little rusty. Anger and confusion curled her toes as she clung to the sides of his drakonte. "Wait — You have other Fire Mates? You're married?"

"No. Are you? I forgot to ask." He conked himself in the head with an open palm. "Are you married? I'll also have to verify with some of your friends if that's okay."

Mirri pinched her lips together. "Of course, I'm not married. How could we be Fire Mates if I were married? Do you even know what an Ah-nis Na Righ is? Where are you from?"

He pushed his lips to one side. "I think we must be talking about different things."

She pressed her face into her palms with a groan. It seemed she had misinterpreted his Arabic several times already. Colloquialisms and slang were far harder to stay abreast of when sequestered within their little outcast nation of snake people. She snapped her head back up, remembering her decorum. As she did, a maroon drakonte barreled its way through the clouds.

Ian. With Urramach on his back.

She cringed and glanced at Havu. Would she have time to jump before he saw? Would it matter with the Eternal Flame already blooming on her skin?

Izkander tapped her wrist and then tapped his own. "What's up with this?"

She groaned again. "It is the bond of Eternal Union granted by the Flame. It is what joins us together and dictates that we have our Eve of Fire."

"Wait, wait, wait, wait, wait. Eternal union?"

She glanced at the approaching drakonte. "Not eternal union," she mocked his drab voice, all her propriety lost in the wind. She needed to get back on the ground. "Eternal Union. With capital letters and gravity. We must marry now."

His eyes widened, bolts of black lightning darting through the green.

Mirri bit the inside of her cheek. "You *are* a djinn?"

He didn't look like one, but with colors flashing in his eyes, he must be. At least partially. Maybe an Ahmaran-Zabriyan mutt. Did purple and yellow make brown? Either way, him being djinn made everything worse.

Izkander Green Eyes laughed and shook his head. "You are a trip, girl. You had me there for a second."

She smacked her teeth together. "Is this some kind of joke to you? Another way to mock our country and take everything we have?"

"Woah." He put his hands up defensively. "Calm down. I'm only half-djinn. And I have no desire to mock or put down your country or take anything. I was just trying to help my boy meet your girl. Be a good wingman." He chuckled. "Get it? Wingman? Do you get it?"

The only thing that tore at her soul worse than his words was Urramach's swift approach. He was close enough now to see the green ribbon tied in his hair flapping in the breeze.

She turned hard eyes on *Izkander*. "You mean my eternal fate and very life are now tethered to a man who jumps another girl's drakonte so he can get his *boy* some?" She clapped her hands together. "There has to be a way out of this."

"First of all, I didn't know you were up there. I thought your girl was flying solo. And second, I was just going to ask her if she wanted to dance."

"Lovely," she said, her words drier than the Ghaluman desert on the other side of the mountains. "I'm glad you're taking things so lightly and all, but what part of Eternal Union with the Queen of Fyre are you not getting?"

"I think I'm mostly tripping up on the *eternal* part." He flashed a grin. "Look, clearly this is just a misunderstanding. We'll just explain to... whoever... that I wasn't participating in the contest. Then we can dust off the desert and walk away. Okay?"

"You're going to go explain... to an unquenchable immortal fire... that it made a mistake by giving us these?" She held up her wrist and shook it.

The fire band didn't move. Its orange glow continued its slow, floral-laced churn around both their wrists.

"Or whatever." He lifted his shoulders contritely. "I'm sure we can come up with something to fix this. Come on, pretty girl. Don't look so down."

"Pretty girl?" Mirri pressed her lips flat to keep from shouting. "I am Fyre's divinely appointed Ah-nis Na Righ. My name is—"

"Mirri?" Urramach pulled his drakonte up next to theirs. His eyes darted between Havu's empty saddle and where she straddled another man's drakonte. His gold eyes brightened as they narrowed. "What is the meaning of this?" he asked, his Gaelic sharp and familiar in the wind.

"I... I don't really know."

Mirri stumbled, not sure if she should be speaking Arabic instead for the stranger's sake. At least Urramach spoke both languages, being a councilman and diplomat. She snapped her jaw shut. She may have lost herself with Izkander, but Urramach was still her subject. Right?

She straightened her back and took a deep breath, staying in Gaelic in case Urramach brought anything inappropriate up in front of the stranger. Her betrothed.

"This is Izkander," she nodded toward the man. "He caught me and took up his seat on Havu."

"Is this your fella?" Izkander pointed at Urramach and cocked a brow.

"Not anymore," she muttered.

"You're joking, right?" Urramach kicked his drakonte closer, so its heavy breath mingled with the air and that of the other two beasts. His eyes narrowed to thin slits that barely showed the gold. "If that's what happened, why are *you* on *his* drakonte?"

The great beast under them tensed and made a low *orgle* in his throat, the threatening sound of a territorial male.

Izkander patted his neck reassuringly. "Steady, boy."

She wanted to cry. Just angry, ugly cry in front of both these infuriating men. But that would be improper, completely un-righ like, not to mention an invitation to have her insides melted by the Eternal Flame. Maybe leaving the stranger out of the conversation wasn't the right idea. At least she would have someone back up her claims. And perhaps it was best if this foreigner understood what exactly he had jumped into.

"Councilman, I request we speak in the djinn-tongue while in the presence of the stranger."

Urramach opened his mouth as if to counter, then snapped it shut. At least he seemed content to obey her for now.

She cleared her throat. "I had to jump his drakonte because he tried to leave after the Eternal Union left its mark on us both." She held up her wrist. "And as you know, if he leaves—"

"You die," Urramach said. But he wasn't looking at her anymore, his eyes were burrowing into Izkander. "You dare try to kill our Ah-nis Na Righ? What are you? Something not fully human, not fully Djinn." His fists tightened over the reins, and he spat into the wind. "You make a mockery of what we hold sacred."

Izkander turned his lips inward and shook his head before a small, genial smile grew on his lips. "Listen, fella. I'm not trying to kill anybody, and I am not trying to steal your girl. I clearly have no idea what is going on here. This is all just a big misunderstanding."

"Son of a djinn." Urramach jutted his chin out.

"You're damn right."

Urramach's lips furled. "Mirri," he growled.

Mirri pressed her lips flat as her thoughts raced about like the drakonte below still enjoying the festival. First things first: not dying. Which meant she had to keep Izkander around until he understood. And she would make him understand. Second things second: maintaining authority. That's what her father would say. She tamped down the unruly beat of her heart and focused on the swell of breath in the beast beneath her.

"Councilman Urramach," she crisped the *ch* sound, so it cut through the wind. "You are not to address me so informally. I am your Ah-nis Na Righ, and you disrespect me."

His brows shot up, lips parted. The look of hurt was more than improper, it stung her chest. He glanced between her and Izkander, slowly closed his mouth, then nodded. "I forgot myself. I apologize. We will discuss this on the ground, my Righ."

The formality was exactly what she was looking for, so why did she feel like she couldn't breathe as she watched him and Ian spiral toward the ground?

"You!" she snapped at Izkander as soon as Urramach was out of sight. "Why?"

Izkander had both his arms wrapped over his stomach and a sharp, painful frown on his lips as his bright eyes followed the maroon drakonte. "Allah's mercy, did you see the look on his face?"

"Yes, I saw it. I'm not blind. Oh, you've made such a mess of things. I ought to feed you to Havu. What are you, a djinn, even doing in the skies of Fyre? That alone is sin enough."

He scoffed. "You don't own the sky. Nobody owns the sky. I was just out for a little flight with Squirt and my bird. Maybe next year you should put up signs or something. *Warning, drakonte chase in progress. Turn the other way unless you want to end up eternally unionized.*"

She laughed, hard and brittle. "You think you're being clever? You think this is a joke? We only hold this festival every twenty-five years. And I have never once seen a drakonte in my airspace that I didn't know about."

"Well, then you haven't been looking 'cause Squirt and I come by here all the time."

"Not here, here. Zabriya? Sure. This mountain range? Okay. But not Fyre. Havu would have smelled your beast *miltean* away." She turned to her shame-faced drakonte. "Have you smelled his beast?"

Well...

"Well, what?" she clenched her jaw so tight it hurt.

I didn't know what I smelled until I saw him... He's got a different flavor than the rest.

"A different *flavor*? And did you just shudder?"

Izkander's drakonte purred, gave his own much bigger shudder, and shook his head hard from side to side.

"You dog," Izkander said and patted his neck.

Mirri closed her eyes, trying to see the fire in the veins of her eyelids to help her calm down. She hadn't behaved so poorly since she was five and threw a fit about having to wear her first set of armor out to play with her friends, none of which were dressed so stiffly. She needed to get back her senses and behave like a righ before they touched down.

"Okay, Izkander Green Eyes. You want to fix the mess you made?"

He batted his eyelashes. "I know they're pretty, but you can just call me Izkander."

"Okay…" She nodded slowly, each swoop of his lashes fanning the flames inside her. "Do you have a family name, then?"

"Izkander ibn Bakr, at your service." He swept his hand to one side and gave a little bow.

She scrunched her brow. "Ibn Bakr?" Her eyes widened. "Your father is Shihala's top general? The one who helped oppress the desperate and starving Vespars?"

"My father did no such thing." He scoffed. "He protected stranded civilians from those rampaging freaks who were trying to make slaves out of all of them."

"That's not the story I heard." Mirri shot him a side glance. "But if I were you, when we introduce you to my parents, I would focus more on the fact that your *athair* is a human and a djinn crusher and less on whose side he fought on. We may have a loose treaty with Shihala, but relations between Fyre and the Nine Kingdoms of Qaf are… tense at best."

"No problem, pretty girl. When are we doing the parent meet and greet? Now?"

"My name is Mirri Naga, Ah… Ah, I don't have the patience for this right now. And yes, now. The festival ends with my capture or the moonset, and with the end of the festival, I am officially righ." A tiny smile crept onto her lips. "I must go accept my place and announce our union.

He nodded and put on a big smile. "Okay."

"Okay?" She shook her head, pushing herself to her feet. "Just okay?"

"Uh… okay, ma'am?"

Mirri groaned and leapt into the air, so Havu had to twist around and catch her. She relished the overwhelming drop in her stomach before landing on the saddle. Izkander laughed and whistled approvingly, and another smile formed unbidden on her lips.

Marduk bless her patience and help her be content. This was going to be a disaster.

CHAPTER SEVEN

Izkander

Izkander followed Mirri and Havu down from the sky. He was too preoccupied trying to figure out what he was thinking and feeling to notice many details of the little gray kingdom of stone. He didn't know anything about Fyre, other than it was where the drakonte originally came from.

The kingdom was an oasis of green surrounded by sharp, white crags that rose so high into the sky that clouds hid their tops. But all Izkander could see clearly was the den of drakonte. He'd never seen so many of the creatures in all his life, and his uncle in Shihala kept hundreds of them as mounts in his army. Scales shone in every color of the rainbow—breeds he'd never seen before.

Squirt's muscles tensed as he made that noise again—that low, gargling noise that quite emphatically said *if any of these sacks of silver mess with me, I will murder all of them.*

Izkander leaned far forward to pat the top of his head. "You're the reason we're in this mess in the first place, so play nice."

He looked down at the intricate ropes of fire wrapped and churning around his wrists like bioluminescent tattoos. They reminded him a little of the Covenant of Shihala, which his Aleamu Jahmil and Aleamat Ayelet wore for one another. That, of course, was a symbol of mutual passion. A mark bestowed by the spirit of Shihala to bless a union that had already naturally formed. But this... this felt more like the Seal of Elm, something stamped on his body without his permission that he had no choice but to adhere to.

Something about Mirri dying, and eternal fire, and not being able to leave. None of that sounded good.

He stole another look at her: Mirri, with eyes like red suns, hair a cascade of fresh lava, and a perfectly curved body under all her tight leather army. Simply calling her pretty was a bit of a misnomer. She was intoxicating. He'd never seen another woman like her, and not only because she rode her drakonte like she was one herself.

He wanted to get close enough to smell her hair, to run his fingers over her impossibly pale skin. It looked so warm.

Mirri. What a name. Soft and feminine and delicate, but with a cauldron of power bubbling under the surface.

At first, he'd had trouble remembering it—such a long rattle of syllables she'd given him when he first asked. It was the same with nobles and royalty everywhere, all so proud of their long, complicated titles. Her real name had only stuck when that man—the handsome one with shiny copper hair and golden eyes, and the long face that cut into his heart like shards of glass—had said *Mirri* in that pain-filled, dejected voice. And she had chastised him for it.

Izkander wondered if it was okay for him to call her Mirri. Or would he get the same heart-crushing lecture? Of course, it wouldn't crush his heart. He didn't have any skin in this game.

Izkander looked down at his wrists. Okay, maybe he had a little skin in it.

Banners were strung between the buildings and from tall posts all about the little stone city, ribbons waving in the chilly wind. People with eyes like drakonte approached cautiously to make a semi-circle around them.

Every vertically slit pupil was glued to Izkander. Whispers permeated the crowd, starting at the front and sweeping back like a high wave moving off the shore. The language was vowel-poor with a *shush-ga-shush* rhythm to it he'd never encountered before. No matter how loudly they spoke, they all sounded like they were whispering.

Izkander hopped down from Squirt's back, landing on his feet in the squishy grass. The discomfort in his gut caused his hand to itch for his sword, but he forced it loose before jogging over to Mirri.

She glanced at him, one hand on the hilt of the sword she wore around her waist and the other stiff at her side. Her back was as straight as an arrow. "The race is over, thanks to you. There's no reason to rush around here on the ground."

"Oh, no. That's just me. I'm bouncy." He bobbed on his feet and flashed a smile. "So, what's the game? What's the schtick? Tell me a story, baby."

"Baby?"

"I mean, Mirri." He bowed his head slightly, waiting for his lecture.

Her lips pressed into a thin line, her eyes trained on the winding path through the onlookers. "The *shtick* is only our most sacred custom that ensures the perpetuation of Marduk's fire and satisfies the Eternal Flame."

"Cool, cool." His smile brightened.

He couldn't call her baby or pretty girl—his mother's voice echoed through his head telling him he shouldn't do that anyway because it was patronizing—but he could call her Mirri. That was all he really wanted.

He cracked his neck and let his gaze slide up to the towering mountains. It was hard to listen to what she was saying when he was looking at those eyes. "So, do you need kindling or something?"

"No." Her lips had all but gone. "Unless you're offering yourself. Long ago my people ceased the sacrifice of flesh in exchange for the Eternal Union, but we can go back if you'd like. I wouldn't mind."

She was picking on him. Those tight veins in her neck said she meant it, but there was something in her voice that sounded just a tiny bit playful.

Izkander put a hand to his chest. "Far be it from me to change the way you do business."

"Really? I got the distinct impression it was the opposite."

"I happen to agree on this one point—ceasing the sacrifice of flesh, that is. In fact, it's the first good news I've heard all day."

"Tinder for you, then. Congratulations." She flicked the fingers on both her hands and pressed her palms together. "When we enter the castle, my father will be there to greet you and welcome you as Subsidiary Righ and my Fire Mate. He does not appreciate jokes."

"Meet the parents time, huh?" He spread his arms wide to stretch his chest. This was all moving very quickly. The word *eternal* nipped at his ears again. He brushed it off like a fly.

"Don't worry. I'm good with parents. I got a couple of my own back home."

"Yes. The Vespar slayer and famed Shihalan Princess. Fantastic. I will meet them shortly as well. Though I get the impression our parents are not of the same caliber, considering the output."

"Redheads, huh?" He winked at her.

"Idiots."

He didn't give a pile of *khanaziri* crap what anybody said about his old man, but normally he'd fight to the death to defend the tiniest slight against his umi. When Mirri said it, however, all he could do was laugh. "That's not a nice thing to say about your own parents."

The vein in her neck twitched. "I wasn't aware you required coddling. Verywell. From henceforth, you shall be known in Fyre as Gaol Aig an Righ."

With a mere glance from Mirri, two of the guards that lined the castle gates hastened forward to pull the cast iron doors wide. Before proceeding, she pulled each of her boots and stockings off and handed them to a waiting servant who acted like that was a perfectly normal thing to do.

He turned around to scan the crowd and the city one last time, walking backward to follow her inside. They were all wearing shoes.

Should he take his shoes off? He looked down at his feet, then back at Mirri, then back at the guy holding her shoes. His umi didn't allow shoes inside, but that was more of a carpeting issue.

Everybody wore shoes at the court at Karzusan.

This was a castle in a foreign kingdom, it made sense that different rules applied. At least, he supposed this gloomy pile of stone was the castle—tiny and unadorned.

His gaze drifted to the high dome of the ceiling, then followed down the carved stone columns, all roughly hewn. It reminded him of his own house, and also not at all. They were equally gray and imposing, but there was no warmth here. No chaos.

His eyes darted to Mirri, who kept a steady pace down the hall.

Her butt was unbelievable.

He gave a soft whistle, then jogged to catch up, his boots echoing on the floor. "Nice place you got here. Reminds me of a mausoleum."

"Yes. I could see that," she said, tone and eyes flat.

Izkander tucked his smile up in one corner. Was that a joke? That definitely sounded like a joke.

They followed a green and gold carpet to the front of a wide throne room draped in curtains that glistened like drakonte scales. With each step, Mirri's body wound tighter, her steps shortened, and her shoulders drew back. Izkander straightened his back.

The stone floor was mostly bare and roughly hewn, a worn path through the center that shone against the firelight. Real fire that smoked as it burned a bright orange. A few thin rugs in rich colors rested beneath wooden benches that lined the wall. And in the very center of the room, a large fountain gurgled. Not with water, but with viscous lava that radiated dizzying heat.

At the end of the room were two people sitting on stiff, metal thrones. He could only assume they were Mirri's parents and the rulers of this strange land. In Shihala, Ahmar, and Vespar—all throughout Qaf and in some places on Ard like Turkey—the monarchs all sat on oversized, comfortable divans when they held court so they could lounge and enforce their will at the same time. Because they're in charge and why should their backs hurt? It made perfect sense.

He'd never understood those pictures his mother showed him of the ghostly pale, human kings of a place on Ard called Europe sitting on stiff-backed chairs and looking very uncomfortable.

Mirri's parents were pale and looked human, other than their snakelike eyes, of course. Maybe pale humans just liked to sit like that.

Side-by-side and stiff as old *pide*, they gazed down at him from their platform. The man was white-haired with a square face and a body to match. Like Mirri, he wore gold and bronze armor. A deep emerald green cape was draped over one shoulder and secured with a matching golden broach that twisted in overlapping triangles.

He wore a tall gold crown and a severe scowl, and his eyes were as red as the veins of Fajar's feathers.

The woman at his side was petite, like Mirri, with vibrant silver hair woven tightly into a braid and the quirk of a smile on one corner of her lips. Her eyes were red too, but lighter with undertones of gold.

Only the man had bare feet.

"Play nice," Mirri whispered.

Izkander smirked. "I'm always nice."

"Then don't be an idiot."

"Ooo, feisty."

She cast him a scathing look. He wanted to push her arm. He wanted her to push him back.

She dipped her head in a shallow bow and pressed a fist against her chest. "Fa Chomhair Righ, Mother. This is Izkander, the catcher of the Righ and my Fire Mate as decreed by the Eternal Flame."

Izkander raised an open palm to wave. "*Salam.*"

The man's jowls stiffened, but he didn't move.

Mirri's mother tilted her head to the side. "Where do you hail from, Izkander Green Eyes?"

"Ard." He offered another smile. That was all he ever told people. Eayima garnered a wide range of reactions from people—from total confusion, to awe, to outright denial.

Ard was good enough. Nobody in Qaf ever asked any follow-up questions when he said Ard.

"A human, then?" The woman's head tilted the other way. "But with strangeness. A mix. Newer. Your blood doesn't know what to do with itself." She squinted and leaned forward. "Some djinn, obviously—which explains your tongue—but also something more. Something with those eyes..." She tapped her lip, and her eyes wandered toward a corner of the room.

He also didn't tend to offer up the fact that he was a quarter *lilu* to people who didn't know. Another subject that brought too many questions, and no shortage of fear and judgment. Djinn and humans alike feared and despised lilitu, and with good reason.

Half-djinn and half-human was good enough. But this woman could tell there was something more. Very observant and educated people often could. But would she be able to figure out what?

The king scowled, his voice growly like a drakonte defending its prey. "A djinn? The Flame has chosen a djinn?"

"Half." Mirri's eyes tumbled to the floor. "He says he's only half-djinn."

"The best half." Izkander smiled, thinking of his umi.

The king's lips curled. "You would be wise to remember the kingdom you are in. You are lucky we do not throw you in the Origin's cusp and dampen your magic so you cannot leave. Or do you make a mockery of my daughter's devotion and her role as Ah-nis Na Righ?"

"You really don't like djinn, huh?"

The king's face reddened. "Don't be mistaken. It is the djinn who don't like us. And if there weren't some human in you, I'd cut you down now and challenge the Eternal Flame with my life to keep you from ruling this country."

Mirri's mother reached across the space between the thrones and patted the spitting man's arm.

Izkander licked his teeth. "I would love to see you try, old man."

Mirri's eyes flicked to his, wide and pleading. "I'm sorry, Fa Chomhair Righ." She bowed her head. "For failing."

"Who's the one questioning the will of the Eternal Flame here?" Izkander lifted his wrists in front of his face and waved them around. "It's not me."

Mirri's father took a clomping step forward, his eyes glowing with all that red. "So you are content to fulfill your duties as Subsidiary and remain in Fyre until the Ah-nis Na Righ passes to the Flame?"

That was one hell of a question. And there was really no reason to answer it.

"Correct me if I'm wrong," Izkander said, "but I can't leave with these things on my wrists or we'll die, right?"

Mirri's mother seemed to pull out of her reverie. "You may leave if she goes with you. But go without her, and you both will violate the traditions and rules that bind her blood, and she will die."

He glanced at Mirri, a little fracture opening in his heart at the thought of hurting her. Still, he needed to know.

"Will I die?"

Mirri's mother shook her head. "You are not bound to the Eternal Flame. It does not animate your spirit as it does hers."

Izkander looked at Mirri again. She kept her gaze on the floor.

"I have to stay then, don't I?" He sighed, reality beginning to dawn on him. "I don't have a choice."

Mirri's neck tensed. "Do not be too burdened by your fate, Gaol Aig an Righ. There are many who would love to marry the righ and serve the people of Fyre. To be chosen by the Origin."

Izkander felt dizzy. "It just keeps coming and coming with all the good news."

Everything that had happened crashed over him at once, like he'd just smacked the ocean in a belly flop from a thousand feet. He downcast his gaze and set a hand on his forehead, shaking his head slowly from side to side.

This was all Squirt's fault. He was going to kill that horny snake.

Izkander forced a tight smile and turned it around the room, bobbing his head.

"What are you doing?" Mirri hissed.

"Being nice."

"No, you're being an idiot. Stop bobbing."

"Don't tell me what to do. I'll bob if I want to bob."

"I am your Ah-nis Na Righ." She tipped her chin up but kept her voice low. "You could at least listen when I'm trying to tell you that you're acting like a fool in a country you know nothing about."

"Well, I'm your *goo wah booboo*, so you could try to be a little more understanding of the rough day I've had. Let a man bob, for crying out loud."

"Enough with this childish prattle," Mirri's father boomed. His cold eyes turned on his daughter who dropped her gaze once more to the floor. "Mirri, are you content with fulfilling the will of the Flame and honoring the Eternal Union?"

She didn't look up. "I am content."

"And you, Izkander Green Eyes? Are you content?"

"That's not the word that leaps to mind." He rubbed his chin, narrowing his eyes at the carpet. "Just for the sake of argument, what if I'm not content? What happens then?"

The man bristled. "Is that a formal request?"

"It is what we on Ard call an innocuous question."

The man smirked. "I am not bound to answer innocuous questions."

Izkander smirked back and shrugged. "Then I'm not bound to answer your questions, either."

Mirri's father jumped to his feet and stormed down the steps. He jabbed a hard finger at the bands on Izkander's wrists. "Oh yes, you are."

Izkander crossed his arms and made a point of sealing his lips.

Mirri twisted to look at him, her eyes scanning his and her face pale instead of peach. "There is far more at stake than your pride, here, Gaol Aig an Righ. Or have you already forgotten?"

"If so much is at stake, I really don't understand why your father won't answer my question. I'm not being unreasonable."

"Perhaps not," Mirri's mother smoothed her way between him and the pulsating king whose face had turned a most interesting shade of pockmarked pink. "But try to look at it from our perspective. A stranger who knows nothing of our customs and values drops in and binds himself to our queen on the day she is declared the official Ah-nis Na Righ. He then meets the king of our lands and speaks with a flippancy unknown here in Fyre. You have shaken us and made us fear for a future left under your care. And now you ask if there's a way you can wash your hands of it altogether. You have wounded this nation's soul."

Izkander sighed, his arms dropping to his sides. His brows lifted in the middle as a little frown grew on his lips that always hurt so much more than he wanted it to.

"I'm sorry for wounding your nation's soul." He kicked his foot on the carpet. "But I didn't bind myself to anyone. It was an accident. And okay, I don't understand your customs. But if you refuse to explain them to me then isn't that kind of a bit your fault?"

The man scoffed. King... whatever. But it was Mirri who stepped forward this time, eyes warily on her father.

"I will speak with him, Fa Chomhair. I will make him understand before we have our Eve of Fire."

"There is only so much that can be done to untangle such a twisted mind," the king said.

Izkander bit his tongue, a snarl growing on his face. He wanted to punch this guy in the face so badly his knuckles hurt.

He bit down hard and didn't call the old king any of the six dozen dirty names that sprang to mind. "Are we done here, or...?"

Murder flashed across the king's face, which Izkander found extremely satisfying. As his old man always said, there was nothing like flippancy to get under the skin of royalty. Baba used the technique on Umi, the princess, all the time to spectacular results.

Mirri grabbed his arm and dragged him out of the banquet hall and down a narrow set of pathways until they reached a giant tapestry with some massive snakes and cowering people on it. She yanked the side open and shoved him in.

"What is wrong with you?"

He wiped a hand over the back of his neck and gave a heavy sigh. "I've had a hell of a day."

"You're not the only one who exists here, Izkander. But you seem to forget that."

"Your old man is a real peach. I'm a big fan of his."

She shoved her fists on her hips. "Why is everything you say a joke?"

He mirrored her, putting his fists on his. "Why is everything you say so serious?"

She clenched her teeth and gave a dry laugh from deep in her throat. "Your mother must be a real gem to put up with someone like you."

"My umi is the most beautiful and wonderful woman ever, and she adores me." He flattened his face and nodded. "That is no joke."

Mirri's thin brows knit together. "Okay."

"Okay." He put back on his smile as his eyes scanned the little space they were in behind the tapestry. "So, this is an interesting change of venue. What kind of stuff usually goes on back here?"

She leaned her back against the wall and banged her head a few times. "The lawfully indecorous."

"Indecorous...?" Izkander flipped through files in his mind, casting himself back in time to days sitting in front of books with his umi when all he wanted was to play in the sunshine. And then the file pulled up and his brows lifted. "Ahh... indecorous. Fun."

"Not fun." Mirri sighed. "Very not fun."

He lifted a shoulder and whispered, "Could be fun."

She shook her head with a scoff, but there was definitely a smile on those pink lips. "Could be."

Izkander's stomach turned in a totally unexpected and weirdly pleasant way. He so wanted to run his fingers through her hair. He had to put his hands behind his back to stop himself and looked down at the floor.

There were so many questions that he felt he deserved answers to. The one burning in his stomach at the moment was probably one of the less important in the grand scheme of things, but he couldn't help himself. "Can I ask you something serious?"

"I would welcome it."

"I knew you'd be game." He winked. "That guy from earlier. The one with the face. How serious are you two? I mean, were you hoping he was going to catch your Havu?"

Her face softened for the first time since he'd met her. "Courtship for a descendant of Marduk, like me—" She bowed her head. "—is different. I did not want him to catch me because I did not want to be caught at all. Not yet. But maybe down the road...." She twisted her lips to the side and pulled herself up from the wall, shoulders back. "It doesn't matter now. Does it?"

"It matters to me." His stomach sank, realizing just how true that was. Mirri was taken. Not technically, but in her heart.

Everything that had happened with Ya'el and her husband earlier that day ripped through him like fire through his lungs. He wanted to ignore the man with the face, however Mirri might feel about him—to do everything in his power to forget all about her.

His umi's voice echoed through his head. *Now that you've helped a woman cheat on her spouse, unwittingly or not, and felt how awful that is, the next time counts.*

His shoulders slumped. "I don't want to get in the middle of somebody else's love story."

"The Ah-nis Na Righ is not afforded a chance to love, at least not in the beginning. And I never said I *did* love Urramach. He is... he is simply the one who has smiled at me for years. Handsome. From a good line. And... decorous?" She looked at Izkander with a tiny smile. "Except for the one time he was not."

"It sounds to me like you're into him." He smiled gently, then shook his head. Little ripples of pain were moving through his guts like kidney stones—guilt and frustration and shame and other things he didn't want to think about because they were stupid and didn't belong.

"I think you just want to be free for a little longer," he said.

"Wouldn't you?" she whispered.

"Girl, are you kidding? Who wants to get tied down so young?"

"Right? I'm a moon's pass from twenty and I'll live like seven hundred years. Why must I marry now?" She bit her lip and blushed. "Besides, I can do everything I need to well enough on my own."

"No truer words." He laughed, an image of her riding high on her drakonte flashing through his mind. "I've got a millennium or two in my future.

"A millennium?" She shook her head, eyebrows drawn together. What exactly *are* you?"

He shrugged with a grin, still wary to share his bloodlines after how things went down with her parents. "It's complicated. More importantly, I'm never getting married. Not unless I find the other half of my soul, which is pretty unlikely."

"The other half of your soul?" Mirri tugged on the end of her silky, straight hair. "What does that mean?"

"Just a stupid romantic fantasy of mine. It doesn't matter." He looked up at her and smiled. "We'll figure a way out of this. And with the way you fly, I don't think you'll need to worry about getting caught until you want to. I mean, so long as I keep Squirt out of the game."

"Your drakonte *is* magnificent. I'd love to meet him. Formally, I mean."

He chuckled. "I'd be happy to introduce you. Just promise me you won't call him magnificent to his face. His ego is big enough already."

"Havu said it enough for the both of us, trust me." She pursed her lips, eyes sparkling.

"They got the hots for each other. I think they'd both be very happy if we chaperoned a little date."

"Alright. We can go down to the hatchery and stables and go for a ride from there. What do..." Her mouth twisted into a nervous grin. "I mean, whaddya say?"

"Yes please." Grinning, he watched her face, warm tingles spreading across his chest. "You are so pretty."

"Ah-nis Na Righ!" a man's voice barreled down the hallway, knocking Izkander from the pretty silver cloud that grew under his feet whenever he looked into those red eyes.

Her face hardened to stone, and her back straightened. She took a step back from Izkander, then slipped out from behind the tapestry. Her abrupt departure felt like being doused in freezing rain. Their ride together would have to wait.

He followed her back out into the hall. A man in uniform bowed to Mirri. His eyes were wide, full of fear, face red from running.

"Righ." The soldier bowed. "*Is e am buklak a th'ann. Tha e air ais aig ar criochan.*"

"I'm sorry. What?" Izkander scratched a brow, the look on the man's face enough to tell him he needed to know what was going on.

Mirri sighed. "He informs me the buklak is back and at our borders."

Izkander turned to Mirri, trying to gauge what in heaven a buklak was from her reaction.

Nothing good.

Her eyes widened before narrowing into slits. "*Cuir coinneamh air dòigh sa bhad,*" she commanded, then glanced at him and said in Arabic, "Arrange a meeting immediately."

CHAPTER EIGHT

Mirri

Relief.

It was the word that seemed most fitting, and one that she had read many times and never really understood. That was until she spoke with Izkander behind the tapestry. The feeling was akin to taking off her armor after a full day of battle drills. But for her heart.

But she had let her emotions take off their armor too soon. The news of the buklak struck a wound deep in her heart. She shouldn't have been playing with a boy when her people were in danger.

A tiny prick poked her ribs with the thought, and she rubbed the itch waking on her chin. Maybe she could turn this around. She didn't know much about this Izkander Green Eyes, but what she did know was promising. That he could ride a drakonte better than most people in Fyre. That he carried a metal sword on his waist and didn't seem bothered by it hanging there. And that his father was a famous Shihalan general. Maybe he could help her with her problems. Or at least, remain by her side while she fought the beast back.

All she had to do was show him her people were devout, hard-working, honest people being attacked on all sides by forces beyond their control. Survivors. He wouldn't deny them his help after that, right? It was worth the price of having a constant shadow. A smirky, sassy, untraditional shadow that was sure to shake the foundation of Fyre every time he opened his mouth.

And one whom she'd fly with later.

She and Izkander walked to the war room as quickly as their dignified steps would carry them. Fyre's drakonte seal had been painted in red over the thick wood door, cast iron stripes of black running horizontal and vertical in a thick lattice above and below. It was the hold. The last resort of her people. And had not been used once. She planned to keep it that way by finding a way to stop the monster in her tracks. Nevermind that her father had been fighting the monster for centuries.

She tilted her head back to look at Izkander. "No talking. Okay?"

"Uh, yeah." He laughed, his shoulders shaking. "That's not gonna happen."

"Okay…" She inhaled as she thought, grateful she could breathe. "Can you at least wait until you speak? Let me have a chance to address my generals and introduce you. The situation is incredibly tense, and there is no time for shenanigans."

"I'll do my best. But you owe me one."

"Excuse me?" She whipped her head to the side with a wave of red hair.

He shrugged. "You owe me one."

"For what?"

"For being decorous," he said in a mock-noble voice.

She almost scoffed, but a pair of servants passed at the end of the hallway. She kept her face straight. Mirri watched them until they were out of sight then flicked her eyes back to Izkander.

He glanced over his shoulder, eyes following to the doorway where the servants had exited. "Interesting…" he said in a low sing-song voice, then he turned back to her.

"You haven't been decorous once since you popped out of the sky."

"No. But I just said I was going to try. And if I'm successful, you owe me one."

"I don't see why I should reward you for behaving as you should. But it seems the best I shall get from you." She gave him one last itch-filled look and shoved the doors open.

A group of twelve men and women stood around a square table with a map of Fyre covering the entirety. They glanced up as she approached, then stood straight and clipped their heels together, hands to their chest.

"Ah-nis Na Righ."

She nodded to each then took her place at the head of the table, Izkander strolling behind her like they were out for a picnic. She blinked to get him out of her mind and focus.

"My apologies for speaking in the djinn tongue." She dipped her head. "The Gaol Aig an Righ must understand what we face. For those of you who need it, a translation will be provided as we go along. Now, I appreciate you all making the sacrifice to be here as the First Moon begins to arch high in the sky. I know many of you would rather be at the festival with your families."

"We serve the Flame," they said in unison.

Izkander stifled a giggle.

She shot him a glare. Decorous her bare foot.

"But it is family that brings us here, today. Children. The *buklak* has returned to our borders and seems unaffected by the Origin's lava we have previously used to keep it back. I do not know which deity it serves, but it is an enemy to our kingdom. We must find a way to chase it from our borders. General Riley, where was the beast last seen?"

"Along the Alsafar River, Ah-nis Na Righ."

Izkander poked her in the ribs, and she snapped her head to glare.

He leaned in and whispered, "Are you going to introduce me? Because this is torture."

"I am not." She sharpened her eyes with a challenge.

"But you said I couldn't talk until you introduced me."

"I know." With her face turned safely away from her generals, she put up a sweet, mocking smile, then wiped it clean. "But if you can't be decorous, admit defeat."

He threw his hands up in the air. "Defeat."

She clenched her fist when the doors to the war room burst open. Two soldiers fell through, one holding the other up and both in the shredded rags of their uniforms.

Mirri rushed forward and barked orders to get the men aid. Then knelt in front of the less-bloodied soldier. "What happened? Tell me now."

"The *buklak*, it's here."

Her chest seized, all the breathing room she had gained with Izkander evaporating. "What do you mean *here*?"

The man spat blood onto the onyx tile. "Coming from the gharb, through the fields of wheat toward the lower village. We believe it recovered from our last stand at Mashrub Sakhin Lake on the other side of the mountain range and came straight from there."

"What happened to the defenses?" Mirri curled her fingers to keep from shaking him. "Yuria's swoop should have been managing the line to the gharb."

The soldier's face fell, golden eyes failing to meet his righ's face. "It came out of nowhere, as if in a shock of lightning. Yuria has fallen."

Mirri jumped up and ran through the doors, calling orders to ready the drakonte. The buklak, the nasty immortal child-eater, now approached the festival.

"Mirri!" Izkander was at her side in a degree, grinning with big white teeth. "Real quick, what's a buklak?"

"Stop smiling," she said, dashing up the stairs toward the balustrades. "And it's a leathery, winged creature with teeth the size of your scrawny little legs that goes around eating the weak and helpless."

"Anything else I ought to know about it? Weaknesses? What it did to those two guys back there?"

"It used to fear the Eternal Flame but has grown resilient, gaining strength from whatever deity it serves. As far as we can tell, the beast cannot be slain by blade, nor arrow, nor lava. It is an immortal plague on my nation that has terrorized Fyre for generations."

"Immortal, huh?" His infuriating smile grew to inconceivable heights. He put his hand out to her, palm up. "I got you, girl. Come with me."

"Right now? When I'm supposed to be leading drakonte into battle with a ferocious monster?"

He cocked an eyebrow. "Do you want to kill it? I mean, *kill it* once and for all."

She stopped in her tracks, bare toes gripping the smooth floor. If she was going to be forced into an Eternal Union before she could prove herself, she at least needed a Subsidiary Righ who could be of use to her. Was she crazy for considering Izkander's proposal? She didn't know where he was taking her, and his glib attitude left her on edge. But she also knew exactly where this next battle would take her and her swoops. To a lot of wounded and dead citizens of Fyre and a monster who would leave just to come back another day. If she was going to be a consistent and good righ, she had to protect her people.

Maybe that meant taking a leap.

She looked up at him, studying his face. "No games?"

"I never play games when child-eating monsters are concerned."

Mirri bit her lip and scanned his eyes, looking for mockery. Nothing but forest green tinged with a few sparks of pale blue and copper.

She reached out and grabbed General Riley's sleeve as he ran by. "Lead the cause. Bring Havu and the Gaol Aig an Righ's drakonte to the front. We will be with you shortly."

The general clapped his hand to his chest and sprinted up the stairs. Mirri turned back to Izkander. What he asked flew in the face of order. Tradition. But none of that had yet killed the monster.

She pressed her hand into his. "Take me."

He looked into her eyes and a confident smile grew on his face. Warm, orange fire wrapped around her like a fog, and the castle faded to nothing.

She had heard stories from a few of her generals who had tangled with djinn and survived the encounter, but none of what they said about how apparation felt came close to what she was experiencing now. It felt like her insides had been sucked into her belly button and left to linger in a white place of nothingness. Surreal. Peaceful. Disturbing. And then her insides were pushed back out, and she stood in a grassy field. She dropped to one knee, breathing in short gasps as a stitch stabbed its way into her ribs.

"Warn a girl next time you're about to pop her through realms, will you?"

"Sorry." His hand—still twinkling with his fire—held tight to hers. He pulled her to her feet. "You've never apparated before?"

Mirri shook her head, still out of breath. "It is forbidden in our kingdom in an effort to keep djinn from finding a way in and apparating their friends back in an invasion we could not stop. We don't employ firewalls or any other of your djinn magic. We rely on the reclusiveness of our nation and the strength of the Origin to keep us safe."

Mirri made sure both her feet were firmly planted beneath her. Wet grass tickled her toes, grounding her. A strange house stood before her. Or maybe it wasn't a house, but a church or library. Its red and white chipped surface implied neglect, but bright curtains hung in the windows in bursts of blue and yellow. The windows were hard rectangles like those in Fyre, but the roof sloped up in arches similar to the palace she'd seen in Shihala when she visited on business with her father. Not quite the same, but it was the best her jostled brain could do. The air felt cold, too, the way it only ever did when she was away from the Flame. And it was bright. So bright.

She cupped a hand to her forehead and squinted at the sky. A solid light-blue dotted with puffs of clouds. No moons. No galaxies. And one beautiful, beaming star.

"Is that the sun?" she asked, breathless. "Are we on Ard?"

"That's right." His cheeks dimpled with a muted smile. "This is España. It's a real nice place if you can get past all the ghouls.

"No time to waste," he said, then broke into a run towards the house, holding her hand to drag her along. It was all she could do to follow without tripping over her bare feet as she stared agape at the beautiful shining circle. She had always wanted to see the sun, and now he was hurrying her through it as a monster ate her people. When they reached a small wooden door at the back of the house, he elbowed it open and burst inside.

"*Que demonios!*" a deep voice cried.

Mirri stepped up behind Izkander into a kitchen with wood paneling on the walls and floor and copper pots hung near a large iron stove. It smelled of butter and fresh-baked bread. A giant of a man with a massive beard and arms like baby drakonte stood at a counter wearing a white apron with lace trim. Flour dusted his cheeks.

"Izkander?" The huge man widened his brown eyes. "*¿Por qué estás aquí? Serap no está en casa. Ella y Cova están comprando mermelada en el pueblo.*"

"Arabic," Izkander said breathlessly in Arabic. "*No hablo,* okay?"

He cleared his throat and switched to Arabic, speaking with a heavy accent unlike any Mirri had ever heard before. "Serap's in town buying jam."

Mirri bit back a grimace. His heavy accent and the swishy way he spoke the Arabic language made it difficult to follow his words despite her education. In truth, as the second royal child, she was never meant to leave Fyre like most of her people and had very little practical application. That she could converse so easily with Izkander was a gift from the Origin all on its own.

"That's okay," Izkander beamed, always undeterred. "I came to see you."

"Why?" The bearded man's voice was flat. "And who is this woman?"

He yanked on Mirri's hand and pulled her in front. "This is the Queen of Fyre."

"And you've kidnapped her, have you?"

Izkander stuck his tongue out at the giant. "Mirri, this is Javier Don DeMario, also known as my uncle, also known as The Immortal Killer."

She snapped her gaze back to the giant man covered in flour, then whispered harshly, "I said no games, Green Eyes."

"No games." His smile reached infuriating brightness, then he turned back to his uncle. "Queen Mirri has something she wants to ask you."

Mirri glanced between the man and Izkander with wide eyes. Was that it for introductions?

Was she authorized to speak on behalf of Fyre? She shook her head. Of course, she was. She was Righ now. As of that day. She could declare war on all of Qaf if she wanted.

"Go on," Izkander nudged her. "You want the monster dead, right?"

She nodded slowly. "Of course I do. But I—You haven't—"

She bit her tongue, upset at herself for once more looking a fool. Her father would never stutter so. Neither would Maron, for all his faults. Even if no one had taught her how to be righ as thoroughly as they had her brother, it didn't mean she couldn't do everything he did. She stopped curling her toes and locked her gaze on the supposed Immortal Killer legends talked about. Her own father had visited this very killer without luck many years ago. The burly man had simply thrown their nation's problem in a hat full of crinkled slips of paper and told them he'd get to it when it was drawn. They'd never heard from him again.

She would do better. She would gain his aid, and then her father would know.

"Immortal Killer." She cleared her throat of phlegm and fear. "I humbly request your divinely bestowed aid to help eliminate the immortal monster killing children in my homeland of Fyre."

"Can't it wait?" the man said, wiping his hands on his apron. "I just put a loaf of challah in the oven."

"What part of *immortal monster killing children*...?" Mirri stuttered before wrapping her hands together to keep her decorum. "Please, it would mean the world to the parents of Fyre who live daily knowing their children could be ripped in half and sucked of their blood by yellow, fanged teeth."

The Immortal Killer tugged on his beard with a pout, leaving powdery fingerprints in the dark curls. "It's bread day."

"Please, *Tio*," Izkander interjected, clasping his hands together and lifting them. "When have I ever asked you for anything?"

"You and your father never cease to ask things of me," the giant grumbled.

"This has nothing to do with Baba. This is about Fyre—a whole country living in, well, fear." He chuckled lightly, then shook his head and refocused. "This is about Mirri and her duty to protect her people. Please."

Izkander set his hand on Mirri's shoulder. She dipped slightly to escape his touch, but his hand moved with her, strong and sure. She bit her lip to keep from blushing and let it stay.

The two men stared at each other, Izkander with a pleading grin and the Immortal Killer with a glare.

Finally, the big man's shoulders slumped, and he untied the strings of his apron. "Fine. I'll get my armor on."

Relief—that before elusive feeling—rushed through Mirri. "Thank you, servant of the Bahamut." She pressed a fist to her chest and bobbed her head once.

"*Sí, sí.* You're welcome." He grumbled as he walked away. "*Si quemas mi pan te despellejas, muchacho.*"

"Hurry," Izkander said.

The giant turned slowly, murder in his eyes. "What did you say to me?"

"Please?" Izkander looked down at the floor, then lifted a couple of big puppy dog eyes. "I mean, thank you. Sir."

"That's more like it." The huge man jutted up his chin, then walked from the room with a grunt.

Izkander turned to Mirri and lifted his shoulders. "He'll just be a second."

She wrinkled her nose. "How come you obey him and not me?"

"Because he's my uncle, and you're just some chick I met."

"I am *not* just some chick you met," she muttered, several more choice words on her tongue that were neither appropriate nor kind. She took a deep breath and met his fine features. "My father made a desperate appeal to the Immortal Killer a decade ago, and he threw us in his hat without another word. But you can just walk in and ask your uncle to kill the monster, and he comes?"

"He's not technically my uncle. His wife is my cousin. Well, actually, Serap is my mom's half-brother's adopted human daughter." Izkander glanced up at the ceiling, his face contorting with thought. "Yeah, that's right. We're not actually related. Like at all. But he and my old man go way back. I've been out monster hunting with him like a thousand times."

"That's infuriating." Mirri's nose twitched with itching. "*You* are utterly infuriating. You half-djinn, part-human with something else in your absurdly green eyes. You fly drakonte like you were born in Fyre, live on Ard, speak like you grew up in Shihala, and show up one day by *happenstance* to become the Subsidiary Righ of a millennia-old nation."

"What are you gonna do?" He smiled and shrugged, infuriating her more.

She pushed down her brows to look angry. But what *could* she do? He had provided her with an answer to a fang-toothed monster that had plagued her people for centuries. Being anything other than grateful would be discontent, and she did not want to burn even so far from her homeland that the wind made her shiver. Never mind that *she* was the righ who was supposed to protect her people and had had no more luck with the man than her father did. Never mind that Izkander didn't even let her try again. He just jumped in and did it himself, thinking her incapable just like everyone else. He may have stumbled into their Eternal Union, but he was wasting no time trying to replace her.

Still, this was about her people and the dying children. Not her pride or her place in the kingdom. She would be grateful, she would be content, but she didn't have to like Izkander or the way he took over things without consulting her first.

She would use his service as the Righ but she would not be replaced by him.

CHAPTER NINE

Izkander

Izkander led the way as they walked around the side of Javier's house to where his uncle always kept a ladder leaned up against the brick. It was important to him that djinn—the bane of his existence—could always make a quick exit. The fire alone was enough for a djinn to apparate from Qaf to Ard, but getting back required the aid of three angles. That is a triangle through which a djinn could pass to harness their fire and catapult themself between worlds.

The sky above grumbled, the sun passing through breaks in gray clouds. Mirri couldn't stop staring at it, a normal reaction from anyone who'd lived their whole life in the moon-drenched land of Qaf. The Ardish sun was truly awesome, though he did warn her she would go blind if she stared too long.

"I am not in the mood for this." Javier tightened the straps on his thick leather gauntlets. He looked like a different man in his head-to-toe black leather armor with weapons strapped to every inch. More what people expected from the infamous Immortal Killer than a flowered man in a flouncy apron who had been known to sing to roasted chickens. "I had to slay the Indestructible Queen of the Marleki yesterday. I am exhausted, and my back hurts."

"No problem." Izkander smiled, a part of him wishing he'd been on that adventure instead of getting accidentally betrothed. "We'll beat the thing down. You just deliver the finishing blow."

"Fine. But make it quick. I have four more loaves to bake, and Serap is not a patient woman when it comes to her bread." Javier grumbled and took one of the long silver daggers from inside his jacket. "I'm getting too old for this."

"You've been saying that as long as I've known you." Izkander set a hand on Javier's forearm, then turned to Mirri with wide eyes and an open palm. "I promised I'd warn you next time, so here we go."

"How decorous of you." She looked at his hands and then back to his eyes, the corner of her lips twisting upward. "Can you make sure we don't pop back in where anyone can see us? I don't want my people to think our security has been compromised. A true djinn has not set foot on our land without magical inhibitors in over six hundred years."

Her words flooded through him with an image of her mother and father sitting on their stiff thrones, glowering down at him. There was a part of him—the showboating part that came straight from his old man—that wanted to pop right into that gloomy courtroom just to stick in the old man's craw. But a stronger part—a part whose origins he hadn't identified—just wanted to see Mirri smile again.

"You think of a place," he said, "and I'll take us there."

She met his gaze once more, then placed her hand in his and squeezed.

What a feeling.

He smiled, and together they all walked together under the ladder that rested against the crumbling plaster of Javier's house.

Izkander focused his fire through Mirri's thoughts of Fyre to bring them where she thought best, and they popped into a field of golden wheat under the arch of a large stone with deep pockmarks.

Already the scene was chaotic. Soldiers mounted on drakonte buzzed the air, their discordant cries so raucous that they shook the dirt under his feet.

A chill licked down his spine. This was his scene. If he was ever going to prove to Mirri that he wasn't an idiot, it would be here and now.

A shattering cry assaulted his senses, this one completely foreign and loud enough to froth the blood in his veins and rend his insides to puree. Izkander crouched and covered his ears. The soldiers did the same, though they seemed to be wearing ear guards, and many of them already had blood dripping down the sides of their necks.

Izkander cast a couple of tiny balls of fire and pressed them down his ear canals, the soft whoosh muffling everything. With the cacophony of noise under control, he took greater stock of the field. Men ran about, bleeding and burnt.

Women wept over small bodies covered with blankets at the edge of the field. Tears streaked their faces. Wails mixed with the hum of night air.

It was easy to forget when fighting at Javier's side the damage some monsters could cause. All the joy drained from him like someone had opened a plug. His hands tightened into fists.

Izkander brought his fingers to his lips and whistled for Squirt. A great shadow rushed through the white clouds overhead, almost as big as Fajar, but deep black and moving in twisting halting circles up in the air.

Cold swelled in his chest, offset by a quickened heartbeat. Whatever fear there was, the accompanying sense of accountability was louder and firmer, even if he wasn't entirely certain where it had sprung from. Usually, when faced with something like this, the sensation competing with the fear in his gut was excitement and adventure, fervor for life and living. And that was there, lifting his hand to his sword, swelling heavy in his chest, and urging his feet forward. But there was a little more to it this time. A feeling that overcame the horror around him and filled him with something light, sweeter, and full of hope.

He had made Mirri smile when they were sequestered behind the tapestry in *lawful indecorousness.* He wanted to do it again. And before she could smile, this thing had to die.

Squirt announced his arrival with a tremendous roar, Havu close at his side. The two drakonte parted ways as they dove towards the field, Havu quickening towards Mirri and his boy aiming square at him. As Squirt's belly grazed the grass, Izkander dodged to one side, then latched onto one of the square, keeled scales that ran the length of his spine. Once he'd swung himself on, Squirt rocketed into the air, never allowing him any time to get situated before throwing him straight into the fire.

Squirt had no patience, no empathy. A ride on him was always a do-or-die proposal, one which Izkander enthusiastically accepted time and time again.

He glanced back at Mirri, watching her move amongst her men as she shouted orders in her native tongue and planned the attack. Every move she made was calm and deliberate whether it was catching a bleeding man who staggered against her or a group of rapt generals leaning on her every word and executing them with precision.

Her eyes met his, speaking silent words he couldn't yet understand before she continued on her path.

Izkander looked back, searching for Javier. There at the edge of the fray, his butt planted firmly on a rock, was the Immortal Killer. The older he got, the happier Javier was to let other people do the hard work for him, then use his gift to seal the deal.

Izkander didn't mind. He was always up for the hard work.

At the very moment Squirt broke through the cloud barrier, another fulminating bawl split the air, like a lightning strike an inch away, the clap of thunder boxing both ears. Izkander's eyes quivered in their sockets like the jelly inside would burst. Squirt veered around, and at last, Izkander got a clear view of the monster, the buklak. The first thing that struck him was it looked far too large to fly. The next was that Mirri had not been kidding about the size of those teeth.

The beast had a flat-leaf, starburst nose like a mole that was bright red, though whether that was natural or merely a smear of blood from recent victims was impossible to say. Four ears pointed straight up from its huge head, transparent triangles of veiny flesh. its great maw hung wide, snarling and dripping with spit, like pink slime from a Giant Cone Snail. Its back was coated in greasy, spiky fur. Three claws longer than Izkander's own body hung like knives in a butcher shop from toes at the end of huge, leathery wings, beating the air furiously to stay afloat. Feet like a sphinx coiled under its muscular torso.

Izkander yanked the matchlock revolver from its holster on his hip and spun the barrel to clear any impurities before he set a little dot of his orange fire at the curve of the serpentine. He jabbed a heel into Squirt's side, his signal to get closer to the beast. He had a range of about four hundred cubits, but every hair past a hundred ate away at the accuracy. Squirt catapulted himself high above the buklak, gliding back down in slow, spinning circles that grew tighter and closer with every pass. Izkander fired a barrage of four bullets at the creature's head. Jets of blood exploded from its head with each hit. It threw its nose back and roared, swatting a massive claw upward. Squirt narrowly dodged.

Below, Fyre's cavalry mounted their assault. Mirri flew at the front, Havu's turquoise unmistakable against the golden wheat below. Mirri stood in her saddle, one hand on the reins and the other holding her sword, aiming straight for the beast. They approached the slashing range of the beast's massive claws. With a swipe, she dropped her blade. The group of riders behind her split into thirds in an instant, one to each side and another down below, their drakonte nipping at the monster and driving it up toward Izkander. Mirri, for her part, charged straight toward the belly of the beast. Havu twisted and turned in sharp angles, dodging several narrow misses as Mirri raked her blade up the creature's stomach. Red poured to the ground below, hot and foul. She shot up to match Squirt in his spiral.

"So when exactly does your uncle move?" She called through the wind. "Or does he just hold the blade while we push the monster upon it?"

"Pretty much, yeah," he called back with a smirk. "We've got to get this thing on the ground."

Mirri wiped the blood from her sword onto her pants and brushed the hair from her face. "Did you hear that, Havu? Make the call. Top to bottom. Drive it down."

Havu *orked* and snuffed in a deep bellow. Like water breaking against a stone, her soldiers changed paths, swarming in a semicircle up, around, then down. The beast roared and hissed, swiping at the drakonte like gnats.

"Squirt, get me close to the wings," Izkander yelled.

His drakonte gave a blasting shriek of agreement and shot toward the beast's left wing, swiping his tail lightly over Havu's as he passed.

"Incorrigible." Izkander laughed as he yanked his sword from its scabbard and cast a sheen of bright orange fire all across the thick steel blade.

What would Mirri do if he brushed her like that? Would she purr the way Havu did?

Izkander shook his head, chastising his wandering imagination. First, kill the beast and make sure no more of Mirri's people were hurt by it. There would be plenty of time for purring later.

Squirt dove straight for the flapping wings, dodging through a swat from the three-toed hand to dip under. The snarling drakonte opened his huge, toothy mouth and snapped the thick, veiny skin, throwing Izkander forward. He pointed his sword directly ahead like a ram on the front of a battleship and sliced the wing. The creature shrieked, and its wings missed a beat. The buklak dipped like a stone for a breath before it caught itself again. Izkander braced his feet against the leathery surface and yanked hard, slowly tearing through the fibers foot by foot.

The monster's feet shot up, trying desperately to claw him away from where he eviscerated the wing when another shriek exploded from the snarling mouth. Mirri had landed on the creature's back and slid elegantly down and around the side where she stabbed her sword into the other wing. Her blade began to glow with the red of an ember. Flames erupted and ate at the bristly hair where her blade tore through the leathery skin.

"Fire. Brilliant," he called with a laugh.

Izkander shot a thick stream of djinn fire into the wound he'd made and relished the scream that tore from the creature's throat. With both wings shredded into flaps of useless skin, the creature began to plummet.

Mirri glanced his way, the light of both their fires bright in her red eyes. She smiled.

He smiled back, a moment without gravity.

Izkander frantically looked behind him, readying to jump, but lost his footing. He started to fall when the creature snatched him in its talons, greasy and blood-sodden.

"Squirt!" Izkander's call was muffled in muscle and sinew, flesh and viscera.

He twisted to yank his pistol from its holster and fired two shots point-blank into a patch of flesh. The creature screamed, and blood and tiny spikes of bone burst up to coat his face. It didn't loosen its grip.

"Izkander!" Mirri called, her bright red hair appearing above him between the monster's sword-like claws.

He spat out a mouthful of acidic fluid and struggled inch by inch nearer to Mirri like a spelunker in a tight cave. He reached for her. She reached back. Their fingers brushed.

She looked over her shoulder, then back at him with a nod and raised eyebrows. Then, she jumped, stabbing her sword straight through the buklak's knuckle. The bone shattered with a spray of blood as she grabbed Izkander's hand and kicked off the beast's chest.

He got his slippery boot against bone and pushed back with her. Free-falling face-first, the ground approached at speed. A line of silver slipped under the two of them, and their bodies slammed hard against Squirt's downy back. Izkander snatched a keel scale with one hand. Mirri started to slip, but he held tight to her hand and yanked her up beside him.

"Are you okay?" he shouted.

Her eyes met his, but before she could answer, the body of the buklak hit the ground like a pail of pig slops, blood and bone exploding in every direction. The sound it made was ungodly, worse than anything Izkander imagined could be found in hell.

Mirri leaned her head against his shoulder, hands pressed over her ears until the worst of it had passed. She dropped her hands, but her cheek stayed warm against his shoulder for several beats of Squirt's wings. Nervously, he slipped his hand around her shoulder and pulled her tighter.

By heaven, she was warm.

"We need to finish it off," she said, eyes scanning the fleshy lump. "We've had it down before, but if we don't move now...."

Izkander brushed his chin against her hair, a close-lipped, lop-sided smile on his face. It was even silkier than he had been hoping it would be.

He pointed down at the ground. "At last, the old man springs into action."

They were so high up, all he could see of his uncle was a slow-moving dot of black making its way across the field toward the splattered remains. He didn't need to watch to know what was about to happen. Javier always did one of two things in these kinds of situations—he either cut the head off or crawled into the chest cavity to get to the heart. Either way, the buklak would not be coming back from this one, not when the Immortal Killer's hand and blade were blessed by the Bahamut to end all endless life.

Mirri flinched when the huge head rolled away from the rest of the body, then pulled herself straight. She tapped on his shoulder.

He looked up at her face, coated in sweat and blood spray, her silky hair wet and her armor shimmering. She was sensational.

"Thank you."

He sucked his bottom lip between his teeth and smiled. He knew he was supposed to say something, but the words were all garbled in his brain. He just smiled and bobbed his head a few times. Then, he tapped a fist against his chest and held it out to her, trying to say *thank you,* too.

She scrunched her nose, lips twitching in the corners. "What is that? The one time I'm okay with you talking, and you don't have anything to say?"

He laughed and leaned over his lap, clasping the bridge of his nose. Then he leaned back, tilting his head towards the sky, and let out a loud *woo.* "We're a pretty good team."

"It's improper to brag."

"In that case, we're a damn good team."

"I can say I've never fought next to someone like you before," Mirri said with the ghost of a smile, "and I wish I had. If nothing else, because it's a lot more fun."

Her words lifted him even as Squirt's wings. He bumped his shoulders against hers. "You are a juggernaut."

She dropped her head against her shoulder, that crinkle back in her nose as she looked him over. "I have no idea what that means." Then she let out a soft giggle.

The sound lifted the warm fuzziness in his chest and cheeks. "It means that you are sensational, a force to be reckoned with."

"Ah." She pulled her shoulder blades back and thrust her chest in the air. "Thank you, Gaol Aig an Righ, and you are a juggernaut, too. For I've never met a red or gold-eyed man who would throw himself at a monster and smile as he flew through the air."

"It's the only way I caught you."

The screech of a drakonte ripped all sound from the air. Havu rushed towards them on her soft, cream-colored wings. Squirt purred a little, but it was weak. The poor boy was tired, and Izkander felt the same way. Tired, hungry, thirsty, and in desperate need of a bath. And maybe some kisses. Not necessarily in that order, though he wasn't sure he'd get the last one later, if ever from Mirri.

He sighed.

Havu swooped closer, nipping at Mirri.

"Oh, you're one to talk, Havu." Mirri scowled. "I still haven't forgiven you for this morning, you know."

Havu clacked her jaw and let out a high-pitched growl.

"Yeah?" Mirri crossed her arms. "You're just moody because you haven't eaten. I'm not stabling you with Squirt. Don't even think about it." She turned back to Izkander. "If you'll excuse me, I need to go have a word with Havu. If you follow us down to the stables, I've got a spot for your troublemaker far away from all my females. And... there's a spot for you, too."

"You're gonna make me sleep in the stables?" He sucked a breath through his teeth. "Damn, girl. I'm not that bad, am I?

"No. You're to sleep inside... If you... I mean..." A blush spread across her chest and up to her cheeks.

Izkander's smile tried to widen, but he bit his bottom lip to try to keep it tight. "Let me send the Immortal Killer back to his kitchen, and I'm all yours."

"You're not going back to Ard, are you?"

He shook his head. "I would never do anything to put you at risk. I mean, other than monster slaying, of course."

She pushed her lips to the side and pressed a hand to her cheek, covering the blush. "I think our bond will stretch that far. Today, at least. I'll finish up with my troops and get Havu settled and meet you at the front gates, yes?"

He wanted to ask more about the stretch of their bond, but it didn't seem the time. Since they hadn't used Javier's mirror to come to Qaf, he couldn't use it to get back. That meant Izkander was going to have to give him a little fire boost. And if he didn't send him home soon, the Immortal Killer was going to get irritated. Besides, he needed to ask Javier to let his folks know what was going on. He didn't want his umi to worry.

He watched as Havu carried Mirri away. Squirt heaved a sigh.

"I guess you heard that, huh, buddy? No females for you." Izkander patted his scales. "You have a reputation."

The drakonte barked and snarled as if to say *give it time.*

Izkander grunted, then the pair of them drifted lazily toward the ground to inspect the extent of the mess they'd made.

Maybe Mirri's baba would be less of a stuffy, self-righteous sack of silver now that Izkander had helped rid the kingdom of a generations-old, children-eating menace.

Nah.

But Mirri had blushed, and that was something.

CHAPTER TEN

MIRRI

MIRRI AND HAVU HAD started and stopped seven arguments on the way to the stables, none of which went anywhere productive. That didn't stop Mirri from starting up again as she unsaddled the drakonte and cleaned the sweat from off her scales for the night. The sweet hay did little to soften her mood, and the gentle glow of the Eternal Flames that always lit the dark stable corridors seemed only to mock her.

"I can't believe you smelled that beast of a drakonte for years and didn't say anything." Mirri scoffed and shot her friend eyes of daggers. "How humiliating for me. For all of Fyre."

Havu snarled. *I told you I wasn't sure what it was.*

"You sure seem to know what it is now." Mirri scrubbed harder than necessary.

Oh, and you're one to talk. Havu bristled, her scales vibrating in irritation so much, Mirri had to stop. *I saw you resting your head on the man's shoulder.*

Mirri threw the hard-bristled brush into the bucket of water she had been using. "I was tired for a moment after the battle."

Is that why you smiled at him, too?

"I'm allowed to smile," she scoffed.

Then how come you never do it around people?

"Because I'm too busy thinking about what a know-it-all brat my drakonte is." Mirri grabbed the bucket, so it sloshed on her blood-splattered pants, and clicked her mouth twice.

Havu grunted her discontent but slithered into the hay-lined corral she roosted in every night. Not because she would leave or because she was in danger, but to set an example for the others.

I'm just saying, you didn't seem so upset about having a Fire Mate out there in the battle.

"How I feel about him is not your concern. You made the mess."

"Feel about whom?" a gentle baritone said from behind. "And what mess?"

She spun around as Urramach stepped carefully through the muck of the stables, hands clasped together behind his back. His crisp green and gold uniform looked out of place, too perfect for the filth surrounding her.

"No one. And nothing." She tried to sound disinterested but there was an uneasiness to her voice that accompanied the itch growing beneath her chin.

He came to a stop in front of her, heels falling in place next to one another. "Now, I'm certain that's not true. You and Havu never fight."

"We fight all the time. I just don't usually let other people hear."

"You fight about no one and nothing?" He raised a brow. "That's interesting."

She took a step back and found herself against one of the beams that dotted the path between the stables. Rough wood pressed through the weak spots in her armor.

"Why are you down here?" she asked, her throat thick. "You never come to the stables when you're not on a task with Ian."

"To see you." His always straight shoulders softened. "To ensure you are safe."

His unexpected gentleness caught her off guard, leaving her stomach squirming.

"It is my job to protect my country. To worry for my people."

"And who will worry for you?" He took her hand and brushed his lips over the top.

A rush of goosebumps covered every inch of her skin from her wrists up through her chest. She had already been touched more today than she could remember and by so many people. None of them had felt like this, whatever *this* was.

None of them had felt like laying her head on Izkander's shoulder, either. They felt almost the same, and entirely different.

"Urramach." She held her breath and pushed her back further into the splinters. "Why are you doing this?"

"*Ta mo chroi istigh ionat.*"

My heart is in you.

She pulled her hand away and wrapped both around the pole behind her. "I am your Ah-nis Na Righ."

"No." He moved close enough she could feel his heat and count his lashes.

She glanced toward Havu's corral, but the prideful little monster had coiled up in the back corner, watching with glowing red eyes and saying nothing, which said everything. *Deal with it yourself.*

Urramach leaned in closer, lips nearing hers.

She turned her face away. "Are you trying to kill me?"

"I cannot."

"You can, too." She looked at him from the corner of her eye.

His golden eyes were serious, his face smooth, and his brows dipped together in the middle.

"You already risked my life earlier today when you stole a kiss."

He inhaled sharply and pulled back a nose's worth. "I would never have done it if I thought there was any chance harm may befall you. And I didn't steal it. It was a gift."

"And now?" she asked, words barely forming in her suddenly parched throat. Her heart beat against her chest, indecorous and unruly. "I am bound to a Fire Mate who is not you."

"It is the same," he breathed, lifting a finger up to tuck her hair behind her ear.

With every movement, she braced herself, certain the moment she felt the burn of love or passion or whatever he clearly felt, she would feel the heat of her skin melting with it.

"You will slay me. I am bound. I have not even had my Eve of Fire. And yet you touch me so." Her lip trembled, and she looked up at him through her zigzag lashes. "This is unlawful indecorousness. And Izkander..."

"Doesn't even want the job. The title. You. He said so himself."

The truth in his words pricked her. Despite her efforts, it did feel as if Izkander was rejecting her as a mate instead of rejecting the entire situation.

She clenched her jaw. "His discontent doesn't change the Eternal Union. It simply puts me at risk. As you do, speaking to me this way, now."

"Is that really what you want?" Urramach pulled back farther, brushing his thumb under her chin.

More tingles spidered their way across her neck and up into her brain, making it difficult to think.

He stepped closer. "To be with a man who doesn't want you? Not just on your Eve of Fire, but every night thereafter?"

She pressed her lips shut, unwilling to answer his question. Unable to. Because of course, that was something she did not want. But there was nothing to be done about it that would also spare her an agonizing death.

She didn't want to commit to Urramach or Izkander. For Marduk's sake, she didn't want to commit to anyone until she proved her worth as Righ. Until she figured out her purpose and proved to herself and her people she could rule without burning from the inside out.

At least Izkander seemed to understand that.

"Mirri." Her name rolled off Urramach's tongue with the lilt of familiarity she had only with him. Warm chills ran up her neck. "If you could be with me and come to no harm, would you?"

"As a Fire Mate?" She turned to face him at last, the question absurd.

He was wrapping her in a dream that wasn't real. That couldn't be. And one she wasn't sure she even had. One she *didn't* have. Being together was his dream. Not hers. Not yet, anyway. So why did she linger? Why did his voice and his touch and the pull of his eyes draw her in so?

"No, not as a Fire Mate." His face fell, golden eyes soft and sorrowful. "I do not know how to change that."

"Then as a cheat?" Her breath caught. "It is—"

"Forbidden?" He shook his head, fingers brushing the gold-plated armor on her shoulder and down the spirals that covered her arm. "What if it isn't?"

She shook her head fiercely, her chest squeezing tight, suffocating her. "Then it would be unkind. Cruel. Dishonest. But it is not possible."

"Why is it unkind? The djinn said he didn't want to get in the way. He doesn't even want to be here. But I do. Without title. Without prestige. Just a man knocking on your door, begging to be let in."

The earnest boyishness that beset Urramach's eyes pulled at her heart. She didn't want to hurt him. And she did want to be touched. She had since Urramach had breathed her name behind the tapestry that morning. Even more, since Izkander had hollered at her when she jumped from his drakonte. It had made her feel something. Like she was a woman wanted by a man.

She had liked the way that felt, the way Izkander made her feel a little free. Even if he did not want her.

Her shoulders slumped.

"I'm going to kiss you, now," Urramach whispered, his words wooing the chirp of the *nimisks*.

"Please." She shut her eyes and pressed her head against the rough wooden beam. "Don't."

"You don't want to? Or you are afraid to?"

Why did his every question weigh her down? She just wanted to fly for a moment. To look down at Fyre and laugh without once worrying who would hear.

"I'm afraid to—"

He leaned forward and pressed his lips against hers for the second time. She squeezed the beam behind her as a maelstrom of emotions burst inside her.

Havu's head crashed over the side of the corral. She snapped the air ferociously, so close her slobber caught the side of Urramach's face. He didn't rush his kiss or cower away. Just finished slowly and pulled back, thumb on her chin, eyes on hers.

"Hello, Havu," he said without looking away. "It's nice of you to join us."

The stream of fanged profanities that flew from Havu's mind and guttural snarls were far more than Mirri even thought she knew. But she was grateful for a chance to breathe and collect her thoughts. To wake up from the thick haze that had just befallen her, clouding her mind.

"I didn't kill her." He glared at Havu, but a confident smile sat on his lips. "She is as well as ever. Perhaps, even better with a flush now in her cheeks."

The words Mirri had been seeking found their escape. "How *dare* you?"

She shoved his chest again and again until they were out of the stables and into the warmed air of Fyre. Snowstorms howled in the distance, as upset as she was that they could not reach the heart of the valley. The fresh air and crisp moon-filled sky helped her breathe.

His brows lifted high along with his hands. "What?"

"I told you I was afraid. But you kiss me anyway? Why does my life seem so inconsequential to you that you risk it for a kiss? Twice! Am I nothing to you?"

He reached for her hand, but she yanked it away. "You are my everything, Mirri. And you are so afraid of breaking tradition that I knew being with you in any capacity would require me to *show* you that you are well. That you can be happy, even bound to some half-djinn oaf from Ard. I bite my pride being second to him, but I do so willingly to be near you."

"And what made you sure enough to take a chance with something that isn't yours?" She punched angry fists down at her sides.

His mouth hitched up in a small smile. "Maron."

"What?" she exhaled, her brother's name knocking the wind from her lungs.

"He slept with half the scullery maids in the castle."

His words shook her, reverberations in a struck sword. She wanted to yell at him that it was not true, but that would be undignified. And the look on his always-earnest face told her it had to be.

She pressed open palms against her stomach. "And he was burned alive from the inside out in the throne room for all to watch."

She shuddered, remembering the pockets of bubbling, red flesh, the pool of her brother on the floor. It made her want to retch, but she forced it down. She always did.

Urramach shook his head. "He wasn't burned because of that."

"How would you know?"

"The sin the Eternal Flame melted him for was egregious."

"Intimacy before Union is egregious."

"I know you think that, which is why I've never brought it up no matter how many times I wanted to." He closed his eyes and heaved, then turned his golden pools on her.

She looked askance as a great itch beset her shoulder blade. She had long wondered what exactly her brother had done to break his covenant to the Origin and its Eternal Flame, wanting so desperately to not commit the same mistake. But the Fa Chomhair refused to discuss it with her, and her mother just went on and on about what tradition really was. Dangerously unhelpful when she was trying to keep her flesh at room temperature and attached to her body.

Mirri took a rattling breath and looked up at Urramach's honey eyes. "If that was not his transgression, then what was?"

Urramach's smile fell with his eyes. "Mirri..."

"Answer me," she said, jutting up her chin.

"We all know he was discontent. That he was looking for ways to get out of being the righ your father wanted. When he wasn't with me or one of the maids—" Urramach smiled apologetically, "—he was in the library looking up how to talk to the Origin, to change his fate."

She clenched her jaw and pulsed. That was her mother's idea, his search for supplication with the Eternal Flame before he was even righ. "He was impulsive and clearly felt entitled to things he had not yet earned. He should have been content."

"Perhaps." Urramach's gaze wandered to the left, then back to her. "Perhaps Maron would have been more content if he had been grateful for what the Origin had given him instead of researching how the Rukh opens the heart of the valley so he could steal a new fate. He was always going on about The Wisdom and The Heart and The Flame, three pieces of a whole he needed to bring together. Perhaps he could have been more grateful for the heart he did have in his life. Yours."

Mirri's heart ached with the words, anger and sorrow, and what felt dangerously like discontent squeezing her chest.

Urramach blinked, eyes soft and wet. He cleared his throat "But perhaps do nothing for us now. And I understand discontent. I get it every time I look at you, knowing I can't be what you need me to be. What I wish to be. You ask a question I cannot answer. I am not the Origin nor the judge of the descendants of Marduk. I am merely a humble servant of the righ. All I know is if his eternal damnation came from his escapades with the maids, the Origin would have claimed his soul many years sooner."

His words burst softly inside her, splashing her insides in cold disappointment. She opened her mouth to ask more, but he stroked his thumb slowly down, catching on her bottom lip.

"Marduk save me, all I think about is you."

"Urramach—"

His warm hand brushed against her cheeks, and he pressed his forehead against hers. His breath tickled her lips, and his nose nuzzled softly against hers.

She froze, unable to move. Not wanting to move, and definitely wanting to. It made no sense, but his proximity, the strange pull in her chest that wanted more but wasn't sure from who tightened and made her too scared to breathe.

"I know you take the law very seriously," he continued, his tenor soft and warm. "And rightly so, but so do I. And I've read it a thousand times. *As concerning the holy state of Fire Mates: The true blood descendants of Marduk shall keep their bodies uncoupled before the bond of Eternal Union has been sealed upon their wrists. Once consummated and presented before the Eternal Flame, they are bound to honor the love and will of their Mate and in all things are equal. At no time may the child of forbidden passion be allowed to live long enough to take the throne."*

His recitation helped slow her racing heart. "I know what the law says, Urramach. If you have read it a thousand times, I have read it ten thousand. I live and breathe and eat and dream the laws of Fyre just to ensure I wake up every morning."

He leaned back on his heels and crossed his arms. "Maron said the law has been misinterpreted for nearly a millennium."

"You mean the Maron whose soul is now burning in the pits of the Eternal Flame?"

Urramach pulled back and looked her up and down, sending a cascade of heat across her bones once more. He smiled. "And yet you stand before me. Kissed and as perfect as ever."

Mirri pressed her fists against her hips. "Just tell me what you're going to say."

"Alright, alright." His grin widened. "What is a coupling?"

Her throat tightened. "The joining of two things to become one."

"And if two things join without becoming one?"

"I don't know." Mirri's toes were curling in her boots, and a thousand tiny itches ran up her skin like little bites.

Izkander and her were two things that joined without becoming one. So what did that make this morning?

"A happenstance?" she muttered Izkander's word.

"Exactly." Urramach beamed, the moonlight catching his gold eyes and brightening his smile. "As long as we have no clear path to or intentions for coupling before your Eve of Fire, we are not breaking the first part of the law. We're just having a happenstance."

His words twisted like a screw inside her.

"And," he continued. "As long as you and the djinn boy don't love each other—and let's be honest about the likelihood of that—"

"It could happen," she tried to say with defiance, though it came out as a pitter.

Izkander would be here any moment with Squirt. What would he do if he found her in such an indecorous manner with another man? Ask if he was her *fella* and say he wouldn't get in the way, most likely. A prick sank into the middle of her heart and spread from there.

"Mirri," Urramach coaxed, drawing her attention. "He doesn't care what you do, but that doesn't have to be a bad thing. As long as he doesn't, we can be together freely after your Union is sealed. You simply must obey each other's wills. If he has no will for you, you are bound to nothing."

"And children?" She shot sharp eyes up to Urramach in a challenge.

He grimaced. "As much as it makes me want to draw my sword, as long as you don't have any heirs that are mine, it shouldn't be a problem."

"So you just want to…" She pushed her tongue out over and over, trying to get the bad taste of the word she could never say out of her mouth. "It is just another way to commit to one another without calling it so."

Urramach's smile vanished, but a tenderness she didn't understand still lingered in his eyes. "Is that so bad? Committing to me? I know I have always seen you before you've seen me. I accept that. But please consider it when you are lonely in your bed without a Mate who wants to hold you. I won't press you. But the thought of you…" He swallowed and his brows creased. "… of you going unloved for centuries is too much for me to bear."

Mirri stood there in the starlight, shaking her head over and over as he kissed the top of her head and bade her goodnight. As the *nimisks* chirped shrilly, waiting for dawn. And as the flap of heavy drakonte wings neared. Only when the heavy belly of the beast landed, did her eyes refocus from the blur her mind had been hiding in. Two paths lay before her. A touch of warmth before the fiery pit of the Eternal Flame. Or a cold bed for eternity.

No.

She refused to accept those were her only options. Maybe there was a third way, a way she hadn't discovered, yet. Maybe offering supplication to the Origin and begging for a change would be enough. Urramach had said something about Maron searching for the Rukh, the famed Wisdom of the Origin that had escaped its heart when Qaf split into the pieces it existed in now. Could she find the Rukh and beckon it to come home?

Every righ was allowed an audience before the Eternal Flame under dire circumstances, which was what Maron hadn't understood. He had been merely a descendant, not yet consecrated. If he had tried to communicate with the immortal being under false pretenses and before he became righ, maybe that was what had burned him up. She *was* the righ, so calling on the Origin wouldn't melt her flesh. She just had to make sure her intentions qualified as pure and right.

Did her contentment being jeopardy count as a circumstance worth waking the Eternal Flame? Or would the very request melt her flesh? Her stomach pinched. It sounded trite just thinking it. But maybe the mystical Rukh was the way. She needed to research. To find out. She could find a way to change her fate without suffering Maron's fate, right? She had to, though only in the deepest parts of her soul would she ever admit that her happiness depended on it.

That her life did.

CHAPTER ELEVEN

Izkander

"So that's the gist of the situation, as I understand it, anyway." Izkander slumped down on a rock next to Javier, gazing out over the dead body of the immortal bat creature.

They were both covered in blood and gore, sticky and thick in the light of the Fourth Moon. The body of the massive buklak lay to their back. It hadn't been dead long enough to start to stink. All Izkander could smell was blood.

Javier bounced his fingers on the end of his long beard. "A prickly pickle."

"You think you can let my folks know I'm okay? They worry. Well, my umi worries. My old man probably hasn't noticed I'm gone. Though, I'm sure he's noticed Fajar."

Javier pushed out his bottom lip and nodded. "Are you sure you want me to tell them the truth?"

"Why not?"

"As Plutarch once said, 'A son ought to take cognizance of the hostility his mother holds for his wife, and try to cure the cause of it, which is the mother's jealousy of the bride as the object of her son's affection'."

"Mirri is not the object of my affection." Izkander scoffed, shook his head, then scoffed again. "I told you. It was an accident. I'm doing what I can to get out of it."

Javier lifted his eyebrows. "By helping your would-be bride slay the monsters that would assail her kingdom?"

His eyes wandered back to the hideous pancake laid out on the wheat field. "I got sidetracked."

"I think you like her."

"I do like her." He laughed at how easily the words came to him, remembering she had laid against his shoulder when the battle was done. Not quite a purr, but he'd surely take it. "She's a juggernaut."

Izkander sucked a breath through his nose and let it out slowly, his body sinking deeper into the rock. "It doesn't matter. She's the predestined queen of Fyre who can't leave this place for more than a jaunt or her heart will freeze or something. *And* we are both way too young to get married to anybody. *And* she has a thing for this guy. Her boyfriend, I guess. By Allah, you should have seen his face when he realized what had happened. His face…"

Izkander lifted a fist to the sky dramatically, then sighed and shook his head, that painful twist in his gut that had come the moment he saw that golden-eyed man's sad, broken expression.

"I don't want to hurt anybody. And I've already made enough of a mess around here. I hope this makes up for it. Mirri is a great… friend."

"If she's just a friend and you're planning on getting out of this marriage, then best not mention it to your mother. She can be a bit… well… especially when it comes to her children… and especially when it comes to you, *mijo*." Javier slapped his thighs as he stood with a low groan. "I'll just let them know you and I were doing a bit of freelance monster hunting together and that you'll be home soon."

"And that Fajar is safe."

"*Sí, por supuesto.*"

Izkander stood and smiled at his uncle. "Thank you for your help. I know it's an imposition."

"Yes, it is," said Javier, his face severe. "Today is bread day."

Izkander laughed and fished in his pocket for one of Fajar's feathers, which he then handed to Javier. All it took was thinking of where Javier wanted to be—home, naturally—and dropping the feather to the ground for the Immortal Killer to disappear back to Spain in a puff of bright orange fire.

Izkander sighed and glanced over the destruction. Several of Mirri's drakonte riders were still middling about, but none of them were speaking to him. He could feel their passive-aggressive stares, all but hear his name in the whispers and long glances they shared with each other. Allah, it was too much. The ice was getting thicker by the moment and he needed to break it.

For Mirri's sake, and for the sake of the bodies lying under bloodstained blankets, he was determined not to behave like an idiot.

He walked up to one of the men—a soldier that had been in the war room with them earlier. "Were there any casualties among your soldiers?"

The man stiffened and turned both his feet to face Izkander, snapping his heels tightly together. He slapped a fist to his chest and bowed stiffly. "Gaol Aig an Righ."

Izkander was about to repeat himself when he paused. Mirri and her parents spoke Arabic, and the nobles seemed to understand it. But everybody else in Fyre spoke that strange *shush-ga-shush* language.

He set a hand to his chest and bowed his head, lowering his eyes to show respect for those who had lost their lives on the field.

The man's expression softened before tightening back up. "Do you have need?" the man asked. His accent was so thick it took Izkander a moment to recognize the words as his own language.

"No. I don't need anything." Izkander shook his head and gazed out over the wheat field. For the first time, it occurred to him to be worried about the plants the ugly bat had died on. "Is this your food supply?"

The man—general—shifted in his stiff armor. "Gaol Aig an Righ."

Izkander nodded, his mind turning back to Mirri. She was the new queen and while slaying an immortal monster was a good start to a healthy reign, letting your people starve was not. But maybe there was something he could do to help, relieve a bit of the pressure pushing down on her. Crushing her bones, as Jahmil would say, who was the only other monarch Izkander knew personally.

Heavy is the head, so they say. Even if Mirri had already found a different man to stand beside her and help hold her up. For the moment, it was his job. The first job he'd ever actually had.

"I don't see any reason why your people should starve or be eaten," Izkander said. "Neither of those are acceptable."

The soldier blinked, but his face stayed the same. Izkander could feel the other soldiers watching them, slowing down their work so they could watch and listen. Fyre was a small kingdom, after all. News traveled fast, and everybody's business was everybody else's business, whether anybody formally recognized that or not.

The man lifted his hand to indicate the mushed corpse of the monster. "It is a blessing."

Izkander nodded and showed a close-lipped smile. "The loss of your grain is not a blessing." He clapped his hands together and rubbed them quickly. "But don't worry. I'll make up the difference."

The man's brows tightened quizzically before smoothing back into their cool, blank expression.

Izkander turned to the land and narrowed his eyes at it, wondering how much a plot like this might produce. The way the beast had scattered itself over a wide area, he figured about a square parasang had been tainted. He knew the average amount a piece of land could produce from autumns spent at Javier's house—helping out with harvest because his baba said it was good for his character and *burgeoning Apollonian physique*. He had to stop and do some figuring on his fingers, and he ran the numbers through his head twice to make sure he'd come up with the right answer. Twenty-six thousand lost bushels of wheat. He could only imagine what something like that would mean to a tiny, largely isolated kingdom like Fyre.

He nodded to himself then looked back up at the soldier and smiled. "I'm sorry, what was your name?"

The man stumbled over his tongue. "General Musharraf."

"Nice talking to you, General Musharraf. Let me know if you need anything," he said and tapped the man on the shoulder before walking away.

Izkander climbed onto Squirt's back, scanning the wheat field one last time and filling his nostrils with the acidic, iron smell of a bloody victory. He made a quick ascending whistle, and Squirt took off at a sharp slither. They didn't fly the distance to the stable, just made their way along the ground like Squirt sometimes liked to do when he was tired or his belly was itching. Izkander could only assume a bit of both after the day they'd had.

They arrived at the stables—a gargantuan three-story building made of wood with stalls each the size of a large temple and stuffed with fresh hay. True to her word, Mirri had had a stall prepared for Squirt far away from the other drakonte. The stablemaster pointed it out after an awkward game of charades. Izkander almost felt sorry for his drakonte as he slithered back into the hay and coiled up, his four massive wings splayed out, comfy but all alone.

He thanked the stablemaster for her help, though whether she understood was anyone's guess, then walked off in the direction of the castle gates. That song was back in his head—the catchy little Mehmet tune that refused to be drummed out. Not by raging husbands, or drakonte races, or accidental engagements, or even massive squealing bat monsters. As he walked along, his eyes greedily taking in the fresh sights of the strange kingdom, he bobbed his head to the beat.

Do, dedo, do, do, do, dedo, do, dedo, do, do, do, dedo.

He came bopping up towards the front gates, a tired little bounce in his step because it was the only way he could keep his eyes open. Several large men were stationed there, two on each end of iron double doors the size of drakonte wings, and forged to look like them as well. Waiting for him with a stiff back and a far-too-typical frown on her lips, was Mirri. Still in her armor and still covered in as much blood as he was. He was grateful for that.

He smiled and lifted a hand out to the side. "Where have you been? Keeping me waiting."

She raised her eyebrows and turned with a sigh, walking through the doors. Her demeanor had changed completely in the fifteen degrees since he'd last seen her, he couldn't help but be a little suspicious. But he stuffed that down deep in his gut along with all the other stupid things he thought about that weren't worth bringing up.

He jogged a few steps to catch up with her, settling in time with her brisk pace to walk at her side. "So, I forgot to ask. Did you get any war wounds?"

"No." She took a sharp turn and headed down a set of spiraling staircases each stamped with a gold drakonte.

"Me neither, thanks for asking. Warms my heart to see you so concerned with my well-being. But you really don't need to worry."

"What do you require for your sleeping arrangements?"

"You are in a particularly good mood."

"How would you know? You've been here a day."

"You can learn a lot about a person in a day." He drummed his fingers together, looking her over with a quirked eyebrow. "Or was this your special festival mood, today?"

"That." She reached the bottom landing and took another hard right through a doorless hallway that stretched before them in a yawn of black.

"Okay." He sighed and shook his head. "A bed is usually customary. A bath seems readily necessary. Some food would be delightful. I also like a warm milky tea before bed and for somebody to tuck me in and tell me I'm a good boy. Preferably my umi, but any nice motherly type that's available will do. How's your mother?"

"Discontent." She sighed again without a glance in his direction.

They reached the end of the hallway where two emerald green doors rose from the floor all the way to the arched ceiling. Two maidservants waited with heads bowed and pulled them open as Mirri approached, shutting them behind him as soon as he stepped into the room. The ceilings in this room curved to a slope at the top, tapestries like the one she had pulled him behind earlier covering nearly every wall. He passed an opening to a bath, the floor tiled in copper marble with twists of gold and a giant tub in the center. Braided rugs softened the falls of his feet, and he realized Mirri was still barefoot.

She sat on the edge of the bed and gestured in no particular direction. "Food will arrive shortly."

He nodded a few times, still craning his neck to take in the bizarre and lavish surroundings. "How come you don't wear shoes?"

"I do wear shoes."

He sighed, his shoulder drooping and his arms hanging limp in front of him. He wasn't sure what had happened between now and when she laughed and laid her head on his shoulder, but no matter what he did he couldn't get the moment back. Maybe he ought to just give up.

She stared at him for a moment, then looked the other way. "It is required of true descendants to remove their shoes on holy ground, which the castle was built upon, so we may more readily feel the will of the Origin and serve our people best."

"Was that so hard?" He walked into the bathroom, narrowed his eyes at the tub, then walked back out. "Can I get some water brought?"

She scrunched her nose. "Why?"

He waved his hands down his body, indicating the filth of sweat and buklak blood. "So I can take a bath."

Her face smoothed with a shake of her head. "We do not bathe here in Fyre and risk putting out our fire."

Mirri stood and slipped her way past him toward a small set of silver levers on the far wall. She flipped the middle one and a rainfall of water poured from little holes in the ceiling across the expanse of the tub. She gestured toward him.

"Ah, Al Madinat-style. Sweet." He took off his sword and his gun and dropped them on the floor in one corner. "Do you think I could get some clothes?"

"Your royal attire has already been placed in the armoire on the left side of the bed."

She stepped closer to him, then ran her hand through the droplets of water. There was something strangely intimate about it, her standing so close and touching his shower water. It ran through his mind to ask her to join him, but he crushed that and seven other similar thoughts until they were compacted enough to shove into his already-aching intestines.

Was all her skin as pale as what he could see or might he find unexpected tan lines where her tight armor showed chinks?

Her lips twitched as if to say something, but she shook her head and passed him once more, returning to the bedroom.

Izkander followed her out, leaving the water running so could fetch his *royal attire.* He lifted a pile of neatly folded drakonte leather and turned the clothes over in his hands. They were very much like Mirri's, though darker and cut for a man.

"These look tight."

She raised a thin brow and pulled her head back. "I'm sorry?"

"I've got really sensitive skin. I chafe. Don't you have anything more… breathable? Cotton? I prefer Egyptian, but Turkish is fine in a pinch."

"I have just the thing," she smiled sweetly, then walked over to the cream armoire on the other side of the bed. She tossed the doors open with flair, pulled out a crisply folded white garment then tossed it across the mattress at him.

He unfurled it and wrinkled his nose at her over the top. "A lady's nightdress, huh?" He tossed it over one arm and bowed to her. "You are too magnanimous."

"Anything for my Gaol Aig an Righ. Breathable. Cotton. Not from those cities on Ard, though, I'm afraid. We can't teleport." Her overly-sweet smile bittered.

"It's perfect. Thank you."

He took the garment and his official clothing, walked into the bathroom, and shut the door.

When he was clean and feeling less exhausted from the splash of water, Izkander first tried on his royal attire. Tight snakeskin pants in iridescent greenish gold that left very little to the imagination, a riding jacket studded with gold and silver inlays that made his skin itchy just looking at it. But he looked like sex on a stick in these threads. The color brought out his eyes and the warmth of his sandy brown skin, and they made every one of his taut muscles pop. His butt was an absolute treasure. But the clothes also made him feel like he was being slowly strangled to death by a bunch of dwarves. Good enough in the daytime, unacceptable at night. He usually just slept naked, but that didn't seem like the best idea.

He took off the skintight suit and washed his old clothes in the shower, hanging them on the towel rack to dry. Then he put on the night dress and looked at himself in the mirror. Just ridiculous enough, but also delightfully comfortable. He put on a smile and walked out into the bedroom.

Mirri sat with her feet up on a red velvet divan next to a table filled with thick bread, steaming stews, and several bowls covered in little blue lids, all of which smelled heavenly. Her hair was wet, though where she had gone to bathe was beyond him, and unlike him, she was dressed in a fresh set of under-armor, the green drakonte scales that flanked the cuffs shimmering in the low light.

When her eyes lit upon him, her cheek twitched. "Lovely."

"Does it suit me?" He did a little twirl as he walked over to the table and sat down in a chair across from her.

"It does, Izkander Green Eyes. Eat up. You earned it."

He piled a plate with a bunch of everything and ate quickly until that pinch in his gut began to fade. Then he sat back and crossed an ankle over his knee, careful to arrange the gown so it wasn't unladylike. He set two fingers on his temple and watched her for a moment before flicking his eyes to the gigantic bed.

"Is this your room?"

"No. It is our room." She cast her gaze around and let it fall back on him. "It was my room yesterday."

He lifted his eyebrows. "So where will I be sleeping?"

"Here." She narrowed her eyes. "Are you discontent?"

"That is such a weird question." He chuckled and shook his head. "Always. Always."

The skin around her eyes creased, and a small frown formed on her lips before she turned away from him. "There is space enough for two in here without you having to be near me."

"The divan looks comfy enough." He smiled and took a few more bites of the meaty stew. Her words boiled in his brain like butter being dropped in a hot pan. Why did she seem so sad? Was she really so upset he would be sleeping in her room?

He wouldn't have dreamed of trying to sneak into her bed.

Well, he might dream about it. In fact, he was positive that was exactly what he'd be dreaming about.

Mirri stood and bobbed her head, waving him toward the divan. Then she walked to the bed, threw back the covers, and slipped in, armor still on.

He walked over to the bed and grabbed a couple of pillows, stuffing them under his arm. He turned back to the divan, then stopped himself and looked down at her. "Are you really going to sleep with your armor on?"

"You have my nightgown." She pulled the covers up higher and curled into a ball. "And the only other clothes I own are these. Unless you count my diplomatic attire, but that would hardly be appropriate for bed, now wouldn't it? They're like a second skin, anyway. Don't concern yourself with my level of contentment."

"You don't have another nightgown?"

"The righs of Fyre are commanded by the Origin to live for the people and not for ourselves. To give freely and avoid excess. I only need one nightgown, so I own only one nightgown."

He covered his eyes with his hand and looked at the floor. "Then why did you give it to me?"

"Because I was concerned with your level of contentment."

"I'll just sleep in my underwear. It's not a problem."

"Keep it. I—I wouldn't feel comfortable wearing it in front of you, anyway."

"I won't look at you. I promise. Come on, you can't sleep in that. If you feel anything like I do after that fight, your bones have got to be aching."

"I know you won't look at me." She curled tighter under the blankets. "And my armor holds my bones together."

He narrowed his eyes at her, unsure what to make of her sudden timorousness. He snatched a throw off the edge of the bed and walked back into the bathroom where he stripped off the nightgown. In nothing but tight, black braises, he pulled the long blanket over his shoulders and walked back out, tossing the gown onto the foot of the bed. Then he went to the divan and settled himself into a little cocoon.

Mirri slipped a hand out from under the covers and touched it to the floor. The stone beneath her fingers warmed to a bright orange, and the fire in the wall sconces dashed from their hold and down to her fingers, leaving all but the glowing stone dark in the room.

Beautiful, and dangerous too. Like everything about her.

Izkander lay still in the deafening silence for about a quarter of a degree before it broke him. "Mirri?"

"Yes, Gaol Aig an Righ?"

He winced at the name which he could only assume meant *Subsidiary Ruler.* "You don't have to call me that."

The sheets on the bed rustled, and the gleam of her red eyes peeked out above the sheets. "It offends you?"

"No. It just isn't my name. I prefer Izkander. Or Skander, that's fine too." He chewed on his lip and tugged on his earlobe. "Does it bother you if I call you Mirri?"

"You are my Fire Mate. You may call me as you please."

"I want to call you as you please."

"My mother calls me Mirri, sometimes. Havu does. Urramach, but no more. Now, you."

He sighed and stretched his arms above him then folded them behind his head, twitching his feet where they hung off the too-short divan. "Just let me know if you want me to call you something else."

"I am content."

"You don't seem especially content. You seem moody."

She sighed. "Urramach kissed me in the stables."

He could feel his fire twist and knew his eyes may be a tiny bit greener than usual. But that was stupid and unfair, especially because Urramach had been there way before him and Mirri had all but said she hoped he would be her husband someday. And the guy seemed nice enough—stiff and a bit pretentious, but that seemed par for the course in Fyre. Still, the sadness in her voice gave him pause.

Friends. That's what he'd told Javier they were. She seemed like really did need a friend. "Is that a good thing or a bad thing?"

"My flesh didn't melt into a puddle. That was a good thing. But, mostly I couldn't breathe." The sheets rustled again, and her shiny hair spilled free from their hold, red against white in the dark. "Is that normal?"

"It can be." He propped a pillow behind his head to sit up a little, gaze shifting between her shadow and the faint light of two moons pouring through the window. "That depends on what kind of not-being-able-to-breathe it was."

"It felt... the opposite of when we spoke in private in the hallway."

He smiled softly, remembering the moment. Her blush and laughter and little relieved sighs.

Friends, he told himself. *Just friends.*

Then again...

"Was it like a tight, pressurized, walls-closing-in, maybe-just-a-little-bit kind of not-being-able-to-breathe?"

She slid off the bed and walked over, then sat on the very end of the divan and curled her knees up to her chest, resting her head on top. "Yeah, like that."

She looked so little, even in her armor. He tucked his knees in to give her some more space.

"I remember this one time I was staying at Javier's house. I guess I was probably like twelve, thirteen? Something like that. And my cousin... well, she's not really my cousin. Javier isn't really my uncle, and she's not really his daughter..." He waved a hand in the air. "Anyway. She kissed me in the barn. I had no idea it was coming. And I got that feeling. Like the walls were closing in on me. Probably because Javier scared the living piss out of me, and I felt like if he caught us he would probably beat me to death with his bare hands. Anyway. I pushed back from her so hard that I fell out of the hayloft and broke my arm."

"So you couldn't breathe because you were afraid?"

"I was afraid. And caught off guard. And..." He ran his tongue over his teeth, casting his mind back to the moment. Of course, the main thing he remembered was the stabbing pain in his forearm as it smashed against the blade of an iron plow. But when he thought about the kiss itself... "It just didn't feel right. I didn't like girls yet, and she was... waaay too much for me."

"I didn't push back. I froze." Her eyes glowed sadly in the dark. "You know how many monsters I've faced down in battle? How many times I've had to stare my father in the eye and perform tasks outsized to my abilities? And then I froze in a stable while my best friend was too mad at me to help."

"Your best friend?"

"Havu."

"Ah." Izkander furrowed his brow so much he could feel the sharp creases between his eyes like an old man. He reached up and fiddled with them with two fingers, trying to take his mind off the cold prickles racing up and down his spine.

"First of all, I seriously doubt there are any tasks that outsize your abilities. I've only known you a day and I can already tell that. Secondly, don't be so hard on yourself. It is a very common occurrence to be thrown off-guard by that kind of thing. Kissing and everything. Especially when someone just springs it on you when you're not ready." He cleared his throat and looked up at the ceiling. "I'm sorry about Havu, too. That's my fault. Well, it's Squirt's fault. But still...."

"Can I sleep here tonight? Would you mind?"

He swallowed a little catch in his throat. "I don't mind."

"Thank you."

"Do you want to lie down?"

She lifted her head. "Next to you?"

A flash of heat lifted his chest and burned his cheeks. It was a good thing it was too dark for her to see.

"Well, I just meant... if you're going to sleep here... I mean... do you want me to move?"

"No. I don't want you to move. To be honest, I didn't come over here for the divan." She squeezed her knees tighter, released them, then turned and lay carefully down next to him, their arms overlapping, hips and legs touching. "I used to sneak into my brother's room when I was little and scared so he would play cards with me and make me laugh."

"You have a brother?" he asked in a croaky whisper, only realizing once the question was out that he already knew the answer.

She smiled softly in the faint light. "We would stay up all night and get chastised by Fa Chomhair for having baggy eyes in the morning. But I did it anyway, again and again, because the only time I ever felt like I could stop fighting was when my brother rubbed my back until I fell asleep." Her smile fell. "But to answer your question: no, I do not have a brother. Not anymore." She pressed a hand over her eyes. "*Susbaint ann an cadal*. Be content in sleep, Izkander."

He smiled gently, the warmth of her body mingling with minty prickles and the knot in his gut to form an entirely indescribable sensation. It ate him from the inside out, aching to twist his bones into strange and painful shapes. It also whispered at him not to move.

His fingers twitched to wrap around her and stroke her back, but he kept them where they were. Her arms rested atop his, her hard armor digging into his skin. Nothing but a thin wool throw stood between his near nakedness and her tight body and soft peachy skin.

His eyes moved over her face. Her sweet berry lips and an almost invisible dusting of freckles on the bridge of her nose that he could just make out in the slant of pale orange moonlight. He was struck with a profound urge to kiss those freckles, those twitchy little lips. But that couldn't possibly have been more wrong, especially with her story of freezing and not being able to breathe fresh in his ears like stinging nettles.

And Urramach. And his face.

He closed his eyes. But he could still smell her—leather and fire and peaches. Or was he just imagining that last one?

His fingers won the fight. He slipped an arm around her shoulder to stroke the bare skin between her shoulder blades. She tensed, and he paused, then the muscles beneath his touch melted, spreading to all of her as she finally relaxed next to him with a little sigh.

"Goodnight, Mirri." He leaned in and pressed his cheek against her silky hair. "Sweet dreams."

CHAPTER TWELVE

Mirri

She woke the next morning with her leg draped over his and her hand and cheek upon his chest. Her first instinct was to bolt upright, but she didn't want to. Not when he smelled so good. A mixture of familiar—probably the soap from her nightgown—and an open field in the spring. And just him. Whatever that smell was. Something spicy and delightful. She puckered her lips. She definitely had to get up now. She tried to remove her leg carefully and ended up sliding right off the side with a little squeak.

Izkander grunted, and his nose twitched, then he settled back into silence.

She spun onto her hands and knees and jumped up, brushing off her armor. Then groaned. He was right. Every bone in her body screamed to be free. She should not have mocked her sore muscles with the closeness of her nightgown while confining them so.

So tight, she cried in silent, constrained little breaths.

Mirri rubbed a hand up and down her lower back as she went into the bathroom for her morning routine. When she finished, stomach relieved and face scrubbed pink, she tip-toed over to Izkander and looked down at his pretty little face. He was as handsome as Urramach, they both had that chiseled-jaw look she found particularly attractive. But whereas Urramach's features tended toward a seriousness she had always respected, Izkander's were soft, like creamed honey. And he had that dimple... Her fingers strayed and brushed lightly through his hair.

She couldn't get her fingers to leave his face, wishing his eyes would open so she could see the green. They always caught her off-guard in her nation full of red and gold. Made her chest catch just a little. Strange and new and completely freeing. But so did Urramach's, in a different way. His golden fires were intensity and familiarity. Safe, yet suffocating. She still wasn't sure what had made her freeze with Urramach, but the way her body responded to Izkander—light and giddy, almost, like the eager flaps of a baby drakonte's wings—had to be due to novelty. That's all it was.

But neither freezing nor flapping was a proper way to run a nation.

She pinched herself on the arm.

What was the point in comparing the two men? One was her Fire Mate who did not want to be and one was not her Fire Mate who did want to be. Neither of their desires changed what currently was.

What was she thinking? Izkander wasn't real. Not in a tangible sense of the word. Or maybe intangible... Whatever the word was for *here today, gone tomorrow, and her forever without.* He had even called her moody. Which she guessed was fair.

She pulled her hand away and bit her thumb so she would stop running her hands through his dark hair and over his thick eyebrows.

She *had* been moody. Had let Urramach's premonitions get in her head. Though he hadn't been all wrong. Izkander had more than readily agreed not to look at her that evening. Not to sleep in the bed with her. And his abject denial of the name she had playfully given him—Gaol Aig an Righ, *love of the queen*—which even now her generals used after the meeting yesterday, had all affirmed Urramach's declaration: she would be unloved.

But he hadn't been all right, either. Because she hadn't slept alone, cold in a bed with a Fire Mate who didn't care. She hadn't slept on the bed at all just to make sure of it. So there.

What really troubled her was why she had opened up to Izkander about her brother, about Havu being petty. And why had she told him Urramach kissed her in the first place?

He does not want to stay, Mirri, she scolded herself. *He doesn't want you or Fyre.*

... and Urramach does.

She held up her wrist and tried to spin the ring of fire that still hovered around her skin, but it did nothing. Now, everyone in the castle—in the entire kingdom—would know they had not had their Eve of Fire because the promise remained on her wrist. Not horribly embarrassing... yet. There were many a nervous bride or groom in the past that waited a few days before joining in physical intimacy with their spouse. Or poor Roimhe who was terrified of what his Fire Mate might do to him in the dark. They waited a month.

Soon, whispers would flow like a mountain spring. And even if she did seek refuge from Izkander's indifference in Urramach's relentless arms, she could never have a child, not if she wanted it to live.

She pressed the bottom of her palms into her eyes and moaned. Time to get it over with.

She leaned over Izkander and slapped his arm softly. He grunted and choked a little, a weird *nyeck* sound coming from his throat. Then, he yawned and stretched his arms over his head, the blanket falling down to show his broad shoulders and the top of his bare chest. He blinked a few times before his big, green eyes came to rest on her face. His lips turned in a little smile.

"Good morning, pretty girl," he croaked.

Her eyes grazed his bare skin, and she bit her bottom lip to keep back an inappropriate smile. Or was it appropriate? Yes... A very appropriate, unwelcome smile.

"Good morning. Sleep well?"

"Yeah, actually." He pulled the blanket back over his shoulders and snuggled down into the pillows. "You?"

"Yes, thank you. Better than I have in a long while. So well, in fact, the First Moon has already risen. We should start our day before gossip beats us out the door."

Izkander stood up and shuffled into the bathroom, humming a little tune as he went.

She shook her head. He even woke up super happy. She had wondered if yesterday was *his* festival mood. It would appear not. But his happiness put a bit of peppiness in her step, too. And as long as her father didn't see, she supposed that was alright.

Her newly-found joy diminished when he came out of the bathroom dressed in his clothes from the day before, clean and dry, if a little wrinkly, and carrying his belt and boots. Another rejection of Fyre. Of her. He walked past her to the divan and flopped down.

"What a charmed life you live," she said, a bit of wistfulness leaking out unbidden.

He stood up and drooped his shoulders with a little sigh. "What can I say? Most things are awesome most of the time."

She stepped behind him and pulled his shoulders so his back straightened. "Until you came here, right?"

He smiled over his shoulder at her, that deep dimple of his forming in one cheek. "Actually, that's mostly been awesome too."

"Even though my generals and people will call you Gaol Aig an Righ instead of Izkander?"

"Considering some of the things I have been called, I don't figure that's too bad." He squinted one eye up at the ceiling. "What's it mean, anyway?"

"Ugly troll king."

"Hardy-har-har." He twitched his nose. "Alright, you keep your secret. But until you start opening up, I get to keep calling you pretty girl."

"It's a demotion for me, but I am content." She placed a hand on the doors and hesitated.

It always got harder to breathe when she stepped out into the castle every morning. And now that her room—theirs, though he did not want it to be—was filled with Izkander's lightness, she worried it would disperse the second the black hole opened. And if he left on top of that? She'd never get it back.

He does not want you or Fyre, Mirri.

And maybe that was true. He wanted to make a difference. To have people give him credit so he could pat himself on the back and move on. That was it. He wasn't committed to the often thankless job of a ruler who served only her people and never herself. She couldn't blame him for that, not really. But she didn't have a choice.

She cleared her throat and looked back at him. "Ready for all the ogling stares and questions surrounding your virility because we have not yet sealed our Union?"

"Yes. By Allah! Yes."

She pressed a hand to her mouth to stifle a giggle. "Come on then, ugly troll king. Let us face it together."

She rapped on the door, and the maid on the other side opened them up with a groan of wood and hinges.

Izakander walked up beside her and put out his arm, the elbow cocked in a square to the side of his body. "Do people do this kind of thing in Fyre?"

"What?" She poked at his arm. "What is this gangly thing you present to me?" She fluttered her lashes at him.

He pulled back the sleeve of his shirt and flexed a rigid, sinewy upper arm. He kissed it, then snapped his gaze to her. "Don't look directly at it. It will burn your eyes out like staring at the sun."

She shoved his sleeve back down while choking down another giggle, then took his arm with a second brush of his hard muscle. "Yes, we do this kind of thing in Fyre."

He pulled her tight to the side of his body. "Let me know if that serpent is constricting on you too hard."

"It's just a little hatchling, no match for a true snake." She winked. "I'm not too worried."

He mimed biting her. "Juggernaut."

"Thank you."

She tugged him through the corridors of the castle and toward the stairwell that led to the balustrades. As they neared the top step, a pair of bare feet waited for her. She almost swung Izkander around and yanked him back down like... well, like Maron would have one of his lecherous maids.

"Fa Chomhair Righ." She bowed her head quickly to her father. She elbowed Izkander, hoping without much hope that he'd do the same.

He bowed, but he was giggling the whole time. She would have stomped on his foot but seeing as hers were bare and he wore boots, it would hardly be a proper chastisement.

Her father took a step down. "Ah-nis Na Righ." His red eyes slid to the fiery cuffs around each of their linked wrists. He smirked. "*A bheil thu toilichte?*"

She slid her arm free from Izkander and pressed her hands together in front of her with another dip of her head. "I am content with the will of the Flame," she answered in Arabic.

His cold eyes moved to Izkander, his lips forming a scowl around the unfamiliar language. "And you, djinn? Has my daughter left you content after your first night together?"

Izkander ran a finger over his lips. "A more than satisfactory experience. Four out of five marks."

She pinched her lips together and shot him a glare. All she ever was to her father was four out of five marks. She had always hoped someday she would overcome. But maybe that's the best she ever could be. They hadn't slept together and had their Eve of Fire, after all. Maybe that's why. She wasn't his type. Too lean perhaps. Or somber. A mere four out of five.

Izkander narrowed his eyes at her. He took a step up beside her, watching her face carefully. "Actually, I'm gonna bump that up to a five," he said slowly before turning his smile on her father, "with strong hopes for many sixes, and perhaps even an elusive seven for our future."

A little of the tension in her muscles began to fade until she saw her father's sneer. For an inexpressive man, he seemed effusive around Izkander.

"Did you need to speak with me, Fa Chomhair?" Mirri asked.

He thrust a small gold coin at her, emblazoned with the seal of Fyre. But when she reached for it, he shoved it toward Izkander.

Izkander flinched, then looked at it and cocked an inquisitive brow at her. She had only half a guess as to what it was, but as far as memory served her, it wouldn't kill him. She nodded.

Pushing out his bottom lip, he shrugged. He wrapped the fabric of his sleeve around his hand before taking the coin.

Her father scoffed. "It's just a coin, boy. An approval for meeting."

"Of course, that's what it is." Izkander pointed at the fabric wrapped around his hand. "But gold gives me a rash."

"Djinn," he muttered in Gaelic, and Mirri winced. "Give it to your parents. Or, the half of them that doesn't fry like a *shmeeno* slug under salt when they touch metal. It is the diplomacy token for Mirri's visit. I expect a seal of approval in return for the histories and official documents."

"You expect a what-now?"

"A sealed approval from your parents supporting your Union and the legitimacy of the Fyre throne." A mean smile shaped his lips. "Is that a problem?"

"No. Why would it be?" Izkander slipped the coin into a pouch on his belt and shook out his sleeve, straightening his shoulders. "My parents are delightful people."

Mirri eyed him, trying to make sense of the different smiles he wore. This one was bright, shiny. *Too* shiny. But now was not the time to question him about it.

"Thank you, Fa Chomhair, for your diligence in managing the affairs of our great nation even as it passes from your purview to mine." She dipped a little lower, hair spilling over her shoulder the way it always did as she bowed to her father. "Is there any other way I may serve you?"

Her father's face smoothed. "Nothing I can't do better myself."

Mirri slowly scraped her teeth over her top lip. "Yes, Fa Chomhair. *Beannaichidh Marduk thu.*"

She grabbed Izkander's elbow and eased her way past her father and up the last few steps, not stopping until the icy breeze of the mountain air whipped against her always-warm skin.

Izkander yanked on her and called over his shoulder. "Hey, Chomhair!"

Her eyes widened, and she tugged against his hold. "What are you doing?"

"I have something to say to him."

Her father's bristling face appeared in the doorway.

"Don't do this, Izkander." She grabbed his shirt and tried to pull him away.

"I just have a question for him." He snapped his head towards her father. "When was the last time you slayed the immortal buklak that has been plaguing your people for generations?"

A deep purple colored her father's face. "What did you say to me, boy?"

Mirri twitched, not sure if she should step in front of or behind Izkander. "He is your—the Fa Chomhair Righ of Fyre," she whispered, voice thick in her throat. "You should not disrespect the great things he's done for our nation long before you arrived." She made sure to speak loud enough to carry over the blustery winds and to her father's burning ears as well as those of the attentive guards.

Her father's eyebrows twitched. "Step away from him, Ah-nis Na Righ. I need to have a word with his wicked tongue."

"It is an innocent question." Izkander lifted his shoulders. "When was the last time you slayed the immortal buklak? Because your daughter and I did that yesterday."

"You think I haven't fought my share of monsters in the three hundred years I've ruled?" Her father growled.

Mirri stepped between them. "Fa Chomhair—"

"Get out of my way, Ah-nis," he hissed, "so I may throw your Fire Mate off the castle."

"It doesn't matter how many monsters you slayed back in the day," Izkander continued, all bravado and no sense. "You should still show a bit more respect to somebody who did so yesterday. If you could have done it so much better yourself, where were you during the battle? Huh?"

"Ah-nis!" Her father's eyes were bulging with rage, clenched knuckles white and shaking.

"Izkander," she tugged on his sleeve. "Leave it be."

"Fine, fine." He put up his hands and took a step back. "Consider it left. I just don't like him talking to you that way."

Her father pulled back his hand, opened the palm wide, and smacked her cheek. Her face stung so much, it numbed despite the bite of the freezing wind. She tasted blood on her lip. She looked wide-eyed between the two men who had refused to listen to her, turned, and with the words *he doesn't want you* ringing in her head, jumped off the side of the castle and into the air.

She didn't want them, either.

CHAPTER THIRTEEN

Izkander

"Bihaqi aljahima!" Izkander cried.

When Mirri's father slapped her, it sounded like two flat boards smacking together. His eyes widened, and he stared, frozen in the moment.

What kind of a...? How could he just...? When she was...? And with no regard for...?

Izkander's mouth hung open. Flabbergasted. Flummoxed.

Furious.

"Bihaqi aljahima!" he cried again when Mirri leapt off the side of the castle.

He darted towards the edge and looked over, breathing a heavy sigh of relief when Havu swept under her like a gentle wind. She caught the drakonte by the neck and slipped her feet into her stirrups as the massive snake arched back into the sky. Mirri's hair whipped around her like quick flames, and she didn't look back.

Izkander smiled watching her. That was what she was supposed to look like—high and free and doing whatever the hell she wanted, not cowering and kowtowing to this pompous bag of hot air.

"Look what you've done!" the old king snapped.

Izkander moved his fingers on his sword and squared his shoulders to the King. "You slapped her in the face for no reason, you tremendous royal prick."

"The Origin and its ever-burning Flame require I guide the Ah-nis in matters of the kingdom until she is wise enough to do so on her own. Your unbridled stupidity was the cause of her chastisement. That, and her shameful inability to control you."

Izkander stomped closer. "You wanna slap somebody, Chomhair?" He lifted his arms to the sides and puffed up his chest. "I'm standing right here."

The king lunged at him, coming in low and spearing him in the gut with a clenched fist that hit like a hammer. Izkander spat out a hard cough. He snatched the king's neck and yanked, twirling him in a circle and pushing him away.

"Come on with it, you buklak-non-slaying, condescending sack of silver!" Izkander shouted and drew his sword.

"It's a duel you're after, is it djinn?" The king sneered and wiped his foaming lips. "Very well. I accept."

Izkander showed a smile like a wild namur about to pounce. "Anytime, anywhere, old king."

The king lifted his hand and called for his sword which a wide-eyed manservant promptly fetched. The man got down on the floor and held up the pommel. Then, the king set his foot on his shoulder and pushed him back to yank free the two-handed long sword. The servant fell back on his butt, then scrambled up and scurried away.

"First blood," the king said, lifting the blade to eye level and swiping it quickly out to one side with a sharp cutting sound.

"Perfect," Izkander sneered.

"If I win, you will speak only when spoken to in the Court of Fyre. And you will defer to me in all things."

Izkander's neck twitched. He wasn't about to show weakness by quibbling over terms. Besides, he knew deep down that he wouldn't be here forever, no matter what they all said. He had friends in high places, very high places. He could get out whenever he wanted to.

Probably.

But he hadn't even tried yet, and that was everything to do with Mirri.

Izkander laid his sword over his thigh and leaned back into an easy fool's guard. Cocky and confident and ready for anything, like his old man taught him. "If I win you are never again to lay a hand on my Fire Mate. And you will speak to both her and me with more deference."

"You presume to dictate my relationship with my own daughter?"

"You presume to dictate my relationship with what is now my own Fire Mate. How is that any different?" Izkander's smile tightened, baring all of his teeth. "But, if you lack the confidence to throw anything worthwhile on the table, I will declare myself the winner by default."

The king's sharp, scarlet eyes widened and tightened all at once. "I will silence that infernal tongue of yours if it costs every drop of my blood."

"Does that mean you agree to the terms?" Izkander cocked his head to one side and lifted an eyebrow.

"Have at, djinn."

The king bent one knee and set the tip of his sword on the ground in front of him in a long tail guard. Izkander's eyes swept over him, sizing him up for the fight. He was a large man. Big-boned, broad-chested, muscles like a male drakonte in heat. And he held the long sword with easy shoulders, though the rest of his body was still tense.

His face held that delightful tinge of infuriated purple.

Izkander took a breath and rolled his shoulders, forcing his muscles loose. The anger that had driven him to say what he had said, that forced his hand to draw his sword, was still burning as bright as the Seventh Moon during glass season, but he knew from experience he could not fight with it. Righteous indignation had to be forced down and pressurized to be of any use in a fight unless the intention was to go berserker. But a duel was far too controlled a practice. He needed to bring the roiling boil of his blood down to a more manageable simmer.

That said, the sound of the slap still echoed in his ears. Over and over, not dimming in intensity. He met the king's eyes—his would-be father-in-law—and lifted his blade into a high guard. The Mamluk saber he carried was shorter than the king's long sword. Lighter, thinner, and much more maneuverable. The slight curve of the single-edge sword made it much easier to execute quick slashing movements and to slip the tip of the blade into unexpected places.

Izkander put one hand on his hip and bent his front knee, turning his body to the side. The king's longsword was so heavy it threatened to tip the man forward like a bird about to drink from a fountain.

Izkander made a feint. The king blocked with a sharp upward thrust. Izkander moved back, shifting his feet one over the other to move in a half-circle to the side before coming in with another feint. This king parried with a hard swipe that threw Izkander's arm wide. The hard block rattled his shoulder. Even with his heavy sword, the king's blows came in more forcefully than he anticipated, a storm in a man that threatened to keel him over.

Izkander shook the reverberations from his shoulder.

Quick, easy strikes. Loose guards. Patience. All he needed was a single drop of blood.

They exchanged parries, the king driving Izkander back in a straight line before Izkander would slip to one side and they restarted the process.

"You contrive and pivot like a woman," the king spat, whipping his sword in for a few quick and exceedingly heavy blows.

Izkander caught each one, letting the force of it roll down the curve of his blade so the force did not shake him as much as the first had. He gave a hard laugh in his throat.

"Your heavy-handed buffets couldn't get the best of a lame Ghaluman lizard."

The king snarled and came in with quick strikes with his long sword. The truth was he was faster than Izkander expected. His blade was also made of metal, which mitigated the advantage Izkander usually carried over the more brittle djinn blades of greater Qaf. Each strike of their swords *clanged* with a ferocity only afforded to shiny, fire-forged weapons meant to kill.

If Izkander let himself get hit, he was going to lose more than a few drops of blood. Even if the blade was dull, which it clearly wasn't, the slab of steel was heavy enough to crush bones. He would have to move faster, wear the king out, and slip in a hit before blocking that giant blade wore down his stamina.

"You are nothing but an obnoxious parvenu." The king lunged, aiming to spear Izkander through the chest.

"And you are a blustering hierophant." He pivoted—*like a woman*, like a person with sense—and snapped back, bringing his sword down in a barrage of quick slashes.

The king dodged side to side with his body, his sword down. "Any man in this kingdom would be better suited as a Fire Mate to the Ah-nis Na Righ."

"Then how come none of them could catch her?" Izkander whipped his blade up in an underhanded circle, the tip poised to slice the king's groin.

The king crouched, smacking his long sword in place with less than a moment to spare.

"Your ignorant swagger will be her death," the old man hissed, tiny bloodshot veins twitching in the whites of his eyes. "The death of Fyre. I will see your skull dashed upon the high rocks of Untar!"

"Little wonder you've managed to convince a hundred million djinn to hate you."

The king came in with renewed vigor. Slash, lunge, slash. A wide swoop overhead. Izkander ducked, the wind of the blow brushing his cheek. Chomp Hair was not going for blood anymore if he ever had been. He was trying to kill him. The power behind his blows amped up. The next time Izkander parried, his shoulders were almost ripped from their sockets. He stumbled. The king brought his blade in again. Another hard parry.

The king kicked Izkander's stomach. He lurched forward in pain, and an elbow smacked the crown of his head. He fell back, landing with a hard thud on the unguarded rampart. His head was hanging over the side, nothing but ten stories of open air below.

Izkander probed his face quickly with two fingers. No blood.

The sword chopped down. Izkander rolled to one side, the steel cutting into the stone which burst into shards at his back. He rolled back the other way. Four times he did this, narrowly avoiding being cloven in two each time.

Snarling, Izkander kicked the king in the knee. The large man stumbled, his sword falling far enough off target he had to stop to pull himself back or risk tumbling over the side.

Izkander rolled to his feet.

The king swiped again with a heavy backhand and a cry of "Death!"

Izkander rolled hard to one side. Another quick exchange of stabs and lunges brought them full circle around the jagged rampart. Izkander hopped up on a tooth-shaped parapet, forcing the king to lift his sword higher to attack. It killed some of his momenta and stole the power from his swipes. With his sword in an underhanded grip, Izkander caught the blade several times. As the king's energy began to wear, Izkander's quickness shined. He parried and threw his own strike in a single exchange, forcing the king to dodge back, and then rushed back in like a fish caught in a heavy swash. The bright-red flush of exhaustion intensified the purple on the king's face.

The king gave a low bawl. He swung his sword at Izkander's feet, forcing him to jump over it. Twice. Three times. Izkander saw his moment. He kicked the king hard in his nose. A splatter of blood burst.

The king stumbled back. He snarled, teeth pink with his own blood, and brought a hand to his face. Izkander stood unmoving on the parapet, chest heaving and his sword still raised. Would the son of a snake ever stop? Probably not. He wanted him dead. Now more than ever.

The king muttered something under his breath in the *shush-ga-shush* language of Fyre, but the tone could not be mistaken. The venom and viscera. The unmitigated and steadily intensifying hatred.

Their eyes met and held one another for a moment that stretched on longer than any he had ever known. Izkander tightened his grip on his sword, back tense, core muscles trembling with anticipation. He expected the king to call the guards on him, as bested kings tended to do. Izkander readied himself to defend against twenty men, either trying to execute him or haul him off to a dungeon. He was ready to fight, ready to accept whatever consequences may come in the wake of his reprimand.

Ready.

The king threw down his sword and rolled back his shoulders, finding admirable dignity even with blood dripping from both nostrils. "As is dictated by the Eternal traditions of the kingdom of Fyre, I concede defeat."

Izkander narrowed his eyes, a curious little wave rushing through his lungs. "You do?"

Fa Chomhair sneered, his eyes an unparalleled embodiment of loathing. It sent a chill through Izkander's sore, tense muscles.

"The Origin as my witness, I am content with the outcome and accept the outlaid conditions."

That strange flabbergasted feeling from earlier was back with a vengeance, though it set a very different flavor on his tongue. Izkander glanced over his shoulder, certain a cavalry of drakonte wasn't coming at him from behind.

Clear skies.

A horrid feeling gnawed at the inside of his chest with the realization that he had gained a tiny crumb of respect for the snarling king of Fyre. Though that did nothing to dim his fiery hatred for the man. And it did nothing to alter the creeping sense of guilt suddenly biting into the back of his brain like a lamprey.

"When next we meet in battle, *mac-cèile ùr*," the king said, his face as yielding as lava stone, "we fight with bare knuckles. And we fight to the death."

Izkander sheathed his sword. He lifted his hands to his chest and cracked a knuckle. "Suits me fine."

His gaze locked on those cold, snakelike eyes, Izkander brought his fingers to his lips and whistled loudly. A few moments later, the distinctive *thwick-a* of Squirt's four wild wings approached from behind. Izkander kept his gaze on the king and waited. It seemed an eternity looking down at the fuming king who moments ago had so gracefully admitted defeat. It left a bitter taste in the back of his throat and a cold suspicion churning in his gut.

The king had essentially just threatened to beat him to death with his bare hands, but it was the unspoken threat living in his serpentine eyes that sent shards of rusty ice licking up Izkander's spine.

When, at last, Squirt was near enough, Izkander ripped his gaze away from his would-be father-in-law and leapt off the ramparts. He landed on Squirt between his two sets of wings, gripping the drakonte's body hard with his thighs and digging his fingertips into the ridges of the scales. Squirt flew away from the castle in a series of lazy 's' shapes, and Izkander leaned forward on his fluffy back and pressed his cheek into the soft feathers.

"Where's Mirri?" he sighed, his voice just loud enough for Squirt's keen hearing to pick up. "Take me to her."

CHAPTER FOURTEEN

MIRRI

IF HAVU HADN'T BEEN saddled and ready for Mirri's morning ride, she would have hit the ground and splattered into a thousand blood-soaked pieces. A servant could have been running behind schedule. Havu could have had an attitude problem or snuck off to go see Squirt, or the winds could have been too rough to make for a decent flight.

But Mirri wasn't thinking about any of those things when she jumped. Embarrassment burned too hot on her cheeks, and anger leaked too readily from her eyes. Her father hadn't slapped her since Maron died and she'd made a scene begging for answers at his feet in front of his generals. He hadn't once struck Maron. *The future Ah-nis Na Righ is the Origin's call and must be treated with respect*, he always said.

So what did that make her?

And then there was Izkander, who just couldn't hold his tongue for the life of him. Who thought playing righ in her little kingdom was a fun game that didn't affect the souls of thousands of people. Her people. And her. And who had convinced her to get distracted by his games, too. Linking arms and giggling. Hiding behind tapestries. Sleeping on divans. None of that was who she was.

She was Mirri Naga, Ah-nis Na Righ, and true descendant of Marduk. And she didn't live in a dream world where breathing was easy and everything was fun. She needed to recalibrate and remember why she had done everything she did. To be independent of anyone. To be a dutiful and content righ.

Havu flew stiffly beneath her and eased Mirri into the saddle, her feathered tail like loose leaves in a sharp wind. Silent. As was she. They kept flying like that, farther and farther from the castle until a burning began to itch beneath her skin. The fire ring around her wrist glowed more brightly, shooting a beam of light back the way they came.

Your Fire Mate is that way it was saying. *Get back to him or die.*

Mirri's shoulders hunched with the reality of her situation. She gave one long whistle and two short clicks, and Havu twisted in a spiral toward the hatchery in the back of the castle. If she couldn't ride free into the mountains to breathe, maybe the little hatchlings would brighten her spirit. They circled over the canvas awnings, white and blue like the sky so the baby drakonte would remember where they came from. Where they should return. Several little purple and yellow snappers jumped and scurried around in the fenced-in field. Mirri waited for Havu to pick a safe place to land.

Round and round and round.

"What are you doing?" she finally snapped.

Mirri. Havu snuffled.

She hunched her shoulders even further. "Yes, Havu?"

I'm sorry.

Mirri shifted in the saddle and said nothing.

I didn't think he'd actually do it. If I had... I never would have let him risk your life like that. I just didn't think... Havu's body shivered beneath her. *I'm sorry.*

Mirri laid her face on the thick, oval scales and wrapped her arms around Havu's massive sides. Havu was all she had to talk to. The only being who understood all her woes, her past, the mess of her present.

She groaned. "What am I going to do?"

With Urramach? Nothing. Havu said flatly. She cast a glance back toward Mirri and shook her head with a snort.

"About any of it, Havu. Urramach and Izkander. Fa Chomhair Righ. Maron..."

Havu twitched beneath her. *What does he have to do with anything?*

Mirri pushed a stray strand of hair from her face and followed it to its end. "You heard Urramach. He said Maron started interpreting laws differently."

And had his face melted off.

"Yes... thank you for that imagery." She shuddered. "But why? I tried to ask Urramach, but his gaze shifted. He looked... discontent. He said he didn't know what Maron's sin had been, just what it hadn't." Mirri pushed herself up, leaning on her elbows as she let the air waft by. "You know, no one's ever told me what exactly he did wrong."

I know.

"Why is that?"

Because it doesn't matter. Once a true descendant dies because of their disobedience, they're not supposed to exist anymore. You know our people's lore.

"It is not so easy to erase someone. Not from my memories."

Don't think about Maron. And don't follow in his footsteps. Which also means no Urramach. A win-win.

Mirri let her heart pinch longer. "You just want me and Izkander to magically work out so you can keep Squirt around."

Not true. Havu whipped in a sharp turn so Mirri slid in the saddle. *I was staunchly anti-Urramach before the festival. Remember?*

"I remember." She sighed, scanning the hatchery below. A splash of snow-white hair coiled over a shoulder stood out amongst the dark, muddy earth. "Take us down. I need to have a word with my mother."

Havu swooped low, thrusting her wings out to the side in slow, heavy flaps so the little hatchlings scattered out of the way. When the coast was clear, she settled her belly into the mud, using her tail to flick away any curious little ones she didn't want to deal with. The hatchery rested in a long oval of drakonte stalls and practice hoops, large troughs full of melted snow on one end, and a tall wooden landing used for forcing first flights on the other.

Mirri slid off, the wet earth squelching between her bare toes. Izkander had quite the quirked brow and off-kilter smile when he asked her why she didn't wear shoes.

He clearly thought it odd. And perhaps it was, but now she would keep an eye out for the smile. That one and the shiny one he used when talking about getting his parent's approval. She wasn't sure what that one meant yet, but she had a feeling it wasn't good. And with how he talked of his *umi*, Mirri was certain she was just another person who would find her lacking.

Her umi, on the other hand, didn't care about anything that wasn't a drakonte or its eggs.

"Subsidiary," Mirri said, nodding her head as she approached. She had slipped back into her native tongue and reveled in the familiarity.

Her mother turned and smiled, white hair shimmering and a hint of sun on her cheeks. "Mirri, good morning."

Mirri ought to chastise her mother for not calling her by her formal name, but what would be the point? Her mother never listened. Not a true descendant of Marduk, she didn't have to. Instead, Mirri knelt down next to where her mother sat cross-legged feeding a new hatchling with little scraps of meat. The little drakonte's orange and red scales cast translucent rainbows on Mirri's arms as it chomped and tore at the flesh with finger-long teeth.

"How are the numbers with the little ones?" Mirri asked, both obligatorily curious and in need of something comfortable to say. "Has the mortality rate improved at all?"

"This batch of hatchlings is tenacious. It appears the Flame is content to let them live."

"*Moladh Marduk*," Mirri exhaled. "Are there enough to keep the den going?"

"For now, but with every generation getting smaller, the gene pool suffers. They do not have their blood cleansed of impurities by the Flame as you do. Marduk blesses us, however."

Mirri scowled. "You mean because of Squirt?"

"I meant the Origin rumbles beneath the castle. Another batch of pure hatchlings has been birthed from the Eternal Flame. The eggs warm now in the lava, waiting to be born."

Mirri's lips twitched in a brief smile. "That is good news."

"But you're not wrong," her mother added with a wink. "This Squirt brings fresh blood. Fresh genes. And supreme ones for all I can tell. Where did your Fire Mate acquire it?"

Mirri frowned. "I will ask. It is concerning that there are drakonte's being bred without our knowledge. The practice must be stopped. They are our main livelihood and the lifeblood of Fyre."

"So it is," her mother nodded.

The little sunset drakonte swallowed the last of its scraps and slithered and slapped away, snapping at a fly. Its body left deep tracks in the mud behind it, a winding path all the way to the stalls. Mirri watched it go, wishing as she often did that a sun existed in Qaf. She had only ever seen pictures of the sun in books from her ancestors before yesterday. Lovely. Yellow. Round and warm. And then, without warning, Izkander had thrust her beneath it, and she hadn't even had the chance to enjoy it. Maybe he could take her again when a monster wasn't attacking? He could apparate, couldn't he? Or would that make him feel used?

She flipped her hair back over her shoulder. She should not be dreaming up plans with someone who did not plan to stay. Especially a djinn. Her father would be furious if he knew she was risking the kingdom by allowing Izkander to apparate in and out. The fact that the Fa Chomhair had not yet slapped magical binders on his wrist to keep him here was the only testament that the title of Righ had indeed transferred, despite her father's consternation.

"Mirri?" Her mother looked up at her. "Why did you really come here?"

Mirri looked askance. "To run away from Fa Chomhair Righ and Gaol Aig an Righ fighting with each other."

Her mother raised an eyebrow. "And?"

"And because Fa Chomahir was content to physically chastise me in front of the guards and my Fire Mate."

With a little *harrumph*, her mother pulled herself to her knees. At three hundred and eighty-nine years old, her mother was beginning to feel her bones. She touched a hand to the wound on Mirri's lip. "I am discontent with that, as I am sure you are, too. I'm sorry."

Mirri bit her lip and looked away. "He never hit Maron. Never once."

Her mother exhaled so far her shoulders slumped. "You aren't supposed to speak of the Lost Ones."

"You, too?" Mirri asked, frustration filling her up. "I thought of all people, you'd be willing to talk to me about him. Aren't you the one who's always telling me to question what I've been taught by the ancestors?"

Her mother's gold eyes softened. "Yes. But there are other things that are just too painful to speak of, lawful or not."

"I want to know what he did." Mirri pressed her eyebrows together. "What did he do, mother, to be melted by the Flame?"

"Mirri..."

"How can I make sure I don't do it if I don't know what it was?" She threw her hands to the side, then cast a nervous glance around to make sure no one watched.

A stable hand moved bags of apples on the other side of the oval, but otherwise clear.

She dropped her arms just in case. "Why is everyone so Flame-bent on trying to get me killed?"

"No one is trying to get you killed," her mother chided.

"You won't tell me how Maron died. Izkander breaks every rule there is. Fa Chomhair slapped me. And Urramach—" She scowled. "It sure feels like everyone would rather I be dead."

"Urramach?" Her mother's lips twisted into a smile. "Do tell."

"He is not my Fire Mate."

"And?"

"Uch!" Mirri curled her toes over and over into the dirt. "And so I'm not with him. I'm with Izkander."

Her mother's eyes slid down to the fiery cuffs on her wrist. "Are you?"

Mirri pushed her lips flat, fighting the strange and utterly indecorous urge to punch something. "I don't really have a lot of say in the matter."

"I don't believe that at all."

"Izkander doesn't want to stay, mother," she exhaled. "He wants to leave."

Her mother patted her cheek as a little group of drakonte slithered between them, chasing one another with hisses and chirps. "So have your Eve of Fire and let him go. Once your Union is Eternalized, he does not need to stay for you to live."

Mirri frowned, a great weight pressing her into the earth.

The ability for the Subsidiary Righ to permanently be apart from the Righ after the Eternal Union had been sealed was something little-known amongst her people. Why would it be? As despised as Marduk's descendants were by the rest of Qaf, they had nowhere else to go. But Izkander had many places to go. His home wasn't even in Fyre. And not telling him he could be free as soon as they had their Eve made her stomach burn and her skin itch. But she also couldn't make herself do it. To let him know he could leave the shelter of the mountains and live his life away from her while she remained alone and barren the rest of her life.

"So you want me to be alone for the next six hundred or so years?" She sighed. "You know as well as I that once I have a Fire Mate, I can never get another."

"What does being alone even mean?" her mother tutted. I have been with your athair for centuries, and I am often alone. And what about you? For all your belly-aching, it sounds like you would still have Urramach."

Mirri's cheek twitched. "But I can't sleep with a man knowing he will just up and leave the next day. I want a Fire Mate who will stand by my side and help me lead the country. How can I be intimate—" Her face flushed hot, and she pressed a hand to her stomach to make sure she wasn't catching aflame. "How can I do such things with someone who doesn't even want to be with me?"

"We don't always get what we want." Her mother shook her head with a look of infuriating sympathy. "I know I didn't."

"But you got me," Mirri looked down at her dirty toes. "I wouldn't even be able to have children. How would the kingdom continue? Who would rule as the embodiment of the Origin's Eternal Flame? I would fail as righ, just as Fa Chomhair predicts."

Her mother sighed.

They stared at each other as a gentle breeze tussled her loose strands and rifled through her mother's braid. The heavy sound of double wings beat overhead, and within the expanse of a single breath, billowed to a landing next to her. Dust and pebbles bumbled past her. She kept her eyes shut to keep the whirlwind of sand out, and when all was quiet, opened them to two lakes of gentle green.

Izkander slid down Squirt's tail, and his boots landed in the mud with a splash. His eyes scanned the baby drakonte, and a small, almost shy smile grew on his lips. His eyes sparkled with tiny flecks of gold like the transient Ardish sun.

"Aww," he cooed as one of the smallest hatchlings slithered closer. He got down on one knee in the mud and made little clicking sounds until the little drakonte was close enough for him to pet.

Some of Mirri's frustration slipped away watching him. He had such a soft way about his face, sometimes it caught her off-guard. And the little sharp-toothed rugrats seemed to like him well enough. The way he fawned over them was borderline adorable.

She should *not* get attached.

Mirri hardened her jaw and lifted her chin, dropping to the unfamiliar twists of the Arabic language. "Had your fill of speaking with Fa Chomhair Righ?"

He sucked in his bottom lip and looked up at her with big eyes, a guilty quirk to his eyebrows. "Yeah, we're all done."

A ruby hatchling pushed against his leg hard, and he fell down on his backside in the mud. The drakonte wiggled onto its back, and he petted its belly with both hands.

Mirri focused her gaze on sacks of apples across the oval so she wouldn't get distracted by the genuine look of utter joy that filled his smile. "And are you finally content?"

He sighed and gave the hatchling a few more seconds of rubbing before rising to his feet. He patted the mud off his backside as he walked towards her.

"Look... uh..." He clapped his hands together and looked up at the sky. "I know you want me to just keep my mouth shut. And he's your father, and it's not really my place to be getting all up in your business." He shrugged, his arms hanging limply before he tightened his shoulders back up. "I just got caught up in the moment with you. And I couldn't handle him being so disrespectful. It just... if you were really my girl I would never let anybody talk to you like that."

Mirri glanced at him and wished she hadn't. His large eyes and contrite little pout poked at her heart while his words poked at her brain.

"I'm confused," her mother said, brushing herself off and speaking Arabic with an accent almost too heavy to understand. She looked at Izkander. "What do you mean if she were *really* your girl?"

His eyebrows shot up as if he hadn't noticed she was there. He watched her for a second then looked to Mirri for some guidance. She folded her arms and pushed up her chin.

He cleared his throat. "I just mean, there's the whole Fire Mate thing, which obviously has its own protocols. But if she were my *girl*, I mean, if I were in love with her, it would be different. That's all."

Her mother smiled. "Of course. Your Eternal Fire Mate certainly deserves less than someone you love."

Mirri's cheeks filled with the heat of embarrassment. How many times did she have to be shamed by her family today? "Gaol Aig an Righ, Subsidiary was wondering where you got Squirt?"

He opened his eyes wide at her, his lips squished together hard like he was trying to hold something in. His mouth twitched back and forth a few times, then he looked at her mother. "I didn't mean to imply that one was necessarily less than the other. But I also haven't heard anybody say anything about love, other than it's basically not something a righ can afford to concern themselves with."

"Gaol Aig an Righ," Mirri snipped, unable to stand them talking about her like she wasn't there. "Where is Squirt from? He is not in our registries, nor is his profile something we've seen in our histories. And breeding outside of Fyre is unlawful."

He sighed out a laugh and shook his head. "Go tell that to all the drakonte in Shihala. There's a wild population in Orkeshi now."

Her heart nearly stopped. "What?"

"That's where Squirt's from. My old man found the egg while he was climbing in Orkeshi. He monitored it for a few days and decided the mother had either abandoned it or been killed, so he brought it home, and we hatched him there."

"Magnificent," her mother breathed, as unconcerned for the welfare of the country as ever.

"Not magnificent," Mirri snapped. "Traitorous. And from our only allies." An itch formed on the bottom of Mirri's foot, and she rubbed it atop the other. "The blood of Marduk spilled across the mountains of Orkeshi without guidance, without containment. And to make things worse, the foundation of Fyre's sustenance rests on our drakonte trade. Without it, we simply would not have enough to survive. We must head to Shihala immediately to address the outrage."

"I don't get it. What's the problem?" Izkander asked with a shrug. "Drakonte aren't just animals, they're very intelligent with free will. You can't stop nature from happening."

"Are you educating me on drakonte when they spring from the same Flame as I? Do you think I don't know how intelligent drakonte are with Havu as my confidant? You condescend to me, and you ignore the livelihood and hungry stomachs of what should be half your people."

"No offense." He shrugged. "I've lived around drakonte my entire life, so I know a thing or two about the insatiable little buggers myself."

"What a blessing it is to have you with us, then. I don't know what we would have done without your expansive wisdom." She curtsied. "Now, go away. I have a diplomatic mission to plan and would prefer to do it without your commentary."

His chin flattened, and he took a few steps closer to her. "Are you mad at me because I'm not treating Fyre like it is my kingdom or because I am?"

"If you think that the blessed descendants of Marduk breeding freely in a land of ice is not a problem and is something that should just *be* because it's *natural*, then there is no way you are treating Fyre like it is your kingdom." She took a step forward toward him as well. "You don't even know anything about us. You laugh at our traditions and make a mockery of our contentment. You don't want this to be your kingdom, and you don't respect what it is. You just want to change it all to be what you know and are comfortable with."

"There is more than one way to skin a namur, pretty girl." He smiled again, making her blood boil. "Just because I don't do things exactly the way you would. That doesn't mean I don't care, and it doesn't mean I'm doing it wrong. *And* if you're planning a diplomatic mission to talk to the king of Shihala, it would be pretty silly not to take advantage of the fact that he's my uncle. But of course, you already knew that because you know everything."

"You don't even want to be here, Izkander." She dropped her voice and shook her head. "This isn't a game for you to get *caught up* in. Fyre is real. I am real. Whether you want to stay or not."

"I know you're real." His lips twitched, and he cocked his head to the side. "Can I speak to you in private, please?"

She flicked her gaze between him and her smirking mother, an itch spidering its way across her back. She didn't want to be alone with him. She always did stupid, inappropriate things when only he was there to see. But her mother's amusement was more than she could bear.

"Mother," she snipped, switching to Gaelic so Izkander couldn't insert his un-solicited opinion yet again. "Send a message to the Peace Council, I want them to assemble our Shihalan emissaries and a few top councilmen and fly toward Shihala. Have them take a swoop of *fad-turas astar nathair* so they reach our disrespectful allies by morning. I want them there as swiftly as possible." Mirri then took a deep breath and turned towards Izkander, straightening her back as far as it would go.

"As you wish, Gaol Aig an Righ."

CHAPTER FIFTEEN

IZKANDER

IZKANDER FOLLOWED MIRRI OUT of the massive corral and through some dusty but very clean stables to an isolated patch of grass at the back. Being around Mirri, he felt like he was starting to understand a bit more of the thousands of pieces of advice his old man had given him about women over the years.

You can never win with a woman, son. Just give up on the idea right now. Because even if you win, you lose. Then the old bastard would laugh and say, *You are completely screwed.*

Then, of course, there was his umi in his other ear, calling his baba a patronizing chauvinist. Izkander had no clue what to believe and what to ignore.

Best not to think of them right now, really. Or any of the things they had to say. He needed to focus on the argument he was actually having instead of replicating a fictional one in his head.

Sighing, he rubbed his hands over his face, then gazed out across the shifting field at the impossibly tall Zabriyan mountains. Their peeks were shrouded in clouds and starlight, beyond even the reckoning of the human eye and swirling with frozen clouds. But here on the ground in Fyre, it was warm. Like spring in Ankara—brisk but bursting with new life. Little white and red flowers dotted the landscape, nipping at each other like baby drakonte on the breeze. A few white wisps of magic danced with black and gold butterflies.

It really was beautiful here.

He glanced at Mirri—at the cold scowl on her face—without turning his head. How much she reminded him of the land itself—warm and bursting with life yet surrounded by icy natural ramparts. He had experienced that warmth too rarely. And it seemed no matter how hard he worked to scale her walls, every time they parted company, he was knocked back and had to start again from ground zero.

"Mirri, I'm confused." He turned his gaze back to the butterflies. "I'm getting very mixed signals from you, and I don't know what to make of them."

"If you have questions, ask them," she said briskly. "I have no desire to withhold information from you."

"Okay." He picked at a little scab on his wrist, focusing on it so much more intently than necessary. "Are you mad at me about your father?"

"No. I am mad that you don't listen to a thing I say. And I know I'm not your Ah-nis Na Righ and never have been, but I *am* queen here. You shame me in front of my people and my father."

"Shame you?" Was that how she saw what he had done? Or was it just that she was generally embarrassed to be saddled with someone like him? Someone who didn't even belong living in her kingdom, let alone ruling it.

"I respect you, Mirri. I do. And I don't not listen to a thing you say. But I didn't realize you expected me to behave like one of your subjects."

"I do if you have no intentions to stay. Which is what I understood from our recent exchange. Has that changed?" She tilted her head and the moons overhead caught in her eyes.

"We agreed we were going to try to break the bond. You said you didn't want to be bonded to anybody. But..." Izkander swallowed a hot lump in his throat. He had been trying to avoid thinking about what he was about to say. As often happened, it all crashed down on him at once and he couldn't hold it back. "What if we don't find a way?"

She chewed the inside of her cheek, glanced his way, then stopped. A light brush of pink warmed the peach of her cheeks. "Are you saying that if we cannot undo the bonding, you would be content staying and ruling over Fyre... with me?"

Izkander watched her bright red eyes, made orange by the glow of the First Moon. Warm tingles and sharp needles competed for dominance in his chest, which left his lungs achey. He looked back at his scab. It wasn't quite ready, but he ripped it off anyway, so a dot of blood bloomed on his skin.

"I don't want your flesh to melt off. And... I don't know, this place is so..." Izkander rubbed away the dot of blood on his wrist and looked up at her. "I can tell you're under a lot of pressure, and I know at least some of it is my fault. I want to help."

A slight frown brushed her lips. "If you want to help... I would welcome it." A crease appeared above the bridge of her nose. "But it is unwise to be so bullheaded about things when you know so little about Fyre."

"Wisdom is not one of my virtues." He glanced into her eyes and offered a little smile before turning away. "And all I can say is that if I were going to live here for the next several hundred years, I sure as Jahannam am not going to spend it tip-toeing around your old man."

Her face smoothed with a small lift of her eyebrows. "He is Fa Chomhair Righ. You are Gaol Aig an Righ. You do not have to listen to him."

"Clearly," he scoffed before the implications of her words sank in. "What exactly does Fa Chomhair Righ mean?"

"The Before King."

"Huh."

He licked his upper lip, the scene from the ramparts replaying in his head in vivid detail. Everything the old man had said to Mirri, and everything she had said back. And that slap, the sound of it so much more than the sight. He would never forget that sound.

"But if he's the before-king," Izkander said, "that would make you the now-king, right? Queen. You know what I mean."

"All rulers, female and male, are righ here in Fyre. But yes. I am the now-righ. King, or queen. It does not matter. Unless you have a preference for the title you take on when we visit other countries." She raised a brow at him, a little twitch on the corner of her lips.

"I gotta be honest, ugly troll king is not in my top five."

"That is too bad." She dropped her eyes to the soft earth and her bare feet. "If you want to be called Subsidiary, instead, I will announce it so."

He jutted out his chin and wiggled his jaw from side to side. "I still don't get it. If you're the righ, why do you let him speak to you like that?"

The skin around her eyes creased, and she turned her head, so a sheet of red hair fell across her face. "Are you able to best your father?"

He grunted. "I get good hits in every time. But I tell you what, I never stop trying to best my father." He punched a fist into an open palm. "Someday I am going to make him cry."

"But he loves you, right?"

He moaned in his throat, long and slightly high-pitched. He and his old man didn't tend to talk about that kind of thing, but he knew the answer. "Yeah, he does. A lot."

She tilted her head up toward the sky, a sad smile catching the dim light. "A luxury not afforded to the righ."

Her words sent his stomach twisting into cold lumps like two undead snakes wrestling through his lower intestines. A blizzard swirled inside his ribcage, bones freezing solid and beginning to crack. He took a step closer and laid his hand on her shoulder, then stroked down her armored upper arm and squeezed her elbow. She let her head fall to the opposite side, watching him with eyes like the dying embers in a fire.

"Love is not a luxury."

"Not for you." The corner of her lips lifted into a tight smile. "Most things are pretty awesome most of the time."

"That's the spirit." He punched her lightly in the shoulder. "And maybe it isn't the worst thing in the world if you occasionally let your ugly troll king do what ugly troll kings do best."

"Steal princesses?"

"Damn straight."

She breathed out a soft laugh, then shook her head. "Is your uncle really King Jahmil?"

He nodded. "And he really is my uncle by blood and everything."

He had been waiting for her to come back around to that. She was so into the whole royalty thing, being a princess... no, queen. He didn't usually go around bragging to people about his aristocratic extended family, but he wanted to let her know he wasn't just some schlub from the wrong end of the Mornish River. He wanted her to be impressed.

But that was ridiculous. He wasn't a king or a prince. He didn't have any power at all other than the favors he could buy with his smile.

"I can see why you were so upset about ending up with me, then," Mirri sighed. "What is humble Fyre to Shihala and the Immortal Killer?" Her face tightened. "I'm sorry about... everything."

Her words felt like dead seaweed slipping between his toes. "Shihala isn't mine. And the Immortal Killer is just some dude I know." Sighing, he turned his gaze back to the horizon. "I don't have anything. And nobody needs me. I'm a bum."

"You are not a bum. You are Gaol Aig an Righ. All of Fyre is yours. And... and I need you... r connections." She smiled at him and tilted her head so her hair swished forward to frame her face.

He smiled tenderly, her words fizzy in his stomach. He sucked all of his preposterous self-pity into his throat and let it out with a long exhale. As he drew in a fresh breath, his smile widened into something more demonstrative.

"Want me to take you to Shihala? I was meaning to go there, anyway."

"I would be very appreciative." She hesitated, then cleared her throat. "You actually would have to come, either way. Remember these?" She held up her wrist with the slow-churning bond shining as brightly as ever. "Every day the tie draws us closer. I am sorry, though."

He glanced down at his own bond and blew out air through his puffed cheeks. "About what?"

"That I haven't yet spent the time to find a way to free you." She bit her lip and released it almost immediately. "To free us. I promise, as soon as we return from

Shihala, that will be my main priority. I assume you want this taken care of before we would end up having to meet your parents. But I must always put the people of Fyre and their safety and well-being above my own personal comforts. I hope you understand."

"No problem." He smiled and shrugged. "We can do the one thing and then we do the other. Besides, my family will love you, I know it. My umi is just as serious and studious as you are. My dad, well, he's a big softie. My siblings love anyone with bones strong enough to climb. Squirt already loves you and Havu. And Fajar loves everyone."

Mirri's face puckered in mock seriousness. "What's a Fajar?"

"Our bird. My baba loves her more than anything."

She shook her head with another breathy laugh. "Are all families outside of Fyre as interesting as yours?"

He showed a toothy smile. "Not remotely."

"Okay." She turned to him resolutely and held her palm out. "Take me to Shihala and show me what you can do. Just..." She scrunched her nose to one side. "I don't know what to call you in official settings. You seem discontent with... all the names. Or shall I call you Izkander Green Eyes?"

"Why not? It's growing on me." His grin softened into closed lips.

Gazing directly into her eyes and the muted tones of sadness that lived within, he was struck with an undeniable urge. He moved in and wrapped her in an embrace. Brushing his fingers down her hair and over her back, he took one deep breath and one tight squeeze before he pulled away.

She dropped her eyes quickly to her wringing hands, neck, and cheeks as red as the flowers that dotted the field. "You smell differently than I had expected... last night and now." Her blush deepened to maroon, and her fingers twisted even more. "Warmer."

She was so beautiful, like a rose growing through a crack between rocks.

"Thank you." He chuckled and reached for her hand.

A shy smile dusted her lips as she slipped her fingers into his. "You're welcome."

He tightened his hand around hers and closed his eyes. "I'll try to move more gently. We were in a bit of a hurry last time. A reminder since you don't apparate often, we have to pass through Ard and go to Shihala. That's how apparation works: you can only move between worlds. Two pull-throughs, but at least you'll get to see the sun again."

Mirri bit her lip and grinned. "I'm ready."

Izkander pulled on the fire deep inside and dusted its power over them both, his mind filling with visions of sunshine and tall, sheer rock faces. He spent much of his time in the human realm dangling from precipices, relying on nothing but the strength in his fingers and the amiability of oncoming blusters to keep him alive. So when they slipped through to the other side of the expansive, white namelessness and into the warmth of brilliant sunshine, their feet touched down at the very top of a towering green bluff in Southern Thrace. A sheer drop led down to a ribbon of sand and then the great blue ocean, winking in the sunlight as sky birds screamed above.

Before their feet fully sunk into the loose grass, Mirri dragged him forward, fingers tightening around his. When she reached the very edge, she let go and stretched her arms wide. "*Bòidheach*!" She laughed, then wrapped her arms around herself and shivered. "I wish Havu was here." She looked over her shoulder at him, the sunlight a halo around her equally bright face. "I'm glad you are."

The last remaining cold lumps in his gut melted into nothing, and he laughed too, hopping up onto a jut of rock beside her on the ledge. "We can bring her some time. Take Squirt and her on a double date. I know all the best flying places."

She bit her lip, eyes sparkling. "I wish I could jump. Feel the wind in my hair and see only the warmth of Ard's sun on the waves."

"Wish granted."

He snatched her hand, pulling her along the ledge, jogging quickly over the round stones and high grass. He kept his eyes trained straight down over the side of the cliff. When his eyes caught sight of three hunks of wood suspended from the side of the cliff on dusty ropes, clumsily tied into the shape of a triangle, he pulled Mirri closer and pointed down.

"That's our way out when you're ready."

Mirri faced the horizon once more, breathless and windswept. The sun traced the shape of her body with light. She kissed her hand and waved it off into the sky, then looked back at him with a mischievous little smile.

"If I fall through the triangle without you what happens?" she asked.

Her hair was begging for him to touch it. He pushed the silky strands back from her face despite the blustering wind. "You'll splatter on the rocks."

"Then you'd better catch me," she said, then turned and jumped.

"Mirri!" he yelled and dove off after her.

He kicked his feet back and straightened his arms ahead, streamlining his body. His heart pounded with numbing fear and panic. She was halfway through the triangle when he finally managed to snatch her ankle.

As they fell through the nameless whiteness, he yanked on her leg to draw her torso nearer his and wrapped her body tightly against his. Hesitant at first, her fingers quickly threaded themselves into his shirt. Her chest shook softly. and she pulled him closer. He wrapped a hand around the small of her back, his eyes trained unblinkingly on hers as he focused all of his energy on angling their descent so they wouldn't come out in Qaf headfirst. He also had to think fast. They were falling fast, which meant he couldn't bring them back in on land.

The expanse of nothingness blinked away as quickly as it had come. Six moons and endless stars flashed overhead as they kept falling, then splashed into the still water of the reflective pool outside of Karzusan Palace. With a few kicks and a torrent of bubbles, he broke through the surface at the same time Mirri did. She gasped for air, spluttering as she ran a hand over her eyes. Wet hair hung in straight lines across her face. Then her eyes met his, and her gasps shortened into a burst of laughter.

He set his feet on the reflective tiles underfoot, the water only as deep as the middle of his chest. He growled and splashed her. "You crazy monkey!"

She splashed him back, still giggling. "I'm not crazy."

"Oh, you are howling-at-the-moon crazy," he laughed.

A few Shihalan soldiers quickened to the side of the long, square pool, spears in hand and barking questions.

Izkander looked up at them and smiled. "At ease, boys. It's just me."

"Sheikh Izkander," one of them said and bowed stiffly before straightening his back and pulling his spear into his side. The other three guards followed suit and took a step back.

Mirri moved closer to his side, placing a hand on his shoulder. Her chin was up and her back straight, staring down the men.

"Shall I call you sheikh, instead?" She bit her smiling lip.

He tilted over his shoulder to look at her. "Nah. I want to be Green Eyes." He grinned and batted his lashes at her. "Have you met Jahmil before?"

"Twice. Once when I was very little—five, maybe?" She followed him out of the pool, accepting his hand to step over the high edge. "And then four years ago. Both on diplomatic trips to negotiate the terms of our drakonte contracts."

He twisted up the bottom of his shirt and squeezed out some water. "Good times?"

She shrugged. "My father was content with the arrangements, and I was treated well, considering."

He cocked a brow at her. "Considering what?"

She shivered a little, brushing water off her arms and scaled armor. But for her hair, she looked pretty well the same. His clothes were clinging to him like a second skin.

"Oh, you know..." She widened her eyes and wiggled her fingers. "That I'm half-snake. Well, a third."

"Terrifying," he said flatly, trying to hold a straight face and utterly failing. "Come on, you crazy snake woman. Let's go get you some arrangements that make you feel better than content."

"You are Gaol Aig an Righ." Her quick smile softened. "Lead me."

CHAPTER SIXTEEN

MIRRI

IT DIDN'T TAKE LONG for the heat from Mirri's skin to dry her hair and for the peach glow to return to her skin. But even with all the water evaporated, the fire in her blood had begun to cool. Just a little, but that was all it took to make her shiver. She had always hated diplomatic trips when she was younger for just that reason. Everywhere but Fyre left her with a chill.

As soon as they entered the palace with its white marble, sloped domes, and golden spires, word of the snake queen traveled quickly. Her diplomatic emissary, *Peacach* Bryden, stationed here in Shihala scurried to meet her. His light-gold eyes were wide, skin pale. She reassured him a dozen times he had not missed her request for arrival and that King Jahmil would not hold it against her, though her skin was afire with just that worry. She sent him off with a harried-looking Shihalan representative to prepare the rooms for the rest of her convoy which would arrive by early that next morning.

Her stomach wrung into a tight ball. The convoy... the councilman...

Urramach. He would be assigned to the diplomatic mission as the highest-ranking sentinel to the righ. She hadn't thought this through, having both of him and Izkander around in a foreign palace while her thoughts and heartstrings were all a mess. Should she warn Izkander? She wasn't sure she could find enough spit to coat the words. But he wouldn't mind, would he? He had made it clear time and again that he did not care about her or what she did, right? Not like that.

Izkander's words about wanting to be a boon to Fyre—to her—had set a strange smolder in her bones. The result of the licking flames of hope and the dampening splash of... well, rejection. He would stay if needed because he wanted to help her people—who desperately needed it—but not for her. Which she could—and would—not hold against him.

Then another thought snaked through her mind, and the heat of her bones went out completely, leaving only the cold of her skin. What about when he found out he didn't have to stay after their Eve of Fire because there was no Flame in his blood? How quickly would he disappear after fulfilling his need to be helpful? She could just *not* have their Eve of Fire if it weren't for the bond that glowed on their wrists, the bond of Eternal Union meant to bring them together.

Today, she had been able to travel a magh-space away from him—or as far as a bon horn's blare carries over the hills—without her blood burning. But every degree clipped the tether shorter and shorter until they would be bound at the wrist. It was the Flame's cunning way of forcing compliance, whether because of a growing familiarity that led to desire, or desperation to separate that formed from the very same thing: a need to couple and release.

Not that this was the time to be thinking about that.

She followed Izkander and his uninterrupted stream of silly jokes and stories through the elegant archways of Karzusan palace. Vague memories of some statue or view of the city poked at her memory. As much as Izkander reassured her, King Jahmil would not be thrilled to see her, an uninvited queen from another land there to accuse him of breaking good faith in their contracts. And maybe that was her people's fault. They had refused to use the seal of Elm because of what the King of Eastern Elm had done to the beautiful Najima, one of the first children of Marduk descended from the race of pure djinn before the Origin and serpentine blood of Marduk cleansed her of the impurity.

It was a matter of honor and pride, but one that often left them vulnerable to the untrustworthy disdain of the djinn.

In fact, every step closer to the negotiation room made her heart beat a little faster. What if this trip was just another irresponsible, indecorous flash of impulse she only ever got when she was around Izkander and his disarming smiles and bubbly laughter? He was like ale. That's what he was. Something that made her mind fuzzy and her heart far lighter than it should be. The only difference was she could hold her ale. But just a few wing flaps alone with her Gaol Aig an Righ, and she was off-her-chair tipsy with undeserved giddiness and inexplicable relief.

Mirri tried to push thoughts of Izkander away. It didn't help that his muscled shoulders moved conspicuously beneath his wet shirt and his eyes brushed over her. She could practically feel the touch of his skin on her back and arm and his body pressed against hers as she fell laughing through the sky or hugged him under the stars of Qaf. Fire spread across her skin that chased away some of the chill.

They neared a large set of domed doors inlaid with rubies the color of her own eyes. Such opulence left her toes curling. She tugged Izkander's shirt.

"Yes, pretty girl?" He turned to her with a sweet, lopsided grin. Pale-blue mist stretched across his green eyes.

Glug, glug. She looked at her bare feet and her heart beat even faster, trying not to drown in the sweet ale.

"Are you sure about this?" she managed to ask. "I'm not even dressed appropriately. And King Jahmil has only ever dealt with my father. Our arrival was sudden, and..." She wrinkled her nose as it warmed with what she knew would be a bright-red heat. "And I don't have any shoes on."

He pouted and grabbed her hand, setting his other on top. "Think of it this way. This is not a diplomatic mission. He's my family, and I'm bringing you to meet him. And, yeah, we have a couple of things to talk about. But there is a secret to dealing with Jahmil, and I know it."

"A secret?" she asked, a healthy amount of skepticism in her voice.

"Mhm." He beamed at her. "Trust me. Jahmil is not nearly as..." He stuck out his tongue and looked at the ceiling. "...the way he seems as he seems to be."

She let out a small smile before tucking it away. "I hope you're right because all I remember is him being like glass. Clear eyes and sharp edges."

"He is glass. What he doesn't want anyone to know is that he is a jar of honey. Actually, you remind me of him a little. Hard as nails on the outside with a soft, sweet center."

She pursed her lips and looked up through the fuzzy edges of her brows. "Just nails. And glass. No honey."

"Mhm."

"Nu-uh." She crossed her arms and shook her head.

Before he could argue—something he seemed perpetually eager to do—she pushed him through the doors and into the negotiation room. Pulling back her shoulders, she stepped up to his side and pulled the fire in her blood into her chest to strengthen her pulse and give her the bravery of Marduk.

King Jahmil stood at the front, speaking with one of his officials, his deep-blue face as stern as she remembered it. He was a tall and imposing man, with a trim beard and eyes of the promised glass. The frown on his face seemed as natural to him as the white fire that often dusted his knuckles.

Her bare feet faltered, but Izkander grabbed her hand and pulled her toward the decidedly tense king.

"Eami!" Izkander walked right past the official to throw his arms around the king.

"*Abn akhti*?" King Jahmil said and returned the embrace, showing the first flash of a smile she had ever seen on his face. "What are you doing here, *habibi*?"

"It's a long story," he laughed. "Actually it isn't that long, but it is confusing." He reached back for Mirri's hand.

Fighting the urge to close one eye and wince, she placed her hand in his and stepped forward, bowing her head in deference. "King Jahmil."

"I believe you know the Ah-nis Na Righ of Fyre..." Izkander bit his lip and looked back at her. "Did I say that right?"

Jahmil's brow furrowed, his gaze shifting quickly between her and Izkander. "Yes, I believe we have met. I see there has been a change of leadership in Fyre."

"Every three hundred and fifty years as dictated by the Flame, Your Majesty." She forced her eyes to stay on the glass, much like she had learned to do when speaking with her father, only his eyes had been infernos. "I thank you for the honor of allowing me to visit your beautiful kingdom without notice and apologize for any inconvenience my arrival may yet cause."

Jahmil nodded. He was perhaps the only djinn in Qaf who had at least a functional understanding of Fyre and its traditions. So it was no surprise his eyes flashed with shivers of white when they landed on her and Izkander's clasped hands and the rings of bright fire around their wrists.

The king lifted his eyes to Izkander. "What is the meaning of this?"

"Ah, that." Izkander shrugged, dipping his head from side to side. "That is a short and confusing story."

King Jahmil clasped the bridge of his nose with two fingers. "Am I to understand that *you* are somehow the new Subsidiary Righ of Fyre?"

"Oh, no," Mirri interrupted, a strange desire to smile cutting through the tension in her bones. "He doesn't want to be called that. He is just Izkander Green Eyes. But the Flame has decreed he become my Fire Mate."

King Jahmil folded his hands together at his waist and sighed, leaning back as his eyes poured over the two of them. For a little while, his face was blank—nails and glass. No honey.

"*Tahanina*," he said at last. "Congratulations."

"Hey, thanks." Izkander took a step to one side, shoving his back in the face of one of the advisors. "So, I was hoping that given the circumstances... I mean, since Fyre and Shihala are now closer allies than they have ever been... we might be able to talk with you about some of the issues between the two kingdoms. Would that be okay?"

Izkander's lack of decorum on such sensitive issues made Mirri's face burn hotter than it ever had before. She clamped her mouth shut over the stream of practiced stately apologies and epithets she had learned to utter since she was three, trusting in Izkander for no other reason than she had already done so this far. The feeling was foreign, but it seemed right. Just as Izkander didn't know Fyre's customs, she wasn't as familiar with Shihala's. Maybe his informalities and impromptu visits were acceptable here. Her best choice was to follow his lead until the negotiations.

King Jahmil's gaze darted between her and Izkander several times. "I suppose that would be alright."

"Sweet. I haven't had supper. What do you say we get Aleamat Ayelet in on this thing and we can all sit down together and hammer things out? I'll tell you all about my adventures in Fyre."

King Jahmil paused and eyed Mirri for a long time before responding. "Very well. But not for supper. I have business to attend to this evening. We will meet in the sharq wing dining hall come first light."

"Thanks, Eami." Izkander slapped King Jahmil across his shoulder blades.

A stomach-churning mix of mortification and hilarity had her pressing her hand against her stomach. At least he seemed to treat all the noble rulers of Qaf the same. Indecorously.

"I appreciate the sacrifice you make meeting with us." Mirri dipped her head again toward King Jahmil. "I know the impositions of ruling a kingdom can be a weight on even the strongest shoulders."

"Hey, don't worry about that. Look at this guy." Izkander clapped his hand on King Jahmil's shoulder. "He's a brute."

"Yes, thank you, Izkander." The king turned and bowed politely with hands clasped to Mirri in the manner of Fyre. "Your arrival is no imposition, Ah-nis Na Righ. I am gratified to see the traditions of Fyre are still holding steady. I am certain that her new righ will do honor by the title. I look forward to our upcoming meeting."

"Your generosity gives me hope, Your Majesty." She returned the bow. "I will strive to be as willing and strong an ally to noble Shihala as Fa Chomhair Righ was before me."

With one more bob of her head, she followed Izkander who, light-footed as ever, turned and strode out of the room. The moment she was out of sight of the king's cool demeanor, a bit of warmth returned to her skin. She turned to Izkander and slapped his shoulder.

"Ow," he said flatly. "What's that for?"

"I thought you said King Jahmil was honey? I thought you had a secret? The fire in my blood almost went out talking to him. I'm so embarrassed."

"What are you talking about? It went great."

She stared at him, mouth open and head shaking back and forth. "What?"

"He's like you. You have to get him away from all that mess. He's tense when he's in the negotiation room surrounded by advisors and scrolls and valets and all that crap. And..." He lifted a finger with authority. "Ayelet is my secret weapon."

"His queen?"

"That's right." He pounded a fist against his chest. "She's his heart."

"Another honey-filled glass jar, hm?" She pressed her lips tight.

"Nah, she's more a sort of..." He bit his tongue and looked up. "Nope. There's no metaphor for her. Or at least, I'm not smart enough to think of one. She's nice. Just try to calm down."

She raised a brow, the last two words making their home inside her brain. Her father had told her to calm down thousands of times, but always when she had been too excited or happy about something. It was how she became *glass* according to Izkander. She had thought with the way he always made her laugh, that he wanted her to be different. To maybe be herself, whatever that was. But maybe there was no hope for her to behave appropriately. Not when her honey center showed through all the time.

Don't be excited. Don't be upset. Don't be anything. She sighed. Izkander was too excited, too happy. And he was allowed to be because there was no Flame in him. No expectations.

"Okay." She looked away from his face. "You've brought us this far, which Fyre is grateful for. And you said you wanted to help in case you are stuck with me. I trust in your knowledge of Shihala and look forward to meeting the nice, non-metaphorical Queen Ayelet."

"Thank you." His smile softened but did not fade. "Now, I need to go get cleaned up. If I stay in these drenched clothes much longer, I'll prune. I don't have magic skin so steaming hot that it dries my clothes for me."

"Oh," Mirri bit her lip. "Do you... have rooms ready for you?"

"Mhm. My room is in the bahamut wing with my cousins. You'll probably want to stay in one of the diplomatic suites." He traced his thumb over his cheek. He wanted to ask. He shouldn't ask.

He had to ask.

"You could stay with me, though." Izkander lifted his painfully sparkly green eyes. "If you wanted…"

"It's fine," she sputtered. "No worries. Or expectations. We're not in Fyre. And this—" She held up her glowing wrist. "Nothing but an inconvenience, right? We can play Subsidiary and Righ around your uncle to get a meeting, but we don't have to pretend in private, right?"

"Right." The word came out like a curse.

Mirri turned away. "I also need to prepare. Fyre's convoy will be arriving early in the morning, and I need to have everything ready. Spending the night apart is for the best."

"Okay. Yeah." He cleared his throat. "No, you're right. Of course."

Her stomach tightened at the thought of seeing Urramach, but she remembered the words of her father, of Izkander, and smoothed her insides back into glass. She would not show emotion in front of a man who wanted to leave or to a nation that already thought her weak. She needed alone time to recoup and strategize and blush about indecorous meetings with two different boys, both of whom she didn't need.

She needed to think in quiet.

Mirri took a few steps away and glanced over her shoulder. "I'll see you tomorrow morning, Izkander Green Eyes. Have a good night."

He smiled, the skin around his eyes wrinkling. "Good night, Mirri Bright Eyes."

She let her gaze linger on his just a moment more before turning and catching sight of her emissary fidgeting noticeably in his thick robes. She would have to fix that. The nervous little man represented everything she and Fyre were, and she did not want him looking weak. She supposed his lack of propriety made sense, though. The Fa Chomhair had assigned the man this position as punishment for violating the rules of Fyre. Five years cooling his heart away from the Flame for selling a drakonte egg to the Magnate of Ghaluma.

Mirri followed him silently, skin cooling, cooling, and she wished for one of those jerboa shawls her soldiers had been wearing up on the balustrades of her castle. Her emissary escorted her to an ornate suite of small rooms on the sharq side of the palace where her diplomatic attire had already been laid out on the bed. She frowned. It had been nearly two full days now since she took off her bone-crunching armor, but the thought of the silky, free-moving fabric in this cold place left her feeling like...

Glass.

"We are not meeting tonight with the king," Mirri turned to him. "I require a different set of clothes for sleeping."

He fidgeted again, twitching this way. "I'm sorry, Righ. As you're aware, our convoy will not arrive until morning, and you and the Fa Chomhair have never stayed here overnight. We do not have another set of Fyran clothing. But if you'd like, I can inquire with the palace servants and find something else."

Every one of his words seemed to tighten her armor and jab it into her ribs. Mirri nearly groaned. Marduk knew she wanted to. But she could do nothing so indecorous while one of her subjects was near.

"I will require no such thing. Leave me, *Peacach* Bryden."

He half-bowed and left, walking backward out of the room before shutting it.

She set her lips and pushed herself forward. Not honey. Honey wouldn't save her in a negotiation with the likes of King Jahmil. Her father had only gained any ground with the proud king by being just as proud. She would be, too. Tomorrow. First, she desperately needed to breathe.

Mirri undid the leather buckles and drakonte-scaled clasps of her gold and silver armor and breathed a silent sob as she peeled the plates off. She rubbed each tender rib, then again, and again. But there was nothing to do for them. Laying in her armor next to Izkander for an entire night would leave her aching for some time.

Not wanting to expose her body any longer than necessary, she slipped on the only clothing she had with her in Shihala, and the one kept in Karzusan for just such stately visits. Made of the shedded and soft scales of newly-hatched drakonte, the shimmery green gown fit her body like snake skin, moving when she moved and completely non-restrictive. Gold trim lined the high neckline in front and framed the deep swoop that revealed her entire back down to her waist. Slips of gauzy fabric touched the top of her shoulder, fanning out with slits so the chilly air could reach her skin before coupling back up in gold, Marduk-emblazoned cuffs at her wrists.

She felt exposed wearing it. Vulnerable. But also free. Her ribs were certainly glad for it. There was a delicate set of slippers to hide her bare feet, so far was she from the sacred grounds of Fyre. It was a completely ridiculous outfit for sleeping in, but so was her armor. Still, it would not do.

Perhaps, she was indecorous enough to sleep in nothing.

Mirri pressed her hand to her stomach when a knock sounded on the door. She opened it wide, expecting her twitchy emissary

"Mirri." Urramach smiled.

She froze.

His eyes swooped down her then back up, a smile playing on his lips. "You look beautiful."

She stared at him like a startled *pukeesh* away from its hole. He stepped inside and shut the door behind him.

Her heart picked up. Her skin itched.

"Urramach," was all she managed to squeak out.

"I'm sorry to drop in unannounced," he said, that apologetic face she hated seeing on him once more before her. "Should I go? I just wanted to wish you luck. You're doing the right thing, standing up for Fyre against these Shihalan takers."

"No. You don't have to go..." She clenched her hands behind her exposed back, as confused as ever about the tightness she was feeling in her chest.

Her conversation with Izkander swirled in her mind. *Completely normal. Not right. Completely normal. Not right.* How was she supposed to know which one was which?

"I appreciate your well-wishes. But how did you get here so swiftly? I wasn't expecting you until morning."

"Ian." He smiled, gold eyes the warm color that heated her from the inside out.

"He's not a long-journey drakonte," she furrowed her brows. "He'd never make the whole trip on his own."

"He didn't fly the whole way on his own. I coiled him and let him ride atop one of the long-haulers for the first half of the journey. Then we used a mounted slingshot to blast Ian and I forward, helping us get the speed and altitude we needed without having to burn energy. He fire-burst here after that. He's completely burnt out and will be for a good two weeks, though. It was a theory I'd had when we played war games before the festival. I've been wanting to try it, to see if it would be of use to Fyre in the future. I want to do everything I can to support my righ."

Mirri's furrowed brows softened. "That is admirable, indeed. The Origin is wise in insisting Fyre be ruled by a righ who serves only the people and never herself. It is ideas like yours that will it keep our nation going, not me."

"You are a great Ah-nis Na Righ," Urramach chastised softly, touching her elbow. "Just look at how much you've accomplished in the two days you've assumed ruler-ship of Fyre."

"That wasn't me. That was Izkander." She shook her head with a sigh. "A foreign interloper has done more for our people than I might ever. It is humiliating."

She shook her head even harder when she realized it was true. All she had done for her country was get caught by a stranger who had swooped in and done the rest. Perhaps, she should be called Subsidiary for all the good she had done. She had wanted to make a stand. To show her people and her father she could rule on her own and do it well. But all she had proven was the opposite. Always the opposite.

"Mirri," Urramach's voice was soft. He took her hand in his, and little warm pricks raced up her arms. "You have prepared for this your whole life. It is your instincts that guide the country into right and wrong. If this..." He paused, then breathed a smile. "If this Izkander has been able to accomplish so much, it is because you trusted the will of the Flame and listened to her wisdom. That is the most honorable thing a righ can do for her people."

Mirri smiled, taking heart in his words. It was little, the honor he offered her, but it was enough. "Thank you, Urramach."

He lifted her hand. "I need to apologize."

"For what?"

"For treating you so disrespectfully. I let my heartbroken soul put you at risk by kissing you, even if I would have staked my own life on the outcome. I will never forgive myself for it." He turned those sad, shining eyes on her, and she yearned.

To step closer. To itch her fingers. To talk to Izkander.

"Will you forgive me?"

She glanced away, then back. "Urramach..."

"Please?"

"Of course, I will." She sighed and tried to smile. "Just don't do it again."

"Don't kiss you? Or don't kiss you without asking?" He stepped forward so his shoes touched her own, and she was grateful she wore slippers to hide her curling toes.

"I don't know," she whispered, feeling exposed and cold and so confused.

Completely normal. Not right. Completely normal. Not right. And Izkander's voice in her head all the while.

Izkander had not seemed upset the first time she brought up Urramach. He had said he didn't want to get in the way. Nothing had changed about the situation except for his willingness to aid the country should he be stuck with it. And she had not yet told him he would be free to leave when—if—they ever coupled. Surely, he'd be gone without a second thought when he found out.

Urramach, though... He would always be in Fyre. He was as much a part of it as she was. How would she know how she felt about Urramach unless she tried? She had yet to melt from his advances. And he smelled like Fyre; heathered moors and the hint of snow. Being close to him and the feel of her home felt like a barrier against the cold.

She cleared her throat nervously. "I suppose you could ask and try your luck."

His bright smile widened. He leaned in, eyes locked softly on hers. "May I kiss you?"

Her heart hammered in her tightening chest, and sweat misted the back of her neck.

A banging sounded in her thrumming ears, and for a moment she thought it was her heart. She snapped her head to the side and rushed to the door. Then yanked it open.

"I heard there was another arrival from Fyre, Ah-nis Na Righ," Bryden said, a twitch in his eye now accompanying the rest of his fidgeting. "Shall I attend to bedding them for the evening?"

"Yes." She nodded vigorously and turned to a crestfallen Urramach. "I'm sorry. You must be exhausted from your trip. Bryden will show you to your chambers and get you anything you need for the evening."

"Mirri—" He reached for her, but she was already hurrying him out the doors and into the hallway.

Before he could say more, she slapped the door shut. Mirri pressed her bare back against the smooth wood, back curving in a slouch her armor would never have allowed.

Marduk sàbhail i. What was wrong with her?

Her fingers grasped the supple dragon scales of her dress, and she wrenched it off, tossing it away from her on the floor. Then she sank down in a naked puddle, pressing her burning hot body against the cool marble floor.

She needed to be a better righ.

To serve her people as much as they served her.

To stop being so confused.

To either commit to Izkander or not.

To either be with Urramach or not.

She needed to breathe and stop hurting. To talk to somebody—anybody—about Maron without them shutting her down and leaving her with unanswered questions.

And most of all...

She needed to talk to Izkander.

CHAPTER SEVENTEEN

Izkander

His bedroom at the palace of Shihala was in the far-gharb wing, just a few doors down from his cousins Lalam and Tabor. He had spent practically every summer there since he was nine so he did have quite a few personal effects in this room that might be worth bringing back with him to Fyre—pajamas, for example.

Izkander was starving, so his stomach was the first matter to attend to. He called on his valet at the palace and ordered one of everything from the kitchen before sitting down to gorge. Mirri had given him dinner last night when he'd asked, but no breakfast had been offered. No lunch.

Did they even eat in Fyre? Or was that something to do with them being part snake, too? Either way, mealtimes there weren't often enough for his voracious appetite.

Izkander wasn't sure how to feel about bringing Mirri to Shihala only to spend the night without her, but it was the right way. They weren't married, after all, and Jahmil did not stand for such things in his palace. Which was why Izkander had started spending less time in Karzusan and more in Ahmar and Al Madinat, where they had much more liberal attitudes towards unsanctioned couplings.

Then again, Izkander had had plenty of unsanctioned couplings in this very room with lots of different women, all under his conservative uncle's nose without once giving a damn what he thought.

But it was different with Mirri.

He'd been vaguely hoping to convince Mirri to slip into her gown that night and cuddle up on the divan again. Having her in his arms had felt strangely natural and the prospect of sleeping without her made him feel like a child that had lost his blanket.

Izkander had just slipped on his soft, Ardish-cotton nightwear and sat on his down mattress, when a soft, rhythmic knock came at his door. His body tightened. He knew that knock, that rhythm.

He crawled over the massive silk-dressed blankets because it was quicker than going around, then yanked open the hunk of hand-carved wood. A pretty purple woman stood before him, her lips like ripe strawberries, freshly sliced and juicy. Her thick brown curls fell over her shoulders in shimmering waves, accented by a long transparent veil.

"Shayla. Hi."

"Sheikh Izkander." She dipped into a curtsy, her eyes fixed on his.

The title struck his ears as oddly as ever. He was welcomed as a prince in Shihala and afforded all the deference that that implied, but he'd never once felt like he deserved it. He was just Izkander ibn Bakr, nothing fancy. Why was everybody always trying to make him fancy?

"What are you doing here?" His eyes swept over her. Her long purple dress was nearly the same shade as her skin, creating the subtle illusion that she was naked from the chest up. Memories and imagination did the rest.

"I go where I please." She batted her long black eyelashes and swept into the room, brushing by him so he smelled her sweet perfume and felt the brush of her silky hair.

For almost a year now he'd been thinking about her, obsessing over her, calling other women by her name. And for her part, the most eligible and beautiful Sheikha in Ahmar loved to give him just enough to get him on the hook so she could watch him squirm while she went out with other guys.

In the last two days, she hadn't crossed his mind once.

"I think this is all very unfair of you." She turned on him and cocked a sculpted eyebrow.

His voice instinctively grew deeper and raspier. "What did I do this time?"

"You arrive in Karzusan and cannot even be bothered to send a missive. I have to hear about it from the servants like a common—"

"Sheikha?"

"Excuse me?"

Izkander bit the tip of his tongue and smiled. "Isn't eavesdropping on the same servants who were just eavesdropping on you like the number one pastime in any palace?"

Maybe not in Fyre...

Shayla pursed her bright red lips, then snatched a pillow off of the bed and threw it at him. He laughed and rolled his shoulder so it plopped uselessly on the floor.

"Still as entertained by yourself as ever, I see." She narrowed her eyes.

"Don't you worry about me."

She swept closer to him and set her hands on his shoulders. "I've had enough of this Izkander. You've made your point."

He smirked. "What point?"

"Your very public declaration that you no longer have any intentions on me." She pouted.

He didn't think what he'd done had been over the top, and it certainly hadn't been planned. Yet another stupid cotillion thrown by the Queen of Glitter. He'd brought Shayla on his arm, thinking everything between them was finally settled. Then after two dances, she was off flirting with a Ghaluman emissary.

So he marched over there and shouted, "You want her? You can have her." Then disappeared in a puff of smoke—off to Ya'el's house as it so happened, to cause even more trouble.

"The queen herself called me to her chambers to talk about it," Shayla continued. "And she told me all about how she used to sleep with your father and that I'm better off."

Izkander tightened his teeth. He didn't like hearing about his father being with any woman other than his mother. It kind of made him want to stab his old man right in the testicles.

"Well, if I have Qadira's sanction..."

"Hardly." Shayla laughed brightly, her whole body quivering with the bell-like sound. "Come now. Let's not play these games."

Izkander grabbed her hands and pulled them off of his shoulders. "Shayla, this isn't a game. What we were doing before—that was a game. But this..." Izkander sighed and looked away from her bright silver eyes. "I don't want to do this with you anymore. People are getting hurt. Lives are getting ruined. And I..."

He trailed off. Usually, when Shayla was near him, he felt like his head was filling with hot air—about to float off into the sky. She left his body aching for her whenever he caught a whiff of her scent. And that was all there still, but there was something else. Something new.

"I think I might be ready for something more..." His throat parched. He didn't want to say the word, but that didn't make it any less true. And like truth sometimes does, it burned on his tongue until he finally spat it out. "...serious."

"What?"

"I think I want something more serious. Like a girlfriend who doesn't cheat on me every chance she gets just to see if she can get a rise out of me."

Shayla stared at him for a few beats of his hot heart, then she lifted a hand and ran her nails lightly through his hair, bringing a shiver. She knew his body too well. It was always what drew him back in.

He wanted to kiss her. He wanted to do everything to her he had ever done. But he was surprised to find that he didn't want it nearly as much as he used to. Shayla used to sparkle like a diamond, but her luster had dulled.

Who needs diamonds when you have lava?

Nervous laughter filtered through his nose. He lifted a stiff finger between them. "I have breakfast with Jahmil and the Queen of Fyre tomorrow morning. I cannot afford to be sleep-deprived and slathered in your lipstick."

She grabbed his hand and lifted it to her lips. He knew she was about to suck his finger into her lush little mouth when she paused and furrowed her brow. "What's this?"

"What's what?"

"Is that a bracelet?" She pulled back his sleeve to reveal the ring of fire around his wrist—the bond that held him to Mirri. When she touched it, the flames ripped through his whole body, burning up everything that was flammable and leaving nothing but cold in its wake.

This woman is not your Fire Mate, it seemed to say. *Go to your Fire Mate.*

Izkander stepped back and tugged his cuff over his wrist. "You and I aren't together anymore, so it's really none of your business."

"Did a woman give that to you?"

He smiled at her transparent jealousy. "It's more like a Covenant. It was given to me by the spirit of a land far away from here."

Even as he said the words, Izkander paused over them. He hadn't spent much time wondering about the nature of the Origin, but comparing the Union burning on his wrists to the Covenant of Shihala—which united two destined souls together in an eternal embrace—he couldn't help but wonder if the Origin of Fyre wasn't such a foreign concept after all. Maybe the Eternal Flame was just Fyre's way of referring to the spirit that animated their land and nurtured the people.

And that meant the laws of Fyre did come from a divine place. Or some of them did, in any case.

Shihala never would have bestowed the Covenant on two people who were undeserving. Did that mean the Eternal Flame knew what it was doing when it encircled his wrist in fire?

Shayla's tiny upturned nose twitched with a wrinkle. "Two days. That's how long it took to replace me?"

He cleared his throat and coughed out a chuckle. "That's longer than the two degrees it always takes you."

"Okay, Izkander." She turned on her heel and clipped to a desk in the corner. She rearranged the objects sitting on top and hopped up to a seat on the edge. "You know it's not nice to give ultimatums."

He watched as she crossed her long legs, revealing a long slit in her dress. Usually, his hand would already be on that thigh. He blinked and lifted his eyes to meet hers. "What ultimatum?"

"That I have to be serious with you or you won't have anything to do with me anymore."

"That is not what I—"

"I shouldn't even entertain this. My cousin has made it very clear that if our association goes any further than purely casual she'll banish me from Ahmar."

"Yeah, yeah." She'd said that before, always using her distant cousin as an excuse for virtually everything she did. It was a good excuse as Queen Qadira was known for being a tad capricious, maybe even a little unreasonable at times. But it was still an excuse.

Shayla swept her hair over one shoulder and petted it absently. "Ask me again."

"Ask you what?"

"To be your wife." She lifted her eyebrows, the corners of her lips tight with a smile. "I can't answer until you ask."

Izkander opened his mouth and closed it. "You want to be my wife?"

"Not the most eloquent proposal I've ever received, but I knew what I was getting into." She flashed a brilliant smile. Like many Ahmaran noblewomen, there were specks of crushed diamonds embedded in her teeth to make them sparkle. "The answer is yes."

Izkander was rendered still. The fountain outside his window slushed and blubbed.

What the hell just happened?

"I... don't..." His voice faltered. He looked up at her eyes, then back down at his bare feet on the fluffy Persian carpet. "I don't trust you."

"Nor I, you." She shrugged and hopped down from the desk, sashaying closer. "Make love to me, Izkander. I've missed you."

Izkander twitched. He wanted to make love so badly it hurt. Being around Mirri these last few days, watching her move and listening to her laughter, his clothes felt like they were getting tighter and tighter with every pass of the Fourth Moon.

He rubbed his wrist and looked down at the floor. Mirri didn't want him, wasn't ready to get tied down. They were just *pretending*...

All the same, he had far too much respect for Mirri to go around acting like a whore while he was still her Fire Mate, whether it was temporary or not.

Shayla stepped up to his chest, leaned in on his tiptoes, and kissed him.

A surge of floral perfume flowed over him. She pressed her palms against his chest, and a very familiar twist touched his stomach muscles then quickly radiated down.

This was the part where he normally threw her down on the bed and ruined her carefully styled hair. But he didn't move.

Shayla had lost her shine.

Izkander took a step back. "I can't."

She looked up at him, red mist like twin galaxies in her eyes and a challenging sneer twisted her lips. "What?"

"I'm sorry. I..." He wanted to tell her that he'd found someone else, but he couldn't say it. Not out loud. Not yet. "I have to sleep. I need to be on my top game tomorrow for Jahmil."

She tongued a tooth, scrutinizing his eyes. "You're keeping something from me."

He shrugged. "Yeah."

"Is it to do with this?" Shayla ran a finger over the back of his hand and over the flame on his wrist.

He pulled it back. He didn't like when she touched it. It made him feel like a creep.

She huffed and put a hand on her hip. "Since when is Izkander ibn Bakr capable of keeping anything to himself?"

"I don't appreciate your tone, young lady."

"What are you going to do about it?"

She stepped nearer and lifted her face to his—so close he could have licked her. One of her hands slipped down his chest and grabbed his belt buckle. She slipped her thumb inside the top of his pants, her fingers pointed down, and tugged, pulling his groin against hers.

"I know how much you hate to sleep alone."

He shivered and looked down at her hand, his body standing at attention. But his body wasn't in charge.

"I want to sleep alone tonight."

Shayla laughed and kissed him again. Slower than before, sliding the tip of her strawberry tongue into his mouth. She was in a mood—the same mood he had repeatedly prayed and given thanks for over the last several months.

Nobody did him like she did. Being with her was like muscle memory, and his muscles trembled with a desire to reminisce.

But his muscles weren't in charge. And neither was she.

He broke off the kiss and took a measured step back with a slight shake of the head.

"As you wish." She pulled back after a moment, then wiggled her eyebrows once before brushing out of the room.

This was the part where he twitched in bed until he couldn't take it anymore and then hunted her down, threw her over his shoulder, and carried her back to his room.

Not tonight.

He shot a little burst of orange fire into the door's handle. A premade enchantment gently closed the door and turned the lock. Izkander stepped up to the wash basin and poured cool water into the glass bowl.

Picking up a goathair mitt, he scrubbed furiously to clean Shayla's dark red lipstick away. He didn't want Mirri to see it.

Izkander let the mitt drop. He caught his own reflection in the shined glass mirror and was surprised by the expression on his own face. "What do you care?

"I don't know." He lifted his shoulders and pouted. "You've seen her out there. That chase she gave when we first met, the fight with a buklak, and today, just jumping off a cliff." He chuckled and shook his head. "She's sensational. And I don't want to embarrass her."

He smacked his lips. "Is that the only reason? Or are you worried she won't like you anymore if she thought you hooked up with someone else?"

"I mean, maybe.

"She thinks you're an idiot.

"So what else is new?

"And she can't leave Fyre.

"Well, clearly she can.

"And what about Urramach? Have you forgotten about him?

"Who could ever forget Urramach? And his face...

"You did that to his face. You did.

"I know, and I'm sorry. But... Mirri doesn't seem too sure about him, anyway.

"She doesn't. That's true.

"And she was smiling at me a lot today. And touching me. And blushing so much. And sometimes I get the feeling that she's bothered by the fact that I don't leer at her.

"But you want to leer.

"I'm trying to be a gentleman.

"Why?"

He scoffed. "She's the Queen of Fyre. Not for leering.

"I think it's because of Urramach. The man whose kiss made her feel like the walls were closing in..."

Izkander sighed, slumped to the door, and locked it. "But that could just be nerves. She clearly doesn't have much experience with men." His body gave a warm shudder at the thought, which made him hate himself a bit, but it couldn't be denied. "Or it could be guilt. I could see her feeling guilty. Maybe she feels like it would be cheating on me." He chuckled at himself. "But that's ridiculous.

"Tell that to your poor lips."

He touched his lips, swollen and a little pink from the vicious scrubbing. "You're being dramatic.

"Well, clearly." He pulled the covers high over his head, regretting his current state of being alone.

He needed to get some sleep, so he'd be fresh in the morning. What he'd said about Jahmil was true—he was full of honey. But that didn't mean he couldn't be prickly or downright rude at times.

He had to be there to protect Mirri from it, to act as a buffer zone the way his father always did for his umi. The Flame of Fyre had chosen him to be her Fire Mate. He didn't want to let either of them down.

***

When Izkander came to the breakfast table the next morning everybody was already seated. Jahmil and Ayelet were together on one long, overstuffed divan with Mirri sitting on the other side of a low table carved of delicate white stone.

Mirri was wearing a slinky dress that barely would have passed muster in the Court of Ahmar, let alone Shihala. Her body curved expertly under every tight turn of iridescent fabric. Her long, silky hair brushed her hips and shoulders, moving in the gentle breeze provided by two servants stood at the edge of the room waving giant fans made of *naeama* feathers. Looking at the curve where her stomach met her hip Izkander had never wanted to stroke anything so badly.

"Izkander Green Eyes." Mirri dipped her head in a little bow. Her hair swished over the porcelain skin peeking through the cutout shoulders of her dress.

He slid onto the sofa beside her and leaned in close. "What are you thinking wearing that?"

She scrunched her nose. "This is my diplomatic attire."

"Now I'm not going to be able to focus on the conversation at all." He let his eyes run over her body, wanting her to feel his stare.

She opened her mouth, then *clocked* it shut, a pretty pink painting her cheeks. She looked away and took a slow sip of water.

Izkander looked across the table at his aunt and uncle. Jahmil looked as regal as ever, perhaps even more so in his simple, yet exquisite, white clothes and his hat made of *farw alqaqim* fur all shining in contrast to his jewel-blue skin. His human wife wore a radiant blue dress — the sun to her husband's moon. Her long black and ruby-colored hair cascaded down her shoulders, gray eyes sweeping the room playfully.

"*Tebrikler*, Izkander." Ayelet grinned, glancing at Jahmil. Though she spoke Arabic well, she often punctuated her speech in her native tongue, Turkish. Izkander didn't speak a word.

"Huh?"

"I never thought you one for settling down. But I used to think that about me, too."

"Izkander picked up his water glass, then set it back down without drinking. "So until I have a chance to explain, I'd appreciate it if you kept this arrow in the quiver when it comes to my umi and baba."

"You haven't told them?" Ayelet shook her head, a smile always on her lips. "That's going to go badly for her."

Mirri shifted in her seat. "For his umi?"

"For you." Ayelet poked a finger toward Mirri.

Mirri's face fell. She straightened her back into a hard line. "I thought your parents were delightful people?"

Izkander shifted his feet under the table. "My father is going to adore you. And my mother is a sweet and lovely woman."

Jahmil scoffed into his glass. If anybody else in the world had done that, Izkander would have kicked them under the table, but Jahmil was his mother's brother so he got a pass.

He better not do it again, though.

"Anyway..." Izkander stared daggers through his indecorous uncle. "Mirri had one or two official things to talk to you about, and I thought given that we're going to be family..."

"Yes, I understand." Jahmil leaned back and threw his arm up on the back of the sofa behind Ayelet.

Izkander turned to Mirri and gestured toward Jahmil with an open palm.

Her eyes scanned his for a moment, like they were searching for something, then turned to Jahmil. "I am unfamiliar with the diplomatic approach Izkander Green Eyes has taken in this endeavor but have accepted his reassurances that you would have a receptive ear. Is this correct? May I speak freely of the affairs of Fyre's state and the relations between our two countries?"

Jahmil gave a deferential tilt of his head. "Whatever is decided here will be declared and officiated at a later date with all proper circumstance."

"You are generous." Mirri pulled her shoulders back even straighter, chin up. "Which is why I'm confused and concerned about the way Shihala has handled the drakonte we have entrusted to your care."

The tiniest puff of orange and black smoke lifted through Jahmil's eyes before they settled back into copper. Trying to decode the colors in Jahmil's eyes was just as difficult as if they were written in gray slate. When every color flashes so quickly and so easily, it leaves nothing to hold onto. But those two colors—orange and black—shame and fear?

Why would Jahmil be feeling that?

"Izkander Green Eyes has told me you have failed to uphold the agreed-upon terms. That drakonte are bred freely here and many aren't tended to at all, left to roam the wilds of a country that is not their own. Is this true?"

"The breeding of drakonte in official hatcheries within Shihala was authorized by your predecessor in exchange for a large annual stipend to your country. During the Vespar Wars, our need for fresh drakonte increased exponentially and has never leveled back out. And in recent years the produce from Fyre had been disappointing, both in number and quality."

"If your numbers have yet to level back out, why do you allow drakonte to roam the wild in your lands?"

"The establishment of a wild breeding population in Orkeshi was an unintended consequence of war."

"It is sacrilege to one of your nation's allies." Mirri's eyes were sharp. "I've come to request all wild drakonte in your land be returned to Fyre immediately so you will not be in breach of contract and so Fyre may bolster its population and strengthen its economy in a time of hardship."

"The wild population in Orkeshi is a safeguard against the possible demographic collapse of domesticated populations." Jahmil cocked his neck and leaned back further to look even more casual. "Whether intentional or not, allowing an errant population of drakonte to breed is a violation of our agreement. That you are safeguarding against my country's failure only reassures my doubts about Shihala's intentions towards an ally of thousands of years."

"The alliance was made thousands of years ago when circumstances in both our kingdoms were very different." Jahmil lifted his brow and rested a finger on his temple, his brooding eyes and lips tightening. "Why should Shihala bolster your economy with our domestically produced specimens when you offer nothing in return?"

Mirri shot Izkander a scathing look that made him feel about half an inch tall. Why did Jahmil have to be so very Jahmil about everything all the time?

"Because your country made an oath of honor. If you will not prove yourself worthy of keeping your bond," Mirri said, meeting Jahmil's crystal stare eyes with her own brilliant red lava, "I will have no choice but to exact the stipulations of the contract."

Jahmil sat still as stone. "Is that a threat?"

"It absolutely is."

"We are not going to war over a bunch of horny snakes." Izkander brightened his smile and turned to Jahmil. "The longer a generation of drakonte are away from the Eternal Flame of Fyre, the weaker their blood becomes. Just like the royal line, it begins to cool and that natural virility that makes drakonte so magnificent in the first place begins to fade. With each subsequent generation, the fire will dim until you are left with a mountain range filled with giant snakes who can't fly, are of no use as battle mounts, and make a nuisance of themselves by eating villagers."

Izkander was talking out of his backside, of course, but it sounded like the sort of thing that might be true. He met Jahmil's acrid stare and doubled down.

"Jahmil, if you'd be willing to allow us to capture the wild drakonte from Orkeshi to bolster the bloodline, and rid yourself of one hell of a nasty vermin problem in the future, I'm sure Mirri would be willing to offer you pick of the resulting litter and then we could all continue the exclusive and mutually beneficial contract that has existed between our countries for so long."

He turned to her and lifted his eyebrows, hopeful that she would see the value in compromise, especially since they were talking to his own family.

She stared at him for a full degree, an actual flicker of flame in her narrowed irises, then slithered her gaze back to Jahmil. "The Gaol Aig an Righ has spoken freely without consultation and offered you far more generous terms than our contract allows."

Izkander's heart caught. He thought he was doing good. Had he stepped on her naked toes and screwed everything up for her? He just wanted to help, to prove that he wasn't useless. That he wasn't just some random dude who happened to own an awesome drakonte. He had connections, he was part of high society.

He was somebody Mirri could actually want to be with.

Izkander held his breath, waiting for her next words.

She forced her clenched teeth soft by running her tongue over them. Her eyes never left Jahmil. "I will honor the terms if you accept right now."

Jahmil stared at him for a long time, too. Izkander had never once been struck with such a strong desire to melt into a wall.

With a smile as natural to her as the ruby highlights in her hair, Ayelet reached an arm around her husband and laid her cheek on his arm. "I think this may be Skander's attempt to share his boot."

Izkander wrinkled his nose in confusion. Jahmil and Ayelet gazed into one another's eyes, sharing a silent conversation like they so often did. He grimaced, she lifted her brows, he shook his head, and she blinked slowly. Then with an almost inaudible sigh, Jahmil's face softened.

"Very well." Jahmil lifted his crystalline eyes, which flickered with a rainbow of emotions as clear as daylight. "I will allow for the capture of the wild drakonte population."

"Excellent!" Izkander almost yelled before he realized he'd cut Mirri off. He pulled himself back and cleared his throat. "That is excellent."

Shihala and Fyre weren't going to war, and that had to be a good thing. But when he looked at Mirri and saw nothing but cold fire in her expression, he knew he had done something very wrong. He just didn't know what.

CHAPTER EIGHTEEN

MIRRI

THE NEGOTIATIONS WITH KING Jahmil had been brutal. Even after Izkander had unnecessarily stepped in, the Shihalan king refused to give anything she didn't pry from his glass fingers.

And to what gain?

If Izkander had just let her remind the arrogant king that she could call *all* the drakonte home if he failed to fulfill the contract, it would have been a very different conversation. One blow from the Origin's lava-cast horn would compel all the drakonte in Qaf to return home. She was being diplomatic, coming to talk to the king at all when the contract was on her side and the drakonte were bound to the will of the Flame.

A safeguard against possible demographic collapse. King Jahmil's declaration that Fyre *offered nothing in return.* Shihala had all but declared their alliance dead. And she had half a mind to ignore the deal Izkander struck and rip the drakonte from this land, anyway.

As soon as they snapped the last words of the deal, she brushed quickly past Izkander and down the cold hallway, spying a slip of curtain she could hide behind like the weak righ she was. Once concealed in a blue and cream brocade, she collapsed her shoulders and sank against the wall, her bare back freezing against the marble.

Fyre could not handle an influx of that many drakonte all at once. And a war with Shihala would be devastating.

And the nonsense Izkander had spewed about the drakonte? She groaned. Clearly being away from the flame had made the wild line stronger. If King Jahmil put that together himself, he would think Fyre was as dishonest as she found Shihala to be. But what was more worrisome, was that what he said *should* have been true. To a degree, at least. They wouldn't lose their wings, but they should be turning wilder. Ferocious. Untamable. Squirt seemed to fit that description, to a point, but if there was a whole den of drakonte out in Orkeshi not ripping people to shreds, maybe that part of her people's lore had been embellished?

She wanted to run. To go back home and be warm. But she couldn't even do that without Izkander anymore.

The brown tips of boots appeared beneath the hem of the curtain. She snapped her back straight. "What do you want, Gaol Aig an Righ?" She used the official name out of habit, but the tease in it stabbed like a sword in her gut.

He cleared his throat. "Can I come in?"

"If you must."

"I don't *must*. I'd like to." The boots didn't move. "Are you mad at me again?"

She focused on the inhale and exhale of her lungs for several breaths. "The negotiations were successful so I am content."

"Okay," he groaned. "I'm coming in and you can kick me if you want to." He pulled back the curtain and stepped inside next to her. His lips held a little frown, and there were lines between his eyes. It made him almost unrecognizable. "What did I do? Was it the stuff about the drakonte? Was it the dress comment?"

"No." The fabric cocoon amplified the warm smell of spring that followed Izkander as readily as winter. "I mean a little about the drakonte. I said I was content."

"But you're not happy. You're lurking in a curtain, and you don't want to look at me."

"Would you prefer I step out?"

"No. I don't mind you hanging out in curtains. I don't mind hanging out in curtains with you, either." He lifted his gaze to hers and tried for a smile, but it looked broken. "I really wasn't going to say anything. I'm trying to get better at shutting up. I'm sorry."

"Fyre is half your charge." She pressed her lips thin. "Your word can bind as well as mine. And I know they are your real family. While I am irritated that you proceeded without me and that your tactics were not incredibly honest, you did secure a favorable outcome. You were wrong, though. You told me your uncle is honey when he clearly is not."

He shrugged guiltily. "Maybe not in any official capacity. Hey, what do I know about kings? You're a complicated bunch."

She sighed, wanting to look into his eyes as much as she wanted to punch him. "You realize that complicated bunch includes you now, right? At least temporarily."

He exhaled audibly and bobbed his head. "I think a thousand years could go by and I would never really get used to that. I just wish that I could... you know..."

She gathered the fire in her blood and looked up at him. His green eyes caught her off-guard every time, and her heart sang a little sweeter. "What?"

"Help your back feel better."

She stilled, her chest feeling tight. Different from when she was with Urramach. *Normal or not right?* She clasped her hands behind her back. "You did. You do."

"Good." He stepped closer until his face was only a few inches from hers, his gaze locked on her eyes. Bright red fires bloomed at the center of his pupils. "And you'll let me know the next time you need help with that, right?"

Her breath shallowed, and her skin greedily drank up his warmth. *Glug, glug.*

She forced herself to speak, hoarse and uneven. "That will be hard to do when you're not around."

He watched his own fingers as he ran them down the length of her arm, his touch so light it tingled. "Maybe it's time I started taking my duties a bit more seriously." He lifted his eyes to hers. "I will always be available for that."

A heat, unlike anything she'd ever known, spread like branches through her body. "What are you saying?"

He bit his lip in a breathy smile. "I'm saying I like you, Mirri. A lot."

She had a burning desire to reach up and kiss him but was seized by an icy chill. If they kissed, what came next? While she was vague on the specifics, she was pretty sure it would lead to her Eve of Fire. And as nervous as she was about that, she couldn't help but think beyond it to the next morning when he woke without the bond on his wrist keeping him near her. Without the obligation to stay lest her flesh melt. Did he like her because he was contenting himself, or was it separate from their circumstances?

"How do you know if it's normal or not right?" she whispered, warm for the first time since she left Fyre.

He sighed, his gaze turning off to the side. "Well, I guess it's a difference between afraid and excited. Do you freeze or do you melt? Are the walls closing in, or are you free-falling?"

She missed his green eyes. She wanted them to come back. A gentle ripple spread through her chest and out through her limbs. "I think... I'm falling."

His eyes turned to hers again. "So am I. And I don't ever want to land."

She giggled and brushed a hand down his chest, plucking at the soft cloth. "You're going to have to eventually. You're the only one who can catch me."

His smile brightened so much it sparkled. He wrapped his arm around her side and rested his palm on the bare skin of the small of her back. "I could hold you in mid-air."

"I know you can." She leaned in closer, drawing fire from his touch different from the Flame. Orange, still, close to her red, but sparkling and far brighter. She could feel it in her blood, timorous at first but growing bold. It tightened her chest with pure excitement, and she wished she really was falling through the skies of Ard with Izkander wrapped around her.

She bit her lip, blushing hard, and rose on her tiptoes. His eyes fell closed as he leaned in.

"Ah-nis Na Righ?" a familiar voice called. Then the curtain ripped back.

She snapped her hands from his chest and pressed herself into the cold wall behind her, too embarrassed to even look at Urramach.

An awful silence cut through her racing heart. She forced herself to look. His golden eyes were wide, framed in low brows and a look of exquisite hurt. He pulled back, the little frown on his face falling into an open mouth. He clipped it shut and bowed low.

"My apologies, Ah-nis Na Righ. Your advisors said you went missing, and I know how you like to collect your thoughts in private." His eyes shifted to Izkander, who was gripping his stomach. "I did not realize you were discussing business."

"Urramach..." she started.

He cleared his throat. "Subsidiary, I would like to speak with you after I have a moment with the Ah-nis. Would you mind?"

Izkander nodded a lot. "Yes. I mean, no. I've been wanting to speak with you, as well. No problem at all." He turned to Mirri with a little smile, shimmers of pink in his green eyes. "I'll see you later."

Izkander brushed by Urramach, careful not to touch him, and walked off down the hall holding his head in his hand and mumbling to himself.

"Izkander—" she called. A sharp gale tore through her as he walked away. And another broke her down as she looked back at the devastation before her. "Urramach."

He sniffed and turned his head to the side, inspecting the weave of the curtain. "Did I interrupt you before your business with the Subsidiary could conclude?"

"No. Yes. It wasn't really business," she said, trying to make it better. The twist in his lips told her she had made it so much worse. "The negotiations with Shihala were successful enough."

"What does he want with you?"

Urramach's abrupt change of course sent itchy tingles across her chest. "What do you mean?"

"The Subsidiary. He was going to fix this. That he wanted nothing to do with Fyre or with you. And now he's negotiating contracts over the very life blood of our nation with parties he clearly has an inordinate amount of interest in and connection to and snaking his arms around you."

"It wasn't like that." Mirri shook her head, knowing that wasn't quite true. "There likely is no way out of it. He's just trying to make the best of his circumstances."

Urramach's face smoothed, and he leaned back with a haughty twitch to his lips. "Oh, I can see that."

That tight, closing-in feeling started to ensnare her. "May we please go out from the curtain?"

"It is the only place you are genuine, Mirri." Urramach's voice had an aching quality to it, low and urgent. "Do you not wish to be genuine with me anymore?"

"I do," she said, reaching for him. But then she didn't know what to do with her hands. She settled on a gentle squeeze of his arm. "You are the first who saw me as more than righ. I haven't forgotten that." She ran her hand down his arm and took his palm in hers.

The pressing feeling was still there, growing and itching. But she was in charge this time. This was her choice, and she was determined to find out once and for all how she felt.

She stepped closer and took up his other hand. "Thank you for seeing me."

"Of course I see you. I always have." He dragged hopeful eyes up. "I love you."

She had no idea what to say to that, so instead, she held her breath and wrapped her arms around him. Smoke and ice and heathered hills. *Familiarity.* He pressed a hand to the back of her head and held her tight. Just breathing and letting her breathe.

When at last he pulled back, he pressed his forehead against hers. "May I kiss you?"

She was surprised when the hooks of betrayal pulled at her heart. Izkander said he felt like he was falling. She had felt that way, too, excited and giddy and her stomach plunging, but she still wasn't sure what it meant for her or Izkander. Or what it meant for Urramach.

Despite the storm brewing inside her, she whispered, "Okay," determined once and for all to find an answer.

CHAPTER NINETEEN

Izkander

He walked and walked and didn't stop until he was outside of the palace, standing in a grove of *'arjwani* trees just beyond the outer wall. When Urramach was ready to speak to him, it would be easy enough to find him. Trying to hide in Karzusan was nearly impossible unless you literally shoved yourself under a bed, or behind a curtain as the case may be.

Purple leaves shivered in a cool breeze and rained down in gentle twirls. Izkander sighed and climbed the mottled trunk, then laid back on one of the wide, horizontal branches. He cast a little ball of fire in the shape of a coin and rolled it back and forth over the tops of his knuckles, his eyes watching the shifting sky beyond the rain of slender leaves.

What was Urramach doing? And what was Mirri doing with him?

There was a horrible twist in his guts, worse than before. A watery taste in the back of his mouth that made him worry if his breakfast was about to come up. He needed to talk to Urramach, man to man. Let him know what he was thinking and get answers from the drakonte's mouth, so to speak.

He didn't like it when people he'd never even spoken to didn't like him. He much preferred to be disliked for his personality, not some unintentional slight. Most importantly, Izkander was as confused about Mirri's feelings as she seemed to be. Maybe Urramach would be able to shed some light on the situation.

He was certain they would be able to find common ground and mutual interests. Their taste in women, for example.

Izkander groaned at himself, the stitches in his side intensifying. Why did he always have to make jokes, even in his own stupid head?

He'd done his best, telling Mirri in no uncertain terms what he was feeling. The last thing this situation needed was more chaos and complexity. He had hoped that it would make him feel better, lighter. And it had for about a degree. Right up until the moment they were about to kiss and it all fell apart.

He felt like he was starving, even as his stomach churned and wanted to come out. He wasn't hungry for food, not thirsty for water. He'd experienced guilt before. Regret, shame, dishonor. He had curled in on himself as physical twinges of galloping empathy ripped through his soul. But he'd never felt quite the way he did right now. He couldn't even name it.

Snatching a ripe 'arjwani pear from a branch, he played catch with himself, throwing the gray fruit high in the air and watching it spin end-over-end in the crystal heavens before coming back down. He tried to keep his focus on all the moments he had shared with Mirri that day. Laughing on the cliff and falling in the reflective pool. The blush on her cheeks. The moment when she lifted onto her tiptoes, her breath on his skin. But it all kept coming back to the moment she pushed away from his chest and smacked her back against the wall. Like she'd been caught doing something wrong. Like she was cheating. It made him feel sick, disgusted with himself, and...

Sad. So much sad.

He needed to be honest with himself and everybody around him. The problem was he wasn't entirely sure what the truth was anymore. He kind of wished Urramach was dead, but he refused to let himself go down that road. And he didn't really wish that. He didn't know the man, and if Mirri liked him, he couldn't be all bad. And he was there first.

But what did that matter? Mirri wasn't an island to plant a flag on.

He wondered if Mirri looked at Urramach the same way she did him. If she snuggled against his chest or unburdened her heart to him in the dim light of the

Fourth Moon. Did she laugh with him until her face was the color of a crushed pomegranate?

What did Urramach give her that she couldn't get from him?

Realistically?

Probably a lot. Someone who shared the same values and the same past. Who understood all the things about Fyre that he didn't even understand well enough to properly ask about. Those kinds of things mattered as much as he wanted to pretend they didn't.

He groaned and let the pear fall past his shoulder to splatter on the ground.

A throat cleared below, and a pair of golden eyes stared up at him. Urramach, looking very pleased with himself.

"Shall I join you up there or would you prefer to speak on the ground?"

Izkander curled up to a seat on the branch. "Dealer's choice."

Urramach rolled his shoulders and jumped, swinging easily into the branch next to him. He twisted so his legs hung off the same side and leaned against the trunk. "You said you also wanted to speak. Would you like to go first, Subsidiary?"

He grunted. "That is not starting off on the right foot. Call me Izkander."

Urramach smiled, easy and relaxed. "Okay, Izkander. Did you have something you wanted to tell me?"

"Actually, at the moment I'm more interested in what you have to say."

"Alright. I would like to start by saying I respect the role you've taken up in Fyre and the great things you've accomplished for our nation." He nodded once, then cast his eyes far away. "That said, I'm concerned you don't understand the implications of what you've stepped into. Especially concerning Mirri."

"That may be a fair concern."

"She is spectacular, isn't she?" Urramach brushed a strand of his hair back and looked at him sideways.

Izkander sighed and nodded. "She is."

"I have known Mirri her entire life, did you know? And have been hiding behind curtains with her since she was fifteen. Talking. Letting her bang her head on the wall where no one else can see."

Izkander narrowed his eyes at Urramach. The way he phrased that—hiding with Mirri since *she* was fifteen—made him wonder just how old Urramach was. He was a senior statesman and a trusted member of the official cabinet. Not something most people could achieve when they were twenty.

Like djinn, the people of Fyre didn't seem to outwardly age very quickly, not like humans who wore that information on their faces and in the curve of their spines. But if Urramach was even ten years older than he and Mirri, that meant he was twenty-five when he started hiding behind curtains with a fifteen-year-old princess.

Maybe that was normal in Fyre, as it was in so many places. But thinking of a man his own age hooking up with Shakira, his fourteen-year-old sister, made him feel like a spiny caterpillar was crawling up his spine.

Izkander wanted to ask Urramach how old he was, but he had a feeling the question might derail what so far had been a perfectly civil conversation. He didn't want it to get back to Mirri that he was the one who was indecorous.

Urramach sighed, his head hanging just enough and his golden eyes unfocused. "There is a lot to Mirri most people don't see."

"Seeing how restrictive higher society is in Fyre, I imagine there is a lot to most of you that most people do not see."

Urramach grinned. "I know our ways must seem strange to you. But when you don't know what little act might kill your righ, you tend to be over-cautious."

"And stagnant."

"Perhaps. But when you only change rulers every three-hundred-and-fifty years, it takes a long time to notice." He dropped a lazy hand in his lap. "It doesn't change the reality of it, though. Her blood is tied to complete obedience to the Flame and could be taken back at any time."

"I don't want to cause Mirri any harm." Izkander plucked a leaf and let it drop. "But all life is a quality that can be taken away at any time for the slightest misstep. I think continuing on exactly as you always have might not be the best option."

"Are you willing to stake Mirri's life on it?"

"I wouldn't gamble with another person's life."

Urramach flicked a ragged piece of bark to the ground. "Mirri's mother thought she could fly in the face of tradition, and it ended in tragedy."

Izkander shrugged. "I don't think you came here to talk to me about the good of Fyre, or Mirri's mother."

"The implication that Mirri is somehow separable from everything I've mentioned reveals your ignorance, Izkander. But I can be more direct. When you first arrived, you said you wanted to null the bond and stay out of the way. Is that still the case?"

It was a good question. Izkander wished he had a good answer. "I'm conflicted."

"I find that answer unacceptable when a nation and Mirri's life and heart are at stake."

"I'm not going to put any more pressure on the situation than there already is. Mirri gets enough of that from virtually every source in her life."

Urramach studied him for a while, half his face hidden in shadow. "You're going to have to put pressure on the situation eventually, one way or the other. Or Mirri will. It would be kinder to just get it over with and not mix all your watery, half-hearted emotions with it. She doesn't need you confusing her and making her think you care when you won't stick around."

Izkander smirked to try to keep that barb from entering his heart. "Subtlety is not one of your virtues."

"Good."

"I disagree."

"Because I care about you not hurting Mirri?"

"You're in love with her. You want me to go away. Why not admit it?"

Urramach turned, so the moon illuminated his face. "Okay. I love Mirri, and I want you to go away."

"Ooo, now we're getting somewhere."

He smirked. "I didn't just drop out of the sky into Mirri's life. I've been here year after year, burden after burden, listening to her and consoling her. I trained for years to catch Mirri in the race and, if I had failed, was prepared to train for another twenty-five years to try again. And after you left the curtain, thinking she may yet like you or some other fool-hardy hope, she and I kissed. And I will do it again and again, as long as she lets me, whether you're her Fire Mate or not."

Izkander tongued his canine and cocked his head to one side. He didn't want to give Urramach the satisfaction of reacting to what he'd said about kissing Mirri, but holding it all back gave him a stomachache. "You couldn't fly high enough to drop out of the sky into Mirri's life. But I did. And, okay, you've been there year after year, but that doesn't make her your possession. I've owned these boots for six years, it doesn't mean I want to have sex with them."

"You are a vulgar man, Subsidiary." Urramach leaned back against the tree, a smile curving his lips.

"I'm an honest man. You ought to study me. Then maybe you would be able to fake that more convincingly."

"Unlike you, I'm not conflicted."

"I'm certain you see that as a virtue." Izkander pressed his lips into a pout. "I may be Subsidiary, but I still outrank you. And I know that sticks in your craw because you really care about all that stuff."

"Yes, I do. But I care about Mirri more. Which makes me feel torn about you."

Izkander crossed his arms. Every word this man spoke was a thinly veiled threat. "I think you love Mirri's title. I think you could put any woman in that armor, and you would love her."

Urramach leaned forward, the gold in his vertical pupils moving with a lick of flame. "The part of me that aches when she's away would disagree. I yearn for her when she's near and I cannot touch her. And I burn when our skin does brush. I would move the world to make her content. Her. And no one else. I see her timid smiles, her intelligent eyes, her silky hair the color of the Origin. The only thing keeping me from running my blade through your heart is because I don't know what it would do to her." He tilted his head toward Izkander in a challenge. "How much of what you think you feel for her is—what did you say?—*liking* the girl rather than the novelty of the situation? I saw that lavender-skinned djinn leaving your apartment earlier. Is she novel, too?"

"First of all, *I* am the thing stopping you from *running a blade through my heart.* Second, all of it. Just all of it." Izkander lifted a tense hand and waved it over Urramach. "And you are too intense. You should go take a bubble bath or something."

Urramach scoffed. "We don't take baths in Fyre."

"Well, there's your problem," he laughed, then he looked down at his knees and shook his head. "I think it's pretty clear what has to happen here, don't you?"

"Enlighten me."

"You and I shake hands like we're supposed to and just stay out of one another's way. If you see me with Mirri, turn the other way. And I'll give you the same courtesy. And she'll make up her mind. Are you secure enough in your intense, everlasting love to mind your own business?"

He exhaled and squared his shoulders, a tiny hint of a smirk playing in the corner of his lips. "Absolutely. Though it might get harder for you to ignore Mirri and me being close as time goes on. What with your shiny bracelet keeping you close together and all. Good luck with that."

"Don't act like you aren't phenomenally jealous of my shiny bracelet." Izkander offered his hand to Urramach.

"I love your bracelet and all that it implies." Urramach gripped his hand hard and shook it twice. "My only regret is that I'll start having to ignore your existence while you're in the room. But I can manage." He grabbed the branch and swung himself onto the ground, landing in a crouch and pulling himself up straight. "Stay dry, Subsidiary. And may Marduk bless your endeavors."

"Thanks. I'm sure he will," Izkander said cheerily.

He waited until Urramach was gone before he popped every bone in his body that would pop and hopped down from the tree. The pain in his gut hadn't changed much, maybe frothier. There was a nagging voice in the back of his head telling him he should be mad, that a flame should be burning under his heels. That he should be challenging the interloper to a duel and trying to humiliate him in front of Mirri and the whole kingdom. That's what his father would have done.

But he didn't want to do that. He didn't want to fight with Urramach or any other man about something like this. It was stupid, and even the few verbal swipes he had taken only left him feeling empty inside.

He didn't want to fight for Mirri. He didn't want to win her like a prize or be bound to her like an obligation.

He wanted her to want him.

Nothing about the conversation had been illuminating, not even the fact that Mirri had kissed Urramach within moments of his departure. He wasn't angry, but all of his internal organs felt cold. He wasn't sure what it meant. All he wanted at that moment was to go home, to lay in his own bed, and try to sort through his thoughts and emotions. To be with his umi—who always made him feel better. But home was a world away. He was tethered to Mirri by cords of fire that would burn away her skin if he left, even for a night. Even for a moment.

For the first time since this whole thing had started, Izkander felt trapped.

CHAPTER TWENTY

Mirri

Mirri wasn't a hair-puller, not since her father threatened to chop it all off for using it as an emotional crutch during a meltdown when she was five. But she pulled it now, behind the curtain that offered her no privacy at all. The silky strands tried to slip from her fingers, so she held tighter, refusing to let go and pulling so hard her scalp throbbed.

She felt like a cheater.

She *was* a cheater, technically, wasn't she? Or was she if her Fire Mate didn't care? But then, she had thought... he said he liked her. *A lot*. And she had only said Urramach could kiss her so she could figure out how she really felt. His kiss certainly hadn't felt like free-falling. It felt like the last bite of apple cake when you're already full. Instant regret for something you thought you wanted because you liked it before. Her stomach ached just the same. Because of the kiss. Because of the almost kiss. And because she hadn't yet been honest with Izkander about everything.

"It was so easy not to" wasn't a good excuse, either. He asked so little about Fyre and the customs, she had at first been offended. But now she didn't want to tell him. Talking with someone who didn't look at her with eyes of pity, undeserved respect, or fear made it easier to breathe. But if she truly cared for him, she would tell him he could leave after their Eve of Fire—which he seemed to suggest he was more than

willing to have. If she truly cared for him, she wouldn't tell him it would mean a life of loneliness for her, and would just let him move on.

Would he leave after he was free? And how quickly? She groaned and let go of her hair.

There was still time left in the day. And as much as she hated it, freeing Izkander was the only way she wouldn't feel like a worm. Was she half-snake or not? And didn't that noble blood count for something?

She straightened her shoulders and marched out, nearly jutting back into the shadows of the curtain as Urramach passed in a corridor ahead. He caught sight of her, smiled with a bow, winked, and moved on. What did that mean? She curled her toes and then smoothed them back out. It was how he always greeted her in public places. Perfectly normal. Even if he had just been talking to Izkander. Right?

She picked up her pace, nearly jogging as she entered the garden that smelled of lime and jasmine.

"Izkander?" she called, then held her breath and waited.

"I'm over here, pretty girl," he called back in a tired voice.

She found him sitting cross-legged under a gigantic tree dripping with soft purple leaves, his hair and shoulders dusted. By anyone else's standards—especially in Fyre—he looked perfectly content, which she knew was all wrong. What had he and Urramach spoken about? She scratched her clavicle, pretty sure she knew the answer. But he had lifted her up when she felt down, and now she wanted nothing more than to do the same. Especially since this was all her fault. Then, when he was happy again, she would confess everything.

She slowed to a walk as she neared him, racking her brain for things he liked, er, *really* liked, since he seemed to like so much.

"Long day, Green Eyes?" she asked, crouching down in front of him.

He watched her quietly for a moment before smiling sadly. "Bits of it."

"Want to go somewhere else?"

"So much. What did you have in mind?"

"I have two places in mind." She held up the matching amount of fingers and wiggled them with a smile. "But I don't have to tell you what they are for your puffy powers to work, right?"

"My puffy powers?" He chuckled quietly then shook his head. "No, you don't have to tell me."

"You don't mind jumping into the unknown with me, do you?"

He exhaled sharply through his nose, and some of the sadness in his smile waned. "No. I'll jump with you."

"Good," she beamed. Then she stood and held out her hand. "Stand up, then. I don't have all day."

"Pretty sure you do." He clapped his hand in hers and yanked to pull himself up. When he was standing at her side, he squeezed her hand a little and looked into her eyes. "You ready?"

That sparkling fire she had felt from him before surfaced again, tiny and unsure but warm. "Nuh-uh. You have to hold me."

"Do I?" He looked down at his feet and swallowed. "Well, if I must." He slipped an arm around her waist and yanked her quickly to his chest. "Better?"

"Oh, yes. Your little hatchling arms are holding up quite nicely." She tried not to shiver when she breathed in his scent, relishing the heat from his chest with as neutral a face as she could muster. "Tally ho, puffy powers."

"Girl, you are asking for it today." He slipped his other arm around her and squeezed.

The crackle of his fire rushed over her skin, radiating from him to consume her. The world slipped away.

She was growing to love the feeling of being between worlds with him, when nothing mattered but being free. But then came the loss as the world tumbled back into focus on the blustery cliffs on Ard. The sun was on the other side of the sky then, as radiant as anything ever was.

"Should I jump first again?" she asked with a grin. "I warn you there is no water where we are headed and you must still be holding me, so answer carefully."

He nibbled his lip and looked far to one side. Then he tightened his grip on her waist. "Best not."

"Wise." She nodded solemnly.

"I'm working on it."

They walked to the edge, and she took a deep inhale before they jumped, feet first and close through the triangle gateway between worlds. She hopped up and wrapped her arms around his neck so he had to catch and hold her as the glow of red and wash of heat surrounded them. They landed gently in a cave full of black stalagmites that burned like embers with orange veins of heat. A wall of lava drizzled down one side, and a cavernous expanse opened up on the other. The air was so hot, hazy lines split the air in blurry waves.

"Ta da," she said shyly, clinging to his neck.

He held tight to her, glancing at their surroundings without moving his neck. "Oh, I see." He grinned. "You brought me here to kill me."

"I would bring you somewhere much more festive to do that. Besides, we don't kill in the Origin." She bent over, careful to keep off the ground as she removed both of her slippers. Then she dangled them out to one side. "Okay, you can put me down now if you want."

He didn't move. "The Origin? Do you mean...?"

"Do I mean what?" She furrowed her brow and pushed out her bottom lip.

"Nothing."

He lowered her down gently and loosened his grip on her waist, then he turned in a slow circle. Bright red reflected in his eyes and on his teeth as he smiled.

She wanted to prod him about his question, so breviloquent was he when he normally couldn't stop talking, but her mission right now was to bring back his genuinely happy smile. The one that wasn't sad, or too tight, or shiny.

"Come on." She grabbed his hand and pulled him down an ashy path. "And for the record, you were never here. There's sort of a strict no-djinn-allowed policy. If we went to war and someone with puffy powers had been here before, they could pop right in and destroy our deity and all of us with it. Understand?"

"I was never where?" He winked.

She turned with a serious face and patted his arm. "I know I'm not your umi, but good boy."

"I like being a good boy."

"Now, come, come. I didn't bring you here to watch Fyre's heart beat. What we want is near the actual entrance."

She hurried him along, a nervousness making her silly. The truth was, no one but true descendants had ever been in the Origin before. The law forbade anyone whose lineage had soiled Marduk's blood from entering. But seeing as Izkander had never had any of Marduk's blood, she was pretty sure he didn't count. The punishment, either way, was the Flame boiling his blood from the inside, and he had none of the Flame either. They took a sharp turn, and little coos and cries echoed off the wall. An oval room lay tucked to one side, soft ash and scaly down making a bed for several eggs. Three little turquoise and orange drakonte hatchlings scampered about, freshly hatched from the Origin itself.

She turned to Izkander, smothering the desire to bounce on the balls of her feet. "What do you think?"

He pouted, turning his head to one side, his eyes sparkling with moisture. "They're so *ooo-sha-boo*." He dropped down into a crouch in the ash. "Oh, my goodness. Look at you."

She giggled, dropping next to him and rubbing under the wide jaw of one of the little hatchlings. "They're straight from the Flame. Not born from any other drakonte. Aside from being hatched in the Origin, you can tell by the colors." She ran a finger along the cream belly and pulled at the orange on the thin wings. "It's Havu's colors. Only made for the true descendants of Marduk. Their genetics are strong and unique, and the eggs only emerge from the lava with a change in righship. They're incredibly sacred and rare and are the only ones capable of teaching a righ how to drakonte-speak."

He flashed her a quick smile, then turned back to one of the babies and clicked at it gently with his tongue until it came slithering closer. The baby drakonte darted out its long, pink tongue and licked his cheek. He giggled, then rubbed it behind its ear holes until its tail was darting back and forth so quickly it rattled.

"You're just a little sweetheart, that's what you are."

She watched him, insides melting at the sweet face he got around the babies.

"Thank you for your help today," she offered shyly. "I don't think I properly said that before. But I couldn't have done it without you. Getting a meeting with King Jahmil, or getting the impossible man to agree to anything. And I'm telling you this so you know you were wrong."

He gazed at her, the skin around his eyes wrinkling. He opened his mouth as if to say something when one of the babies headbutted him playfully. He turned to it with a laugh and swatted at its head a few times. "You want to fight, little lady? Come on with it."

He danced around with the hatching for a little while, its darting tongue tickling him so many times that his shirt sleeves were wet. It wrapped around his leg and started weakly constricting. He pushed a hand on top of its head and looked back at Mirri.

"What was I wrong about?" he laughed.

She took a seat, burying her feet in the cool ash as she took in his warm smile. She had missed his laughter. "You were wrong about nobody needing you. Because I very much do."

Izkander's brow lifted. He stopped to uncoil the hatchling before taking a step toward her. "Go on, you. Go play with your brothers." He had to throw a rock so the snakelet excitedly chased it before he could make it all the way over.

He sat down on the rock beside her, eyes locked on her face. Then he bit his lip, gave a little sigh, and looked down at her feet. "I've never known anybody like you before."

"You mean someone who's howling-at-the-moon crazy?" she asked, her voice almost too soft to hear over her racing heartbeat.

"That's part of it." He pushed out his bottom lip and nodded. "Just one part."

Mirri wiggled her toes in the ash, trying to cover them up. The smile she had brought to his face hadn't lasted nearly as long as she had hoped. "I'm beginning to think the other parts aren't so good."

He slipped down onto one knee in the ash in front of her, his face tilted towards hers. Then he brushed his fingers through her hair. "Now, who's wrong?"

His simple touch sent a river of heat through her, a mixture of the Flame's red and his sparkling orange. She shivered and looked away, afraid if she stared into his eyes any longer she would start falling.

"I'm sorry," she said, voice husky.

"For what?"

"For binding you to Fyre. For not being as forthcoming as I should. For... for kissing Urramach." She wrapped her arms around her chest and rubbed her arm to keep away the cold spreading from her selfish heart.

"It's okay." His hand dropped to his knee, but he stayed knelt before her. "I get it. I think I get it."

"I just wanted to see..." Her bottom lip trembled, and she squeezed her arms tighter, missing his hand in her hair. "I've been so confused, and I wanted to figure out how I really felt."

"Did it help?"

She stole a glance his way, and the mossy calm of his eyes brought breath into her lungs. Thoughts of Urramach and the guilt that came with them flitted away. All she wanted was to be closer to Izkander.

"I don't yet know. I was interrupted in my data collection and have nothing to compare the kiss to."

"How frustrating. Anything I can do to help?"

"There is..." Mirri loosened her arms and slipped them over his head and around his neck, hoping he didn't feel the little tremors dancing beneath her skin. "You said you were willing before... to kiss me. To fall. I'm hoping that hasn't changed."

He lifted nearer to her and slipped an arm around her back, his hand resting on the nape of her neck. His tongue twitched behind his teeth as if eager to say something though he wasn't sure what.

He laughed and shook his head. "Oh, to hell with it."

He pulled her close and kissed her.

Fire stung her cheeks, and she couldn't breathe. Eagerness snatched up all her air and used it to fan the flames. She tightened her hold around his neck, yanking him closer so hard she nearly fell backward. His grip tightened around her, and he pulled her onto his knee, his fingers moving over the bare skin of her back. His heart hammered in his chest, pulsing in his restless lips and the tips of his greedy fingers. The languid rush of lava, the coos of the drakonte, even the silky ash beneath her feet faded into nothing as she drank in the scent of spring that lived on his skin and the taste of fire that coated his lips.

She was free, and she was falling, and she never wanted to stop.

CHAPTER TWENTY-ONE

Izkander

ALL THE TENSION IN his body burst free the moment his lips met hers—an oral orgasm, unlike anything he had ever experienced. He'd heard some people talk about butterflies in their stomachs or fireworks bursting in the sky. But there was a herd of drakonte taking flight in his gut as the most powerful volcano in two worlds erupted.

His breath was short, taking her in with every desperate gasp. Her skin, like silk under his fingers, was hot and eager to be touched. He sucked on her bottom lip, then pulled back enough to look into her eyes. Her wild eyes of pure fire, tiny dark-red flames dancing in waves around the vertical pupils. His chest swelled—flashes of pleasure touched by tiny white-hot needles that only served to heighten the feeling.

He combed her hair back from her face with his fingers and kissed her again, slower and deeper. Drawing her breath into himself and shivering with the flavor, the heat. He wanted to rip her clothes off and devour every inch of her body. To hear the gentle moans in her throat grow louder, deeper, and raspier. To taste her sweat. To jump in with both feet and be alive with her as he had never been before. To fall and keep falling.

But he refused to rush. Not with Mirri. If he moved too quickly, he might miss something. And he did not want to miss a single moment.

He pulled back and brushed his lips lightly over hers, relishing in her little shivers and hurried breaths. He kissed along her jawline, and her head rolled back. He sucked on her earlobe, drawing both his palms up her back, lifting an arch in her spine.

"Mirri," he breathed and moved down to her neck. He brushed her hair over her shoulder and stroked her throat before kissing it.

"Mmm?" she asked, more moan than question. Her hand fluttered against his chest, tracing the edge of his neckline and using it to tug him closer.

He smiled against her skin, then brought his lips to hers. He nibbled lightly on her bottom lip and spoke in tiny, breathy gasps, "How's your data set?"

She giggled, nipping his lip. "I don't have nearly enough."

He fell onto his butt, pulling her with him. She giggled as he grabbed one of her legs and pulled it to one side so she was straddling his lap, then yanked her closer and kissed her again. He grabbed her thighs, pushing his fingertips in to massage the skin as he moved slowly up and down. Pulling back, he looked into her eyes again. He wished he could kiss her and see her eyes at the same time.

Pressing his hand against her back, he lifted her higher so he could kiss her chest and shoulders. He yearned to taste the peachy, tender flesh under the fabric. His hand snaked behind her neck and undid the clasp on her high collar.

She inhaled sharply and sat up, pressing a fist to her chest. A look of uncertainty washed the blush from her cheeks, and she turned her head away so he could only see a sheet of her fiery hair.

He bit his lip and set his hands on her waist. "I'm sorry," he breathed heavily. "I shouldn't have done that."

"No, it's—I don't know..." She shook her head so a small ripple spread down the length of her hair. "This feels like what the whispers say about the Eve of Fire." She eased her eyes back to his, cheeks and the bridge of her nose pink once more. "Is it?"

His vision was blurry, hips wiggling in the ash because he was forbidding them from grinding against her. "I don't know what an Eve of Fire is," he said hoarsely. "But I feel fiery."

She dropped her gaze to his chest. "It's when a man and woman join their bodies together and seal a Union."

"Then, yes. It has that potential." He took a deep breath and gnawed on the edge of his bottom lip. "But it doesn't have to be if you don't want it to be. I'm happy to kiss you."

The fist Mirri held to her chest loosened. "I just don't think anything can be done to undo the bond once the Eternal Union has been sealed, and…" Her eyebrows dipped in the middle. "I don't know if that's something you want."

He moaned and rested his forehead against her chest. It was so unfair. What he wouldn't give just to be with her, to enjoy the high, and to experience all the new and exciting things she made him feel without the constant implications of Eternity and melting flesh.

He wanted to ask her if she still wanted to break the bond, but he also wasn't sure he wanted to hear her answer. Her voice echoed in his ears, telling him she *very much needed him.* And that had been exactly what he wanted to hear.

He wanted something serious. He wanted the other half of his soul. But if she was his other half, why was she still kissing Urramach?

"I am… conflicted."

Mirri nodded, a small frown marking her pretty face. She patted his chest, then pushed herself to her bare feet and stepped over him, smoothing her skintight dress. "It's… a little chilly in here, don't you think?" She rubbed a hand up and down her arm and watched the baby drakonte sleeping in a pile near the back wall.

"*Al'ama.*" He punched the ground and sat back, then rested his elbows on his knees. "I don't know what to say. We were in agreement about not wanting to be eternal the last time we talked, but I feel like things are changing…"

She looked over her shoulder at him, a deep sadness in her shining eyes. "I, too, have been… conflicted." She gave him a pitiful little smile, and he couldn't handle it.

He hung his head in his hands and laughed the most painful, little sobbing laugh of his entire life.

"You laugh at me?" she asked, a quiver in her voice.

"I'm laughing because I don't know what else to do." He pressed his hands over his face and looked up at her between his fingers. "It's just so unfair."

"What is unfair?"

"Just this whole situation. It's stressful, and it's frustrating." He shrugged and let his hands drop to the ground. "I just want to be with you. I think you're amazing. I have never met another girl like you. I never thought I would. And I wish I could just think about that, and feel it. And know…"

She stared at him for a few moments. "If you didn't have to be with me eternally, if these—" She shook her wrist and the fire ring around it. "—weren't binding you to me. What would that mean?"

"Like I just met you normally?"

"Sure."

He sighed out a tiny smile and slumped his shoulders. "I'd be following you around like a puppy, girl."

"But not forever, right? Ayelet teased you about your loyalty."

Izkander tensed. "That is because everybody in my family—everybody I know—thinks I am charming, attractive, and entirely useless."

"I don't think that…" Mirri sighed. "I need to tell you something. You see, my mother recently explained to me some nuances of the bond I had not been aware of." She paused, chewing on her lip and tugging at the ends of her hair. Then she straightened her shoulders and lifted her chin. "Namely, that once the Union is sealed, you are no longer required to stay in Fyre or by my side. My flesh will not melt off and neither will yours."

"What?" His eyebrows lifted so sharply it stung. "Then what does it do?"

"It seals the promise of Marduk into the blood of the Subsidiary which allows for children of the Eternally joined couple to ascend the throne. Though, most rulers don't have children until the end of their rule, which is several hundred years away."

He scratched his chin. "That is a really long time to have to wait to have kids."

Mirri walked toward the wall of lava, leaving footprints in the ash. She ran a hand under the molten liquid and shook it off like droplets of water. "Are you content?"

Dragging himself to his feet, he crossed the distance between them, stopping just far enough away that her lava shower wouldn't splash on him. He watched her caress the molten rock like some kind of ancient fire goddess. She was beautiful, but his chest was tight, like he had just inhaled two lungfuls of campfire smoke.

"Why are you mad at me?"

Another cupful of lava filled her waiting hand and splashed out. "I'm not mad at you."

"You are so."

"I'm not mad, Izkander." She took a small amount of lava and rolled it back and forth in her hand so it started to cool into a sticky black ball. "I thought you'd be happy about the news, and you do seem happy."

"Okay, you're not mad." He put his hands on his hips and looked up at the incredibly sharp stalactites overhead. "Are you sad at me?"

"Are you asking if I'm discontent?" She raised an eyebrow.

"I mean... no. That wasn't what I was asking. But, okay. Are you discontent, Mirri?"

"No." She flicked the cooled ball of lava into the ash and pressed it into the ground with her big toe. Then brushed off her hands. "Are you ready to go?"

Her words struck him like a full-frontal landing on jagged rocks from half a parasang up. He grabbed his stomach. "Why won't you talk to me?"

She inhaled slowly then exhaled in one quick breath and turned her eyes to him. "What do you want to know?"

"What do I want to know?" He groaned and turned away from her. "See? This is why this whole situation sucks."

She pressed her lips together, her eyes shiny with the reflection of lava. "I don't see why you're so upset right now. I told you that if you commit to the Union, you are free to go. The only ones who will know anything about it are the citizens of Fyre and, unfortunately, your parents. Without finding a mystical solution that will make it as if the bond never happened, I don't see how I could mitigate this any more than I have."

"Yeah, I heard all of that. It's not really the point, though."

She sighed. "Then what is, Izkander?"

"Forget it. I already told you. But it..." Izkander choked on a lump in his throat and folded his arms. It was hotter in here than any other place he had ever been, but he was beginning to feel the chill Mirri mentioned. "It doesn't matter."

Little wrinkles formed above the bridge of her nose, then smoothed into glass. "You're upset because things are unfair, right? And that you have to commit to anything at all right now?"

"I'm upset that I *have* to. I don't want to *have* to. I want to *want* to. I want you to want to. I want the other half of my soul."

She glanced at the ceiling with pursed lips. Then dropped her fiery eyes to his and stepped close, pressing an open palm to his chest. "You seemed like you wanted to before I stopped you."

"I did. I do. I still do."

"Then what's the problem?" She raised up on her toes and brushed her lips against his.

He closed his eyes, a heavy sigh leaving his chest before he pulled back. "Mirri, what would you want if these things didn't exist?" He lifted his wrist to eye level and twisted it.

"Would that include not meeting you and having you bring blessings to my country? To me?"

A warm fuzzy rope wrapped around his heart and squeezed until it hurt. "Do you really feel that way?"

"I know the Eternal bond has burdened you... and I'm sorry about that. But despite my misgivings, you have only brought warmth to me and Fyre."

He pulled her closer and wrapped his arms tightly around her. She hugged him back, rubbing her nose into his chest. Her fiery scent was an analgesic. It flowed through his blood, numbing the pain that had flared so suddenly. He kissed her hair, then lifted her face to his and kissed her forehead.

"You are content?" she asked.

"Ugh, that question."

She pouted. "What's wrong with it?"

He kissed her pout and hugged her to his chest again. "It just sounds so... bleh. It doesn't really mean anything."

"It means everything to me." She pulled back and shook her head. "The moment I am no longer content is the moment I become ungrateful to the Flame and lose the life it gave me."

The conversation he'd had with Urramach under the *'arjwani* tree flared in his memory. While Urramach saw no real separation between the woman and the country she ruled, perhaps Izkander was making too great a separation. He didn't want to be like everyone else in her life, trying to force her to fit what he wanted her to be. She put enough pressure on herself, along with everyone else in the kingdom. He wanted to relieve her pressure, to be a soft place for her to lie down in. "I want you to be content. I want to be content, too. I also want you to be happy."

"Okay."

"Okay..." He hung his head.

"I mean," she cleared her throat and put up a beaming smile. "That's easy. Everything's awesome most of the time, right?"

Now it was his turn to pout. "Are you making fun of me?"

"Never," she said, then kissed him. "How could I make fun of a puppy?"

He giggled. "I want you to meet my parents."

"The delightful ones who will think I'm a dagger in their backs?"

"Just my umi." His shoulders drooped. He wasn't entirely sure why he had blurted that out, but there it was. And it was true.

"They're two of the most important people in the world to me. And I want them to meet you."

"I'm teasing, you know," she offered, patting his head. "You've met my parents and, from what I heard recently, tried to stick a knife in one of *their* backs." She raised both her brows at him. "If you want to introduce me to your family, I am happy to go. I need to get their approval so I don't die, anyway. Two birds, one stone kind of thing. And I know how much your family likes birds."

He chuckled. "I don't want you to die. That has been well-established at this point. But that's not why I want you to meet them."

"Why do you want me to meet them?"

He looked down at his feet and kicked some ashes. He didn't want to say it. He had to say it.

"Cause I want you to be my girl. For real, you know?"

Her cheeks bloomed to a pink that matched her lips. "Then I'd be honored, Gaol Aig an Righ."

CHAPTER TWENTY-TWO

MIRRI

MIRRI TRIED TO HIDE her growing anxiety as she waited for Izkander to finish playing with the little drakonte before they left for his parents. Despite his assurances, Queen Ayelet's words of warning and King Jahmil's coldness lingered in the forefront of her mind. She had been so preoccupied trying to make Izkander happy, she hadn't had the time to wonder what would happen to her if his parents refused to give them their blessing.

Izkander had laughed and told her not to worry about it, but there were a great many things he laughed at that definitely warranted worry.

Worrying about the upcoming disaster was better than thinking about the one that had just taken place. Izkander had bemoaned *having* to do anything with her and had looked so relieved when she explained he did not. How could she have ever told him what the effects of him leaving would be on her when he smiled so?

She had felt so much heat when he was touching her, his skin hotter than lava. If that was what *completely natural* was supposed to feel like, the reserved way she felt around Urramach couldn't compare. But it had also left her feeling a little uneasy. Like she was out of control, and her body had taken charge. *A weakness*, her father always said, *to let the flesh of man take over the mind of Marduk and the fire of the Flame.*

If it weren't for the guilt she felt, she wouldn't have cared. Which made it all the more frightening. Guilt for kissing Izkander because of all the years Urramach had spent caring for her. And guilt for kissing Urramach because of the place in her life Izkander won by taking a random leap in the air. So what made the difference? And was one really better than the other—skin-twitching sensations aside? If Izkander left, would she wonder century after century if he would ever come back and feel guilty over the familiar, cool embrace of Urramach? And if he stayed, could she stand Urramach's torturously sad face every time she held council?

What was worse, based on Izkander's surprisingly confident lips and hands, she suspected he had been like Maron—wonton and liberal in his ventures—which made her seethe with jealousy over a past neither of them could change. Her stomach coiled at what that might mean if—when—he did leave her in the future. Would he be off enjoying one embrace after another not caring that she had only shame and Urramach to share her bed?

She scratched the itches on her upper back coming in uneasy waves. "Careful, Green Eyes. If they get too attached, you might start hearing their thoughts in your head. And the royal line tends to be pretty snarky."

"Snarky I can handle." He palmed one of the hatchling's heads, batting it playfully from side to side. "I'd love to be able to talk to these little demons."

"Give it a month, when they're old enough to leave the Flame, and if you're... around, the girl is yours. She's expressed the desire, and the Flame will not deny my request."

His eyes widened, the reflection of lava sparkling on the surface. "You mean it? I can have the baby girl?"

She couldn't help but smile seeing that puppy-like innocence on his face. "It is rare, but not unheard of for a righ to share a sacred drakonte with their Mate. And I know you will do right by her, wherever you are."

Taking her by the hands, he kissed her cheek. "Thank you. You're amazing."

"Tell that to your mother and her knife." She forced up another smile, the muscles in her cheeks sore from overuse. "Maybe we shouldn't go... Just cross our fingers and try to break the bond. We haven't even hit the library yet. Then we could just let another twenty-five years pass before we have to think about anything again."

Just saying the words made her throat constrict. Following Urramach's dissection of the law, if she and Izkander weren't Fire Mates, the only way they could be together without melting her flesh was by her *not* wanting them to be together—a painfully impossible notion to convince herself of at that point.

A sadness filled Izkander's eyes, tinges of pale-purple mist in the green, though his smile remained unchanged. "Don't be nervous. She's a great lady. She just worries about me. A lot."

"Well, that's understandable." She squeezed his hands, a million other worries tumbling through her heart. "The suspense hurts worse than sleeping in my armor." She winced, then widened her eyes as the ease of movement she was feeling registered. "Is what I'm wearing okay? I forgot I wasn't dressed in something more practical. Is my diplomatic dress too much? Are my bare feet too little?"

"My mother was a diplomat back in the day, so I'd say it's perfect. Besides, you are edible in that dress and your toes are adorable."

She tried to give him a scolding look but ended up breathing out a laugh. It was *that*— that way he could make her laugh without worry—that made her stupid-believe any of this could work.

"Okay. Take me to your umi."

"You got it. But first, we need to stop by the mountains and grab my dad's bird."

Mirri quirked a brow. "Your family's fondness for the avian species is beyond my understanding."

"You'll get it when you meet her."

He winked, then moved them into the place between worlds. They came out on Ard in a different space than before, a vast forest of tall, skinny trees, sunlight filtering through green and yellow leaves. He dragged her a step forward under a fallen limb, and the world shifted again so they stepped out into a biting gale. Snow circled all around them, the sparkling skies of Qaf just peeking through slants in the heavy white clouds above. She could feel the pulling heat of Fyre close by. Izkander put two fingers to his lips and whistled so loudly, the echo cracked like a whip over the high peaks of the Zabriyan mountains. He put his hands in his pockets and bobbed his head.

A moment later, a light as bright as the Ardish sun dawned between the jagged crests of two snow-topped ridges, followed by a bright *caw*. An enormous bird swooped past, its wings burning unmistakably with the Eternal Flame. She lit the sky with a trail of rolling fire and angled back around.

"*Mìorbhuileach*," she breathed, grasping Izkander's hands so tightly it hurt. A shiver of nervousness spread across her chest and made her stomach flip inside her. "Your bird—you didn't tell me your *family pet* was the immortal Rukh."

He offered a sheepish grin and shrugged. "Baba prefers we keep her a secret to keep her safe. I'm impressed you knew what she was, though. Other than glorious, of course."

Mirri couldn't take her eyes off Fajar. "Not know her? She is a piece of the Origin, broken off long ago when the Eternal being split into three. The Heart, the Wisdom, and the Flame. The Flame lives in me, and the Rukh returns to our skies every few decades or centuries, blessing the land as the Origin kisses a piece of what once was itself. It is the Heart that's missing. But the Rukh..." She bit her lip so hard it stung and she had to let go.

Izkander cocked his head to the side, his eyes tinged with worry. "What about her?"

"The Origin opens to kiss her, to invite her home. And if the Origin opens..." She looked at him with hopeful eyes, her stomach biting her at the same time. "The acting Righ is invited in as well. It is what Maron was looking into when he became discontent. A way to use the Rukh to gain a meeting with the Origin. It would be our chance to plead before the Eternal Flame and ask for our bond to be broken."

"Are you saying Fajar is our ticket to breaking the Eternal Union?"

She nodded, her chest filling as quickly as her stomach sank. "If she were to fly over Fyre, we would have our best chance at changing our fate."

His eyes shifted between her and the flaming bird who circled down from the skies, drawing closer with each pass as she looked for a place to settle on the rocky surface of the wind-swept cliffs. Colors played in his eyes, far too many for her to keep up, but they set her on edge.

"Izkander?" She stepped closer and touched his shoulder.

He shook the colors from his eyes and smiled. Tightly, this time. Without a hint of shine. "We can't have her fly over Fyre now. We have a dinner appointment with my parents."

Disappointment rattled her chest, but she supposed the point was fair. Best to tend to the matters that were solid and had timelines before wandering into legendary suppositions.

"You still want to show me to them even though... even if..." She couldn't force herself to finish the sentence and looked down at her bare feet melting the snow beneath her.

"Yes, I do." He cleared his throat and waved Fajar over to a spot between crags that had a bit more wing room. When he returned, he brushed a few snowflakes from her hair, making her blush. "Want to meet her?"

Mirri's eyes widened so much they hurt. "Me?"

He chuckled. "Do you see anyone else up here in the deserted mountains of Zabriya?"

Her body trembled all over, but she managed a tingling nod. "Do you think she'll like me?"

He squeezed her hand in return. "I really do."

The Rukh circled one last time, her massive wings spread wide to show the patterns of embers that sparkled in her flight feathers. Then with a beat of wind so heavy it made both Mirri and Izkander sway on their feet, she landed on the edge of the cliff. Her talons crunched in the stone, tearing through heavy granite like it was dough. She leaned closer, her neck whooshing in the air, and pushed Izkander with her beak.

"I'm sorry." He laid his hand on the very tip of her beak. "You had a nice time, though. Right?"

The downy feathers around the Rukh's collar ruffled as rhythmic twitters rose in her throat. She pushed Izkander with her beak again so he stumbled. Laughing, he fell against her and hugged the side of her face. Then he turned back to Mirri. "This is Fajar. Fajar, I want you to meet Mirri."

Mirri bounced on the balls of her feet and mustered a shy little wave. "Hello, Fajar." She glanced at Izkander who nodded with a smile. She stepped closer and stretched out her hand. "I'm Mirri Naga, the Flame, and your sister in the Origin."

The Rukh cocked her head far to one side with a little *coo*.

"Go on," said Izkander. "You can pet her. She says it's okay."

Standing that close, she could feel the Origin in the bird. Separate, different, but a piece that once belonged to the same whole. With every step closer, her skin tingled and her blood bubbled inside her, as excited and eager to be near the bird as she had been to be close to Izkander. She brushed her fingers through the soft, radiant feathers of Fajar's head, and a jolt of fire shot down to the bottoms of her feet. She gasped, clinging tightly though the pain begged her to let go.

"Are you okay?" Izkander asked, walking closer and setting his hand on the feathers near her.

The pulse of radiant, celestial heat from Fajar intensified, accompanied by a sensation like being wrapped in a warm blanket after hours of walking naked through the snow. An image pooled in the backs of Mirri's eyes, a single moment captured in every detail so that it filled up her senses. Fajar settled in a nest, a tiny green-eyed baby snuggled in the feathers of her neck being rocked to sleep by her breath.

Tears streamed down her face from pain, from fire, from the beauty of the memory. From love. She turned to Izkander, the edges of her vision blurry. She felt half-certain she would die right there. All her muscles tensed in shock, and she could feel herself filling up with the Flame, new and old, like a cup about to overflow. Then, as if her shell had ruptured, just enough of the heat burst out and flowed back to Fajar so that she could pull her hands away from her. She dropped to the ground and shoved them under the snow, knowing it wouldn't help at all. Her heart pounded in her ears, and she felt like she could run a thousand miles and never weary.

"*Mìorbhuileach*," she breathed again.

Izkander crouched down in front of her. "What's the matter?"

"She is so beautiful. So powerful. I could feel my beginning in her. The Flame. Only kind and gentle. I also feel like I might have been struck by lightning."

He set a steadying hand on her shoulder and smiled softly. "That sounds painful."

She looked at him like he was crazy then laughed, ripples of fire still buzzing throughout her. "It was." She stood back up, keeping a little distance from Fajar. "She loves you."

"I know." He downcast his eyes, his smile soft and shy. "She is love."

"She is Wisdom," Mirri corrected.

Izkander smiled. "Maybe she's both."

He lifted his shirt to show his stomach and pulled his pants down an inch. A golden tattoo shimmered on his abs just to the right of his belly button, one of Fajar's feathers with all the shifting tones of glowing embers. The power of the Eternal Flame radiated from it in the same soft, kind melodies of the Rukh.

"She marked me when I was a baby."

Mirri sucked in air and bent over, tracing the lines of the feather and feeling that sparkling, orange fire she felt every time she was close to him.

"Pah! It makes sense." She let her fingers linger on the sinewy muscles of his abs, a sadness filling up the places the extra fire had left empty. "I have one, too. But not so beautiful. And not from love." She pulled her hand back and tucked it behind her back. "You are blessed."

He tucked his shirt back in. "You have one too? What does that mean?"

"It is a mark from the Flame. But not from the piece of wisdom that broke off and made Fajar back when the world was forming. Mine came from the Origin. It means the Eternal Flame has an eye on us, I think. Though I don't know for sure. Not all true descendants get one. My brother, for instance…" She twisted a strand of hair around her finger. "Mine is smaller than yours, though."

"Can I see it?"

She let her head flop to one side and mustered a smile. "Depends."

He showed her a half-cocked smile and took a step closer. "On what?"

"On whether you can find it, of course."

His grin widened, and he set a hand on her hip. "And when am I going to get an opportunity to look?"

The tingle of Fajar's Flame warmed her where he touched. "That depends entirely on whether you're a good boy and I'm still alive after we visit your umi."

She grabbed his shirt and pulled herself closer, trying to be playful, to smile, to be the jar of honey he wanted so he would stay happy. So he would stay when everything fell apart... or came together. It mattered more than ever now that she had so eagerly spilled the truth of the Rukh before she had time to decide what she wanted.

"That is a pretty big carrot." He tapped her nose with one finger. "I'll do my best."

He held her close for a moment, then entwined his fingers with hers and looked back toward Fajar. He plucked one downy feather from her breast, held it out in an open palm, and blew on it. It rocked gently as it fell to the ground, then a flash of orange fire and golden smoke engulfed them.

It smelled amazing. Like the Origin and the fields of Fyre and fire and something primal that spoke to her blood. When her feet landed on the soft squish of cloud, she reached for the smoke and tried to grab some, but her fingers filtered through, and she felt a loss. Then the view hit her. Expanses of sky, of towering clouds as wide and tall as the mountains that surrounded Fyre. And the sun, a white halo of rays stretching around it like arms. She wished Havu were there so she could jump. She raced to the edge and leaned over to see the sparkling ocean far below and to feel the salty, wet air evaporate on her skin.

"Where in Qaf did you grow up?" she asked over the whip of wind.

"Nowhere." He beamed and widened his arms. "This is Ard, pretty. Eayima, the floating sanctuary of the Seal of Sulayman."

"It's amazing," she called to him over her shoulder, hair whipping and stinging her cheeks.

And she meant it.

It all made sense. Easy-going, always-happy Izkander Green Eyes and his pet bird that was actually a minor deity. Of course, he grew up in a floating palace in the sky, looking down on everyone else as the sun kissed his cheeks.

She turned, a giggle in her throat. "Why would you ever leave this place?"

He laughed. "Company?"

"You're howling-at-the-moon crazy!" She waved her hand dismissively. "With this view and Fajar, I don't think I'd ever come down."

Fajar took flight, swooping lazily around the circumference of the island. She let out a loud cry that rippled through the air like sunshine and dove beyond the crest of a craggy ridge.

"Baby girl?" a distant voice cried.

Mirri did a double-take. If Izkander himself wasn't standing with Fajar, she would've thought the man who came galloping out of an old, stone temple that sat in the middle of a verdant twist of plants was him, down to the chiseled jaw and stunning green eyes.

She stepped back from the edge and to Izkander's side, her shoulders pulling back and her chin jutting up in the way her father had taught her to do when addressing people. "Is that your brother?" she asked, fighting the urge to hide behind him.

"Everybody always thinks that." He rolled his eyes. "That's my old man."

A smile twisted on her lips as several things he had said over the last few days registered in a concrete thought for the first time in her dense skull. "How long exactly are you going to live, Green Eyes?"

He shrugged. "I'm the first one of my kind, so I'm not entirely sure. But the lilu blood says probably a few thousand years."

"Lilu?" She nearly coughed the word.

Those beings were as old as Marduk. As old as the lost race of pure djinn and the human Adam and Eve, only they were very few and lived forever. They were nearly as old as Qaf, which formed from the burble of the Origin, the kiss of the Celestials, and the swish of the Bahamut's tail.

"Are you impressed?" He smiled, and she swore the sun could wink off those teeth in the middle of a storm. "My dad's half, so I'm a quarter. But what that does for longevity, I'm not sure. The telltale sexy man looks didn't dilute, so I'm thinking the lilu blood is dominant."

"Poor thing." She shook her head with a smile, trying to process everything she had learned and felt in the last ten degrees. "I didn't know the lilu bred. That's fascinating..." Her thoughts wandered as Izkander's father roughhoused Fajar in an impossibly weighted match. "I can see why you hesitated to tell me and downright refused to admit it to my parents. Though I can see where you get your free spirit."

Izkander grinned and wiggled his eyebrows, then whistled loudly. "Hey, old one! Come here."

His father looked up, and Fajar snatched him in her talons. She flopped down on her back, the impact shaking the ground with a deep *boom*, then held him up above her like she was playing with a ball. Mid-air, Izkander's father turned toward him. To Mirri. His eyes widened.

She tried with everything to pull her eyes away from the worshiped Wisdom of her people playing like a namur kitten and raised her hand in a nervous wave.

Izkander's father pried himself out of Fajar's grasp and landed deftly in the grass before breaking into a jog toward them. "Where in hell have you been, boy? Your mother has been jabbering on about you for days."

"Allah forbid somebody actually gives a crap." Izkander rolled his eyes.

"Who's this?" Izkander's father turned his eyes to her again. There was a suspicious lilt to his voice and an angle to his friendly smile that looked just a bit worried. "This can't be the infamous Shayla?"

Mirri snapped a glare at Izkander. Shayla?

He furrowed his brow and shook his head. "Heavens, no. This is Mirri. The, uh, Ah-nis Na Righ of Fyre. Mirri, this is my baba."

Mirri glanced at Izkander and rubbed her tongue against the top of her mouth. While she appreciated the formal introduction, it did not seem very, well... *Izkander* of him. She worked to let it roll off her like lava from drakonte scales. It was probably nothing.

She dipped her head. "It is an honor to meet the father of Izkander Green Eyes."

He cocked one thick, dark eyebrow. "That's a new one."

"Shut up," said Izkander. "Please."

"The Righ of Fyre, hmm?" Bakr bent down to examine her face more closely. "Wow. I've never actually met anyone from Fyre before. Your eyes are beautiful."

She couldn't help but grin with those jade eyes so close and him calling her nice things. "Yours are, too."

"Aww, shucks." He smiled and rolled his head to one side. "So, are you and my son here an item?"

She almost glanced at Izkander but didn't want to find an answer that would break her heart. Best to get everything out in the open. "He is Gaol Aig an Righ and my Fire Mate."

That dark eyebrow went up again, higher this time. "What's that mean?"

Izkander smiled and slipped his hand around her shoulder. "She's my girl."

"Your girl or your fire mate?" Bakr's eyes widened. "That's a pretty important distinction."

"Fire Mate does not mean the same thing in Fyre as it does the rest of Qaf." A shy smile touched Izkander's lips. "It's a lot more important."

"The most important." Mirri nodded. "The Eternal Flame of Fyre has decreed we enter an Eternal Union. That is why we have come. To announce our marriage to you and your beautiful wife and gain a token of your approval for the historical records and to show my father your intentions for Fyre are pure."

Bakr's eyes widened, and he turned to Izkander. "Eternal Union?"

Izkander smiled brightly. "I mean, yeah. That's what's up."

She scrunched her nose at the cavalier way he answered, but he had also somehow managed the intense negotiations with King Jahmil and convinced the stodgy old Immortal Slayer to help with the very same attitude. Maybe this was the best way to handle his family. Maybe they all had absurdly strange customs and even stranger personalities.

She smiled weakly. "Is that a problem?"

His father pulled his chin into his neck and shook his head with a little grunt. "Why would it be a problem? There's no problem. Everything is super." His eyes snapped to Izkander, and he wrapped his arm over his son's shoulders. "Will you excuse me and my son for just one moment please?"

Izkander looked down at Mirri and sucked his breath through his bottom teeth. "Just one moment, okay?"

Her heart threw a fit, but she forced it to cool. This was what she had expected. The news of an Eternal Marriage for a son who had recently been with the *infamous Shayla* would probably be very alarming. He had said they were lovely people. Many, many times. Too many times? And with a very shiny smile. She forced up a smile she knew looked like a grimace. Everything would be fine. Because most things were awesome most of the time, right? According to his dad, they were downright *super*.

Her hand twitched. It was all she could do not to face plant into her palms with a groan.

"Of course," she said, her throat as dry as the Ghaluman desert. "I'll just be enjoying the spectacular view with my sister, Fajar, your pet bird god..."

She laughed nervously and turned toward the sky, all the absurdity of the day finding her bones. Marduk forgive her if she ever disbelieved. How could she be discontent after this?

She wanted to laugh and cry and jump and fly. To reach the sun with her fingers and sing.

And who knew... standing beside Izkander as *his girl*, maybe she could.

CHAPTER TWENTY-THREE

Izkander

When Izkander finished his story—confessing everything that had happened since he left—his father's entire body drooped over the rock on which he sat until his knuckles were on the ground.

"Well done, idiot."

"Screw you."

"Screw you back." He chuckled and shook his head. "So, what's your plan?"

Izkander's neck twitched and he folded his arms across his chest. He was still riding a high from what had happened with Mirri. They were together now. Officially. Forget about Shaya, Ya'el, and all the stupid games. Mirri needed him. She thought he was a blessing. And that was more serious than anything he had ever known.

All of this filled him to the brim with hopeful anxiety that hurt almost as much as it felt good. His skin seemed tight, uncomfortable. He wasn't sure exactly why, but he felt like something was about to go horribly wrong, or like something already had and it just hadn't caught up to him yet.

Izkander laughed at himself, nervous and raw. He'd never been cynical a day in his life and he wasn't about to start. He was just nervous. Nervous because he had never been in anything approximating a relationship. He wasn't sure how he was supposed to behave.

"I don't know why I need a plan." He lifted his gaze to meet his father's pale jade eyes. "Just act naturally. Do what feels good, what makes sense in the moment. Do everything you can to make her smile and to make her back feel better. And try not to make her mad or sad at you."

"Simple enough." His baba nodded sharply. "But weren't you just here telling me how you would never get married?"

"I don't know what to tell you." Smirking, he lifted his shoulders. "Things change."

"What's changed? Other than you got yourself roped into a magical contract in spite of the thousands of times your umi and I warned you not to."

The bubbles in Izkander's chest pooled and rose to the surface. He shivered and smiled. "But I like her."

His old man clapped a hand to his forehead. "Izkander, you've known her for three days."

"I know. But—"

"You cannot marry someone you have known for three days."

"Sometimes you can, old man. Look at Ayelet and Jahmil."

His baba clenched his teeth and sucked air through to make a squeaky noise.

"I know it's crazy, okay? You don't need to say anything. I know."

"I know you think you know..."

"Everybody thinks I don't know anything."

He looked across the field at Mirri, her hair floating in the wind like cascades of lava as she gazed out at the shimmering waves and pastel sky. She lifted up onto her tiptoes, raising her hands in the air as if about to jump. His insides warmed and churned. Drakonte taking flight.

"I'm more than just a pretty face." Izkander stiffened. "I can be useful. And I can make my own decisions."

His old man scoffed. "You are free to make all the stupid decisions you want. I have always supported that."

"Why are my decisions automatically stupid?" Izkander snapped, his eyes narrowing. "I thought you of all people would be on my side."

"And what side is that exactly?"

Izkander sighed, his face slumping with a grin that felt both heavy and effervescent. "Just whatever side I land on."

"Fine." His old man's eyes rolled so far back they could have fallen into his brainpan. "But your mother is *not* going to be happy."

Izkander's jar tightened. "I wish everybody would stop talking about Umi like she's this mean, unreasonable woman. It's not true, and I'm going to punch the next person that says it." Wiggling his jaw from side to side, he loosened his fist. "Umi is..." He sighed and shook his head. "She would never do anything to hurt me. She wants me to be happy. And when she sees Mirri makes me happy, she'll be happy for us."

"Oh, my sweet, innocent, stupid, stupid, little boy. Alright. I'm going to go brace her. You go talk to your... Fire Mate." His baba slapped his knees and stood. His old man took a few steps away before he turned back. "I am on your side, okay? Just figure out what the hell side you're on, and I'm there with sword drawn and banner flying."

He smiled softly. "Thanks, baba."

Izkander jogged across the field back towards Mirri. A white fog had crept in—stray bits of cumulus clinging to his hair and clothes. Biting his lip, he sneaked up on Mirri from behind and snatched her by the waist.

She yelped, then turned. With a glance over his shoulder, she got a scrunched-nosed smile and leapt up into his arms. She coiled her legs and body around him, the skin-tight dress surprisingly stretchy as it pulled up above her knees.

"You're lucky that I'm colder away from Fyre. I'd hate to set you on fire now that I'm starting to like you."

He wrapped his hands under her thighs, holding her up. She weighed nothing, and even if she did, it was a good weight. He wanted to hold her little bare feet off the ground forever.

"I'd like to see you try, missy. I'm less flammable than I look."

She gazed at him intently for a moment, leaning back against his hold so she could place both hands on his cheeks. "Last chance. Are you sure in what you want?"

The look in her eye was so fierce and focused. Fire and drakonte and the most impassioned things he had ever known or imagined. It took his breath away. He couldn't answer other than to nod and kiss her with everything he had. She responded in kind, eager hands slipping behind his neck as she pressed herself against him.

He held her like that, kissing her and drinking her in as the sunset colored the sky around them and clouds nibbled their skin. He never wanted to stop and only did so when he heard a barrage of snorts and girlish giggles behind them. Pulling back, he shot a glare over his shoulder at the triplets—Amina, Amara, and Adira—all fresh off their tenth birthday and quickly becoming giant thorns in each other's sides as they moved towards puberty.

He smirked at them. "Go away."

"Skander has a girlfriend," said Amara, a blush on her pale turquoise cheeks.

"Yeah, I do."

Mirri's skin warmed noticeably against his, and she looked away with a clearing of her throat. "Maybe you should put me down."

"Killjoy," he scoffed and set her in the grass, his hand slipping to the small of her back. "These are my irritating little sisters."

"Hello, I'm Mirri." She bent low, straight hair cascading forward and nervous lines around her eyes. "You have lovely eyes, did you know? All so pretty and sharp."

They giggled, and Amina whispered something to Adira, who burst out laughing.

Izkander summoned a ball of orange fire and threw it at them. They jumped aside, giggling and grabbing at each other. Two of them took off across the field, Amara calling over her shoulder, "I'm telling Umi!"

Adira lingered, chewing on her knuckle as she stared at Mirri. "What's up with your eyes?"

Mirri cocked her head to the side and glanced at him. Then she flicked her eyes back to Adira. "Why, you've never heard of the snake people of Fyre?" She puckered her lips and shook her head. "Shame on Izkander for not telling you he's met the queen of snakes. That doesn't scare you, though, does it? I can tell by the shine of your eyes. You're far too brave to be bothered by the likes of me."

Adira blushed and looked down, her sparkly black curls falling over her pale blue face. "You're a queen?"

"I am. Mirri Naga, Ah-nis Na Righ, at your service." She bowed low.

Adira mirrored the bow perfectly. Then she bit her lip and looked up through her lashes. "What in Jahannam are you doing with Skander?"

He growled. "What part of *go away…?*"

Mirri giggled and leaned in towards Adira, hand cupped to the side of her mouth like she was telling a secret. "Don't you know? Snakes love the heat. And though he likes to play tough, your brother has a pretty warm heart, don't you think?"

She bit her tongue and tipped her head from side to side. "Yeah, he's okay, I guess." She flicked her eyes up to him, a bright smile filling her face. "We finished learning the Orlarna dance. You have to come and see."

He grinned at her and nodded. "Sure thing, bitsy. But I gotta go talk to Umi, first."

She clasped her hands in front of her and rolled back and forth on her feet. "Can I come?"

"Not a great idea." He stretched his lips and dipped his head to one side. "Do me a favor and keep the Giggle Brigade away for a bit, okay? Then, I'll come to see your dance."

She pouted but nodded. Then looked back at Mirri and gave the practiced little bow again. "Bye."

"Goodbye," Mirri said, smiling softly.

Amira turned and bolted off across the grass in the same direction the other two had gone.

"Sorry about them." He smiled guiltily and slipped his fingers into hers.

"How many siblings do you have?"

"Twelve. Too freaking many." He rolled his eyes. "I'm the oldest."

She pressed a finger to her bottom lip. "So you wouldn't want that many children?"

"Not all at once, no. Maybe like five or six."

Her face pinched before smoothing back out. "Is that very important to you?"

He ran his fingers over her cheek, then combed them into her hair. "It's totally negotiable."

A visible amount of tension released from her shoulders. "I am only allowed two... but you'll live longer than I, so when I'm gone..." She looked down at her feet.

The *when I'm gone* part of her statement stabbed at him like rusty needles, so he decided to just ignore it. "Two is a good number. Nice and symmetrical. Besides, I'm going to have about ten thousand nieces and nephews. The Bakr line will not be dying out any time soon."

"And I'm guaranteed a boy and a girl, so... you'll get one of each?" She winced out a smile. "I mean... if things go okay with your umi and the whole Rukh thing doesn't... you know..."

"I think this has been built up way too much." He tugged on her hand. "Come on. Let's just get it over with, so you can relax."

She followed after him, brushing her feet off as they walked up the set of cream-colored steps toward the arching front doors of his ancient-temple-turned-domestic-abode. "Is there anything I should know?"

Izkander chewed on his lips as he led her into the main foyer, trying to come up with anything useful to say. The last thing he wanted was to make her more nervous.

"Just be yourself."

CHAPTER TWENTY-FOUR

MIRRI

BE HERSELF? SHE WOULD have scoffed if he hadn't been pulling her through the vast hallways so quickly. Wasn't he the one who told her she was honey and glass? So which one was she supposed to be now? The revelation that his mother had once been a diplomat had done little to quell her nerves about her dress and instead lit little flickering embers inside her stomach.

For all his father's smiles, he also had not seemed thrilled about her being there. And there was a conspicuous lack of curtains for hiding behind in this temple of a house. Just mural after mural of scenes on Ard and Qaf as beautiful as the sky outside. She squeezed his hand as they neared a room with the distinct sound of quibbling voices. Now was no time for self-pity. Was she a queen like the little girl had asked, or was she a coward? A snake or a worm?

Izkander shot her an encouraging smile as he swung the doors wide and pulled her into a massive, airy room with him. Bakr stood at the head of a long rectangular table, one hand leaning against the cherry wood and the other mid-articulation. Next to him, in a high-backed chair and as regal as any princess she had ever seen, sat Izkander's umi. Her skin was a turquoise that rivaled Havu's brilliant scales, lips a dark red, amber glowing eyes, with those same sparkles in her black hair that had been in Izkander's sisters'. A silk head covering the color of summer plums draped loosely over the back, blending seamlessly into the shawl and dress she wore, all fit to perfection.

Mirri sighed. She should have worn the shoes.

"Hi, Umi." Izkander's face lightened with a smile. He went to his mother's side and kissed her cheek.

"Skander," she smiled back, lifting a hand over her shoulder to pat his hair. A surprising softness filled her sun-colored eyes when she looked at him. "You had your father, and I worried when you disappeared so quickly after just returning home."

"I'm sorry. I don't know if Baba told you, but I got a little caught up. I asked Javier to come let you know I was okay."

His umi pursed her lips. "He mentioned a monster, which I assumed you vanquished." She smiled tightly, eyes only on Izkander.

Mirri fought a twitch, the distinct impression his mother wasn't talking about the buklak settling over her mind.

"Was I wrong?" his mother asked, her shapely eyebrow rising.

He smiled warmly and nodded. "I did. Well, I had some help..." He straightened and crossed the short distance back to Mirri, setting a hand on her back. "Umi, I want you to meet somebody."

The woman's eyes barely grazed her before locking back on Izkander. "I don't think there's any need to rush introductions. I've barely had time to catch up with my son, and we haven't eaten yet. Isn't that right, Bakr? That we haven't eaten."

"Zan..." he moaned and rolled his shoulders back. "No, we haven't eaten. I'll go get food. Yep, that's what I'm gonna do."

"Don't move, Bakr." The woman clipped, eyes still on her baby boy. "There's no chance in Jahannam that you're getting out of this."

If Mirri's insides weren't twisted in thorn-filled knots, Bakr's crestfallen cringe might have made her giggle. Bakr gripped the back on his wife's chair hard enough that the wood squeaked. His head fell forward, defeated.

"Umi," said Izkander, that soft sweet smile on his face unchanged as pink and pale blue sparks glittered in his eyes. "This is Mirri, the Ah-nis Na Righ of Fyre."

The woman's golden eyes lingered on Izkander for so long, time ached. Then, she sighed and finally graced Mirri with her attention.

Mirri quickly bowed, far deeper than tradition would dictate but probably not far enough. "It is a great honor to meet the mother of Izkander Green Eyes. He speaks less of angels than of you."

"Aw, isn't that sweet?" said Izkander's father. "What a nice girl."

"A girl, indeed," his umi said, face a perfect mask of nothingness that far outdid King Jahmil's glass. The family resemblance was terrifying. "How old are you, Ah-nis Na Righ of Fyre? You have the face of a child."

Mirri pressed her lips tight so she wouldn't wince. "Half the Seventh Moon's pass from twenty."

"And how long have you been the Ah-nis Na Righ?" The title rolled off the woman's tongue like silk when so many others stumbled.

"Three days." Mirri tilted her chin up high, ready to meet the challenge. "But I've prepared for the call of the Eternal Flame my whole life."

"Have you?" his umi asked softly. "And yet you were caught in the Dragon Ride during your first Founder's Festival. Did you forget to prepare for that as well, or were you planning to break the traditions of your people by marrying so terribly young?"

"Hey, that's no slight against her. It's a testament to the bloodline." Bakr walked over to Izkander and punched him in the arm. "I'd like to see the vixen that can get away from this fox."

"Why he has to chase after vixens at all is beyond me," the woman replied with ready crispness.

Her husband winced again.

Mirri forced smooth the wrinkles that wanted to crease her brow. She had expected some knowledge of Fyre from the woman, considering her diplomatic past, but that she knew so much left a lot less wiggle room for what she had planned to say.

"Preparations aside, I am content to do the will of the Flame and—"

"Content?" A smile plucked at the woman's lips. "You come here to my home on my tender son's arm because you are *content* to follow fate like a blind lamb?"

"I *am* content to follow the Flame, but I'm here because Izkander asked me to come."

The sunny eyes left her for Izkander, and Mirri couldn't help but exhale in a brief moment of relief. "Skander?"

"Yes, Umi?" His smile brightened, hand not moving from Mirri's waist—firm, but not tight.

"You did the right thing bringing her here like this. It will be much easier to find a way to reverse the bond with both of you present."

"I didn't bring her here to reverse the bond," he said sweetly. "I just wanted you and Baba to meet her."

The woman's bright red lips twitched, and Mirri knew all too well the internal struggle his mother must be having, trying to keep her conviction with that persistently candid face staring at her.

"And now we have, sweetie. But we really must address the situation from a practical, technical standpoint and break apart this tether that holds you down."

Izkander chuckled nervously. "Umi, you don't understand—"

"I am so hungry," said Bakr. "I could eat Ghaluman food. Are you sure you all don't want some food? There's half a wild steer in the kitchen, I think. I'll just go tell Ana to heat it up."

His umi's hand flashed up and grabbed Bakr's wrist. "Honey?"

"Yes, darling?"

"Remember that time I made a deal with a demon?"

He clenched his teeth and spoke through them. "What about it?"

"If you leave, I can't guarantee I won't do it again. Okay?" She said the last word with scary brightness.

He let out the growling sigh of a tired drakonte but sank into a chair at her side and set his elbows on the table. Mirri would have smiled but for the *buklak* of a mother staring her down. The *old man* and Izkander were both so genuine and soft. If his umi could be loved by a man like that, maybe a part of her was a jar of honey, too.

"I apologize," Mirri offered contritely, stepping toward the pristine woman with another bow, "for not approaching this situation with the gravity it deserves. Let me start over." She took another step forward. "I am Mirri Naga, Ah-nis Na Righ of Fyre and have come to meet with the Eayima's Queen. Are you the woman I should be speaking with?"

The woman's eyes glittered, even more yellow than at the start. "You may call me Sheikha Sezan. Plead your case."

Mirri glanced toward Izkander who still had a warm-hearted smile on his face and eyes that shone for his umi. It was enough for her to swallow her pride and sink to one knee, grateful for the stretch of the soft drakonte down of her gown.

"Sheikha Sezan, in accordance with the traditions of my people, I have come to secure the blessings of my Fire Mate's lineage so that the Eternal Union through which we are bound may be sealed by Marduk and the will of the Flame."

"No."

"Umi." Izkander took a step forward. "Aren't you even going to ask my opinion?"

Her face softened just enough to lighten the creases next to her eyes. "You have such a tender heart, Skander. I worry you may confuse one strong emotion for another. But I always want to hear your opinion."

A flash of hurt touched his eyes and his smile dimmed a little. "I've decided to go through with it."

A streak of white cut through Sheikha Sezan's amber, and Mirri couldn't help but feel compassion for the woman. She, herself, had had the same reaction when the fire formed around her wrist. It was only being around Izkander that made it into a blessing and something she wanted. This woman had to hear the same news, except instead of gaining Izkander, she was losing him.

Sezan looked at Bakr, lips parted and eyes wide enough to betray her feelings.

He reached out and laid a hand on her arm, his face pinching. He turned to Mirri and raised his brow. "Is that it? Is that your entire proposal?"

She didn't like that look.

It was the same one Izkander gave her when he wanted her to *talk to him*. To be vulnerable. And she already felt exposed and self-conscious in this Flaming dress. But she needed to do this, not just so she could live, but so that she could live with Izkander.

"Sheikha Sezan," Mirri started again, itchiness spreading across her ribcage. "I felt similarly when Izkander unexpectedly fell from the sky and onto my drakonte. That we are too young. That we don't know so much about each other. But can you begrudge me for falling for the same wonderful things you so clearly love about him, too? I am not asking for your blessing so my flesh won't burn, I'm asking because I want to be with him."

She paused, the truth of her words emboldening her heart. It was true. The Rukh now offered hope of a bond that could be broken, and still he wanted her there. She smiled and bit her lip, then looked up at Izkander's umi.

"I want to be with him all the time. Anywhere and everywhere. And he says he wants to be with me." She took a shaky breath and waited for Sezan's eyes to meet hers. "He loves you more than anything in the whole world. Even Fajar, which I hear is difficult to do."

Sezan's lip twitched.

"It would mean the world to me if the person he loved most trusted him enough to give me a chance. I know I'm not a lot, but I can't go on living in Fyre without him. And I don't want to."

Sezan's sharp brows dipped in the middle, and her softened eyes wandered from her to Izkander and back to Bakr. The two men had the same tender expression on their faces, the room awash in sparkly green eyes. Bakr squeezed Sezan's arm, and the muscles in his neck twitched.

His umi looked past them to the door they had first walked in through and held out her palm. "I presume you have the customary token?"

"I got it," said Izkander, wrapping his hand in the fabric of his shirt before reaching into his pocket. He fumbled and almost dropped it, then laughed at himself and set the golden coin on the table.

Sezan stared at it for a moment, then two. Then pulled a delicate, white silk square from a pocket and picked it up. The nails of her free hand drummed on the table over and over. *Click, click, click, click.*

Mirri's heart thrummed along with them. If her father saw her now, kneeling before a djinn princess like the beggar she was, he would be disgusted. *Maron would never degrade himself so.* But then what had killed her perfect brother in the first place?

Sezan snatched the cloth closed, coin inside. "You may have it tomorrow."

"What?" Mirri fell out of her thoughts.

"Your token of entry and approval. You may come back tomorrow to retrieve it with Bakr's and my mark of approval."

Bakr's eyes widened, and his gaze snapped to Sezan. "Really?"

"Yes," Sezan said, sounding a smidge irritated. "If they come back at sundown tomorrow and feel exactly as they do now, I will acquiesce."

Smiling, Izkander went to his mother's side and hugged her. He kissed the top of her head and said something to her too quiet for Mirri to hear.

Sezan pressed a hand against his cheek. "I know, dear. I would like to speak with you in private, though. After I have a word with the Ah-nis Na Righ, of course."

He nodded and leaned in so she could kiss him. More quiet words.

But while they had their tender moment, Mirri's heart sank. She had the feeling the *word* Sezan was about to have with her would be far from pleasant, and she found herself desperately hoping Bakr would stay.

No luck.

Bakr practically loped to get out the door, while Izkander paused to brush her upper arm with his fingertips. He looked into her eyes, a soft, close-lipped smile on his face she had never seen before. His eyes were misty, glowing like sunlight through the canopy of Sharta forest in summer—the purest green sparkling with blue and copper and crimson. He stood fixed, gazing into her eyes for so long his father had to snatch his arm and drag him out of the room.

Mirri looked out a small round window across the table on the far side of the room. Fajar must be off flying somewhere because she felt the unmistakable cold of being away from home for the first time since arriving. She shivered.

"Ah-nis Na Righ?" Sezan cut right in.

"You can call me Mirri."

"So informal?"

"We are not in Fyre, and I am certainly not your queen."

Sezan smiled. "Why is the bond still on your arm?"

"This?" Mirri lifted the burning circle and twisted her wrist back and forth beneath it. "Because we have not yet sealed the Union."

"With sex?"

Mirri winced at the word she could never say, wanting to crawl under the table, knees tucked in tight to hide. "Our Eve of Fire."

"I'm sure that's not for my son's lack of trying."

"No," Mirri looked up. "It's not like that. He was very respectful."

"Because of the Eternal part?"

Mirri dropped her eyes to the marble floor. "Maybe."

"And now he says he wants to be with you forever, yet the bond remains unfulfilled." Sezan leaned on her elbow, eyes glittering. "Why?"

"It's a newer development..." Mirri said weakly.

"Is it?" Sezan asked softly, sharply. "Or are you afraid that once the bond is gone, Izkander will be, too?"

"I didn't say that."

"You didn't have to."

"I trust him." Mirri pulled herself off the cold floor and straightened her aching back. "I trust him to stay."

"And yet the bond remains."

Mirri clenched her fists. "Did you have anything else you wanted to say?"

"No." Sezan leaned back in her chair, shoulders as straight as the wood behind it. "You may go. I look forward to seeing you and the bond on your wrist tomorrow."

Mirri shoved the growl on her lips down. It rattled in her chest, instead. She gave a stiff bow and marched out of the room, only remembering to slow her steps as she approached Izkander and Bakr, who were chatting with their feet up on a set of woven chairs tucked neatly away in a corner. Bakr had a bottle of some pungent alcohol in one hand and was rubbing a heavily furrowed brow with the other.

Izkander jumped from his seat when he saw her, his cheeks dimpling with a wide grin.

"Your turn," she said briskly, passing them with barely a glance and heading out into the fresh air.

What did that woman know, anyway?

CHAPTER TWENTY-FIVE

Izkander

Izkander sat down on the table, his legs dangling. He drummed his fingers against the wood, then used his thumbnail to scrape off a little imperfection in the paint. His heart was pounding, blood moving far too fast to keep track of. Dizzy, restless, ready to explode into ten-thousand splinters of hot flesh and bone. Everything Mirri had said was pounding in his brain, his heart, his lungs. Over and over and over, a meteor shower of shimmering syllables bashing in his skull with cascades of glitter.

He crossed his ankles and swung his legs to keep his balance, but it wasn't working.

"Why do you look so nervous talking to your umi?" his mother asked, lips tucked into a pout.

He laughed and shook his head. "I'm not nervous."

"You're twitching more than Squirt did when he got into that barrel of Niri wine."

Stretching his arms over his head, Izkander laughed again. Like little bubbles at the bottom of a waterfall, soft and unstoppable. "I want to run. Just run as fast as I can."

She smiled. "And where would you be running to?"

"Nowhere." He shook his head. His cheeks were aching he was smiling so much, but he couldn't stop. "I just want to run in a big circle."

She chuckled, then shook her head. "A circle around Mirri, I presume?"

"No. She'd run with me." He giggled and looked up at the ceiling. "Or I could pick her up and run."

"I know love can be exciting at first. And I'm glad you get to experience that. But…" His umi sighed.

"That's it, isn't it?" he whispered and shook his head. "I'm in love. I love her."

The words were like a balm on sunburnt skin. A blast of frozen air on the surface of the sun. He hopped down from the table, turning an open-mouthed smile to the ceiling. He walked to the window because he had to see the stars, just see them and be near them.

"I wish I could reach up into the sky, wrap my hands around Ursa Major, pull her down here, and kiss her. I've found the other half of my soul."

"Izkander," his umi said in her tired-mother voice. "Your soul is so young. It's just now figuring out what shape it wants to be. And… and you just met her. She's lovely, but what do you really know about her?"

"Oh, enough." Sighing, he let the side of his head clonk against the windowsill. "She's sweet, and loving, and tough, and confusing, and crazy like the moon."

"I thought you had been seeing that Shayla girl for several months now. What about her?"

"She doesn't matter." He laughed at just how tiny she suddenly seemed. "She was never good for me. Playing all these games, dragging me into it. When I was with her, I did things that made me feel bad about myself. Because that's the world she lives in—Ahmar, complete with lies and intrigue and backbiting. But Mirri? When I'm with her, I feel like I could actually be somebody. Somebody worth being."

"I love you, honey, but are you sure you're not confusing loving Mirri with loving what it means for you to be with her?"

He furrowed his brow and turned to look at her, his smile unchanged. "What do you mean?"

"Well," his umi said, drawing out the word as she stood and walked over to him. "I know you've been trying to find your place in both worlds and do things that matter. Then you fall into Mirri's life and find a needy, little kingdom and a wide-eyed young queen who both recognize your strengths and tell you they need you. But you can do good anywhere. You don't have to commit to eternity to find your place now."

"Isn't that what people do when they fall in love?" He laughed again just hearing the word come out of his own mouth. "Like you and Baba. You're together for eternity. That's the way it's supposed to be, right? And I love her. By Allah! I love her."

"And if she didn't call you a blessing? If she and her kingdom were like Shihala or Ahmar and didn't need your constant help? Would you be content staying there as Subsidiary with Mirri and having nothing else to do?"

"But we'll have plenty to do. Her and me and Squirt and Havu. I mean, Squirt fell in love with Havu at first smell." He sighed and shook his head. "I could kiss him. I will next time I see him, whether he wants me to or not. And the two of them can have babies, and I can take care of the babies. Oh, you should see the little snakelets, Umi. They're so stinking cute."

"I'm sure they are, sweetie." She pressed a hand to her eyes, careful not to muss her makeup as she squeezed the bridge of her nose. "And that sounds like rip-roaring fun for the next twenty years. But what about the hundred after that? And the four hundred after those? Mirri has a kingdom to run, and she can't leave Fyre for very long. Can you be truly happy bound forever to a little kingdom running off a flame in the middle of the mountains when you're so used to having adventures?"

"We'll still have adventures. Mirri can leave Fyre. I mean, granted not for very long. But she can leave." He looked down at his wrists and rubbed each in turn, imagining the fire he knew burned under the skin. "Once we're bonded, I can leave on my own if I want to. Come up here and visit. Or we could expand the kingdom. I don't know."

"And how do you think that will make Mirri feel? You leaving to live another life while she's stuck in Fyre by herself? I know I would be terribly lonely if I were stuck here while your baba went off with his beautiful eyes and charming smile, just like yours." She pouted and smoothed the front of his shirt. "You don't want that for Mirri, do you?"

"You like it when Baba leaves sometimes."

She pressed her lips together, a touch of pained purple, like nebulas around her pupils. "You are not used to staying in one place. Being with one woman for so long. It is different."

The sorrow in her eyes cut into his bursting heart, cracks radiating into his veins and over his skin the longer he looked at them. "I'll build you a house in Fyre. You can come for a visit anytime you want."

"You are the sweetest, son, but I wouldn't dare." The yellow in her eyes had nearly vanished, consumed in the violet clouds.

"Umi…" He grabbed her hand, panic spreading through his body with every new whisper of purple. "I'll be the king. I'll make them be nice to you. Or I'll just… I'll come home a lot."

She squeezed his hands, a sad smile on her red lips. "I'm not worried for me. I'm… I'm worried for Mirri, which makes me worried for you."

"What do you mean you're worried about her? I'll be good to her. I'll do anything she needs, anything she wants. I know I can make her happy."

"I know you'd be good to her." His umi pressed a palm to his cheeks. "Too good. But do you know much about the righs of Fyre before Mirri?"

He scoffed. "I know her father is an epic prick."

"He's also one of three to live long enough to pass the throne on when tradition dictates. Out of thirty."

Izkander furrowed his brow. "Why? What happened to them?"

"They burned." She gave a helpless shrug. "Or melted. The history books aren't clear other than it involves the Flame and is gruesome. One wrong step by Mirri, or by you when bonded to her, or by anyone else in the court could mean her demise. And you were born to be free, Izkander, not to walk on eggshells your whole life for a curse that isn't your own."

"But I thought once the whole fire wrist thing was done that she would be safe." He ran his fingernails over his scalp. "What do you mean by a wrong step? What is a wrong step?"

She pursed her lips, fingers back on the bridge of her nose. "Any number of things. Her bare feet, which I noticed. Behaving unlawfully, I suppose. They have hundreds of laws the righ must follow. When she eats. Where she goes. It even dictates that she must cleanse herself by shower instead of bath, lest the flame in her blood extinguish." His umi exhaled. "To be honest, I don't think they even know which rules will kill the righ or won't, so they just obey them all. Fulfilling your Union will keep her from being burned for that, but the rules regarding the Flame are obsessed with *contentment*. And I can't imagine she'd be very content if you were gone all the time."

"I never said I would be gone all the time," he said because he couldn't argue with anything else she had said.

He swallowed a foul-tasting lump. Contentment. He was really starting to dislike that word and everything it meant. Every time Mirri said she was content, she looked like she was dying a little, and he felt it deep under his ribs.

"Why? I don't get it. Why does a flame give a crap what anybody does?"

His umi shrugged again, one hand palm-up to the side. "That is beyond the research found in Elm's libraries. The people of Fyre are as old as any here in Qaf. The King of Eastern Elm's wife was one of the first descendants, and the Flame they worship came before that. To be honest..." She shook her head. "Nevermind."

"What?" he asked, unable to force back the anxious rasp growing in his voice like rust.

"You're just going to go causing trouble and heartache for that girl if I tell you."

"Umi, that's not fair. You have to tell me."

"Will you promise not to be an idiot?"

Izkander pressed his lips together. "I'll try."

She fidgeted with his shirt some more, fingers moving restlessly to straighten the already straight cloth. "There was a contract I found in Elm's libraries when I stayed there during the Vesparan Wars. One that involved the Fa Chomhair Righ. Mirri's father."

He widened his eyes, waiting. And waiting.

"Umi?"

Her fingers froze, and her perfectly straight shoulders sunk. "I didn't understand all of it. But he made a deal with someone named Urramach to give the original

Ah-nis Na Righ Maron a drink of the Origin's blood. All I know after that is that Mirri is now the Ah-nis Na Righ. Not Maron."

"Maron was her brother. He died." Izkander's eyes shifted around the room, unfocused. "What does it mean to drink the Origin's blood?"

"I believe it is a true test of contentment and truth before the Flame, but I don't have any idea what that means, sweetheart. All I can assume is that a shady deal was struck under Elm's Seal in a land that hated djinn, and so death followed. Maybe not all the righs died because they offended the Flame. Maybe the Flame is just a burning lava pit under the city like you would find under a hot spring. Or maybe it *is* a god, and this Urramach and Mirri's father knew her brother wouldn't pass the test."

"Urramach." Izkander sank down onto the window ledge. "That man is a blight on my existence."

"What do you mean? You've met him before? In Fyre?"

"Yeah." His shoulders slumped. "He was kind of, sort of, not really Mirri's boyfriend type thing before I showed up."

His umi narrowed her eyes. "You mean Mirri is close to the one who presented Maron with the blood test that killed him?"

"Yes."

"And now she's in power, and he's as close to her as ever?"

Izkander bobbed his head a few times, then snapped his eyes to hers. "That is what I mean."

"We're undoing that bond on your arm."

"What are you talking about?" He jumped to his feet. "I have to tell Mirri. We can just get rid of him." He punched a fist into his palm. "That relentless, self-righteous sack of silver. Do you know how guilty I've been feeling over him?"

"I don't care." His umi folded her arms tightly across her chest. "You're not going back to Fyre. And you're not telling Mirri. For all we know, she's a part of it, and you'll have Origin blood burning your skin off, too. No. Not my son."

"Mirri isn't a part of it. She would never do something like that."

"How do you know?" She jutted her chin up exactly the same way Mirri always did. "Royal families are brutal. Just look at Ahmar. Or *Fyre* for that matter."

He clenched his eyes shut and shook his head. "She loved Maron. She told me so."

"I know you love her." His umi sighed, her fingers now tapping against his chest. "So I will trust that I raised a son who isn't a gullible fool. But how do you think she's going to respond to you telling her that her almost-betrothed, whom you don't like and are in a rivalry with, could be the reason her brother is dead? Oh, and that her father could very well be a part of it, too? Do you see that going well for you?" She ran those drumming fingers over her forehead. "What am I saying? Why am I rooting for this? You have me all confused with your father's eyes."

He snapped his fingers and pointed at her. "What if I got that contract? Then she'd have to believe it."

"King *Chupkin* closed the library when he took over. He was tired of people asking him to do his job and look over the contracts, the handsy little wisp, so he just shut the whole thing up and hid the key."

"Well, get him to reopen it."

She scoffed. "Talk to Serap, then. Or your father. Chupkin's not a fan of mine. And the feeling is mutual."

"You know who else Chupkin likes?" Izkander smiled brightly and pointed a thumb to his chest. "This one-hundred percent, prime-cut hunk of Qafian man meat right here."

His umi laughed, somewhere between amused and pained. "I told you not to go off and be an idiot."

"I'm not being an idiot. I'm trying to solve the problem with the endowments Allah gave me."

"The problem of Fyre's burning flesh?" She scrunched her face in disgust. "Is there any possible way to dissuade you from this foolhardy need you have to be useful?"

He bit his tongue and looked up at the ceiling. "Nuh-uh."

She groaned. "Then... at least don't drink anything while you're there? And stay away from Urramach. And don't talk to Mirri's father. And... Allah—" She fell into a string of muttering.

"What is it, umi?"

"Just please... don't die. And—" She bit her lip, smudging her lipstick. "And if Mirri ends up... dying. Don't blame yourself, okay? There are too many things going on. It could be something she did, or it could be a contract or a discontent god. I don't want you self-hating like your father does. Not my beautiful boy."

"Don't worry." He laid his hand on her shoulder and smiled gently. "I won't let anything happen to Mirri. I'll be decorous."

Her eyebrow flicked up. "Decorous?"

He folded his arms and leaned back. "Yeah. I can be decorous if I wanna be."

His umi pinched the bridge of her nose and sighed. "Allah, help that poor girl."

CHAPTER TWENTY-SIX

Mirri

Mirri burst through the front doors of the palace and sat in a huff on the top step, elbows on knees as she glared at the sunset.

Sheikha Sezan—Izkander's *Umi*—was just like every other royal djinn she'd ever met over the years. Conceited. Entitled. Hard as glass. How Izkander could speak of Shihala's royal line with so much joy on his face was a testament to his character. But she also understood it, at least in regard to his mother. Considering the tension in the woman's face, Mirri thought she had come off rather restrained, if not harsh and blunt and presumptuous. And a know-it-all.

And like she loved Izkander more than coal loves the Flame.

Everything she had said had been a challenge to Mirri. About her age and how long she'd been righ. About her and Izkander's devotion to each other by holding onto the coin, as if their feelings would change as swiftly as the silver Second Moon. And her questions about the bond on her wrist. As would be expected of a true diplomat, nothing Sezan said was culpable on its face, just needling and passive-aggressive. It made Mirri's blood boil, her skin steaming in the ocean-swept air that trickled up to Eayima.

Soft footsteps padded through the door she had left open, and she straightened her back. The spicy smell of agarwood flowed over her as Izkander's father hopped down and took a seat a few steps below her.

He swung a leg up on the stair and rested his elbow on his knee, then peered at her over it. "Salam."

"Hello," she replied, eyes on the bloom-shaped clouds softening the sky.

There were no galaxies twisting black into flecks of starlight. No nebulas bursting with green and purple or a handful of moons cutting their paths through the heavens. But it was no less beautiful in its simplicity. A creamed blue with just a touch of clouds, like Ard's Celestial sun was breathing.

Bakr sighed and joined her in watching the sky.

"I've always wanted to go to Fyre," he said at last, breaking the silence. "I've seen it a few times from afar, up in the Zabriyan mountains. Fajar loves to fly around there. It always looked beautiful. And I've got a soft spot for those moody flying snakes of yours."

"It is beautiful. Especially deep into Zabriya's winter when the mountains are shrouded in pure white. The valley's verdant hills steam, and the waters glow soft orange as the Flame heats the quartz beneath." She pulled her gaze to him with a sad smile, feeling even colder with the memory. "You are welcome any time."

"If you and the boy are going to be married, you're going to have to get used to this face, I'm afraid."

"I feel like I am already used to it. You and Izkander look so much alike. You wear your hearts on your face the same way."

"Yeah, it's a burden. But it's better than egg." He smiled at her. "None of my other kids look like me, really. I mean, some of them have the whole heart-on-their-face problem, but they're a lot more djinn-y. Izkander is my little clone. I always figured that's because I carried his fire inside of me for a while when he was still in the womb."

Mirri raised a brow, brushing her hair back over her shoulder. "I didn't know you could separate a djinn and its fire. Is that... a normal thing for a father to do?"

"No. It is not normal at all." He tapped his hand against the side of the step, an onyx ring on his finger clicking. He coughed and looked away from her. "There was a demon trying to steal my wife's fire and turn her into a slave. So she gave me Izkander's fire for safekeeping, hoping the demon wouldn't take it and harm him, too. She would do anything to keep that boy safe."

Mirri couldn't help a small smile. "She was fighting for him before he was even born, huh? No wonder I didn't stand a chance."

"She's a wild namur." He turned his eyes back to hers. "And she doesn't pull her punches. But damn, that woman loves like nobody I have ever known."

"I knew there had to be a reason you stuck around." Mirri tossed him a wry grin. "And a reason Izkander talks about her the way he does. I wasn't exaggerating in there. I only hope to achieve half her status in Izkander's eyes in my lifetime."

"Tell me about it," he scoffed.

She sighed, dropping her hand and running her finger along the edge of the step. "She doesn't believe we care for each other. She doesn't believe this is real."

"She's skeptical, but she can be persuaded. She'd deny it, but I know she fell in love with me the first time we met. She told me so. And so did I. I just didn't realize it at the time because, well, I've got issues. Less now than then." He shrugged. "But rest assured that you could have been an angel of love sent down from Allah with Cupid's arrow sticking out of your butt, and Zan would still try to talk you out of it. She loves that boy. Since he was a baby she has been swearing up and down that the first time he brought a girl home she was going to throw her off the edge of the island."

Mirri glanced behind her, running a strand of hair through her hands. She turned back with a grimace. "It's a good thing Izkander is the only one who can catch me then, or I'd be in trouble." She scooched down another step to be closer to Bakr's smell and smile, both enough like Izkander's to warm her against the chill. "Can I ask you a question?"

"Another one?" He grinned.

"Izkander is... impossibly optimistic and cheerful and so easily excited about... everything." She tucked in her eyebrows and looked into Bakr's jade eyes, searching for confirmation.

He chewed on the inside of his cheek and nodded. "I've been protective of him, maybe overly so. I am of all my kids. I never wanted to see any darkness take hold." He sighed and narrowed his eyes at the horizon. "It's hard to wash away once it does, no matter how much light you shine on it. Especially for somebody like him."

"Someone so tenaciously innocent?"

He smiled sadly and dipped his head to one side. "Yeah."

"That's what I'm worried about." She pressed her toes against the marble so they turned white at the ends. "It makes me feel like the worst person in both worlds."

"What do you mean?"

"Your namur of a wife may have... I don't know. Seen right through my glass jar? But there's no honey inside like Izkander thinks. There's lava and darkness that greedily eat up everything he gives, and a whisper that I and Fyre are just his next big high. That he won't stick around. And then I see his eyes... and I want to throw myself into the Flame for thinking it."

Bakr stroked his stubbly jaw, letting out a low groan. "Just a hypothetical, but what if it wasn't going to last forever? Would you still want him for as long as you could get him?"

"Of course, I would. I think I've forgotten how to breathe when he's not around. Which is why I'm terrified."

"You should be. Anybody who thinks they're falling in love and isn't a bit terrified is either really stupid or just plain wrong."

"Great," she breathed out a cold laugh. Then sobered and trained her eyes on his. "Do you think he'll stay? Really, truly, one century after another? Or even a decade? Or a year?"

"Did he say he would?"

Mirri pushed her lips to the side. "He's said he likes me. A lot. That he wants me to be his girl. That he's conflicted about this—" she raised her wrist "—and wished he didn't *have* to do anything... But he talks like he means to. Makes plans for our future. Children. How he wants to change the kingdom." Her face twisted, hot and cold battling inside her. "What do you think?"

Bakr leaned his hands on the step behind him and stretched his back. "He also braved what I'm sure he knew was going to be a very uncomfortable conversation with his mother because he is prepared to enter into an Eternal Union with you. Call me old-fashioned, but that sounds pretty committed to me." He sighed and slumped over his lap. "Izkander is very honest. It's one of his many flaws. If he's talking about children, then he's thinking about children. If he says he wants you to be his *girl*, then you are the girl he wants. He's never been in a real relationship before. I think he tried a little with old what's-her-name, but clearly, that didn't work out. I'm sure this is all a bit new and confusing for him."

"I believe all those things. He's as genuine as the first bloom in spring. But blooms grow, stretch, spread their pollen, then pass on. I worry eternity is a long time for his first relationship when only I will burn if it fails."

"Eternity is a long time. It's such a long time I don't know if it is even worth thinking about. I think you're worrying so much about the future, you're letting the present pass you by."

Mirri uncurled her toes, weight shifting inside her.

"There are no guarantees in life," Bakr continued. "You could get hit by lightning tomorrow or choke on a *dajaj* bone. And yes, your feelings could change. It's always a possibility. Maybe in twenty years, or a hundred, or five hundred, Izkander and you will grow in different directions. Or maybe not. It also depends on how much work you are willing to put into making sure you stretch and move together. I recommend against spreading your pollen to other flowers. That can be a bit of a deal-breaker in my experience."

She tried to stifle a groan, but it came out anyway. "What if I put in all the work I can, and we still grow apart? He has the option of moving on. I don't. All that would await me is Urramach and a constant fear of melting. I don't think I could bear it."

"What's an Urramach?"

"The man who tells me Izkander will leave me in a cold empty bed without any love and who has offered to fill it."

Bakr lifted his eyebrows. "Okay. First of all, it sounds to me like he might have ulterior motives. Second, keeping a side guy waiting in the wings in case things don't work out with Izkander don't work out is a sure way to make certain they won't."

"I didn't ask him to wait there," she snapped defensively. "He just *is*. All the time. Making it difficult for me to breathe. He's always been there. Long before Izkander. But I want Izkander."

"Then you need to tell that to this Urramach guy in no uncertain terms. And tell him to stop waiting for you. When you get into a relationship, terrifying as it may be, you absolutely cannot keep a backup. It will kill it. Or, if Izkander has even more of his old man in him than I ever realized, he will kill him." He bit his cheek and dipped his head. "Though probably not. He's much nicer than me."

"*Daingead*." She huffed. "I think I'd kill whoever *Shayla* is if she ever came around." Then her toes curled, so the nails scraped against the stone. "He's had a lot of Shaylas... hasn't he?" She kept her eyes on the ground.

"You're the only one I've ever met."

"Which is why you looked like you were sucker punched when you saw me?" she asked, her lips twitching into a grin.

He winked at her.

"Okay." She slapped her knees a few times. "Stop worrying about the future. Izkander is honest. Don't ask how many Shaylas there were. And tell Urramach very clearly to go away so Izkander won't fall into a jealous rage. Anything I missed?"

"Izkander is more likely to fall into a jealous cone of guilt, shame, and self-pity. But yeah, that's pretty much it."

"Out of curiosity—Izkander being so much like you—do you like being a glutton for punishment? I feel like all the people Izkander gets shiny-eyed about are super prickly. The Immortal Killer. King Jahmil. Your... beautiful wife." She gave a toothy smile.

"Oh, I am a deeply masochistic and self-harming individual." He giggled and rolled his head on his neck. "What can I say? There is nothing more gratifying than winning over the super prickly ones. When a person everybody else thinks is a mean-spirited, hard-core pain in the ass is just sweet as pie to you—I mean, that's special."

"I see," she said with a chuckle.

"Those kinds of people usually just need somebody to storm their ramparts and make them laugh. And then you end up with the most loyal friend you could ever ask for."

"Then I guess it's a good thing Izkander's willing to do the work. I'll just sit back and scowl with the other half of your family while you, Ayelet, and Izkander rub elbows and make us laugh."

"As a shameless and unapologetic showoff, you are welcome in my audience anytime."

She giggled, feeling the weight of her meeting with Sezan lifting. Too soon. Her shoulders slumped with a little sigh. "Thanks for sitting down with me."

"Anytime." He slapped his hands on his knees and hopped up from the step. "I think I'm going to have my work cut out for me reminding my wife how important she is tonight. I had better get started. If you'll excuse me, *abnataya*."

She jerked her head to look at him, a flicker in her heart when he called her daughter. "Really?" she whispered. "You would call me that?"

He lifted one side of his mouth into a kind smile and nodded. "If my little boy loves you, I'm sure I do, too. I just don't know it yet."

She sprang to her feet and threw her arms around him, entirely embarrassed and not caring at all. She breathed in the agarwood, fire from Fajar, and the salty breeze that clung to his skin and committed it to her memory.

"Thank you."

He squeezed her tightly then pulled back, his hand still on her arm. "You're a sweet little thing. I get it. I get it."

"Hey, you guys," Izkander said from the top of the stairs.

Bakr smiled at her once more, then turned and jogged up towards him. "Scale of one to ten, how mad is she? What am I looking at?"

"One?" Izkander shrugged.

"You're cute, *habibi*, but you're full of crap." He leaned in close to Izkander and said something into his ear, then slipped through the doors into the house.

Mirri waited for them to click shut, then jumped into his arms and kissed him.

He wrapped his arms tightly around her, kissing her deeply for a long moment before he pulled back and set his forehead against hers. "Does that mean you're okay? I know that didn't exactly go awesome."

"It went a little awesome," she said, Izkander adding warmth onto the ember of *abnataya*.

"Thank Allah." He brushed her hair back and cupped the sides of her face. His eyes looked intense, somber, dotted with pink and silver mist. "Everything is going to be okay, Mirri. I promise."

"I know." Her smile fell. "I can get your umi to come around. And your father is so kind."

His eyes fell shut, and he nodded. Then he kissed her again, slow and heavy, but only for a moment before drawing back again. "Should we be getting you back to Fyre?" He squeezed her closer to his chest. "I don't want you getting cold."

Wrapped in his toasty arms and feeling the emotional whiplash of the last several degrees, she hadn't noticed the shivers drawing heat from her bones. Without Fajar nearby, she had, indeed, been away from Fyre and the Flame too long.

But a part of her didn't want to leave this beautiful place. Especially because the promise of love lingered in every tug of the breeze. Izkander's love. Fajar's. A father who did not reprimand or shame her. But she also needed the warmth of the Flame to live. A bubble of discontent began to form before she squashed it as hard as she could and ground it to nothing between her teeth. There was no way she would die now that she had found her other half.

"I am getting cold. And I have some very important matters to attend to." She nestled closer, listening to his heart and worrying over the look on his face. "I know everything will be okay. As long as I'm with you."

CHAPTER TWENTY-SEVEN

IZKANDER

IT WAS WELL PAST the setting of the First Moon when Izkander brought them back to Fyre. The dim yellow of the secretive Fourth Moon was high in the sky—the night moon, as it was often called because it was so pale, it disappeared under the shine of the others and only revealed itself in eventide.

He brought them into Mirri's room—their room—with its tapestries and plush carpets. The large bed that he never would have dreamed of going near on the first night they were together, and the divan where he had stroked her back until she fell asleep in his arms.

There was no point trying to go anywhere except to bed, but as Izkander looked at it, his nerves flared. Everything he and his umi had discussed was ringing in his ears, but even that sounded muffled compared to the hammer of his heart. The pounding rhythm had started the moment Mirri said to his mother, "I want to be with him. All the time. Anywhere and everywhere." And it had intensified to a cacophonous series of thunderclaps when he realized he felt the same way.

He was determined to do things right, whatever that meant. He would not be the one to gamble with her life; nothing in two worlds was worth that. Not when it came to the Origin of Fyre and the deaths of twenty-seven righs before her. He would protect her even if that meant swallowing his pride, suffering indignities, or biting his tongue. It was so little to ask, considering.

As much as he longed to, he could not indulge in their Eve of Fire yet. He wanted to make sure every *markleki* was in a row first, poised and ready to be shot. He needed the official approval of his parents, which his umi was still determined to hold captive until the following morning. He needed to show Mirri that he cared about her country and respected her position, that Fyre was not a game to him. And he needed to handle the situation with Urramach and her father, to get down to the truth of it and blow it open.

But his mother was right. He couldn't just tell Mirri what he had learned without risking coming off as jealous or grasping. She still had affection for Urramach—a corkscrew twisting into his belly button. But now, the sad golden eyes did not sting at him at all. The words Urramach had said—the history, the familiarity, the time spent hiding in curtains—it didn't matter anymore. Mirri was his now, and he was hers. She'd made her choice.

It should have been enough.

When he contemplated the implications of the contract his mother had found, it twisted Urramach's devotion to Mirri from heartbreaking to despicable. It twisted every moment that had passed between him and the golden-eyed man since they met. And those kisses... the ones that made Izkander's eyes greener and left Mirri cold and unable to breathe... took on new meaning too.

He had no proof. From Elm, from Fyre. From any source whatsoever. And no matter how this situation turned, it had the potential to break her heart. And he would not do that lightly, and certainly not based on hearsay. He would get proof one way or the other.

Until then, and until the First Moon rose, he just wanted to be with Mirri.

His ponderings must have shown on his face because she watched him with a little pinch in her brow.

"How's your back feeling?"

"Tired." She sat on the edge of the divan, crimson eyes trained on his face. "Are you okay? Did your umi say something about me?"

Izkander shook his head. He took off his belt and laid it on the ground along with his sword and gun. Then he sat down on the edge of the bed and took off his boots. "She said she feels bad for you for having to put up with me."

Mirri scoffed. "I'm sure that's exactly what she said."

"Verbatim." He pulled off his shirt and scooched back on the bed, crossing his legs.

Her eyes widened, and she stood abruptly, walking her way to a tapestry where she ran her fingers down the weave. "I don't believe you for a second, Izkander Green Eyes. I know you think your umi is a goddess, but there's no way she changed her mind that quickly."

"No, not so quickly." He lifted his arms over his head and stretched, releasing with a little sigh. "But I can be very persuasive."

"And how easily persuaded are you?" She turned and leaned her shoulders back against the walls, eyes studying him carefully.

"I think you already know the answer to that." He bit his bottom lip and widened his eyes, then patted the bed next to him.

She didn't move. "I can't get in bed in my diplomatic attire. That would be absurd."

"Do you need help taking it off?"

Mirri tilted her head, eyes slightly narrowed. Then she marched to the foot of the bed and raised her arms. "Yes."

He got up on his knees and moved in front of her. He looked in her eyes as he reached a hand around her and undid the clasps. His hands moved over her shoulders and over the curve of her waist, then her thighs. He grabbed two fistfuls of the stretchy fabric and pulled the dress up over her head. She shivered a little as the green and gold slipped free of her creamy skin, a defiant look on her face despite the blush that colored her cheeks. She looked up at him through her lashes.

He ran his fingers down the line of her neck, his eyes pouring over her. The dress had hugged every line, taunting him from the moment he saw her in it. And now with every inch of skin revealed, kissed by pale moonlight and accentuated by sharp shadows, he realized his imagination was unforgivably deficient. She was beyond beautiful, or magnificent, or amazing. Awesome, that's what she was. And he wished he hadn't cheapened the word by using it so often to describe common things. He wanted it to mean everything it was supposed to mean. He was awed by her.

"Let's see if I can find that tattoo." He smiled, whispered laughter in his throat, as his fingers moved gently over her collarbone, tracing the edges of her small, lively breasts and then down the contours of her stomach. He stopped when his fingers touched the top of her underwear. He bit his lip and looked up at her eyes.

Entwining his fingers with hers, he tugged gently, silently inviting her into the bed. She followed, her body willing as she slinked onto the sheets, one knee at a time. She inched close to him so her stomach was touching his, skin to skin and impossibly warm.

"I want my Eve of Fire," she whispered and skimmed a single finger down his chest.

He pressed his hands against her back, fingers greedy for her skin as his heart thrashed in his ribs. His eyelids felt heavy. He brushed his lips against hers.

"I want everything to be right. When we have our Eve of Fire, I want every bit of your attention on me."

"I am rapt and ready." She placed both her hands on his shoulders, fingers pressing into his skin, and leaned the little distance forward so her breasts brushed against him. "So why do we wait?"

He ran one hand through her hair, the other tracing long, light lines on her back. "We have eternity. I want to take my time. And I want you to know what it feels like to know pleasure without consequences."

"I always have consequences." She kissed him, then moved lower, brushing her lips down his chest, to his belly button, and then back up again, light as a feather and just as soft. "I can't eat or drink or dance when I want to. But I can have you."

He moaned, and his head fell back. "I want you to have what you want."

"I want you." She kissed his throat. "And I want everyone to know you want me, too."

"So much..." A little shiver licked through him, threatening to shatter his resolve. "And the approval from my parents? That won't cause problems?"

She paused in her kisses, then pulled back. "I... don't know. Approval has always been granted on the day of the Ride. Who wouldn't want their child to marry a righ?"

She looked down for a moment before bringing her gaze back up, flecks of fire in her eyes. "Let's find out."

"I'm not going to gamble with your life. Not like that. Jumping off a cliff, sure." He ran the back of his hand over her cheek. "Tomorrow morning, we'll have it. Until then, there is still so much we can do. I don't mind waiting. And I'm not going anywhere."

Her eyes rounded, and the fire in them snuffed to a dark garnet. She collapsed back into a sit, head hung low so her face was hidden by her waterfall of hair. She stayed like that for a moment, her head sinking until it touched the sheets. Then she crawled off the bed and wandered silently into the bathroom without looking up.

"Mirri?" Izkander sighed and sat back on his heels. He pressed his face into his hands, suppressing a loud groan. "Mirri, I'm sorry."

He waited a while, and when no response came, he slunk off the bed and walked to the bathroom door. He slumped his weight against it and tapped lightly but insistently.

"Mirri?" Again he waited. Another sigh ripped through him, and he let his back fall against the doorframe. "Will you come out of there, please? You're killing me."

A muffled bit of rustling came through the door before it wrenched open, nearly causing him to lose his balance. Mirri stepped out, fully dressed in her drakonte armor down to the silver band on her hair and the gold swirls down her arm. Her feet were bare as ever, and her sword hung from her belt. Her face was pale, devoid of any blush, and she refused to look at him.

"Why are you being this way?"

"What way?" she asked, striding to a small desk by the door into the room and rifling through a stack of ink-scratched papers.

He took a few steps after her. "What did I do wrong? I was trying to be respectful of your culture for a change. Now, you won't even look at me."

"I'm embarrassed." She rifled more fervently so the dry *thwick* of the papers filled the silence.

"There's no reason to be embarrassed." He walked closer and rested his backside against the desk and set a hand on her wrist. "Mirri, I want to do unspeakable things to you. You know that, right?"

Her bijou lips puckered with a tremble. "It is better this way. There was something I needed to do tonight, anyway."

Izkander's stomach hurt, but he bore it without a wince, eyes still trained on her face. Allah, he could not leave things like this. He needed to tell her what he was thinking.

"I just wanted to rub your back. And kiss you everywhere. Feel your body next to mine. And fall asleep holding you."

"Perhaps that is not such a good idea."

"Yeah. I'm getting that."

Her coldness was like two lungfuls of frozen smoke. And suddenly, it was his turn to be embarrassed. He let go of her and walked into the bathroom, shutting the door behind him. He pressed his back against it and slid down until he was sitting on the cold tile. Drawing his knees to his chest, he folded his arms on top and let his head fall against them.

The universe was blasting in his eyes, caustic and cold. And a voice kept repeating the same words: *Useless idiot.*

CHAPTER TWENTY-EIGHT

Mirri

Watching Izkander's crumpled face as he slunk off tore like drakonte teeth through her chest. And she wasn't sure what to do about it. Her thoughts and emotions were whipping around inside her in bursts of hot and cold, threatening a cyclone.

She had lied. She wasn't embarrassed. She was mortified. Humiliated. The sting of his rejection sunk its icy venom into her very core. Maybe it was because he had been with so many others. To him, being intimate was as normal as eggs and barmbrack, but it had taken everything she had to stand before him like that. To be vulnerable and a breath away from naked when her whole life she had been stuffed into armor.

That was the cold.

The heat came with her anger. Because it wasn't fair to feel that way. He said he had stopped because he wanted to keep her safe. To respect Fyre's culture. So much so, even with the promise of Union on their wrists and her willingness to give all of herself to him, he wouldn't give her their Eve. *Just in case. Just in case.* And she was sick of it.

Which terrified her. It was why she crawled off the bed like a wounded animal and crunched herself back into her bone-holding armor. She could not be discontent. She couldn't. She wouldn't. For that was the only thing in all of Fyre's laws that she was certain of. A discontented righ was an ungrateful righ. And the ungrateful must burn.

Which meant no back rubs. No kisses. No sleeping in his arms until morning. Because deep down and in the tingles of her flesh, she wanted more. She wanted all of him. And teasing her soul with just a part, however divine, would melt her into nothing. Even thinking of it could.

But she couldn't leave him like that in that bathroom. Not before she left to talk to Urramach.

She walked to the door, inhaling and exhaling with each step. Then knocked twice. "Izkander?"

"Hmm?" he called back, his voice quiet and raspy.

"You know I want to do unspeakable things to you, right?"

He gave a barely audible, breathy chuckle, and a soft *thwunk* sounded against the door as if a heavy head had just hit it.

She sighed, pressing her fingertips against the wood and tracing the lines as high as she could reach. "Thank you for not wanting to kill me. It's a low bar, I know, but so many righ have died in the past... I was being selfish."

"You didn't do anything wrong, pretty girl. I'm an idiot. So I'm just gonna crawl in a hole and lick my wounds, and then I'll be all better."

His words were nettles in her heart. "Protecting your girl is not idiotic." Her throat thickened, squeezing her next words. "It was my fault. I... I was not being as content as I should have been. I need you. And I'll be more grateful for your kindness in the future. Okay?"

The door groaned as if weight were being pulled from it. "I'm just going to shower, okay? Everything is fine."

Mirri bit her lip. He didn't sound fine. It sounded like he was in the *cone of guilt, shame, and self-pity* his father had warned her about. But she didn't want to push him.

"Okay." She rubbed a smudge in the wood. "I have something to speak to Urramach about while you're rinsing, then I'll bring you back some food. Do you want something warm or cold?"

"I... I don't care."

"Izkander..." Her heart tightened so much, she felt pain in her hands. "Please don't be sad. I'm sorry. I'm sorry I'm not filled with honey." She thumped her fist weakly on the door then turned and rubbed her face in her hands.

Thoir matheanas dhi, Marduk. Why couldn't she just be content?

Mirri stood still as she listened to the shower water turn on. She wanted to burn the door down and beg at his feet like the shameful, desperate little girl she was, but he clearly didn't want to see her. And the door of the sacred castle was made of petrified wood, it wouldn't burn, anyway. She had crushed him. Now, all she could see was an image of his mother smiling, smiling, as they returned tomorrow with feelings changed. Maybe his umi had seen right through Mirri. Maybe this whole time she had been undeserving of Izkander's love.

He did love her, right?

She pressed a hand to her stomach, harder and harder though it did nothing to help. She wanted to eat something, to eat so much of a loaf of bread she felt sick just to take her mind off of everything, but she had eaten in Shihala, and the snake and Flame in her said that was more than enough for a good week.

She glanced once more at the shut door of the bathroom, then trudged into the hallway. It took several averted gazes from passing nobles and servants before she realized she was behaving with impropriety. She forced her aching shoulders into a square and swallowed the thought of missed back rubs and kind words. But her mind trailed back to his breath on her skin, his chest pressed against hers. Her lungs cracked with silent cries.

Would he still want her in the morning? Or had she broken everything? She had been so afraid to lose him *after* their Eve of Fire and so determined to prove to herself — and his mother — that she wasn't, that she had ended up losing him before it even happened.

Her blood chilled with the thought.

She followed the winding paths of black-bricked hallways until she reached a little nook behind a set of tasseled emerald curtains not too far from her room. The bond on her wrist tugged back the way she came, persistent and uncomfortable like heartburn on her skin.

Your Fire Mate is the other way, the glowing rings warned. *Go back. Go back.*

She stayed, wincing against the sting as she placed a hand on the center brick and lit it with her fire. On the other side of the wall was Urramach's room. He would see the glowing orange signal—he always did—and come.

Not a quarter of a degree had passed before his light hair and pressed uniform slid into the space. His golden eyes were soft and warm, so different from Izkander's ocean green, and his smile was the playful one he always had on when she summoned him.

"Mirri," he breathed. Then his face fell with concern. "What's wrong?"

Her mind slipped with the familiarity of it all. She wanted to divulge her woes to him like she had so many times in the past, and for a moment, she forgot why she had come.

He touched a light hand to her elbow. "I don't think I've ever seen you so sad."

"I am content," she said, the words instinctive.

"You can be content with being righ and still be displeased with other things. You are allowed to feel, Mirri."

She met his gaze. "I don't think I can."

"Because of Izkander?" he asked, face smooth and patient.

"Because—" She turned away. "Because of everything. The Drakonte Ride. The rules. This." She held up her wrists and the bracelet of fire. "I don't know what I'm doing anymore. And that was the one thing I could claim before. That even if the rules of how I must live are out of my control, at least I could choose what to do with them. And now?" She threw her hands up and leaned her back against the rough wall.

Urramach turned his head, brows knit in thought, and she remembered how much she admired his perfect posture and neatly tied hair ribbon, his square jaw and warm eyes. How decorous and polite he was, even behind curtains. None of that had changed. But something had. Something that had brought her here in the first place.

He looked sideways at her, face serious. "Who your Fire Mate is doesn't have to decide your life for you, Mirri."

"I disagree."

"Why?" He faced her once more and raised both his brows, mouth open in a slack smile.

"Because they're going to be with me for eternity." She raised her chin. "Because if I mess things up with them, I could die. Because they're the only way I can have children who can assume the righship after me. And because... I'm a person who has feelings."

"Feelings?" His voice dropped.

"Yes." Mirri tried to look at him and failed.

She gazed past him at the tiny tufts in the velvet curtain. Heat scalded her cheeks, and it took everything in her to keep back a bitter laugh. Her whole intimate life was on display for anyone who wanted to see, but admitting she actually cared about it was what tripped her up.

Urramach tilted his head. "Hm."

"What?" she asked.

"Is that why you're sad?" He shook his head like he was pitying her.

She bristled even though it made sense. No, *because* it made sense. She was behaving pitiably. Pitifully. Worst of all, a small part of her wanted to be pitied.

Urramach touched a finger to her chin, eyes creased. "Has he hurt you?"

"Of course not."

"Mirri?" he pried, his tone disbelieving.

"No." She forced her gaze up to his.

"Then why are you here hiding with me instead of in bed with him? And at such a late hour?"

"We're fine," she snapped, feeling turned around and entirely unsure of how it happened. "He is good. And kind. And decorous."

Urramach shook his head again. "That man is anything but decorous."

"Oh, yeah?" Mirri glared. "Then why is this still here?" She waved the bracelet in his face.

Urramach smirked.

She blushed.

"It seems you need time to think." He reached forward, hesitated, then brushed her hair back from her face.

"No." She pulled her head back from him and tried to collect her scattered thoughts. "I came here to tell you something."

He pressed a finger to her lips. "There is nothing to tell. Not yet. You have a large burden to bear, and I see it wears on you."

"Urramach—"

He darted in and stole a kiss, her body freezing as it always did. Then he pushed the curtain aside and clipped down the hallway. "I love you, Mirri. And I'll always be here for you."

All the air had been sucked from her lungs, creating a cavernous pit that pulled everything into it. She was certain she was going to die that way.

But she did not.

And the first thing to unfreeze was her hand, which she clenched into a tight fist. The rest followed in a torrent as she yanked her hair and kicked the wall and tore at the curtain. *Stop waiting for me. I don't want you.* That's what she had come to say. *I don't want you.*

All that came out had been drivel. Too easily had she slipped back into old patterns, confiding in him about things she shouldn't. Stupidly inviting advice when Bakr had warned her of his *ulterior motives* and how keeping someone on the side ruined relationships. She had let her fear that Izkander would leave make her a pitiful, ugly person.

It was her.

If he left, it would be because of her. Because she couldn't be content. Because she couldn't be brave when she wasn't in front of a snarling monster. Because she couldn't stand nearly naked in front of him and be enough. And because she couldn't go back to their room. Not even with her wrist turning red as the bond chaffed and chided her for not being closer to him.

How could she? After she had shamed herself? After she made him feel ashamed when it wasn't his fault? After she had failed to tell Urramach to stop waiting and instead let him steal a kiss that left her cold and dead inside?

No.

She slid down, the rough stone of the wall tugging at her hair as she pooled on the cold floor. She would sit. Sit and wait for morning. And pray she didn't burn before then, though a part of her wished she would.

CHAPTER TWENTY-NINE

Izkander

ALONE WITH HIS HURT in a stream of water warmed by underground lava flows, all he wanted was to go home. He wanted to lie his head in his umi's lap so she could comb her fingers through his hair. He wanted to cry, and in all his life he had never once cried when she wasn't there to hold him.

A few moments of solitude to collect himself, and yes, wallow in self-pity, was all Izkander needed to feel like himself again. But the fire around his wrists ached, mirroring the pain in his heart. He just wanted to be close to her. But he had been too bold, too presumptuous.

He wouldn't let it happen again.

Izkander emerged from the shower to an empty room, which he was both glad of and devastated by. When she said she was going to go talk to Urramach, Izkander had wanted to scream. But he bit it back. He shoved it all down into his gut to fester with a thousand questions he wasn't sure he wanted answers to.

Once again, after sharing such an intimate moment, the woman he loved had left him to go find comfort in the arms of another man. A man whom she'd known her entire life. A man who claimed he would wait for her for eternity, who hid in dark corners ready to pounce any time Izkander made a mistake.

A man who may yet be a traitor.

But according to his umi, Izkander couldn't risk telling Mirri that without risking turning her against him. He hated being dishonest in any context but keeping something from Mirri hurt. Allah, it hurt so much.

Izkander scoffed, stomped over to the wardrobe, and ripped it open. He was Izkander ibn Bakr, damn it. He was not going to melt into a useless puddle. All the guilt and shame and worry, all the humiliation in the world was not going to dissuade him from being with Mirri. She was the other half of his soul.

That had to be why this all hurt so much. He'd had his heart and his pride wounded plenty of times—not the least by Shayla—but the pain had never been this bad before. Because this feeling came from Mirri, it was more.

He thought he'd been reasonable, respectful. He thought decorum meant everything to her. He'd wanted to show her he was taking her, and all of this, seriously.

But it wasn't enough.

And that meant he had to do more. Whatever he had done wrong—he wasn't a hundred percent sure what—he was going to find a way to fix it. She had said that if they slept together that the bond, which even now was searing his skin like twin silver bracelets, would disappear. Then he would be able to go home, leave Fyre, and do whatever he wanted.

The only clothes Izkander had were the same he'd been wearing for days. None of his plans to bring his possessions over from Karzusan or Eayima had come to fruition. Izkander's eyes slipped across the room to land on a pile of thin drakonte leather. He picked it up, running the thin, yet strong, fabric through his fingers.

Maybe this was all a test. She wanted to see if he was really committed. If he was capable of being the kind of man she would want by her side.

He looked down at the leather and tightened his grip. Maybe living in Fyre meant being just a little uncomfortable all the time. He could get used to that. For Mirri.

Izkander pulled on the skin-tight clothes, pausing every few seconds to adjust so the leather laid just so. The greenish-gold riding jacket accentuated his broad shoulders and the inverted triangle of his torso. The tight, iridescent pants hugged his legs and made his butt look so good, he wished he could twist around far enough to take a bite out of it. His muscles popped, his skin glowed, and his eyes shone like backlit emeralds. Sex on a stick, decorous as all hell, and so uncomfortable.

Izkander pulled on his boots and strapped on his weapons. With a fresh shave and oil in his hair, he felt like a new man. Ready to handle his business and do what needed doing. It was still dark out, and *al'ama*, he was so tired. Using a trick his umi had taught him, Izkander drew two tiny balls of fire to his fingers and flicked them into his own eyes. It stung like a couple of bee stings, but it did the trick. He was ready for another two days straight. Five. He didn't need sleep. Or food. Or sex. He was running on borrowed time, and he needed to get this *khara* over with.

Throwing open the door, Izkander walked down the hall with his shoulders back and his head held high. The few servants bustling through the hallway at such an hour paused to look at him. The widening of eyes and the parting of lips was everything he needed to know.

He didn't know his way around the castle. He had only been to the throne room, Mirri's room, and up on the ramparts, and he couldn't remember how to get from one to the other. It made him feel like an idiot, but he crushed that thought before it could fully form.

He walked up to a servant, a young woman down on her hands and knees washing the stone floor. She flinched and looked up at him, a look of fear filling her expression that he didn't need djinn fire to interpret.

"Excuse me." He smiled prettily. "But how do I get out of this castle?"

Her bottom lip quivered, and her eyes darted about the room as if he had just threatened to eat her firstborn.

"Don't be nervous." He lowered himself into a crouch in front of her.

She dropped her sponge and scurried back a few feet. "Gaol Aig an Righ."

He wanted to correct her. To tell her to just call him Izkander for crying out loud. But that was indecorous. And it wasn't what Mirri wanted. "I don't care about the manner of exit. The roof is fine. Any help at all would be much appreciated."

Finally, she pointed with a wrinkled finger down the hall. He followed that way for a while and got lost again, then asked another servant. And another. Finally, he came upon an old man repairing some mortar in the hall who just led him down to the main entrance.

Izkander wanted to go to the stables to visit Squirt. He wanted to make sure the grain shipment they had secretly finagled from Jahmil had arrived. He wanted to pick a few bouquets of those red wildflowers, one for Mirri and one to give to his mother when he saw her later that day.

He wasn't two steps out of the door when a pain, like hot iron seized both his wrists and drove him to his knees.

Izkander retreated back inside the threshold and pressed his back against the wall, breathing hard. How in Jahannam was he supposed to do anything for Mirri if he couldn't even go outside without her?

But if his wrists were wrapped in searing pain, then hers probably were too. His stomach stabbed and contracted. He couldn't do anything right. Why was he so stupid?

Izkander turned and rushed back inside. Using the pain in his wrists as a beacon, he wandered the halls, searching for the place it hurt the least. Waves of needles pricked his skin, and his heart was cold and heavy. What if he found her with Urramach? What if she was kissing him again? Allah, he didn't think he could handle it.

Cold logic and his own pride told him that if he found just such a scene, then that was it. He would drag Mirri back with him to Eayima and let his umi do what needed doing to break the bond. Then, he would just tell Mirri what he knew about the traitor and let her handle the situation as she saw fit. If she was so duplicitous that she would run off to be with Urramach after the evening they had just shared, she wasn't someone he ought to give his love to.

That was logic. And logic was a joke. Because the thought of leaving Mirri—of never seeing her again—hurt even worse than the stab of betrayal thinking that she would never be loyal to him. And that thought—*that* fact—terrified him. He would stay even if she wasn't loyal and let her tear his heart to pieces over and over for eternity. How long would he be able to tolerate it before he snapped and cut the golden-eyed weasel into small chunks and fed them to Squirt?

A shift in the fabric of a deep blue curtain caught his eye. As he approached, the pain in his wrists faded to nothing and the bright. red light dimmed to its usual soft gold.

He stopped when he was within a finger's breadth of the curtain and rested his shoulder against the wall. He opened his mouth to speak, but his tongue felt stiff and dry. He wiggled it about and gave a long exhale, trying to force out his excess tension.

"Did I ever tell you about that time I was ironing my curtains and fell out of the window?"

The curtain rustled.

He cleared his throat and kicked one foot behind him. "I once wrote a story about a ripped curtain. It went through a lot of drafts."

Another rustle. A peek of toes out of the bottom. "Was it any good?"

He smirked. "It was long-winded."

A muffled sigh.

Izkander checked his fingernails. "I got a thousand of these. I can go all night."

The toes disappeared, and the curtain pulled open, revealing a tired-eyed Mirri sitting on the obsidian tile. She didn't look at him, staring off into nothing. "Did you have a good shower?"

"A bit lonely, but what are you gonna do?"

"I would have joined you," she said softly, her eyes still unfocused.

He smiled and wiggled his eyebrows. "Next time. I'm holding you to that."

She glanced at him, little lines between her eyes. "A little water is all it takes to make you shiny again, huh?"

"Do you like the new digs?" He stood up straight and brushed the sleeves.

"Crisp." She leaned her head to the side. "Handsome."

"That goes without saying." He offered her his hand.

She accepted and pulled herself to her feet, still leaning back against the wall, then let go and brushed off her drakonte-skin pants. "Did you come looking for food? I... got distracted. I'm sorry."

The word *distracted* stung. *Distracted... with Urramach.*

Izkander smiled and rolled his shoulders. "It's a good thing you've got this whole queen gig locked down because you have no future as a waitress."

"I suppose that's true. Though if Maron hadn't died, the siblings of the Ah-nis Na righ end up in the hatchery with the Subsidiary. I suppose I would fare better there."

His guts twisted, and he set a hand on her shoulder. "Don't do that."

"Do what?" The lines on her face deepened.

"Put yourself down like that. You are going to be the best queen Fyre has ever had. And I should know. I'm constantly around royalty."

"With you here, I won't have to do a thing." She gave him a small smile that didn't reach her eyes and brushed her hands across the shoulders of his kingly attire. "And either way, I am content with my lot."

He bit his lip and glanced out of the window where the crest of the First Moon was rising over the golden field, the snowy mountains a radiant backdrop. "You know, you never got around to answering my question about that."

"Oh?"

"What happens if you're discontent?"

"Oh." She turned away from him and rubbed her arm. "Same as anything else. Death and the return of my ungrateful soul to the Origin where I will suffer eternity with an angry Flame."

He looked down and kicked his foot against the stone. "I find it hard to believe that the same entity that created Fajar could be so cruel."

"Is it cruel to take back life given to someone who is ungrateful for it?"

"Absolutely. If that were the worldwide policy, most kids wouldn't make it past two for how readily their mothers would be murdering them."

A light breath left her throat. A laugh? "Then perhaps Fajar took all the goodness when she broke free, and the rest of the descendants are watched all the more closely so we don't do the same."

"That's an interesting theory. What do you think would happen if Fajar were to go into the Origin?"

She looked at him over her shoulder, one slender eyebrow raised high. "There's a story about that. A prophecy, maybe? A legend."

"I'm all ears."

"Why?"

"Why?" he echoed incredulously. "Why wouldn't I be?"

She shrugged. "You haven't asked a lot of questions since you got here. And it's a story only told during the *gealach foghair* when the soldiers are very drunk."

"I want to understand everything about you. And that means understanding everything about Fyre, too. So tell me. Please."

"Okay, Gaol Aig an Righ. There is a story of a righ. The one who would raise our people up. Who would let the Eternal Flame burn freely by returning the lost pieces to the Origin. The Wisdom, which is your Rukh. The Heart, which is missing. And The Flame, which never left. But it's just the drunken hope of tired soldiers and desperate righ. Though my father thought it would be Maron."

"Why? What was so special about Maron? Other than he made you laugh, which puts me firmly on his side."

"My father said he was his heart. His shining boy. His one and only and the true heir to the Flame." She dipped her head, and the shadows cast long across her sad eyes. "Maybe he thought that would be enough? Though the Flame clearly disagreed."

Izkander was quiet for a moment, her words pooling in the back of his brain and blending together with the incongruous story he'd gotten from his mother. "What happened to Maron? I mean, which one of his discontent actions caused what happened to him?"

She stared into nothing for a moment, then snapped her eyes to his. Straightening her shoulders, she said, "No one will tell me. All I know is Urramach said it was something egregious and that my mother says it is too painful to talk about."

Izkander scoffed. His tongue wanted to leap on the whole Urramach subject, but he forced it down. More festering in the pits of his stomach.

"They don't think that might be something you of all people really ought to know? Can't you just order them to tell you?"

"We are not supposed to talk about the Fallen Ones. They are not supposed to exist."

Izkander clenched his teeth and tried to swallow his next question. He didn't want to disrespect her laws or her. He also didn't want to keep quiet when he might be able to help her find the answers to questions that had been burning in her brain for years.

"If you knew what happened to Maron," Izkander said, "wouldn't that help to protect you from the same fate?"

"I have asked." She shook her head, her hair rippling in burning waves. "I have asked... but not commanded. How do you command your own mother to speak of things that hurt her heart? And Urramach..." Her face scrunched tight, and she clenched a fist, turning away from him. "I can say nothing to him these days without it turning into a mess."

Izkander leaned his back against the wall and crossed his heels. He entwined his arms over his chest and gazed levelly at the rising moon. "You came out here to talk to him, right?"

He bit the side of his tongue. Curse his voice for that stupid quaver.

She glanced sideways at him, eyes half-concealed by her lashes. "I was honest about that."

"Can I ask why?"

She didn't move at first, everything tight and poised like a snake waiting to strike from the brush. Her chin tilted slowly up. "Your father gave me some advice, and I was trying to act on it."

He sighed and shook his head. That could mean so many things. His old man was a cornucopia of advice. And some of it even made sense. "You don't want to talk to me about him, do you?"

"I want to talk to you about it more than anyone in both worlds. But I don't want to hurt you." She groaned and hid her face in her hands.

He ran his tongue back and forth over his bottom lip, swallowing one comment after another until he finally landed on what he really needed to say. "It hurts me more this way."

She pressed her hands against her eyes so hard, they whitened at the knuckles. "If I tell you... will you still rub my back?"

He turned his eyes to her and showed a soft, lopsided smile. "I promised I always would, didn't I?"

Her hands drifted down to her sides, and her whole body went rigid. She stared at him, face as pale as the fourth moon. "I came out here to tell Urramach to go away and that I didn't want him," she said, words gurgling out in a breathless rush. "But when he showed up, I got all confused, and his words wrapped around me so I couldn't breathe, so I didn't say what I wanted to say, and then he kissed me, and I froze, and he said he loved me and left. And then I pulled my hair and sat behind the curtain and tried my hardest not to die of discontent."

The soft clatter of a servant walking past them down the hallway pounded in his ears. He waited, saying nothing as the old woman with the wash bucket passed by, all the way until she disappeared at the other end of the hall and they were alone again.

"Do you still want him?"

"No."

He raked a hand slowly through his hair. "Then why were you confused?"

"He knows me, Izkander." Her face twisted, but she kept her eyes on him. "We've had so many talks together. I've told him so many things. He knows how to trip me up. To make me feel bad. To make me feel good. And he talks so quickly, I... I get lost. And all I could think about was how upset you were at me. How I ruined everything. And he made me believe that was true."

Pain tightened across his chest, his lungs aching and constricted in these clothes. He wrapped his arms around her shoulders and drew her close. "You didn't ruin anything. Don't be crazy."

She melted into him, hands grasping his shirt as she rubbed her face into his chest. "I tried to tell him. I wanted to tell him. I opened my mouth, but he covered it up."

Izkander kissed her hair, then pressed his cheek against the top of her head, tightening the embrace. Only then did the last of the lingering pain in his wrists finally subside. He breathed out a sigh. "Urramach is tenacious. And manipulative." He set his lips against her forehead. "I'm not upset with you." Pulling back, he looked into her eyes. Then he lifted her chin and kissed her. "I need to go to Elm. Will you go with me?"

"Elm?" Her pink lips tightened. "The birthplace of djinn and the abusers of our first ancestor, Najima? They not only sneer at our legitimacy as a nation of Qaf, but they also refuse to put us on their maps. Why do you need to go there?"

"I need to visit their library."

Her face smoothed except for a quirky smile. "The library?"

"What's so funny?" he scoffed and folded his arms. "I library from time to time."

"Often enough to turn the word library into a verb. I underestimated you."

He pushed out his bottom lip and nodded. "That is a dangerous thing to do, missy."

A bit of the sadness washed from her eyes, replaced by dim sparkles. "I need to leave orders for my generals and advisors for the morning's agenda. I will be back before then?"

"I expect so. I just need a quick chat with King Chupkin so I can get permission to find what I need."

"King… Chupkin?"

"Sorry, Zayne. King Zayne."

She pouted and looked down at her feet. "Can I go in my armor, or do you think I should put my diplomatic attire back on?"

"Whatever makes you happy, pretty girl." Unable to resist, he stroked the curve of her waist down to her hip. "I'm happy to lust after you either way."

She glared at him but giggled. "Then armor it is. And I'm going to wear boots. My muddiest boots. There is nothing sacred about that place."

"Hey, don't cause trouble. I need a favor. And you know how princes can be about their damn rugs."

She pushed her lips to one side, then stood on her tiptoes and leaned in so her lips nearly brushed his. "Don't worry. I'll be decorous."

"Indubitably." He pecked her lips and pulled back, then reconsidered and kissed her for real—the way he wanted to be kissed. Soft and humid and hot and breathy. He yearned for the sensation inside that only came from kissing her, from sharing one breath.

Izkander leaned back to look into her eyes, lacing both his hands around her waist. "You *are* going to tell Urramach, right?"

Her smile faded, and she dropped her gaze. "Yes... though I may need you by my side."

Nodding, he kissed her forehead. "Eternally, Ah-nis Na Righ."

CHAPTER THIRTY

MIRRI

Izkander's warm fire curled around her, and she breathed in every last drop she could get. It smelled so much of the Flame and Fajar and him that it filled every piece of her being. So much so, that as her booted feet landed on what sounded like a bustling thoroughfare, and the shouts of djinn surrounded their sudden arrival, she could do nothing but lean in and catch the last of the smell with her eyes closed.

She pulled away with a sigh as the muggy air of Elm enveloped her, suppressing the heat in her skin and coating it in a thin mist. They stood on a crisscrossed path of light gray stone that led straight to the epicenter of the city, the gargantuan King's Palace. There, King *Chupkin*—whatever that meant—sequestered himself away from the people he was supposed to serve. If he had been a descendant of Marduk, he would have burned alive long ago. But his line followed the more liberal and less pure race of Ramliabad who cared far more about themselves than their people.

The evidence lay before her in the garishly overdone state building rising from the streets before them. One-quarter of the palace was larger than her own castle in Fyre, and every gem-covered doorknob and window pane could have fed her people for months. Unnecessary. Wasteful. But in the end, what could she say? His people held all of Qaf in its shadow, djinn so distrustful of others, they needed the King's magic to make them behave. It was for this reason alone, the people of Elm seemed to lack for nothing. The opulence and gluttony also made the insecure part of her feel like a terrible righ.

She gritted her teeth and yanked herself back as a dark-green djinn woman with ridiculously high hair hurried past with a snarl.

Why did Izkander need to come here? Especially when it was the middle of the night in Fyre and the place he wanted to go was a library. Elm was known for being the city that never slept. Everything was always open, or it never was. But he had looked so earnest and had forgiven her so easily about Urramach, what else could she do but follow him to the ends of Qaf?

She groaned and took up Izkander's hand, missing the cold, dry air of Fyre and Zabriya. At least in Elm's balmy climate, her heart would be warmer for a little longer. If not wetter.

"Are you sure you want to visit the library?" she asked, trying to sound playful, though it came off like a child wearing itchy shoes. "Books have no legs, no eyes, or free will. Any tomb you're searching for will still be here come Fyran morning."

"Don't be nervous." He started down the path toward the expansive palace complex. "Chupkin loves me. It won't take but a moment."

"I'd ask if everyone in all of flaming Qaf loves you, but aside from my father and… well, it seems to hold true."

He sighed dramatically. "It's exhausting being so popular."

"Alright, alright. Deflate the ego and take me to the palace so you can show off."

"You are one lucky lady." He pulled her closer, slipping her arm around his as they walked. "There are women crying all over Qaf about this thing with you and I."

"This *thing*?" She turned her head and pulled her chin back with a harrumph. "And unless those women can wield a sword as well as I can, it would be best not to mention them around me, hm?"

She tossed him a sharp smile, ignoring an ugly stare from a passing djinn man. Or at least, she tried to ignore it, but it slopped into her stomach like fresh lava. The reserved, almost prissy nature of Shihala was one thing—it kept the people there from behaving too poorly on account of being spiritually *above it all* while not actually caring about any other country—but Elmarans were proud of their judgemental heritage and permanent sneers. And the second they saw her drakonte eyes, they were more than happy to share just exactly how they felt.

Mirri pressed herself closer to Izkander and pulled him along to hasten their arrival. She breathed a sigh of relief when her feet found their way up the expansive staircase that led to jeweled doors. She curled her toes as she walked even though it hurt.

"Do you think I should mention who I am?" she asked Izakdner. "Or keep it to myself? Would that be an act of war?"

"What?"

"Espionage."

"Don't be silly." Izkander walked up to one of the many armed guards standing in attendance at the enormous double doors and introduced her and himself in a loud and confident voice, requesting an audience with the most powerful king in Qaf as if it were owed to him and should have been given to him yesterday.

The green-skinned guard didn't respond. He went and spoke to his superior, who then went in through a small door to the side of the main entrance. Izkander and Mirri were left waiting for a long time, as courtiers, lawyers, and judges bustled through the palace complex all around them. The Elmarans leered at them as they passed, some stopping in their tracks to do so. Everybody she saw had that natural deep-green skin. Izkander and she stood out like plague sores, even to those who hadn't caught sight of her eyes.

Finally, a little *agha* with a heavy white beard came through the double doors, his tall black turban almost brushing the frame, and led them inside. Izkander held her arm tightly as they followed through the serpentine halls. Every wall was draped in finery—tapestries, paintings, displays of crystal and fire, and a range of weapons going back centuries.

They were brought up a staircase twice as wide as her own bedroom, fashioned of stone so white it seemed to glow under her boots, and twice as tall as her own castle. When they reached the top, the *agha* asked them to wait and passed through another set of tremendous doors which were carved with a Seal of Elm that glowed faintly green with shifting djinn fire.

Another long wait and even Izkander had begun to fidget. Pink light shimmered on the surface of his eyes.

"Maybe we should just go," she whispered to him, jutting her chin up at the next glaring djinn who passed. "It's not like the books won't be here later. What's the rush?"

He bit his lip. "Is it okay if I explain that to you after I find it?"

The lava in her stomach started to boil, little pops of hot air bursting through a crusty black layer that had formed on top. The large doors at the other end of the room opened before she could inquire further, and a suave-looking man with black hair, matching eyes, and surprisingly cool-blue skin brisked into the room.

The man straightened one of the cuffs of his sharp black suit and stepped towards them. "Ah-Nis na Righ," he said, tipping his head to her.

She bobbed her head back.

"Sheikh Izkander. What can I do for you?"

"You're not Chupkin," said Izkander.

The corner of the man's lips tipped in an almost-imperceptible sneer. "His Majesty King Zayne is not currently receiving diplomatic envoys. My name is Alwazir al'Aezam Rehan Huriya. And I have two-and-a-half degrees, so if you please." He made an open gesture towards the door.

Izkander's eyes widened, the pink deepening. "I'm not a diplomatic envoy. Chup... Zayne is a friend of the family."

"Appreciated, but I fear that does not change His Majesty's circumstances." The Grand vizier walked past them, his steps soft on a massive and colorful rug woven with such intricacy, it could be studied for days and not give away all its secrets.

The grand vizier took a seat behind a large stone desk at the end of the room. He tented his fingers and pushed until his knuckles cracked. "What can I do for you two?"

For once, Mirri was grateful for the harsh reprimands her father gave her telling her to behave more like a righ. To hold her tongue, look into the eyes of those speaking to you, and swallow the first three comments on her tongue. Elmarans were the worst—litigious, fastidious, stuck-up, and utterly convinced of their own superiority. This grand vizier, though he wore the pale blue skin of a Shihalan and Vespar, clearly had Elm in his soul.

Mirri went to square her shoulders, but they were already locked into place, tense and straight. "Our apologies for the unexpected visit. I know the arrival of rulers from foreign countries can be a strain. But Sheikh Izkander is correct. We are not here on a diplomatic mission. We simply wish to use the library of archives your country so generously holds for Qaf. Is it possible for you to help us with this very pressing matter?"

The grand vizier's eyes focused on her, his face as smooth as river stone and his eyes pure black with a pale sheen of copper.

"I'm afraid you'll have to be more specific." He leaned back in his seat and crossed his legs. "Our kingdom is home to several hundred libraries and archives."

"The one that holds old contracts," said Izkander. "Chup—King Zayne shut it down when he took the throne."

"You mean the Immortal Royal Archives." The vizier glanced at Izkander like he was a fly before turning back to Mirri. "They were never *shut down*. Their access has been drastically restricted after a few incidents involving Qafian nationals abusing their privilege. I'm afraid no one except for licensed Elmaran judges are permitted access to the Archives, including the noble houses of every other kingdom in Qaf."

Mirri stared at the cool mask of the vizier, matching it with one of her own. "You do not have access to a library under your charge, even as the Grand Vizier of Elm?"

"I am the Supreme Judge of the High Court. Of course, I have access to it."

"Then I don't need to hear about the Elmaran judges and their subjective licensing. I am willing to accept you as our guide."

"Forgive me for being obtuse." He drummed his fingers on the desk. "The answer is no."

"But I'm friends with the king. He'd let me in in a heartbeat." Izkander stammered, an expression on his face like he'd just seen a drakonte sing a sea shanty.

The vizier gave Izkander a brief and subtle, but utterly withering look.

Izkander's eyes bulged, shocked and confused.

So much for everyone in Qaf liking him.

The large doors of the office swung open, and a man with long jowls poked his head inside. "Alwazir al'Aezam, your wife is here."

The Vizier took a very expensive timepiece from his jacket pocket and glanced at the crystal face. "Tell her I will be with her in two degrees."

"Yes, sir." The massive, elaborately carved door shut with a powerful boom.

"That's a beautiful chain you have for your timepiece," Mirri said with a nod. "And I wasn't asking for permission. You will take me to the archives."

He set an elbow on his desk and ran his fingers over a beautiful white silk runner. "And why exactly would I be inclined to do that?"

"Because Fyre is not a kingdom in Qaf, so the rules don't apply."

A tiny line formed at the edge of his lips, almost a smirk. "Fyre may not be one of the Nine, but it is in Qaf, and it is a kingdom."

"You are incorrect. But the Elmarans have a very limited set of knowledge from which they teach their students," Mirri said, allowing a line to form in her own lips. "Fyre is not in Qaf. Fyre is in the Origin. Qaf is also in the Origin. But they have nothing to do with one another other than that."

"Your religious convictions are fascinating but legally immaterial."

Mirri had no answer for that, and Izkander's shiny smile told her he wouldn't say any more than he already had. But it wasn't her religion she was speaking about. It was the truth. And her lineage was as old as this *Chupkin's* and far older still.

"I will remind you that the Immortal Archives were created by two immortals, not one. And both gave their blood to build it. As such, as a direct descendant of Marduk and the wise Queen Najima of Elm, I have as much right to access the Archives as King Zayne, himself."

"Perhaps there was a time when that was true, but the lineage of Najima has not had any official status in Eastern Elm since the Schism that divided our kingdoms over two thousand years ago. Perhaps you would have better luck in Western Elm where they still hold your Najima in high regard, except... that's right. They squandered all of their archives, didn't they?"

Mirri allowed another line to crease her face, but she suppressed the urge to grab his arm and burn his flesh with the Flame. "Thank you for making what I need to do very clear. I appreciate that in a grand vizier. The rulers of Fyre are the rightful heirs to the throne of Western Elm. And while we have not bothered with the country because it is so close to… yours, I am happy to call on the Flame beneath it and take back what is mine so that I can read in your library."

The skin around the man's obsidian eyes tightened. "Were this an official diplomatic meeting, I would be forced to take that as a declaration of war."

Izkander's eyes widened. He leaned in close to her. "You're not declaring war again, are you?"

Mirri kept her eyes on the vizier. She had meant her threat. And she could fulfill it, though it would take some time to call the wrath of the Flame so far from home. Still, Elm was part of Qaf and Qaf *was* part of the Origin, which meant its veins of lava—even little ones—ran under this city, too. The Flame would hear her call.

"That depends entirely on whether we get an escort to the Archives." She leaned in and let out a full smile. "How much trouble would it cause if a river of fire opened up in the middle of your palace?"

The only good things that had happened to Fyre since she became righ were because of things Izkander did. If she couldn't do this one thing for him, then what was her purpose? Why was she even righ? And if she couldn't even fight for him with Urramach, when would she start fighting for him? She bent over and removed each of her boots, then plunked them on the ground in front of the vizier. Even so far from home, she could feel the faint pulse of the Origin beneath the earth, warming her toes, however faintly.

The vizier stared at her, his keen eyes without fear or any expression at all, but it was clear he understood her threat—he was one of the few djinn in all of Qaf who knew exactly what the righs of Fyre were capable of.

He set his thumb and finger to his cheek, the intensity of his stare betraying his casual pose. "Are you certain you would declare war on the most powerful kingdom in both worlds?"

"If this were a diplomatic mission, I would tell you I was absolutely certain. Are *you* certain you want your palace destroyed and an international war started because you refused to give the Ah-nis Na Righ of your sister nation a library pass? Especially with your wife in the palace, so close to all the trouble?"

The vizier tapped his fingers on the desk in slow succession. *Click, click, click, click.* He glanced at the door, then took out his timepiece and sighed when he glanced at the crystal.

He snapped his eyes to hers, displeasure clear in the minutiae of his face. "As a diplomatic courtesy, I will allow fifteen degrees with an official escort. And all requests for copies must be approved by the Master Archivist."

She bowed her head in the haughty way her father had also taught her, her eyes never leaving the vizier's face though a swath of joy burned inside her. "You are wise and serve your people well. The kingdom of Fyre thanks you. And your wife is a blessed woman."

He stood and walked around the desk towards them, then returned her haughty, little head bow like a professional. "It was a pleasure to meet you, Ah-nis Na Righ. Allah's blessings upon you and your people. My assistant will secure you an official escort to the Archives."

She picked up her boots, making a show of tossing them over her shoulder instead of putting them on her feet so her threat remained. With one last practiced look at the vizier's practiced expression, she took Izkander's hand and followed the man with the long jowls through the door into the hallway.

When they were out of the room and clipping down a hallway, she let out a sigh. A wash of jittery nerves raced to the ends of her fingers and into the curl of her toes. "Ha."

Izkander grabbed her, picked her up, and twirled her quickly in the air. "You are a fire goddess."

"Only a third," she giggled, lit by his smile. "You're my boy. I will always fight for you."

His eyes filled with golden mist, his dimples as deep as she had ever seen them. He kissed her, deep and passionate, and enough to make her melt. Then, he snatched her hand and jogged after the squat man who lumbered down the massive hallway without them.

"Izkander," she said between breaths, squeezing his fingers. "Why did I just almost declare war on the most powerful nation in Qaf for a trip to the library?"

"Because you're the most wonderful and trusting girlfriend ever."

His answer dampened some of the happiness and pride bursting within her, but she had already come this far following him blindly, and he hadn't yet let her down. "I think Fire Mate is a step beyond girlfriend, don't you?"

"You are beyond anything I have ever known," he said, a seriousness in his voice she hadn't expected. "And I will tell you everything as soon as I find that contract. Okay?"

Mirri sighed, the thrum of fire and blood in her veins matching beat for beat with their hurried footsteps. "Okay."

CHAPTER THIRTY-ONE

Izkander

The Archives of Elm were even larger and more serpentine than Izkander's mother had told him. Then again, some six-thousand years of Qafian history were contained on those shelves, so he wasn't sure what he had expected. The shelves were all on wheels so they could be pushed aside to make room to look between them, like hangers in a wardrobe. Twenty-five stories high with a footprint that went for eternity in every direction, Izkander could have wandered the Archives the rest of his life and never found anything.

Their official escort was none other than the master archivist herself, a burly woman with a rough, egg-shaped face and shoulder pads almost as wide as the hallways. He had to ask her about seven-thousand questions to even find the section that held Fyran documents— on its own more books than he had ever seen in his life—and several thousand more to get to a section from the current century.

From there, he was on his own. The grand vizier had only given them fifteen degrees in the archives, so he skimmed one scroll after another and tossed them aside in a hasty pile. Mirri left to take advantage of her hard-fought time in the library on her own, saying she wanted to see if she could find anything more on the Rukh and the Flame.

Izkander had almost given up when he finally came upon a section devoted to the now defunct Righ of Fyre, ol' Chomp Hair. Even then, he only knew it was the correct righ because of a document announcing first Maron's birth, then Mirri's.

Most of the documents, however, related to trade agreements with Shihala, who depended on the Seal of Elm just as much as any other djinn nation. That was until he came upon a slip of paper too small to be rolled. It read:

On the ninety-seventh day of the three-hundred-and-forty-ninth pass of the Seventh Moon in the year of the Thirtieth Righ, Urramach Salach DeNaga agrees to pass in secret a Goblet of Origin to Prionnsa Maron Naga, Ri Tichd Ah-nis Na Righ of Fyre, to be drunk by the Prionnsa in the presence of the Royal Court. In return, Ah-nis Na Righ Fenz Naga of Fyre, the Ri Tichd Fa Chomhair Righ and agrees to allow said Urramach unfettered access to Bana-Phrionnsa Mirri Naga of Fyre.

Both parties had signed at the bottom of the little slip of parchment alongside Elm's unbreakable seal.

This was it.

Izkander's joy was short-lived when he glanced down the aisle at Mirri. He had found what he was looking for. It really existed. Which meant the story his mother had told him was true. And that meant he had to tell Mirri.

He handed the letter to the official escort so that a copy could be made by the Master Archivist. To his relief, the Archivist returned with the completed copies post-haste and with no further questions. When Izkander had the official copy in his pocket, Izkander and Mirri were guided from the Archives. Some fifty guards escorted them to the edge of the palace complex, their eyes trained on Mirri until Izkander summoned his fire and took them through to the clifftop in Thrace.

It was night in Ard, but the sky was cloudless and the moon full, bathing them in a shimmering white light bright enough to read by. He had been hoping the contract would be a little more damning, but after reading it, he wasn't sure what it meant.

What was the Goblet of Origin? And why was it being passed around in secret? Could it have been what killed Maron, or was he completely off? Maybe Mirri had been right, and he should have been asking more questions about Fyre. But before he hadn't known what he was looking for well enough to ask. Now, he had plenty of questions.

Mirri stood at his side, watching him with wide eyes. Expectant.

Smiling nervously, Izkander took the folded paper from his pocket and tapped it against his fingers a few times.

"You are making me nervous," she said, scrunching her nose and squishing her lips to one side. "And not just because you wanted to visit a library."

He sighed and bit his lip, then scrunched his eyes closed and thrust the paper toward her.

She pinched the parchment with two fingers and tugged it from his grasp. "Is there anything you want me to know before I read this? You look the worst I've ever seen. And we fought a monster and faced your mother together."

"I just want you to remember that all I want is to help. Okay?"

She frowned, looked at him a moment longer, then flipped up the paper and read it. He held his breath the entire time, his eyes unable to settle on anything. The moon, the ocean, the twist of grass in the soft wind, or the expression on her face. He especially did not want to look at that because the temptation was too great to analyze every twist and curve, every twitch.

"Why... did you know this was in the Archives?" she asked, at last, her voice quiet against the *shashoosh* of waves.

He rested his hand on the guard of his sword, squeezing tightly and then letting go. "My mother told me about it. She resided a few years in Elm, and most of that time she spent in the Archives. She was studying up on Shihalan contracts, which I guess led her to Fyre. That particular contract she found weird, there being so few sealed contracts from your nation, so she remembered it."

"Okay..." Mirri's head was nodding. "Okay." She folded the piece of paper and held it between her flat palms. "But why are you showing it to me?"

"Why am I showing it to you?" He lifted his eyebrows. "You don't find it interesting?"

"Of course, I find it interesting... but worth a middle-of-the-night trip to a country I had to threaten with war? I disagree. It seems..." She sighed. "Superfluous."

"It does not seem superfluous to me."

"If you're trying to hurt my feelings, then it is not superfluous at all. But I don't see how it changes any of my decisions. Are you trying to hurt my feelings?"

"How could you even ask me that?" He rubbed a hand over his eyes and shook his head. "Look at the date, Mirri. Does that date mean anything to you?"

"What are you trying to insinuate?" Mirri asked, a flicker of fire in her scarlet irises. "About my family? About Urramach?"

"I'm not insinuating anything. The reason I needed to go to Elm in the middle of the night is I did not want to insinuate. I didn't write that date."

"Then what did your *umi* insinuate about it that made you want to go and fetch?"

His ribs felt like they were caving in, stabbing into his lungs. He swallowed hard and forbade himself from bending into the pain. "Your father and Urramach made a deal about you and your brother, something neither of them ever told you about. And the deal took place the same year your brother died. How could I let something like that pass me by without going to try to confirm or deny it?"

"You want it confirmed or denied? Fine." She flicked the paper open and held it up. "Yes, my fa... the Fa Chomhair Righ and Councilman Urramach made a deal concerning my brother that I didn't know about. Hence the hurt feelings that you claimed you didn't want. And yes, the date coincides with the day Maron disobeyed the Flame and became a Fallen One. What is the point?"

"With the very day?" His eyes widened, and he shook his head hard. "What if this is the reason he's dead?"

She scoffed. "The Origin doesn't kill the true descendants of Marduk. It strengthens us. And it is given to all the righ before they ascend to the throne. I've drunken from the Goblet of Origin, and I'm not a pool of flesh and lava on the floor."

"Can you explain to me what the point of this kind of deal would be then?" His eyes kept drifting to the edge of the cliff. Why did he suddenly have the urge to fling himself off the side? "If drinking the Origin is so normal, why make a clandestine contract about it? Why should Urramach have given it to him in secret?"

"I don't know." Mirri pressed her lips together, the flicker in her eyes now a full flame. "Maybe there were rumors. Discontent fomenting in the Council."

"What kind of rumors?"

She glared at him, then turned to look at the cliffside. "Fifteen righ ago, the descendant of Fa Chomhair Gòrach and next Ah-nis Na Righ stood in front of Fyre's people and drank the Flame for the induction ceremony." She snapped her head back to look at him, her hair swishing side to side. "His flesh melted in front of the entire kingdom, and civil unrest ensued. For how dare the righ try to ascend an untrue descendant of Marduk?"

"An untrue descendant?" Izkander echoed and looked down at her bare feet. He couldn't remember her ever having looked at him like that before. Like she was hoping he would burst into flames. "You mean like a bastard?"

Her lips curled. "Yes, I mean that. And Maron was not. But if a councilman expressed discontent to Fa Chomhair, he would see fit to prove Maron before the induction to ease their nerves about another civil war. A mild formality that Urramach took advantage of to be close to me." She flinched before regaining her composure. "And you've made your displeasure with him very well known."

He shook his head. "This isn't about him. Or me."

"Are you sure? Because the two people you seem to dislike of everyone in all of Qaf are the Fa Chomhair and Urramach. And now you throw this in my face, so I am wounded by them both."

"I'm not throwing it in your face." Izkander gripped his stomach and pushed back the acidic bile trying to rise from the sting of her accusation. The one his mother had warned him she would make. "And if it was just a formality to quell unsubstantiated rumors, then why make a secret contract? Why not do it publicly? And why did he die that day?"

"Watch your tone, Izkander ibn Bakr." She twisted sharply to face him. "My brother was a true descendant. And he was the shining star of my father's affections. If the Fa Chomhair felt the need to challenge the bloodline to appease his petty councilmen, he probably did it as a secret so Maron wouldn't find out and be heartbroken. Your father loves you, you should understand."

"I don't." He pressed his face into his hand. "If somebody called me a bastard and there was some simple and very public way it could be proven otherwise, I would want as many people watching as possible. And so would my father."

"And he would get that at the induction ceremony. We can't all be as perfect as you and your floating family. Fajar doesn't grace Fyre with her presence. The Flame does."

He set his hands at his sides, clenching and unclenching fists just to feel the sting in his knuckles with every stretch of skin. "The day your father decided to secretly test him, he died."

"Because he was discontent."

Fire was rising in Izkander's gut, mixing with the bile and the ache, and fanned by her cold stares and colder accusations. "What if it's all nonsense?"

"Excuse me?"

"What if the stuff about content and discontent and all your rules are nonsense? What if none of them are true?"

"You think Maron melting by divine will is nonsense?" She stared hard at him, eyes flaring and skin visibly steaming in the muggy air. Then she held her wrist up. "Is this real enough for you? Or do you think it is all subterfuge? That somehow my kingdom and I—who never asked for you to come along and mess with our business—tricked you into thinking the burn from this bond is real?"

He clenched his teeth. "I'm not saying there isn't magic in the Origin, or Fajar, or the drakonte, or you. I'm not saying that. I'm just saying what if your ancestors have been manipulating the belief in that magic for so many thousands of years, that you've ended up with a giant stack of laws that only exist to control you? What if what's written has no bearing on the true will of your Flame?"

"Then my life, my religion, my family, and my kingdom are all a joke. But you love jokes, don't you?"

He flinched at her insult. "No. That's not what I'm saying." He lifted the painful circle of fire on his wrist. "This is real. The flame put this here. And your father, and Urramach, and you, and all these people who know the laws so well can't explain why the Origin would choose someone like me."

He looked into her eyes, but they'd taken on that smothered-ember quality. Eyes that threatened to burn.

Izkander looked away. "Maybe it doesn't really care what you eat for dinner. That's all I'm saying. Doesn't it seem a little weird that it would care about that?"

"The Flame gave me my life and gives me laws to ensure I take care of it properly. Is it weird that your mother made you eat your vegetables growing up?"

"My mother never threatened to burn out my insides if I didn't. She never forced me to live a gray half-life filled with torment because I constantly have to be content with everything." He ground his teeth hard enough that they made a noise. "The drakonte were fine in Orkeshi. Healthier than the ones here. Doesn't *that* seem weird?"

"No," she snapped, the gold wrapping around her arms now glowing orange with heat. "What seems weird is that you claimed you wanted to stay and do something good for my kingdom. *Our* kingdom. And yet you seem Flame-bent on burning it and its rulers to the ground. You love Shihala so much? Fine, take the drakonte and go live with them. I'll be a pool of lava either way."

"I don't give a damn about Shihala!" He punched himself in the thigh because there was nothing else to punch. "And I have been to the Origin, or as close as anyone can get. You took me there, remember? And it felt good and right. It did not feel like the petty creature I assumed it would be based on all your laws."

He turned away from her, throbbing pressure rolling down his spine like sharp rocks. "And for the record, it is getting really old being accused of wanting to murder you every time I dare to question anything."

"*Marduk thoir maitheanas dhomh,*" Mirri's face crumpled, and she looked away. "I took you into the Origin. I took you... discontent."

She pulled free the light sword she kept on her belt and stabbed it into the ground. Then she knelt and slid her finger on the blade, so a flower of red bloomed on her skin.

"*Tha mi a 'tabhann iobairt, Marduk,*" Mirri prayed, then sat back.

She lifted up her bare foot and pressed the blood of her finger to the bottom where the glimmering tattoo of a flame colored her skin, much like the one Fajar had given him.

He wanted to ask what she was doing, but her strange actions and stranger words, both performed with religious solemnity, had rendered him still. An inferno raged inside of him for everything he had said and every cruel thing she had accused him of being. He wanted to run away, but his feet were glued to the spot. Never mind the tether on his wrist.

The tattoo soaked up the blood streaming from her finger and flared red in a small blaze that crackled the air. She cringed and waited, eventually opening one eye and then the other. She expelled a sigh of relief, then rested her head on the hilt of her sword.

"I am sorry for my discontent with your words," she said over the soft and ever-present *shashoosh* of waves. "It is hard for a child to hear such things of her father and of her closest confidant. But I understand our ways seem peculiar and distasteful to foreigners. And because I live even now before you, I know the Flame has accepted my plea and understands your naivete as well."

His lips parted. He glanced far askance then turned back to her. "What just happened?"

"Your words are treasonous and ungrateful to the Flame, and I feared for having brought you into its very heart with such thoughts in your own. So, I made supplication with a sacrifice of my own blood and admission that it was my fault, and the Flame has accepted."

He grabbed at his wrist, rubbing at the chain of fire which he had largely ignored until now, so convinced that in the end, it wouldn't matter. Firstly, because he thought he could break it, and then because he decided he wanted it. But her blood-infused supplication for his sake—the grandest form of apologizing for him and his stupidity that was possible in either world—made him feel like he wore an iron manacle.

He wanted it off.

She looked up at him, exhausted eyes widening. "You pull at your bond." She pushed herself to her feet and reached out a hand. It lingered but a moment before she dropped it. "You think I'm crazy, don't you? Or deranged? Or frightening?" There was so much hurt in her voice, each syllable cracked as she said it. "You think those things and want to leave."

He snapped his trembling jaw closed and ran his tongue over the roof of his mouth. "I think you're scared. And I think you're in denial." He sniffed hard, feeling a sting in his eyes and utterly defiant of it. "And I think you think I'm an idiot. You think I am a jealous, petty idiot who is going to get you killed and has ruined your life. And you wish you never had met me."

Her hair whipped in the breeze. Only *shashoosh, shashoosh, shashoosh* and silence.

"You ask me with one letter and a few days of knowing you to forsake my country and my god," she whispered at last. "To brush away my entire knowing and way of life. You, who has done little to understand me or my people and who makes light of it with jokes. And then, you accuse me of denial when I don't." She swallowed hard, body shivering with the next breeze. "That is not such an easy thing to ask. It is not a fair thing to ask."

"I know it isn't." He swallowed hard and wiped his dry lips. Allah, he was thirsty. "But what you ask of me isn't fair either. To blindly accept everything when my entire life is being torn to shreds so that I can be with you. My mother can't even come to visit me in Fyre. You all hate djinn. And there is a part of you that hates that part of me, too."

"And I cannot visit all of the rest of Qaf without djinn hating me." A mist formed along the rims of her eyes, evaporating quickly from the heat of her skin. "Do you really think I hate you? That I think you're an idiot djinn?"

"I think you think your way is the only way. And I think you wish I would just shut up and get with the program. Well, you know what? I'm trying." He sighed and dropped his gaze to the ocean below. "I am trying."

"If you want out," she whispered, chin tilted high towards the moon and hair a curtain of red behind her, "then fly the Rukh. Let her pass over my nation so the Origin yawns open to accept her. I read in the Archives another confirmation that it is true. I will descend and speak with the Origin and let you be free of me and Fyre. I will not be the chains you accuse me of being."

He bit his bottom lip.

I love you. It was on the tip of his tongue, but he couldn't say it. Not here. Not now.

"Did the Flame seem offended that I was there at the Origin?" he asked in as firm a voice as he could muster. "If it was, couldn't it have just killed me? Or you? Why hesitate?"

"No, it didn't seem offended." The flames reflecting in her eyes died out, leaving her usually vibrant red nearly coal-black. All the heat, too, seemed to have vanished from her skin. She shivered. "No more questions tonight, Izkander ibn Bakr." She took up her sword, the splash of blood still upon it, and held it out to him.

He looked at it then back to her darkened gaze.

"Take it. Then take me home." She pulled back and squeezed the cut on her finger so a few more drops hit the reflection of the moon that shone on the blade. "It is a trick Fa Chomhair Rhoime used to delay his Eve of Fire with his Fire Mate. My blood will let us part for half the First Moon's pass before the Flame in it fades and the bond realizes we are apart. That should be enough time for you to fly the Rukh so we may speak with the Flame if you want out."

If there was any part of his heart still holding intact, it shattered. He looked at her and wanted to say something more. To ask her, for the last time, what she really wanted.

No more questions. He was a fool and a foreigner, and all he had managed to accomplish since coming to Fyre was to insult her and breed discontent. It was clear what she wanted. And he wanted her to have what she wanted.

He took the sword. He didn't have it in him to deal with the djinn triangles, so he took one of Fajar's feathers from the pouch he kept on his belt and dropped it. Even the embrace of her fire was not enough to warm the ice inside of him.

CHAPTER THIRTY-TWO

MIRRI

THE MOMENT HIS HAND clasped around the hilt of her blade, fingers briefly brushing hers, she died inside.

He took the sword. He took the sword. He doesn't want you. He never did.

Mirri spun deftly away from him on the ramparts, the frozen wind whipping her skin and sinking into her bones for the first time. She didn't look back. What was the point? It would be another memory of his face she would have to scrub from her mind for the next seven centuries. If she lived that long. And she didn't care if she did.

She took a sharp turn away from the doors into the castle and headed toward the edge. Then stood for a moment on the rough stone, staring out at the beauty of her kingdom. A warm heart surrounded by cold. A waste.

She jumped.

And as she fell, she considered briefly not calling Havu at all. But that third of her that contained pestering human nature and its desire to survive kicked in halfway down. She whistled sharply and curled into a ball. Too late?

The grunting huff of her drakonte cut through the whirling white blizzard, reaching Mirri before she saw the flash of turquoise and orange. Havu spiraled closer, easing her back against Mirri's front and brushing the flowers on the ground with her belly before jutting back up.

Mirri gasped with instant relief.

Where have you been? Havu chastised, a clicking sound rasping deep in her throat.

"Does it matter?"

Havu's blocky head turned back to look at her, the flaps of skin on the sides of her face flaring with concern. *What's wrong? And where is your Fire Mate? How are you so far apart?*

Mirri leaned forward, pressing her face against the drakonte's unyielding scales. "I pulled a Fa Chomhair Rhoime and let Izkander go."

What? Havu cut a sharp turn that would have knocked Mirri off if she hadn't been expecting it. *Why?*

"Why? *Why?*" Mirri sat up as her temper flared inside her aching and exhausted body. "Because he doesn't want to be with me, Havu. He doesn't want this." She spread her arms wide to embrace the view of Fyre. Then pressed a hand to her heart. "Or this."

A hiss and guttural clacking rumbled beneath Miri's hands. *I don't understand. You seemed to be getting along. Was it his family?*

"No, Havu. Apparently, it's mine."

Havu flicked Mirri's back with the feathery ends of her tail like she always did when she thought Mirri was being evasive. Perhaps, she was.

"He dragged me to Elm in the middle of the night and showed me a contract between Fa Chomhair Righ and Urramach. A contract that said Urramach would give Maron a cup of Origin in exchange for lawful indecorousness with her."

A snarl ripped from deep within Havu. *I'll tear that man's face from his body.*

"Why?" Mirri asked, that dead feeling inside of her solidifying in ice. "What's the point?"

The point is Urramach's a sniveling, backstabbing, cheating little weasel.

"Who loves me."

Havu nose-dived toward the ground, coming to a hard landing in a field of blue flowers next to a glowing stream. She flipped her back hard to the side so Mirri tumbled off into a heap of grass and armor.

"Havu!" she cried, angry flames licking her barren chest. Her elbows and knees stung with dirt and torn flesh. "What is wrong with you?"

What is wrong with you?

"Nothing."

Everything, Havu said, adding a vocal *hiss* for emphasis. *You just defended a man who treated you like property and made a deal with your father behind your back.*

"At least I know why he did what he did." Mirri stood and ripped off her boots, throwing one and then the other at the haughty snake who flicked them easily aside with her tail. "At least he cares about me and will always be there for me."

You're in denial.

"Stop saying that!" Mirri grabbed a few clods of dirt and threw them at Havu before storming to the lava-warmed stream and kicking her way to its center. She had hoped the shock of heat would help ground her, but there was nothing to ground. "You don't know what you're talking about. You weren't there. With Urramach. With Izkander."

I'm all ears, Mirri. You're just too busy having a tantrum to tell me.

Havu's words rang so close to her father's, they opened a chasm in her chest. The heat from the lava-kissed quartz beneath her bare feet coursed through her body as her blood sucked it up.

"Gaol Aig an Righ—" The name stuck like honey in her throat. The honey she was supposed to have inside but didn't. Her voice cracked. "He accused Fa Chomhair... my *father,* of murdering Maron, the son he loved more than anything... more than me. Urramach, too."

Havu snapped her jaw, a groaning chatter rattling her scales with a shiver.

Mirri turned wet eyes to her closest and only friend. "How could he do that?"

The water gurgled and babbled around her knees, and the smoky scent of Fyre's spring ruffled her hair.

Havu groaned. *What reason did* he *give?*

Mirri looked down at the contract crumpled in her hands. The words were creased now, and the corner of the paper soaked with her blood, but the message was clear enough to read to Havu verbatim. Date and all.

Havu slithered closer to listen, and when Mirri finished, reached her head over the water and nudged Mirri's shoulder with her triangular nose. Mirri reached a hand up and pressed the drakonte's face against her own. They rested like that, cheek to cheek, as the moons of Qaf made progress on their courses through the sky.

"What am I going to do?" Mirri whispered.

Havu breathed out a gravelly breath. *About the contract or about Izkander?*

"Either. Both."

I think it's clear what to do about the contract.

Mirri groaned.

Come on. Havu slithered the saddle and stirrups on her back closer to Mirri, water gushing away from the massive snake's body.

Mirri hoisted herself up, moaning and growling the whole way though it didn't make her feel any better. Havu's strong wings had them in the air in three flaps and headed towards the hatchery to see her mother.

"What about Izkander?" she asked, slumping forward and letting her hands fly languidly in the air.

You let him go, Mirri. I think the only thing you can do at this point is hope and trust that he comes back.

"And if the Rukh flies?"

Havu said nothing.

When they neared the blue and white awnings that marked the hatchery from the sky, Havu glissaded down with a flourish, smacking her tail into the dirt to announce their arrival. Several bleary-eyed stable workers poked their heads out with perplexed irritation before the white-haired braid of her mother appeared.

"Mirri?" she asked, wiping the distinctive yellow goo of a recently hatched egg from off her hands with an apron. "What are you doing here so early? The first moon has barely touched the sky."

"You are always at the hatchery," Mirri said. "You are never in the castle with father."

Her mother's hands slowed. "So you came to see *me* at this hour?"

"Why are you never with Father? The last time I saw you in the castle was before the Drakonte Ride. And the time before that was... was back when Maron was still alive."

Her mother's golden eyes widened.

Mirri pressed two fingers to her forehead, thumb pressing into her temple. "What happened to Maron? What did he do?"

"Mirri," her mother scolded. "We've been over this."

"No. We haven't." Mirri shook her head and pressed her thumb harder, so a pain began to radiate next to her eye. "No one has been over it with me. He's been dead for a year, and still, no one will tell me what happened."

Her mother took a step back. "It is too painful."

"Tell me what happened, mother."

"Mirri..."

Mirri growled, Izkander's words floating in her head. "Fa Chomhair Subsidiary Ban-Righ, I command you as Ah-nis Na Righ to tell me why Prionnsa Maron died."

Her mother's brows shot up, and her hands wrung nervously in front of her. "He offended the Flame."

"Because he was discontent?"

"Because—" Her mother hesitated.

Mirri leaned in, desperate for some sort of answer that didn't make her want to jump off a cliff.

"Because I was."

Mirri exhaled and nearly fell forward. "What?"

"I told you I've been lonely."

"What has that to do with Maron?"

Her mother stared at Mirri, who looked back with brows cinched. Staring, staring, chin pulling downwards as her forehead rose up. Mirri's eyes snapped to slits.

"Mother... what has that to do with Maron?"

"There was a man..."

"*Thug Marduk mathanas dhut!*" Mirri spat. "You cheated on father?"

Her mother's lips hardened into two flat lines. "He is a hard man, Mirri."

"Yes. A hard man that *you* chased down in the Drakonte Ride. If you didn't want him, why would you do that?"

"Things are not always as they seem."

"So, what?" Mirri threw her hands up. "You didn't chase him down on your magenta drakonte with the Fourth Moon at your back and your white hair flying like in the stories everyone tells?"

"No." Her mother sighed. "I did do that. I was caught up in the glamor of marrying a righ and had just had my heart broken by a councilman. I didn't think I'd *actually* catch him... but apparently, your father had an eye for me and made himself an easy win."

Mirri groaned, each of her mother's words a spear of ice stabbing out from her core and connecting with things Izkander had said. Her blood chilled despite the Flame.

"Are you saying—" She took a raspy breath. "Are you saying Maron... wasn't father's?"

Her mother dropped her gaze faster than Havu's landing.

"What... what did you *do*? How could you let Maron—*everyone*—think he was a true descendant when he was not? You... Do you know what you've done?" Streaks of white shattered Mirri's vision and a burst of dizziness threatened to knock her down.

"It was never my intention to hurt Maron," her mother said quickly, reaching out and touching Mirri's arm. "I took every precaution to keep him safe, even giving a rib to the Bone Witch in the swampy marsh between Ghaluma and Izrak to change his eyes and hair so they would match the Mardukian lines."

Bile rose in Mirri's throat. "You did *what*?"

"Everything." Her mother said resolutely, raising her chin for the first time since Mirri had accused her. "I did everything I could so my son could rise to the throne."

"Except for realizing that nothing you did would ever be enough because he doesn't actually have the Flame in his blood." Mirri sneered. "Were you really that stupid, gambling his life like that?"

Her mother's face hardened. "Don't talk to me like you know, Mirri. You are your father. So fearful of the Flame that you follow the law to the letter in everything you do."

"Of course, I do!" Mirri shouted, her voice echoing around the nearly empty oval outside the hatchery. "It is *my* life that will end if I don't. I don't have the luxury you and Izkander do as Subsidiaries. I can't just go around challenging traditions when my blood could boil at any moment."

Her mother's sharpness fell away to a look of pity that had Mirri clenching her teeth. "Aside from the drink of the Origin and the Eternal bond you wear on your wrist, none of it makes any difference."

"Then why did you think Maron could get away with the lie of being a Marduk? He would have to drink to become righ."

Her mother's chest heaved, and her shoulders sank. "Because I thought that was a false belief, too."

"But the Fifteenth Righ—" Mirri started.

"I thought was a legend. A myth." Her mother shook her head. "So much of Fyre's laws and stories are."

Her words were little blades slicing at Mirri's heart, her eyes, her mind, her skin. "And how could you possibly know?"

"Because the last time the Rukh flew by nearly one hundred years past, I spoke to the Flame."

Mirri's eyes widened, and every part of her skin itched except for the tattoo on the bottom of her foot. "What did it say?"

"That change was coming—" her mother whispered. She lifted her eyes to Mirri's, haunting and gold. "—with the end of the Marduks."

CHAPTER THIRTY-THREE

Izkander

Izkander watched Mirri fall, his heart catching exactly as it had the last time she leapt from the ramparts. But Havu—beautiful Havu—swooped under her a moment before she hit the ground and climbed into the sky.

With a sigh that emanated from recesses far deeper than his bowels, Izkander plunked down on the side of the wall and dangled his feet off the edge. His stomach roiled, desperate for food and drink. His head lolled, sleep a forgotten memory. He couldn't go on like this.

When Mirri said that he could leave, how far exactly did that mean? Did it mean he could be on the other side of the castle? Could he go to the surrounding peaks? Farther?

Could he go home?

She had said he ought to go find the Rukh and fly it over Fyre if he wanted to get out of their arrangement. Which was her way of telling him he should do just that because deep down *she* wanted out. Once again, she was shifting everything onto him, all the blame. Like she had done from the moment they met. Telling him over and over that he would leave. Cutting him down. Robbing all his words of power. He had thought it was because she was insecure, because she wanted him to stay. But what if the whole time she had really been trying to convince him to leave? And to do so in such a way that he was the eternal bad guy, so she could save face with her people.

Then she could marry Urramach—the manipulative snake—close her eyes and ears to anything that didn't agree with what she had already decided was the truth, and just forget him.

Forget him.

He ripped off the suffocating jacket and threw it over the edge of the castle. Then he wiped a finger over the smear of Mirri's blood on the blade of her sword, collecting all of it like the precious substance it was. He pulled down his collar and smeared it on his chest. He didn't know if it would make any difference, but just in case it did, he took up her thin sword and cut a line on the back of his forearm, gathering his blood on the blade. Then he pointed the tip of the sword down and dropped it so it impaled in the dirt below.

Standing, Izkander brought his fingers to his lips and whistled. He waited, his eyes scanning the country that lay below. The red and white snapdragons. The golden fields of wheat—more than half of it crushed and soaked in the buklak's blood and viscera. Streams of smoke rose from the small, yellow-topped houses of the peasants. Sitting in the bailey, Izkander spied thousands of bushels of wheat piled together in massive containers. Jahmil had come through. There had never been any doubt.

Squirt gave a bright and virile cry as he swooped into the air, his silver feathers and scales catching the light of the cresting First Moon. Izkander leapt from the ramparts and landed on his neck. Catching his long, shining horns, Izkander led him in a wide circle, taking in a final view of the kingdom. He took a feather from his pouch and dropped it. From such a height, they were able to make another half-pass on the circle before the heat and smoke overtook them.

They sliced into the air above Eayima. Usually, when the jagged cliffs and swooping valleys of his home filled his eyes, he was struck by an immediate sense of relief. But the emptiness was still inside of him, gnawing at his liver. It had flooded his body the moment Mirri offered him that sword and told him what he had to do so they could be rid of each other.

He brought Squirt in to land beside Fajar, who was pruning her feathers. He leapt to the ground before Squirt could even touch down. The massive drakonte made a sad purring sound, asking him what was wrong and why had they left and when were they going back. Izkander ignored him.

His brothers were out in the field playing blast ball—Idris, Raja, Rasheed, Bakr Alaibn, and Kahleed—all turquoise-skinned, dark-haired, brawny boys between the ages of fourteen and nineteen. They called out to him, inviting him to come and join them as he had done so many times in the past.

Izkander ignored them too, trudging by with his head held down and wishing he could just be invisible.

The door of the house hung open, letting in fresh air and warm sunlight. He walked through the main foyer, dodging past his sister, Yamina, who no doubt had a thousand questions about why she hadn't seen him on the concert scene these last few days.

Izkander kept walking, his heart a beacon leading him exactly where he needed to be.

He found his umi sitting on her own in the back solar, the brightest room in the house filled with vibrant plants given to the family over the years by his Aleamat Lila. She sat on a low, blue-striped divan, a large book in her lap and a steaming cup of tea on the table beside her.

She started when he walked in and looked up. "Skander?"

He met her eyes, feeling the tingle of fresh and eager tears. He blinked, and two identical droplets broke free and slid down his cheeks. "Umi, I'm sad."

"Oh, my sweet one." She stood and opened her arms wide. "What happened?"

He fell against her, slouching so he could set his head on her shoulder. "She doesn't want me."

Her lips pursed with a *tsk tsk*. "Who? Who could not want my beautiful boy?"

"Mirri." Her name hurt his throat. "She doesn't love me. She doesn't want me around. She thinks I'm an embarrassment."

His umi wrapped her arms tightly around his shoulders and head, stroking his back and hair. "That's impossible."

"I went and got the contract, and she got so mad. She accused me of being jealous and petty, just like you said she would." He wrapped his arms around her and closed his eyes.

"Of course, she did, Skander…" His umi laid her cheek on top of his hand. "If your father had come to me and told me *my* father had a plan to murder Jahmil, his shining son, back when we were just starting to see one another, I would have laughed him out a window."

He sobbed and hugged her tighter. "She fell down on her knees and begged her god for forgiveness for taking someone like me to their sacred place. And she gave me her blood so I could go get Fajar so she could break the bond."

"Oh, sweetie, sweetie." His umi pulled him closer and rocked him side to side. "I ache for you. This… I feel like this is partially my fault."

"No." He shook his head against her shoulder. "It's my fault. I'm an embarrassment."

"You are not, Izkander." Her soft tone took on a reproachful sharpness. "Did she say you were an embarrassment to her?"

"She didn't have to." He took a step back and sank onto the divan, letting his arms fall limp between his knees and hanging his head. "She never listens to anything I say. And she repented with her blood for the one time she trusted me enough to share all her sacred Eternal Flame stuff with me. She wants to be with Urramach."

His umi sat down and patted his knee. "I'm going to put this Urramach business on hold for a moment because I don't like seeing your eyes that green and ask instead: why do you think she doesn't listen to you? Didn't she go with you to get Javier to fight the monster? And didn't she—against what I would call better judgment—go with you to deal with cranky Jahmil?"

"Yes."

"And it sounds like you found the contract. With that bond of yours keeping you close together, she must have gone with you to Elm, too. Fyre and Elm hate each other. In fact, most djinn who are aware of Fyre hate her as much as her people distrust djinn. That can't have been easy for her to do, but it sounds like she listened and went, right?"

"Yes. I guess she listens sometimes." He wiped his nose on the back of his hand. "But if I have anything to say about Fyre or its stupid traditions, she treats me like I'm an idiot."

"Hm." His umi nodded for a moment, her yellow eyes glowing slits framed by a sparkling waterfall of hair. "Did you know I left your baba in a hot spring on Ard once because he talked about Fajar like she was some graceful, loving, sentient being?"

He furrowed his brow. "But she is."

"Yes," she smiled sweetly. "And a lovely one. But I had never met her, and even though I loved your baba with everything I had—and maybe *because* I did—I couldn't understand. I thought he was crazy, and it made me... angry."

"But how am I supposed to live in Fyre all my life if I'm just supposed to keep my mouth shut about everything? That's not fair."

"No, it isn't." She shook her head in commiseration. "But your baba still has Fajar, doesn't he? And me? Together." She squeezed his knee and turned marigold eyes misted with silver onto his. "He just... had to show me. And trust that I would see, when I was ready, the truth of what Fajar really is."

He thought about what she was saying, possibilities bursting in the back of his brain even if they all seemed stupid. "It's different. I can't show her without her thinking I want her to die."

"I love you, sweetie, but I really don't think that's what she thinks."

"She doesn't want me. You always wanted baba, but she doesn't want me. Every time I think things are going well with us, she runs off and kisses Urramach."

"Okay," his umi said flatly. "I'm just going to ask this once because I'm getting déjà vu. Is Urramach a lilu or any other sort of sex demon?"

"No. I'm the sex demon here. So, why would she go kiss him when I'm right there? Why would anyone?" He let his body go limp and fall against the back of the divan, his head thumping against the wall. "It doesn't make any sense."

His umi pushed her lips together and raised a tastefully sculpted brow. "I thought the reason the bond was still on your wrist was that she was afraid of losing you?"

"I've been trying to be a gentleman," he said in a halting pulse.

"Ha!" His umi laughed and shook her head. "I thought she had made that up. Are you saying, then, that she has been willing to break the bond, but you haven't?"

"She has, but I was worried about not having your approval yet. I didn't want her to think that I didn't care if her flesh melted off. I thought she would appreciate that. But she got really weird and then ran off and kissed Urramach."

"I thought you said she was upset because she felt like you were trying to kill her? It sounds like, in that instance, she was upset because you were not."

"I don't know. I don't even know. I'm so stupid." He leaned forward again and cradled his head in his hands. "She hurts me. I ache."

"Baby," his umi crooned, scratching his back softly. "I didn't realize how far she reached into your heart. I think you were right. That you do actually love her."

"I love her so much." He wiped more tears on the heels of his hands. "She makes me feel everything all at once, and I just want to make everything better for her. But I keep screwing it up."

"Because she kisses this Urramach and sends you away to fetch Fajar?"

He groaned, shaking his heavy head. "Why does she keep kissing him?"

"Well..." His umi's hands paused in their circular rotation on his back. "I'd say there are three likely answers. One —" She raised her eyebrows high. "She doesn't love you at all and came to meet your scary mother and ask to marry you even though there was a plausible way out for no reason. Two, she feels a confusing sense of guilt and connection with this man and falls into old habits, which—" She cleared her throat and smiled tightly. "—your father can explain to you if you don't understand. Or three, she isn't kissing him. He is kissing her, and she doesn't know how to make it stop." His umi leaned closer and resumed her scratching. "Do any of those sound right to you?"

He sighed and rubbed his hands over his hair. "She says he keeps kissing her. And that it makes her freeze. And that she can't breathe. And she feels like the walls are closing in."

"Well, that sounds utterly terrifying for her. Why haven't you stepped in and been the boy I raised you to be?"

He dipped his head from side to side. "Because he's her friend. Her *close confidant.* The guy she was kind of hoping would catch her drakonte before I dropped in out of nowhere, not that he stood a chance in Jahannam. I didn't want to come off like a presumptuous prick."

"And that's very admirable." His umi reached over and rubbed a thumb over his cheek. "And when you first showed up and she told you about it, I think that was right. But if she confided in you every time he kissed her and told you she felt so awful and scared and trapped, I think it's okay for you to step in. Even if she's mad at you about it later. Even fierce queens who slay monsters at night can get scared about standing up for themselves, especially around *close confidants* that *we* know are manipulative murderers. Don't you think?" She blinked at him expectantly.

He sat up straight, pressing his hands between his knees. "Do you think I should go fight him?"

She chuckled. "You are Izkander ibn Bakr for sure. And I'm sure your baba would tell you to go do just that. And maybe you should. But it sounds to me like you should talk to Mirri about it and see if you can help *her* fight him."

"He's a creeper, isn't he?" He rubbed his chin hard, a cold smile growing on his face. "I have been letting a creepy creeper creep on my girl out of some weird misplaced sense of propriety. I ought to cut his head off."

"Izkander," his umi said, sharp and flat. "Don't you go starting trouble. Cutting heads off is a last resort. Preferably a last-resort if it's not a ten-eyed, yellow-fanged monster."

"But he's a murderer. I can feel it in my blood. He helped kill Maron and then comforted Mirri about it for the last year." He shivered as if snail slime had been painted all over his skin. "I shook hands with him. I wish I could go back in time and punch myself in the head."

His umi sighed, long and slow, and with a shake of her head. "Before you go punching or cutting off any heads, shouldn't you decide what to do about that bond on your arm? I doubt whatever is allowing you to be so far from her with it on will hold forever."

"Half a high pass of the First Moon..." He rubbed a hand around his wrist. "Do you think she might still want me?"

"What did she say when she sent you off for the Rukh?"

"I don't know. She gave me her blood and told me about the spell and said to go get Fajar and fly her over Fyre if I wanted out." He bit his lip and lifted a finger. "If. She said *if.*"

"She said *if.* And she said *you.* Which sounds to me like I might be stuck with her as an *abnataya.*" She sighed as if the news were a great burden.

"I have to go back."

"Yes, you do." His umi leaned forward and kissed his cheek, then rubbed it off with her thumb. "Just be careful. Fyre is a strange and old place. And if Fajar came from their Flame, then it is something you should be respectful of, even as you sort out all the mess the people of Fyre have heaped upon it."

He bobbed his head. "I do respect it. I felt something in that place. And with the fire-born hatchlings. Oh, Allah, so stinking cute."

She chuckled. "You and your father and those drakonte. I shouldn't be surprised at all that the woman you fell in love with loves the slobbering things as much as you."

He smiled and shook his head, then pushed himself up to his feet. He headed out the door when a horrible stabbing pain ripped up from his stomach. He grabbed at it. "Umi, I'm starving."

She hurried to his side with a chuckle and put her shoulder under him to help hold him up. "My poor baby amongst all those snake people. Let's get you something to eat."

CHAPTER THIRTY-FOUR

Mirri

Mirri wanted Havu to barge straight into the castle and squeeze her way through the corridors to find Fa Chomhair, but she still couldn't shake the fear that doing so would be sacrilege and melt her bones. Which left her with no other choice than to go alone on foot.

The clip of her feet echoed around the cold walls of her home. Each step, the tick of a timepiece, drove home the words her mother had said. About Maron. The Flame. The doomed fate of her bloodline.

How? How could it be true?

But how could it not be? Maron drank the flame the same day he died. And her mother had no reason to lie and implicate herself as a traitor to the crown. But what about the rest? Her mother's insistence that the laws didn't matter? That Mirri had walked a line her whole life, going to bed every night in fear so she could wake up with it in the morning. Why would she let Mirri live her life that way? Did she, too, only care for Maron?

Why did no one love her?

No one but Urramach?

Her stomach ached like it hadn't eaten in months. She pressed a hand to it the same way Izkander always did, and the thought of him made it so much worse. She stopped at the bottom of the set of stairs leading toward the war room and leaned against the wall until the pain lessened.

Was what Urramach felt for her even love? Or a zeal to rule? To keep things the same way they had always been? And what, then, did Izkander feel if he was the one who left when Urramach stayed?

The deep growl of bickering men carried down the hall from the war room, her father's voice unmistakable in the fray. She exhaled slowly, knowing she was weak around him. That she always cowered and did as he asked out of fear and out of respect. *A good righ garners both in equal portions*, he had always said. But she was righ now, and he neither respected nor feared her. Fear she could do without, but respect was necessary to rule a kingdom and required something she had yet to find when confronted by her father. Courage? But she had that in spades when out in the field. It was something else...

"Ah-nis Na Righ?" General Riley's scruffy head poked out from the ironclad doors, the tufts of his slicked white hair backlit by the chandelier in the room behind. "Our great respect and honor to the blood of Marduk, but we have been waiting for you to lead the morning meeting. It is already five degrees past time."

Mirri blinked. She had completely forgotten, wandering her way here in search of her father, who also happened to be inside. But that was irresponsible. Despite all the turmoil serrating her heart and all her mother had said about the kingdom and laws, she *was* the righ of Fyre. And righs couldn't just grab swords and disappear to go live a different life. A life they liked better. They stayed and burned with the castle and were *gu forneartach* content about it.

"Thank you, General Riley, for your desire to serve Fyre so dutifully." She swung her hair behind her shoulders and marched through the door. If she was going to burn, she was taking the Fa Chomhair Righ with her.

Her father's red hair and redder eyes glistened when she entered the room. Half her generals and commanders stood, mid-bicker with their hands outstretched across the table. Chaos and anger thickened the air in palpable streams of heat that radiated from those in the room with purer lines of Mardukian blood. She glared at the Fa Chomhair. He could have run the meeting. He had for many centuries before. Strategizing ways to keep back the Ghaluman bandits from their borders was something he was good at. Something he enjoyed. But whatever fight had happened between him and Izkander must have changed that, because now he sat back, arms crossed and legs kicked up, letting the war room squabble itself into disarray.

His eyes met hers, a flicker of fire and bitter challenge in his serpentine irises, clear as the first moon's peak on the horizon. Her skin prickled under his stare, and she glanced away. That's when the gravity of the situation fully settled on her shoulders.

The room wasn't full of just her generals, but her councilmen, too. All of them. Including Urramach.

She was falling head over heels toward jagged rocks to splash raw in the ocean of political discontent. Her stomach twisted. Her vision swayed. She shut her eyes to regain her balance. Her composure. To find whatever piece it was she was missing so she could be the righ she was supposed to be. At last, she exhaled and snapped her chin up.

"Generals and councilmen," she quipped, her voice hard and cold as ice.

The room fell silent, various shades of reddish-gold eyes all turning to look at her. Many of their faces were smooth, expectant, but a few carried the trace lines around their lips that spoke of frustration. Of *discontent*.

She moved her gaze around the table, meeting the hard stare of each man and woman one at a time and skipping Urramach so she ended with the burning glare of her father.

"Speak." She opened her palm and gestured around the room. "I can feel the wills of you, my councilmen and generals, through the Flame that burns within me. You are at war with one another instead of at war with the Ghalumans. So, enlighten your Ah-nis Na Righ. What makes you so ungrateful to the Flame?"

Silence. A shift in the dark corner of Urramach. And a smirk from her father.

Then, General Riley—*Marduk beannaich e*—spoke. "My humblest apologies, Ah-nis." He clapped a fist to his chest and bowed, shooting an uneasy glance at a few other generals at the table. "But there have been rumors circulating concerning the legitimacy of the Mardukian line."

Her back stiffened. How had everyone found out about Maron when she just had? Or, if they had all known like her mother and father and Urramach, why was it coming up *now*? She forced her hand still and lifted her chin.

"If this is concerning the Fallen One, Prionnsa Maron, the Flame has already addressed the issue and cleansed the bloodline."

She paused. Calling Maron an *issue* sat like old soup in her stomach. Her hand drifted over and pressed her stomach. She wished with every throbbing pulse of her heart that Izkander was here so he could step in and rile everyone up while strangely calming the situation down. But he wasn't. Because he left. Because she wasn't enough. Because everything that made her worthwhile to her people made her worthless to him.

A stray cough filled the tense silence. General Riley winced and looked at his unhelpful comrades for what to say next. Itches spidered across the back of her knees. The Fa Chomhair Righ's smirk widened.

"Speak." She snapped. "Or may the Flame consume your discontent tongues."

General Riley grimaced. "Again, our deepest apologies to the honorable Ah-nis Na Righ. It is not the fallen righ that stirs up contention. But the current."

His words stilled her blood, and she snapped her gaze to her father's cold face. "You challenge my rule as Ah-nis?" she whispered the words, slow and careful so each one cut the air in the room with threats. "After I have consumed the Origin in front of you all and had the Flame bless me with the Eternal Union afforded only to the righ?"

Riley tugged the collar of his crisp green uniform, causing the dark-blue bands that ran down the length of his jacket to bend. "There have been rumors... Rumors that what you drank for the ceremony was not the Origin."

She scoffed, making her eyes burn with the fire that lived in her blood. "The insolence is unfathomable. But if my subjects so doubt the fire inside me—"

She smacked her hand on the table and burned the wood beneath with the Flame's heat in her hand. Tendrils of black smoke curled around her fingers.

"—bring the Origin now, and I will drink. And for every one of you who doubts me after that, I'll pour the sanctifying fire down your own throats."

"It is not just that," General Riley said, his voice squeaking like water forced through dry pipes. "It is the very bond of Eternal Union you spoke of that has many councilmen concerned about your legitimacy."

"What?"

"A few councilmen have expressed concern over the choice of your Fire Mate; a foreign man who has no fire in his blood whatsoever. Not even filtered down and muddied into golden eyes like mine." General Riley dipped his head apologetically.

The itching sprawled its way up her back and across her clavicles, and Mirri yearned to strip herself of her armor and scratch. Instead, she flicked her gaze at Urramach, for who else would complain of her Mate?

Urramach's face was long, soft, and pitying, as it so often was with her. He pushed himself from where he leaned against the wall and stepped forward with a sharp click of boots. "Honored and blessed Ah-nis Na Righ." He clapped a hand to his chest, and his ribboned hair slid over his shoulder. "I have tried to quell their concerns regarding the Subsidiary, but some of their concerns in regard to *your* safety have caught my ear."

"Urramach." She hissed through clenched teeth. "What is the meaning of this?"

He took another clipped step forward. "Your Fire Mate is not from here. He laughs in the face of the traditions that keep you safe. He laughs at our laws and challenged the Fa Chomhair Righ to a duel over his right to help oversee the kingdom. Even now, when your bond should be pulling you together, he is nowhere to be found."

The flare that had fueled her courage began to quiver and wane. She pulled what remained into her core and stoked it inside her heart, but her thoughts had scattered and spread through the wind. Should she defend Izkander after he had left, perhaps forever? Should she agree with them all and declare she had found a way to fix it? Should she fight for Izkander or give up on him?

"Our dear Ah-nis Na Righ," Urramach said, placing a hand near where hers still burned the table black, "it is your Mate's lack of Flame, as your wise general pointed out, that taints your legitimacy. The Eternal Union binds what is the same between two Mates. It is supposed to elevate and cleanse the blood of the Subsidiary and bring it closer to the level of Flame in the righ. But if Izkander Green Eyes has none... then what did it do to your blood to bind you to him?"

Each word that slithered silkily from Urramach's tongue poured a pail of water over the dwindling fire in her heart. She curled the tips of her fingers into the table

What *had* the Union done to her? Because, as much as she hated it, Urramach spoke the words of the law regarding the Union. And the Eternal Union was one of two conditions for being righ her mother had said held true. Was she now as illegitimate as her brother? Even though the Flame responded to her call and burned the wood beneath her fingers? Would ending the bond with Izkander by means of Fajar fix the problem if her blood had already been thinned?

But if it had been thinned, why did she feel as strong as ever? Hotter. Angrier. She had even been able to feel the small veins of the Flame beneath the cold and defiled city of Watali in Eastern Elm. The heat had flowed easily into her while she waded through the stream. And whenever Izkander was near her, her blood pulsed and boiled inside her veins and rushed in her ears. She didn't feel her heat leave when she touched him. She felt his heat pour into her.

Her eyes widened. She yanked her hand up, a blue flame of intense heat burning in the center of her palm. "The bond of Eternal Union sealed Izkander Green Eyes, the Gaol Aig an Righ, as my Fire Mate because, like me, he carries the Flame. And far more of it than any of you could muster even twenty generations back."

A ripple of anger and blatant discontent spread through the room. Most of the generals—those who had fought next to her and Izkander against the buklak — took up her side, while a majority of the councilmen—Urramach's peers—stood decidedly against her.

Urramach's brows furrowed and his mouth fell slack.

Her father stood and stormed to the front. "You defile the bloodline just as your mother, bringing mongrels into the line of the throne," he spat.

"I do not." She raised her palm higher.

Anger bubbled at how easily he insulted her beautiful, kind brother; the only person in the whole kingdom to make her laugh until equally tender Izkander. The flame on her hand burned brighter into a mini conflagration, nipping and licking the air higher and higher until it brushed the arched ceilings in the room. The men and women in the room backed away from her.

"Izkander is from the family of the Great Rukh, the sacred firebird of the Flame's Wisdom that broke free when the world first formed. He is marked by the Flame just as I am, the Origin's blessing imprinted on his very skin."

The room broke into a roar of chaos. Spit flew, fingers jabbed, and a volley of cacophonous vitriol poured through clenched jaws and teeth.

"General Riley," she called through the rabble.

He pushed his way to her side and bowed. "My apologies, Ah-nis Na righ."

"You are forgiven," she clipped, eyes connected across the room with her father's infernos. "Assemble troops and make sure this discontent does not leave the castle. Lock up anyone who stands against me and announce a meeting for the first degree after the High Moon."

"Yes, Ah-nis." He put his hand to his chest. "What shall I say the meeting is about?"

"This." She waved her hand palm out toward the mess she now ruled over. She flicked her eyes to him. "I plan to settle this blatant show of discontent. And anyone who is unhappy with my answer after that will be thrown to the Flame."

"Ah-nis?" he gasped.

"Do it." She narrowed her eyes, then turned back to find her father.

His belligerent form no longer shadowed the back wall. And when she finally found him, he was nearly upon her, face purple against the red of his beard. She stepped back, reaching for the sword she had left with Izkander. He pulled his own broadsword and raised it high, bringing it down as she scrambled away. A great *shing* of blades colliding caught her ears. She looked over her shoulder, stumbling as her heart pounded painfully in her chest.

"Urramach?" The name ripped the air from her chest. She stared wide-eyed, the back of her hand to her lips.

He beat her father back with two more blows until several of the other generals stepped in and pulled him back.

"Remove him to the dungeon," Urramach commanded, shoulders back and in full glory as the savior of the Ah-nis Na Righ. "Quell the insurrection before it leaves the castle while I take the Ah-nis to safety."

"I don't—" she started, but he grabbed her arm and jostled her out the door, pulling her down the hallway at a near run. "Stop it!" She finally managed to yank her arm away.

He flipped around, his face a mask of calm while the small portion of Flame that lived in his blood betrayed his eyes with flickers. "What in the Flame are you doing?"

"Leading my country and quashing a rebellion," she snipped. "What are *you* doing fomenting it?"

"I would never lead your people against you." He looked stung, fingers to his chest as if she had wounded him right in his heart.

"Were you not just in there challenging the legitimacy of my rule?" She took a step back and yanked on the ends of her hair, not caring if it made her look weak.

"I challenged the pathetic bloodline of *Izkander Green Eyes*. Not you." The sneer forming on his lips softened. He took a step towards her, hand outstretched. "Never you."

She smacked his hand away. "We are the same now. We are one. What aren't you getting about that?" She raised her wrist and shoved it in his face. "*We* are Fire Mates. Izkander and I. *Not* you and I."

Urramach's top lip curled before he gained control of it and smoothed it back out. "He has been here only a few days and already he weakens you. Your legitimacy. Your bloodline. Your mind."

"My *mind*?" she spat. "You've always thought I was weak-minded. It is why you thought you could kill Maron and win me in the Drakonte Ride, isn't it? Did you think I would be your puppet for the rest of my life?"

His eyes widened before crushing into little slits. "You don't know of what you speak."

"Then what's this?" She ripped the paper out of her pocket and threw it at him.

He flapped it open. Glowered. Then crumpled it up and threw it in the fire sconce on the wall. "Nothing."

"Burning it doesn't mean I didn't see it. How could you *do* that?"

"For the kingdom."

"For yourself," she spat.

"For you."

"For *you*!"

"Mirri," he growled, his decorum breaking. "Maron would have burned one way or the other, you realize that, right? At least by drinking the Origin before his induction we spared the country a civil war."

"Did we?" The strange power Urramach had to soothe her nerves when they shouldn't be soothed began to creep in. She flicked the blue flame back onto her palm to remind her of the piece of her that was missing. "Because that war room had its own war raging inside it. And it sounds like you were part of the insurrection. Which makes you a discontent traitor."

He sucked air through his clenched teeth. "I would never betray this country."

"Only me?"

"Never." He snarled, deeper in his throat. He snatched her wrist and squeezed hard, fingers clasped through the golden bond that burned undisturbed. "I love you."

"Urramach!" She yanked at his hand, but he didn't flinch.

Instead, he dragged her down the hallway.

"You will see. You will see that I do this for you."

"Then, why do you hurt me?" she gasped, nearly falling as she matched his pace, and tried to rip her hand from his.

More than her blood stained the sword she had given Izkander. Her pride and only defense lay with it. What if Izkander didn't return at all? What would happen to her then? That pitiable, pitiful feeling that drowned her whenever Urramach was around began to lick at her neck, her chin, trying to seep in and end her there.

"I am so sorry about this, Mirri. I am." He ripped her around a corner.

Her heart thrashed against her chest when she realized where they were. He opened the door to his room and threw her in, hand still on her wrist so her elbow twisted painfully.

"But if you let this ugly discontent continue to rise in you, you will perish. And Izkander won't even be here to see it. Because he doesn't care."

"He will cut you down," she snarled.

Urramach smirked and yanked her closer. The blue flame in her hand began to crawl around her palm and over her fingers to get away from his hold. It was forbidden by the Flame to hurt her subjects with the fire that burned in her blood. She could only use it to protect them. But what if the threat to her citizens was one of her own? And what if Izkander was right? Her mother? What if none of it actually mattered? It was still Urramach... the man she had thought was her friend. Her confidant. Her potential future just mere days ago.

Urramach glanced at the flames and smiled. He leaned in and whispered, "He can't do that if he's gone. And he can't do that if he's dead,"

His lips moved toward hers like they had so many times before. She screamed and slapped her flame against his cheek.

The blue flickers eagerly danced from her fingers to his face, curdling the skin into blisters in the shape of her hand.

He threw her to the ground and grabbed at the smoking wound, yelling and cursing as he grasped his cheek. He turned the inferno of his eyes on her and spat on the floor by her feet. "Izkander will never show, you ungrateful *boireannach grànda*. You will be mine. And after a century of forcing you into a lonely and cold bed with only the derision of your parents and your people to keep you company, you will realize that I alone love you. You will welcome me then."

He stepped toward her once more. She flinched. Then, he shook his head and turned. When he reached the door, he sighed and looked back, eyes as horrifically and deceptively soft as they always were when he looked at her.

"I'm sorry it has to be this way. I will make it right." Then he smiled tenderly and left, hand still cupping the blackened handprint she had left on his face. The one that matched her fury in the war room.

She threw herself at the door and pushed all the flame she had into it, but like all the chambers in the castle, it would not burn.

She screamed and banged her hands on the door, then slid down and let her head *thud* against it, telling herself over and over that Izkander would come. Even if she sent him away. Even if she had broken his heart. He would come. He would come.

Would he come?

CHAPTER THIRTY-FIVE

Izkander

The biting winds of the Zabriyan peaks whistled all around him, flecks of ice nipping at his exposed skin while bright white clouds swirled above in heavy spirals. But the giant avian bonfire to his back was enough to combat all of that.

Izkander turned from the panorama of mountains. Fajar tittered on her feet. She wanted to take to the sky—to swoop and dive. She looked like she might take off at any moment.

"Now listen here, young lady." He stepped closer and tried to catch Fajar's smoldering eyes. "Are you listening?"

Fajar ruffled her neck feathers and made a series of playful coos. She cocked her head from side to side in a little dance, then she pushed him with the edge of her wing.

"Stop it," he groaned and stumbled, swatting her away with a smile. "You cannot let Mirri see you here. I will never be able to recover from it if she sees you."

The bird looked wounded before she lifted her head in the air and shook it out with a frisky *wah-wah* noise that told him she understood. She backed up into the large cave behind her and flopped down on her fluffy tummy. She settled her head over one shoulder, burying her beak into her own feathers, and closed her eyes. He didn't know if he would need her, if Mirri would insist that he do what she had asked, or if she might want Fajar for some other reason. But he was determined to be prepared in any event. Until then, though, he didn't want Mirri to think *he* wanted anything of the sort.

Izkander patted the side of Fajar's face, relishing the tingle of her sparkling feathers, then turned back to the gale. Down below, almost too far for the eye to see, rested the green and gold dot of the Kingdom of Fyre. He took a breath through his nose, the unyielding cold filling his lungs with a crisp calm that radiated through his body.

He hadn't decided what he was going to say or do, only that he was going back. Maybe that alone would be enough for Mirri to understand how he really felt. And just how seriously he took her.

With a running start, Izkander leapt off the side of the cliff. As the wind rushed over his face and combed his hair, a smile grew on his face that felt as natural as his own name. A thousand memories of falling from Eayima filled his heart, followed by the unbridled joy and accompanying terror of watching Mirri plunge from the cliffs of Thrace.

He arched his back and spread his arms wide, the rush of frozen wind cleansing the last of the fiery cobwebs from his mind and the fear from his heart. No, he wasn't sure what exactly he was going to do. But it wasn't going to be like anything he had done yet.

Squirt swept under him, and he caught onto the long horns, jamming his heels into the natural holds formed by the crests in the armored plates.

Izkander was through being decorous. After all, being a fat-mouthed part-sex demon had gotten him this far. And he hadn't decided yet if he was going to cut Urramach's head off or not, but he was very tempted to rip off that pretty ponytail of his.

Maybe Mirri would be mad about that too. She could just add it to the list of his infractions because it was happening. The man was a creep, and creeps have bad things happen to them. It was a natural process of the world and a cherished tradition of the al-Eayima clan. They had to try to respect one another's cultures, now didn't they?

Squirt wasn't even halfway to the ground when a familiar bone-shattering shriek filled the air. Turquoise scales carried on creamy, orange wings ripped through the sky towards them. His heart caught as he searched for the familiar flicker of red waves on her back, but Mirri wasn't there. Havu rushed closer and bumped up against Squirt, running her head under his chin. They purred and hissed at each other, long slimy tongues brushing together. A kiss.

Havu reeled back, then swooped in close again. A twittering roar filled her throat that sounded frightened and sent shivers down Izkander's spine.

She settled into flight alongside them and gestured with her long, snakey nose for him to hop on.

Was Mirri in trouble? The thought lit a fire under him and he rose to his feet, then leapt from Squirt's back towards her. She dove under him, and he caught the strap of her bridle in both hands, snapping his feet into the stirrups. "Where's Mirri?"

More twitters, a grumble deep inside her throat that radiated down her body like a chill.

"Take me to her."

The drakonte dove, angling perpendicular to the ground. Wind rushed him so quickly, his cheeks flapped and his eyes went blurry. When she was equidistant from the ground and the ramparts of the castle, Havu's spine curved, and she snapped back up. Izkander jumped, twisting into a ball in the air and spinning before he came down hard on the cobblestone path that led towards the entrance. Both his feet struck the earth at once, sticking the landing as his father had painstakingly taught him.

Peasants, servants, and common soldiers milling about the front of the castle all turned to gawk at him, gasps radiating through the crowd. Without pause, he turned and jogged towards the palace.

The soldiers waiting at the large double doors pulled them open as he approached. He hurried inside and up the steps. He still didn't know his way around the serpentine castle, but he could feel the bond on his wrist beginning to pulse. No pain yet, but warming. A burgeoning heat yanking him back to the place he was supposed to be. To Mirri.

Raised voices and the sounds of a scuffle reached his ears like echoes through a series of caves. He'd never heard any such noise in the dreary, oh-so-restrained castle—dissonant and brimming with a threat of violence. A soldier standing in the hall spied him and shot off in the opposite direction.

"Gaol Aig an Righ!" he cried, but it wasn't a greeting or show of respect. He was sounding a warning.

Izkander set his hand on his sword, his shoulders starting to tense. Had Mirri set her men on alert should he return? Was his mother wrong in telling him to attach meaning to such miniscule words like *if* and *you*? What if Mirri had been hoping he wouldn't come back?

He tensed every muscle in his body, then relaxed them one by one. If she didn't want to see him, if she wanted him gone for good, she was going to have to say that to his face. Plainly, evenly, and with no room for misinterpretation. No more deflection. He would know everything he needed the moment he saw her. Whether honey or glass, her eyes would give her away.

He quickened his pace down the hall and turned the corner. The voice of Mirri's father cut into his ears, guttural and ragged. The clang of metal and the low grunts of soldiers accompanied it. Izkander rushed forward, and after a few twists and turns through cold stone halls, found himself staring at some six soldiers dragging a snarling and foaming Fa Chomhair Righ down the hall. His arms were pinned behind his back by two men, the others forming an armed escort. They had their swords drawn, gazes shifting.

One of the soldiers glanced at Izkander. His eyes widened, pale as the Fourth Moon. Leveling his sword, he called out to his companions, "Izkander Green Eyes!"

The three other soldiers who were not actively restraining their former king turned on him with pointed swords.

Izkander's hand tightened over the handle of his own blade, and he took an easy step forward. "For the record, I am not entirely against whatever is going on here."

"This is your doing, you filthy, inbred mongrel!" Fa Chomhair fumed, yanking hard with his shoulders. The men restraining him stumbled.

"How is this *my* doing?" Izkander furrowed his brow. "Wait a moment. Did you call me inbred?"

"Relinquish your weapons," cried the pale-eyed guard.

"I am not inbred." Izkander put a hand on his hip. "I am outbred. I am a loaf pan."

He giggled at his own joke, then refocused.

"Relinquish your weapons!" the pale-eyed guard shouted.

"Where is the Ah-nis Na Righ?"

The guard lunged forward, bringing the sword in with a sharp thrust. Izkander tucked into himself and rolled. He snatched his sword from its scabbard and took a quick step back, squaring himself to the wall. The gun on his hip whispered empty promises of a quick victory, but he couldn't use it in such close quarters without risking a nasty ricochet.

"Is your righ aware that you are attacking me?" Izkander asked. Mirri may not want to see him again, but commanding her guards to attack him? He couldn't have upset her that much.

Then again, here was her father, bruises on his face and being dragged down the hall by a bunch of soldiers. Had Mirri done that?

None of the guards answered him, forming a loose half-circle around him. The space was too narrow for them to come at him all at once, so they attacked two at a time. The one-handed bastard swords they wielded were more maneuverable than the longsword Fa Chomhair had used but still slower and clumsier than Izkander's Mamluk saber. He traded quick parries with them, waiting for openings and then slashing at their legs and arms. One went down and another fell off balance and slapped his shoulder into the wall. Izkander cut his legs out from under him. Steamy bright-red blood splattered the wall.

Fa Chomhair gave a heavy bellow, and Izkander looked up to see him throw aside one of the guards. As they struggled to grapple him, he headbutted one. The guard's nose burst open. The old righ snatched up the sword that hung at the soldier's hip. He kicked the first guard in the knee, then sliced the sword into the other's shoulder, leaving a nasty chew in the flesh.

The other two guards made their volley at once. Izkander parried one and dodged the other. He summoned a ball of fire to his hand. Jumping back to avoid a lunge, he closed his eyes and snapped the ball.

The fire slammed hard into the ground and burst like a flash of lightning. The guards stumbled, blinded.

Izkander opened his eyes and slashed at their hands, disarming them. One fumbled closer, bent over as he reached to retrieve his weapon. Izkander kicked him in the face full force, driving him to the flat of his back. He walked to the other man, palmed the side of his face, and smacked his head against the wall, knocking him out cold.

His eyes darted up to Fa Chomhair. Two captors lay dead at his feet, the one with the huge chunk taken out of his shoulder still twitching. The old righ met Izkander's eyes. He was permanently gray-faced, even with the tinge of fury purpling his cheek. His eyes of fire blazed, steel lips curving into a hideous sneer.

Lifting his sword to point at Izkander's chest, Fa Chomhair growled. "To the death, defiler."

Izkander raised his blade and widened his stance. "You killed your own son, didn't you?"

"He was never my son!" Fa Chomhair raised the blade high and rushed in—another man fighting with his emotions instead of his brain.

Izkander leapt to one side, sneaking his blade in to catch the old king's stomach. The drakonte armor caught the sword, dampening the strike. Chain-mail split and the leather splintered, but no blood.

Repositioning, Izkander lifted his sword and twisted his wrist down to bring the curve of the blade to protect his face in a high guard. He had no armor, just his ordinary Egyptian cotton pants and kurta, which he'd changed into when he was at home. A strike like he'd just given the old righ would spill his guts across the floor. He just needed to make sure he didn't get hit.

Izkander drew back and repositioned. "You admit you killed him?"

"His own impure blood killed him. That and his mother's befoulment of the sacred line of Marduk. Just like your blood will be the death of you and my wretched daughter."

Fa Chomhair bared his teeth and came in with a quick succession of slashes. The power in each swipe was enough to remove limbs. Izkander dodged and weaved, avoiding parrying the heavy sword.

Fa Chomhair brought the sword down in a chop. Izkander pivoted, and the blade smashed hard against the stone, sparks flying.

"Hold still, you twirling djinn!"

Izkander pushed off the wall with one foot and jumped behind him. He sliced at the exposed flesh on the back of his neck, but Fa Chomhair snapped up so the blade hit armor. The drakonte leather sucked up the strike.

Izkander didn't want to kill him. The last thing Izkander wanted was to add *killed her father* to the litany of infractions Mirri could level against him. Even if the old righ was a blustery filicidal hierophant.

"He *was* your son." Izkander took a cross step to one side. "You raised him. From everything I hear, he was your golden boy. Everything Mirri wanted to be. How could you just turn on him because he had the wrong blood?"

"He was an abomination. Just like you. And just like you have made my daughter. I will end the Marduk line before I see either of you on the throne." He lifted his sword in another heavy chop.

Izaknder rolled away and swung inside, aiming for the same dent he had made earlier when suddenly his wrists were seized with fire. The sword ricocheted. He screamed and drew back, the intensity of the burn driving him down.

The spell was up.

His shoulders hit the wall, the sword dropping from his limp hand. Fa Chomhair laughed and raised his sword like a spear.

CHAPTER THIRTY-SIX

MIRRI

PAIN, SEARING AND EXQUISITE, overtook Mirri's wrists, rolling in stabbing waves throughout her body. The bond warned her to return to her Fire Mate, which meant that Izkander hadn't yet used the Rukh to break their Union and that he had not returned to her.

Mirri had no mind to think about it as she clawed at her wrist, trying with all her might to break the bond, but her fingers filtered through the flaming light as they always had before. She screamed out a raspy whisper, her vocal cords spent begging and commanding to be freed from the room in which Urramach had trapped her. Either no one heard, no one cared, or no one dared. And the last one was the worst. It meant there was far more corruption in her castle than she thought. Whether from her father or Urramach—or both, for that matter—she couldn't tell. But it was clear her allies were far fewer than she had 1assumed.

Not that it mattered if she ended up burning to death. She stumbled away from the door and to the small set of square windows that looked out on the valley below. She had tried to melt the bars with her fire, but the fastenings were connected to the castle walls, which in turn were connected to the sacred earth it was built upon, which made it immune to the Flame's bite. Tables. Chairs. The curtains she had already turned to ash would all burn. But nothing structural.

She tried to channel the flames growing hotter on her wrists, soaking them into her fingertips and pouring the resulting flare out the window in a steady stream of hot blue. A small relief, if not exhausting. But what would Izkander do with the fire that nipped at his skin? If he had been on Eayima with Fajar, could the immortal Wisdom reduce his pain as well?

On the other hand, what if he had chosen her? Where was he? Would he be able to find her? She made the outpouring of fire larger, hotter, blurring the view of Fyre's spring below and getting lost in the bright and wavy lines of heat.

A shrill cry snapped Mirri from her pain-drenched trance. The flare pulsing from her fingers lessened as the stabbing in her wrists surged. Then, her heart stopped, and all the fire in her hands died out in a quick, chilling huff. In the distance, red on white, flew the unmistakable wings of the Rukh.

She grabbed the bars on the window and yanked herself to them, pressing her face out into the cold. There was no mistaking the beautiful creature, and as she watched, the consuming pain that reddened her flesh faded into nothing. She used that blessed reprieve to scan the skies around Fajar, searching in a harried back and forth for Squirt. For Izkander. Dreading to see them though they were her only hope.

Nothing. No sight of them at all. And as sensation crept back into her consciousness, she realized Fajar was headed toward her and the castle, not the Origin which lived below the center of Fyre. The Rukh was coming to her, to the Flame she had pushed out in a stream like a beacon. Fire for fire. Flame for Flame. She had called her sister.

A skip of hope spread through her. She clung to the bars with white knuckles and fought away the pain that sprung tears in her eyes. The firebird swooped closer, its gargantuan wings blocking the moons and shadowing the window as it passed overhead. She reached for it, able to feel its magic and warmth from where it flew far above her. It eased the burn in her wrist, too, The Flame recognizing that the bird was as much a part of Izkander as he was a part of her.

"Fajar, please!" she cried as the Rukh screeched.

A hand touched her shoulder. She spun around with a gasp.

"Mirri, Mirri, it's just me," her mother said, hands up and eyes wide. Dark bags rested beneath her eyes and her usually sleek braid had loose tufts of hair sticking out from the weave.

Mirri's eyes stung. "Mother? How did you get here?"

"I have a few loyal to me in the castle yet. They told me where Urramach had taken you when the insurrection began."

"But..." Mirri shook her head, certain her mother did not care. How could she after all she had done both to Mirri and Maron?

"We must go." Her mother grabbed Mirri's wrist.

She flinched, the skin on her arm raw and angry. "Where?"

"Out of the castle. Into hiding. Urramach is rounding up those loyal to you, claiming he's gathering support."

Clammy sweat clung to Mirri's neck and hands, thickening with every skip of her heart and drop of her stomach. "What do you mean *claiming*?"

Her mother dragged her to the door she had left open wide. "I don't know. If he thinks he can be with you, he might very well be strengthening a coalition of support for your return to rule. But if he finds you are no longer useful to him... he may be planning a massacre."

"My people..." Mirri said, tripping out of the room as another daze threatened to settle in a fog over her mind. "Father would never allow it," she said, regretting her decision to lock him up earlier. "We must let him out of the dungeon. He can stop this."

Her mother scoffed. "Your father was dragged away like a lunatic, raving against *you*, and has now disappeared. He is not your friend in this, Mirri."

"Then what am I to do?"

"Run."

Her mother yanked her behind the very curtains she used to hide in with Urramach so two wild-eyed guards could pass by. Mirri wanted to reach out to them, to command their loyalty and ask what was going on, but if what her mother said was true, she didn't know who she could trust, and she didn't have the heart to burn all those who stood against her. What if it was her entire kingdom? Would her own soldiers turn on her when she had done everything she could to serve and honor her people because they were worried about her Fire Mate's blood?

Izkander was right. She exhaled sharply. The whole thing was absurd. The Origin wanted its people to survive, not to kill each other. And certainly not over something they couldn't control. And if Izkander was here... if he had brought the Rukh and planned on speaking to the Flame... maybe she could get there first. Speak to the Flame not on her behalf, but on behalf of her people. She could convince Izkander to stay with her, couldn't she? If she begged. If she promised to let him leave. If she promised to be good. Or to not be, whichever he wanted. To save her people. Because he had a good heart.

"I must get to the Origin," Mirri said, tugging on her mother, so she spun around. "I must speak with the Flame."

Her mother pursed her lips, worry creasing the corners of her startled eyes. "They will be expecting that now that the Rukh flies. It is possible your father heads there even now. Or Urramach if he has figured out where the entrance lay hidden."

The thought of either of them defiling the Origin sent a shudder down Mirri's back and into the tattoo on the bottom of her foot. "Then we must hurry."

Her mother searched her eyes, then nodded. "Come."

They broke into a sprint, the pain in her wrist waxing and waning as the Rukh—the Wisdom of the Flame and its connection to Izkander—flew in circles overhead.

She overtook her mother, eager to get out of the castle and to the Origin, but as she turned a sharp corner, she hit a wall.

Not a wall.

She fell back, head pounding. Then looked up at a pressed green uniform, gold stripes tapering to the bottom and topped with coppery gold hair tied with a matching ribbon.

"Urramach," she gasped in horror and clambered back to her feet.

"Mirri?" Shock filled his eyes before he gained control of them.

The black handprint on his cheek had faded to a tender, bright red. A hint of glowing blue indicated the use of a minor healing potion they had stolen from the djinn. A healing potion kept in the righ's private stash. His brows dipped in the same look of worry he had fed her since the day her brother died as if nothing had happened between them. As if he hadn't locked her in a room and threatened her with a century of cruel loneliness. How little effect she had on his ambitions, even when she tried.

"What are you doing out here?" he asked. "It isn't safe."

She had at least three scathing retorts, but she swallowed them like the obedient little righ her father raised her to be. If her mother was right, how she responded to Urramach would mean the difference between a slaughter and a celebration. And while the second made her stomach cringe with implications, it was her job to protect her people at all costs. Love was never something a righ could afford, and she had been prepared to set it aside her whole life to be a good leader. That was until she met Izkander and found she was discontent to be away from his arms and his happy green eyes.

Discontent. *Discontent.*

Even thinking the word felt liberating. She *was* discontent with her life for as long as Izkander had not been a part of it. But she could hide it now for the sake of her people and pretend she wasn't. She could swallow the acrid bile that filled her mouth every time she looked at Urramach and play nice long enough to save her people. To find a way to get to the Origin. She had been pretending her whole life, anyway.

Mirri bit the back of her tongue. The fire in her wrist ebbed with another pass of the Rukh. She stretched her face in a look of alarm and prayed Urramach's hubris would be enough.

"Urramach. You're here," she flung herself forward, then lost her nerve. Instead of attacking, she wrapped her arms tightly around his straight back and narrow chest.

Mirri held him like that, face pressed against the familiar scent of Fyre's rolling hills as she tried to come up with an excuse for why her mother was with her. But her mother never stumbled around the corner. Even as Urramach's hands crawled their way around her back and brushed the bare skin of her back between her armor. Maybe her mother had had the good sense to hide? A small amount of relief loosened the muscles in Mirri's neck as a horrid urge to itch overtook her entire body.

"You were right, the castle isn't safe." She kept her face pressed to his uniform and spoke in a muffled voice. "A group of soldiers found me in your room. They tried to kill me, and I barely escaped."

"Soldiers?" Urramach's arms stiffened briefly before scooping her closer, like he was gathering armfuls of hay and bringing them into the safety of the barn. "I thought I had gathered them all up..." He pulled away and pressed both his hands to her cheek, brushing a bit of hair from her forehead. "I'm so sorry. My only desire is to keep you safe, and I have failed."

She bit back the poison on her tongue and widened her eyes with a tremble of her lips. "I was so frightened. Please, don't make me go back."

He pulled her in for another hug, resting his chin on top of her head. "There, there, Mirri. I'll keep you safe."

It took every slap her father had ever given her for reacting poorly to suppress the shiver Urramach's words sent down her spine.

"What are we going to do?" she asked, forcing her fingers to cling to his shirt. "My own soldiers are trying to kill me. What happened? Why are they doing this?"

He pulled her to the side of his chest and walked her down the hallway away from his room. Thank Marduk for that.

"That half-djinn, Izkander, challenged your father to a duel the other day and humiliated him in front of his people. In retaliation, the Fa Chomhair Righ has decided that you are not fit to rule the kingdom and insists he remains in charge."

"And when he dies, who would take over then?"

"I don't think he cares," Urramach said, leading her the fastest way to the throne room. "That is why we must secure your rule and stamp out all the opposition."

She tried to pull away to analyze his face, but he yanked her back to his side. She would not try that again. Nothing to risk angering him when so much hung in the balance. When there was so much she didn't know.

"What do you mean stamp out the opposition?"

"Mirri," he took on that pitying tone again. "Don't you worry. I will make the hard calls. All I need from you is your loyalty."

"*What?*" She broke her mask.

He wanted *her* loyalty? That *no breugach dìleas*. She bit her tongue and closed an eye, waiting to see how he reacted.

He chuckled, setting her nerves on fire. "I know how it sounds. And it is only for a short time, Mirri."

They reached the ornately decorated throne room doors with their flowers of cast iron and buds of gold. The fountain of lava spurtled and churned, aggravated into movement by her presence. She could feel the Origin there, thrumming and bubbling, waiting to see what happened. He spun her to face him, placing his hands on both her shoulders with far more weight than necessary. Her red handprint caught the shadows of the sconce nearby, making it look as if it were still on fire.

"I just mean, I need you to trust me."

Mirri squashed the curl forming on her lips. "In what?"

"We are going to go in front of the contingent of those loyal to you and tell them you and I are to be Fire Mates."

"You and I can't be Fire Mates." She twisted her glare into a look of sorrow.

"We can."

"We can't."

"The Flame blesses us, Mirri." Urramach smiled wide, too much hope in his wheat-colored eyes. "The Rukh flies. We will announce our intention to entreat the Flame and secure a more favorable Union for the good of Fyre. Our Union will keep those content with you content, and the end of Izkander Green Eyes will help sway the favor of those who are discontent with the power he has seized."

Again, she had to swallow her first several retorts. Maybe going along with the plan wasn't the worst idea. If she played nice, she would have a chance to see which of her council members were loyal and also have an opportunity to get close to the Flame. It sounded like Urramach didn't know where the Origin lay hidden, or he would have already gone himself. He needed her to get there. And she needed him to not kill her people while she figured out a plan. If Izkander headed to the Origin, too... maybe the will of Marduk would prevail. Or maybe she would die and the line of Marduk would end with her, just as the Flame had told her mother.

The second thought singed her through with acid, and she pressed a hand to her stomach. Thinking of Izkander and closing her eyes, she said, "I will plead our case before the Flame and do what is best for my people."

Urramach's hands cupped her cheeks, and his lips brushed hers, unwelcome and cold as ever. Her hand lit with fire, but she clenched it at her side. When he pulled back, he scooped up her arm and tucked it into his. "You make me the happiest man in the world today, Mirri."

"Yes."

"I knew from the moment I gave you the token before the Drakonte Ride you would be mine and I yours. It is the Flame's will."

"Yes," she said again.

His reminder of the token killed the last of anything good she ever remembered of him. She extinguished the Flame, placed her other hand on his arm, and squeezed the rough fabric of his uniform.

Urramach had known Maron wasn't a true descendant. Which meant he knew when he kissed her it wouldn't hurt her because the laws were all false, not because of some different interpretation or loophole.

Urramach knew all along, just as her mother had, that all the rules and traditions that oppressed and hurt her were false. He had chosen to keep her bound.

She pushed her chin up high and let the fire burn freely in her eyes. They opened the door to the throne room and stepped in amongst anxious and staring eyes.

She would be free of Urramach. Of the arbitrary laws that controlled her life. Of anyone who stood in her way. And she would make them all burn.

CHAPTER THIRTY-SEVEN

Izkander

Izkander dodged. The top of the old righ's blade scraped against the wall. A foot hit the back of his knee, and he stumbled. The fire around his wrists burned like lava, stealing strength from his muscles. Fa Chomhair swung from overhead, looking to split his skull like a melon.

Izkander caught the hilt in both hands. The force drove him to his knees. He kept his elbows locked. But the pain was driving him down. The old righ had the strength of a drakonte. He hissed and spat, foaming at the mouth as red eyes flickered.

"Fa Chomhair," a man called.

Izkander turned to see a contingent of soldiers at the end of the hall, the familiar face of General Musharraf at the head. He gave an order, and soldiers advanced. Izkander's strength gave way. He relinquished the sword and fell to his knees, trembling with pain and eyes blurry. He couldn't fight anymore.

Fa Chomhair fought the oncoming soldiers with all his might but was soon overcome by sheer numbers. A tall guard wrenched the sword from the old righ's hands, another restrained him, and the two dragged him off down the hall.

Izkander folded over his wrists, hissing in pain. Hands snatched his arms and ripped him to his feet.

"We must get him to Ah-nis Na Righ," said the general, sheathing his sword. He put a hand to his chest and bowed. "Your Highness, Councilman Urramach is leading an insurrection. He has vowed to have you executed and to unlawfully bind himself to the Ah-nis Na Righ. He claims the Righ supports him and their Union will take place. He refuses to wait until the next Drakonte Ride."

The man said the last sentence like that was the part Izkander ought to be upset about. Izkander wanted to snark, but the pain stole everything from him, including his wit.

The general grabbed Izkander's sword from where it lay on the ground and returned it to the scabbard on his hip. Two soldiers draped his arms over their shoulders and dragged him down the corridor.

He wished his stupid hands would just fall off to be rid of the pain. They continued through several twists and down several straightaways until they came into a massive domed antechamber draped in gold and red banners. A large doorway led into a packed courtroom and a familiar voice echoed in the acoustics—as smooth and honest as a shadow.

Urramach.

Dozens of men in plain dress stood guard at the door. When they saw Izkander and the group of soldiers surrounding him, they gave a call of warning and rushed them with drawn swords.

The searing pain in his wrists had faded to a dull burn the closer they drew to the throne room. Mirri was inside. He could feel her.

With a deep breath and a hard shake of his head, Izkander drew the gun from his hip. The antechamber was just big enough to justify it. Besides, he didn't want to leave any questions as to who was out here causing trouble.

He set a fire to the wick, leveled the barrel, and fired into the oncoming soldiers. Five shots left five men on the ground and a sixth pressed against the wall, gripping a wounded thigh. Screams ripped through the throne room. Swords drawn, the general and his soldiers ripped into the remaining guards. Familiar faces filled the hall—councilmen, nobles, courtiers, and Allah only knew.

The flood of bodies knocked him back, threatening to pull him downstream. He summoned a ball of fire in each hand and threw them in succession at the ceiling. Great flashes of orange exploded when they hit. The crowd screamed and scattered.

Izkander stooped, tightened his shoulders, put out his elbows, and plunged into the crowd. Taking advantage of the confusion, he cut through the frenzy like an iron plow, leaving aching bellies and bruised arms in his wake.

He burst into the throne room and turned his gaze up to the platform.

Mirri stood before the throne with burn marks on her wrists and a twist of pain in her expression that hurt nearly as much as the searing flames had. At her side was Urramach. The piss-eyed, ponytail-wielding sack of crap was looking better than usual on account of a nasty black burn on his cheek and a look of utter fury on his face.

Across the chaos, his gaze met Mirri's. Her eyes widened, sparkling rubies from that distance, and her lips parted. She took a step towards him, and Urramach snatched her arm.

"Kill the traitor," Urramach bellowed. "He's come to kill the righ."

Izkander drew his sword and stalked forward. "I am going to tell you this one time before things get downright brutal up in here. Get your creepy, frosty hands off of my girl."

"*Your girl?*" Urramach's face reddened around the burn on his cheek. "She is the Ah-nis Na Righ, ruler of Fyre, and made for me. *I* made her what she is. And it was *I* who stood painstakingly by her side while she became something more than a sack of pitiful bones and breasts."

"Urramach..." Mirri winced and shrunk, almost as if a physical pall hung over her head.

"Quiet, my love," he snapped.

Izkander chuckled and mimed wiping a tear. "I always knew you were charming. Honestly, I can feel my clothes melting off."

The line of soldiers at his back broke. Izkander turned to see dozens of Urramach's men filtering into the room. General Musharraf's troops engaged them, but their true target was clear.

Izkander caught a strike leveled at his head and spun it out, turning in time to parry a chop to his thigh.

"Mirri, hold on," he called, trying to glance back at her. The chamber flooded with swordsmen all out for his blood. "I'm coming."

If he'd known he was walking into a war, he would have brought his old man, and Yamina, and Idris, and maybe even Javier so long as it wasn't bread day. For now, he was on his own. Even with loyal soldiers fighting on his side, he was outnumbered ten to one. And say what he might about Fyran soldiers, they were decent swordsmen every one—a disturbing portion far better—all with metal swords as strong as his own.

"Izkander!" he heard Mirri cry.

A guttural yelp from Urramach followed.

Izkander blasted the floor in front of him with orange fire, giving him a moment to glance in the direction of her voice. She had both her hands wrapped around the hilt of Urramach's sword, where it hung still in its sheath. One of the pig's hands wrenched at hers to keep her from pulling it, and the other wrapped itself in the snarls of her hair.

The fire-blasted soldiers pooled in the space he'd made, weapons held to strike. Izkander reached into the pouch at his hip, snatched out one of Fajar's feathers, and threw it down. Heat and smoke wrapped around him, shifting his body from one spot to the next with no emptiness between.

He popped into existence at Mirri's back and punched Urramach in the face. She managed to unsheathe the sword as he fell back, whipping it across her body and down to her side in three quick *zings*. Then, she turned to him.

"We need to go to the Origin."

He nodded and snatched out his last feather, then threw it down. He filled his brain with thoughts of the little turquoise and orange hatchlings and wavy heat. The haze overtook them, and when he opened his eyes, he gazed at the waterfall of lava Mirri had dipped her hands in the other night.

He turned to her, brow furrowing. "Are you okay?"

"No." She stepped back, running her fingers through her hair like a comb and wincing all the while. Her hands gave up and dropped to her side, the flow of lava glistening in her red eyes. "No."

His hands itched to reach for her. Even that small distance between them caused the bond on his wrist to ache with a dull pain that matched the uncertainty in his heart.

Had he screwed up again?

"What can I do?" he asked.

She closed her eyes and took a slow, deep inhale. When she opened her eyes again, steady flickers of fire spread from her irises like sun rays. "I need you to not be mad."

"Done." He smiled weakly. "Anything else?"

Mirri squared her shoulders to him and tilted her chin like she always did when she felt the matter was serious. "I know you brought the Rukh because you want to be free, but I beg, as the Righ of Fyre and your... your Fire Mate, that you let me use our plea for another matter entirely." She knelt before him on one knee, stabbing Urramach's sword into the ash, and dropped her head. "Please."

His heart pinched, ice growing like needles under his skin. The heat of the lava ate at his lungs. "Okay."

"And..." She bowed lower. "I know I don't deserve your loyalty and that you don't want me, but I need you to help me. Even if what I ask sounds howl-at-the-moon crazy.

"Why do you think I don't want you? What does a man have to do? You're the one who..." He bit his tongue and pressed a hand over his eyes. "I'm here, Mirri. I want you to have what you want. Tell me what you need me to do, and it's done."

She tilted her chin to look up at him, the fire of her hair receding from her face. "I thought... because the Rukh flies..." Pink colored her cheeks and the bridge of her nose. "That you came to the castle to fetch me because you didn't know the way."

He scoffed. "You think I stormed a castle by myself so that I could break up with you?" His mouth hung open, and he blinked a lot. "I brought Fajar because I thought you might... insist. And I didn't want to be a presumptuous prick. I *don't* want to be a presumptuous prick. Why does that get me in so much trouble?"

Her eyes widened briefly before crinkling into half-moons. She giggled. "I don't think that's what gets you into trouble."

His shoulders slumped, arms hanging limp at his sides. "I am at a loss, pretty girl."

"Your face." She stood and brushed the back of her fingers against his jaw. "And your inability to ignore injustice."

Her touch caught his skin like sparks, hot shivers racing through his veins. He watched her eyes, nervous to blink because he might miss a unique flicker that would never come again.

"I love you." He tried to swallow the lump in his throat. "You should know that. Whatever you decide you want to do with me. I just want you to know that."

"I love you, too," she said, eyes softening. "And I want to do unspeakable things to you."

Izkander grinned, his cares flooding away so quickly he felt dizzy. She loved him, and that meant everything else was going to be okay.

"First... I want you to walk with me." She laced her hands with his and turned him toward the wall of lava. "Through there."

He coughed out a noise akin to a nervous laugh. "You know, you don't have to kill me. A simple *no thank you* will do the trick."

She bit her lip, still smiling, though an anxiousness shadowed her face. "I don't want to kill you. I want—" She straightened her shoulders once more. "To listen to you. I want to free Fyre."

He looked up at her eyes. His heart beat in places he'd never known were possible—the tip of his nose, his eyelids. His hands grew clammy in her grip. Every vertebra tightened like drying concrete.

He closed his eyes and let out a sharp exhale. So this was what it was like to be scared all your flesh was about to melt off.

Tightening his fingers around hers, he lifted his gaze. "Should I take my shoes off?"

A beautiful brightness washed over her face. "It would be the right and sacred thing for Wisdom to do."

"Wisdom? That's me?" He sighed from the pit of his soul as he dropped to a knee to pull off his boots. "Oh, boy. I'm gonna die."

Mirri laughed and shook her head. "You are not going to die. You and I are going to live."

CHAPTER THIRTY-EIGHT

MIRRI

HER HEART WAS FULL to bursting as she watched him tug off his shoes. It was a small thing, or at least she imagined it would look that way to people outside of Fyre. But it meant everything. That he had come back, Rukh in tow because of his ridiculous nobility. That he brought her to the Origin when she asked without a second thought. That he loved her...

And now that he was willing to walk through a sheet of lava because she asked him to. A large part of her felt the same way as he looked. Nervous. Unsure. But as she stood before her people with Urramach, about to do what he wanted and suppress how she felt, she realized what the missing piece of her was.

Belief. In herself.

After everything that had happened, she felt certain she had the answer. And though it sounded crazy, the fact that Izkander believed in her too, gave her wings.

She extended a hand to help him up. "Don't worry, I won't let you get too hot. I'm saving that for our Eve of Fire."

He looked at her hand and smirked before taking it and pulling himself to his feet. His toes curled in the ash. "Just in case I die..." He laid a hand on her cheek and kissed her softly. He pulled back and looked into her eyes, then gave a little nod before squaring himself to the lava flow.

Mirri wrapped her fingers tightly in his. "I figured it out when my councilmen were asking me to kill you." She couldn't help a teasing grin. "That you have the Flame in you, too."

He flicked his gaze sideways at her. "I do?"

"Mhm." She slipped a hand up under his shirt and traced the lines of his tattoo, following the brush of fire. "Fajar gave it to you at the same time she gave you this."

His eyes crunched into slits, lines forming between his brows. "Are you trying to say I'm part fire goddess?"

"More Eternal Flame than anything, but... yes?" She scrunched her nose, then shook her head. "It is why our bond worked. It is why I tingle with fire when I touch you. And it is why you are going to walk through the lava with me and not get hurt. So we can return the Wisdom—" She poked his chest. "—The Flame—" She touched her own. "—And the Heart back to the Origin." She held up their intertwined hands. "So Fyre can be free."

He squeezed her fingers. "I trust you."

She took a moment to breathe in his words. Then tugged him toward the lava. "Ready?"

"Come on with it," he growled.

She stepped back into the lava flow, heat pouring over her like a warm shower and splashing off just as easily. When all but the hand that held Izkander's had pulled through, she held her breath. With all the belief in herself she could muster, she tugged his hand. He sucked a hissing breath through his teeth. Like a rock in a stream, the lava parted around his perfect skin, a deep V forming in the flow as he stepped through. Lava ran in rivulets from his hair, his skin, and clothes, burning nothing until it puddled in a cooling, crusty pool at his feet.

She laughed, her heart so full it hurt, and almost threw her arms around him before remembering the solemnity of the place.

His eyes were crunched shut, teeth clenched. He opened them one by one. His grimace eased into a smile, and he let out a loud, "Woo!"

She turned around to where a deep pool of bubbling lava the colors of Fajar's feathers swirled in the center. Altars filled the domed walls around it, built in different materials over different millennia, some rough-hewn and ancient and others newer and cast in sapphires and bronze. One built each time the Rukh flew. Her heart skipped a beat, realizing she brought nothing to offer, then beat twice as fast when she realized there was only ever one thing she could offer, anyway.

She knelt down on both knees in the ash outside the pool where the footprints of her past ancestors still lay undisturbed in the earth. Then patted the ground next to her.

Izkander came to his knees beside her, his eyes and smile both sparkling as he took in the surrounding cavern. She watched him for a degree, loving the joy he found in everything he did. Loving him with all her heart.

Then she turned her eyes back to the pool and touched two fingers to the lava. "*O, lasair shìorraidh mhòr,*" she began in the way her prayers always did. In the supplication of the righ. "A piece of your infinity has returned home to you this day to buoy you up, offer strength, and enhance your Wisdom. In the dawn of your rejuvenation, we, the true descendants of the Flame, come to make a plea before you."

A great warmth settled over them like a blanket left by the fire and set on aching legs. It stung at first, then released the tension in her body one knot at a time. Permission to supplicate. She snuck a peek at Izkander. He watched her, tiny orange flames licking around his pupils in his evergreen irises. The mark on his stomach glowed so brightly, she could see the details of it through his shirt. He glanced down her body then back up to her eyes and licked his bottom lip.

She smiled at him, the skin around her eyes wrinkling softly, then turned back to the Flame. "Through the ever-abounding life and fire given to me through the Flame and the infinite Wisdom and compassion given to Izkander through the Rukh, we ask for the rules and constraints upon the righ and the people of Fyre to be lifted. That discontent be allowed so it may create discourse and foster practices that are best for your people to thrive. And we ask that you forgive the sins of the Mardukians and their corruption of your beautiful power so that they could remain in their own as rulers of Fyre. Wipe the laws clean. Give Fyre a new start. And purify the Marduk line into blood that is merciful and true. The Flame, The Rukh, and The Heart united under Mirri Naga and Izkander Green Eyes and sealed by my body, his wisdom, and our love."

She pressed her forehead to the ash before pushing herself to her feet. Then, she stepped in front of Izkander and turned. With a shy smile and the Flame roaring in her ears, she pulled him to his feet. Piece by piece, she unclasped her gold-plated armor and let it fall, next, the thick drakonte skin she wore beneath, its pearlescent scales shimmering in the soft red glow, and lastly, the slip of her underwear, until she once again stood before him, this time in nothing but her skin.

Izkander's gaze poured over her with eyes that glowed almost as red as hers.

Mirri took a step back, dipping her foot into the pool of lava so it swirled in warm slushes around her ankle. "I love you," she said, swallowing her nerves as the lava swirled thick as honey.

She took another step back. The soothing heat lapped around her calves, gentle waves of heat pushing and pulsing hot against her skin. Every part of her ached for him to join her in the rhythmic beat of her heart and this place. To feel him press against her and fill her with fire.

"I want you." She tugged on his fingers, inviting and pleading as her eyes locked on his and a shiver teased her skin. "Will you help me seal the promise of the Flame with our Union? Our love?"

He stood fixed for a long moment, his bottom lip trembled in a muted smile like a cat watching a bird. Red and green eyes moved from her to the caldera to the jagged ceiling of the cavern. He lifted his arms high and clasped the back of his neck then yanked off his shirt. Walking towards her, he let his belt and weapons fall into the ash with a clank that lifted a soft plume and stepped out of his pants.

Naked, his skin shined like polished bronze and his feather tattoo glowed like the Ardish sun. He reached forward with nervous uncertainty to clasp her arms. He licked his lips, eyes drifting down her bottom before lifting again to her face. "Mirri..." he breathed, hoarse and smokey.

"Please?" She leaned forward and kissed him, soft and delicate. "I need you."

"You have me." He combed his fingers into the hair at the nape of her neck and pulled her back to his lips. His other hand wrapped around her back to press her body flush with his.

Her breath caught, everywhere their skin touched far hotter than the lava they stood in. She grinned, sloppy and unfocused as every brush of his fingertips clouded her mind with tingles and want. Pulling him farther in, she slipped her arms around his neck and stared into the perfect green pools of his eyes.

Being this close, this vulnerable with Izkander brought her a strange and intoxicating sense of power. Like nothing in both the worlds mattered more than this, their Union, and that to her nothing ever would. But even with that strength finding its roots in her blood, a twinge of nervousness made her hands tremble as she ran them down his chest and across his defined abs.

He brushed her skin, his fingers pulsing with ten identical heartbeats. She could feel his stress, the same fluster of nervous excitement that lived in her own body. A sharp shudder raced through him, and a carnal smile overtook his face. He snatched her thighs and picked her up, kissing her fiercely so she could feel the licks of fire mingling in their breath.

She wanted to breathe his name, to have the taste of it on her tongue, but she couldn't. Her lips were occupied. Her tongue busy. She pressed her thighs tight around him, yearning to be closer, closer. He would never be close enough. Then she let her head fall back so he could kiss her neck, her clavicles, her breasts. She sighed with a giggle.

He stepped deeper into the lava, so it licked at their thighs, then rested his forehead against hers as he pressed inside of her. She let out a little gasp and tensed, expecting pain amidst all the tightness, but feeling instead a wave of pleasure without consequences. She stayed tense, then, afraid that if she moved, she would lose the sensation, clinging to his strong shoulders and pressing her fingers into his bronze skin. She remained that way, holding onto him like a boat in the tide as wave after wave brought him back to her. The golden bond on their wrists burned brighter, expanding out in a halo of power and light, growing and growing until it burst when they did.

A shiver raced across her skin and deep down into her belly, and Izkander lowered himself into the heat so that the thick liquid washed her back and shoulders in warmth. She shivered again, resting her cheek against his chest as she watched the last of the golden light fade back to the red of lava.

His breath was heavy, skin dewy with golden sweat. He rested his forehead on her shoulder and nibbled on her neck, whispering little bits of nonsense that were swallowed in the surge of hot wind and churning fire.

His lips brushed her earlobe. "Sorry," he whispered, his breath shuddering with his veins. "I'm excited."

She breathed out a soft smile, enjoying the affection. "Sorry about what?"

"Nevermind." He chuckled weakly and squeezed her tighter. "Just... I can do better."

"I thought it was perfect," she said and kissed his chest. "And I wish I could stay here with you forever."

He ran his fingers through her hair and rolled back his shoulders. "Me too."

She sighed with a little groan. "What are we going to do about the mess in the castle? Even with the blessing of the Flame, at least half the people there want us both dead."

"Huh. I forgot about that." He let his head fall back to gaze at the twisting heat in the dome of the cavern. "Quell the rebellion. Execute some sacks of silver if we have to. Crush them under your delicately turned little heels."

"It's the quelling part I'm concerned about. I want to harm as few of my people as possible, and we barely snapped out of there in time last time. Our generals were surrounded and Urramach—" The name choked out of her throat, and she shuddered.

He sighed heavily, then leaned closer and kissed her neck for a little while before resting his cheek on her shoulder. "That's up to you, pretty girl. Personally, I think we should cut his head off for high treason."

She grinned. "Did you see where I slapped him with the Flame?"

"I was really, really hoping it was you who made such a vast improvement to his face." He sat back, hands still tight around her waist. "I'm sorry I didn't help you more with him. I was trying so hard not to be jealous, and to be decorous. But if I'm honest, I've kind of wished he was dead since the moment I met him."

"That's because you are Wisdom." She tapped the end of his nose. "And I'm sorry I didn't see it sooner." Her playful smile fell. "We've known each other so long, he grew into what he now is without me seeing it. Not until your handsome face showed up."

He smiled softly and ran his fingers over her cheek. "Don't beat yourself up about it. The fact that you're able to trust people and try to see the good in them is a beautiful thing, especially considering your father."

Every relaxed muscle knotted instantly. "He wants to remove me and rule Fyre for another three-hundred-and-fifty years. My own father wants to kill me just like he did Maron." Her lips quivered in a puckered frown as she let herself feel discontent. "Why wasn't I good enough for him after an entire life of obeying, when yours called me daughter simply because you loved me?"

"Because your father is a cruel, power-hungry, murderous lump of *alqarf*, and mine is a good judge of character." He smiled, his eyes tender and laced with wistful silver. "What do you think your rebellious, unappreciative people might think if their glorious queen rode in to quell their revolt on the back of a minor deity?"

A sunny smile spread across her face. She grabbed his cheeks and yanked him in for a hard kiss, then pulled back. "The Wisdom, the Flame, and the Heart. We'll bring them all back to Fyre. You're brilliant." She kissed him again, little pecks all over his nose and forehead, ripples of excitement spreading goosebumps across her skin. "And I've been itching to call the veins of the Flame since I threatened to in Elm. Let's go cause some trouble, Gaol Aig an Righ."

CHAPTER THIRTY-NINE

Izkander

He had never wanted to leave the place, that great churning pit of fire that had scorched and consumed his soul, remaking it as something new. Something almost exactly as it had always been, but brighter. Hotter. Wiser, even. Because now she was in it, woven through him like veins of gold into rock.

They had all the time in both worlds now, the rest of eternity to do every unspeakable thing to one another that his imagination could dream up, and thousands of others he hadn't thought of yet. He tried to quell the twitching inside with promises of a long and largely naked future. His body was usually pretty good about listening to reason and being patient, but it was in rebellion like everything else seemed to be. He didn't want to quell a rebellion—his own or Fyre's—or establish dominance, or even take care of Urramach and Mirri's father for the last time. He just wanted to take her to bed—to their bed—and stay there for days. But their bed was in the castle and the castle was full of discontents.

The thought pushed him on, helping to bring his steaming brain back online. That, and the aurora of a smile she had given him when he suggested riding Fajar. She was his queen and deserved the total loyalty and respect of her people. Nothing less from this moment until eternity.

He was out of feathers, so he had to use his *puffy magic* to bring them from the depths of the caves below Fyre full circle into a small cave in the mountains high above. Another cloudy, blustery day, exactly as it had been the day they met. It seemed like a lifetime ago and mere moments at the same time.

Tightening his hand around Mirri's waist, his eyes scanned the expanse. He called out to Fajar with his mind, beckoning her closer. He could feel her still circling the sky, riding on the currents and warming her belly on the Flame that boiled below. Her cry cut the air, and he felt the wind from her massive wings before the light of her body burst through the clouds.

Fajar landed hard on the cliffside, talons tearing into the rock and crushing it like a child's hands on a fresh loaf of bread. Graceful as she was in the air, she was a beast about her landings. That was when her sheer power was most clearly on display—her size and weight and physical strength could not be denied. She could have snatched an adult drakonte in one talon and dashed its head against a rock before swallowing it whole, and to her, it would have felt like nothing more than breakfast.

Laying a hand on her neck, Izkander ruffled her feathers. The heat and power in her rushed into him like never before, leaving him unsteady on his feet. He clenched his eyes shut and shook his head, then turned to Mirri with a smile. "Up you go."

She gave him a nervous smile, her shoulders shaking in a cute, little shiver. "Hello Fajar," she said and brushed one of the Rukh's feathers before giving her a little kiss.

With a running leap, Mirri scaled Fajar's side and nestled into the soft down of the bird's back, her eyes as bright as stars with fire.

He chuckled and shook his head. "You're a natural." Sighing, he ran a hand over Fajar's chest and gathered another handful of downy feathers, loose from her recent molt. He shoved all but one in the pouch and looked back up at Mirri. "I'll go warn the people."

Mirri nodded. "Make sure no one is in the throne room or the path that runs through the main gate. It is one of the Flame's largest veins and the one I'm going to pull. And, Izkander?"

"Yeah?"

She folded her arms and leaned against Fajar, laying her head atop them. "I love you."

"I love you too, pretty girl." He winked at her. "You're gonna light them up."

He watched her eyes for a moment longer, then let one of Fajar's feathers fall to the ground. The smoke and flame overtook him like a muted sigh, and his feet touched new ground as soon as they lifted.

He stood in the throne room again. The fight seemed to have cooled down, but as he scanned the combatants, he realized it had not gone well for Mirri's allies. He felt momentarily guilty for having snuck off with her to do what they had done in the Origin, but the feeling struck him with a sense of sacrilege. What they'd done was for the good of the kingdom; he could sense it in the fire in his blood. Nothing was the same as it had been a moment ago.

When Izkander looked down at his bare feet standing on the warm stone, a sense of belonging and duty boiled inside. This was his kingdom, the kingdom of his unborn children. The ancient legacy of Queen Najima. The Origin of Fajar, and drakonte, and Mirri, and everything he loved most in the world.

He cleared his throat so those standing in attendance turned to look at him. Eyes widened, murmurings began, and not a few men drew their swords. A call of *"Gaol Aig an Righ!"* rushed from one end of the room to the other.

Smiling, Izkander laid a hand on the hilt of his sword and took a step forward. "Traitors!" he called in a loud, deep voice. "Traitors, villains, and malcontents. You are the shame of Fyre, the weakness that comes from cooled blood. For years The Origin, your wise and loving creator, has indulged your ignorance and your deficiency. But now you have thrown in your lots with the murderers of honored Prince Maron, namely Fa Chomhair Righ and Councilman Urramach. Now, you all must burn."

The door at the far end of the chamber burst open, and there stood the man himself—Urramach without his perfect posture, without his practiced eyes of dejection. The black handprint on his cheek could have been silver for how it shined to Izkander's eyes, accentuated by the purple swelling of a broken nose. He had on fresh armor, but a hunch in his chest and stoop in his back could only have been caused by Mirri's quick assault.

Snarling, Urramach staggered forward.

"Councilman Urramach," Izkander declared in a loud, strident voice, "you are a disgrace to Fyre, an insult to all men and women of loyalty, and a blight upon your Righ." Izkander yanked his sword from his scabbard. "Fall on your knees and beg forgiveness from the Wisdom of the Eternal Flame, Gaol Aig an Righ, and I shall be merciful. Do it not, and every man and woman standing in this throne room will suffer the full wrath of the Origin and Ah-nis Na Righ, the only true descendent."

"The Wisdom of the Flame separated itself from Fyre when the world began," Urramach sneered loud enough for the room to hear. "And if it came back, it would not be in an idiot like you."

"Bet your life?" Izkander smirked and lifted his gaze to the gathered crowd. "This is your one and only warning to vacate the throne room and the path leading into the castle. There's something outside I think you may all be interested in witnessing."

Nobody moved.

Izkander shrugged. "Suit yourselves." He hopped down from the platform and took a step towards Urramach. He lifted his wrists to eye level and cocked an eyebrow. "Have you noticed anything different about me?"

Fire flared in Urramach's eyes, and his face paled. "You defile the Righ," he spat. "Now she is tainted, her blood thin, and her body worthless. You will die for that." He lifted his sword and lit it with a dim golden flame, nothing like the inferno that roared from Mirri's when they fought the buklak.

Izkander looked at his own sword quizzically and cocked his head. He'd just walked through a wall of lava and lounged in a caldera like it was a hot spring, all based on Mirri's conviction that he had part of the Flame inside of him that burned as bright as her own. If he could do that, surely lighting a sword should be easy.

With a deep breath, he reached down inside of himself. The fire he'd inherited from his mother still burned bright as ever, but it now paled in comparison to something much greater. As did the lilu in his blood. Something greater had flooded in ever since he met Mirri and was first touched by the Eternal Flame. Bright red, boiling, hotter than a bolt of lightning. He didn't speak the language, didn't know the proper words to say to bring it forth. But if he was Wisdom, and he must be because otherwise, everything that had just happened in the Origin would have killed him, then maybe he could rely on his feelings to lead him in the right direction.

He focused on his blood, on the heat that pulsed through his veins like molten rock, and touched a finger to the steel of his blade. An inferno of red fire erupted from his finger, so sudden and bright, that it frightened him. He stumbled back, nearly fumbling his sword. He laughed at himself and looked back up to see a flame as bright and red as Mirri's drakonte eyes dancing on the sword.

He looked past it to Urramach and grinned. "You were saying?"

Urramach released a harsh battle cry, spit flying from his mouth. He swung his sword in rapid, rounding arches, advancing on Izkander in a sprint. Urramach's first strike demolished the last of the happy haze Izkander had carried from the past two hours. He worked to parry the quick assault. Another decent Fyre swordsman. Alright, more than decent. Whatever.

Izkander worked to draw the fight about in a slow circle, turning his back to the door that led outside. A sharp *caw* cut through the air, loud and near enough to make the stone underfoot shiver. Izkander caught Urramach's sword mid-strike, twisting his curved blade to hold it locked. He kicked him in the knee, then turned and darted through the door.

Urramach took up the chase. Izkander knew he would. He hoped the spectators would be interested enough in the fight to do the same, to get out of the line of fire. Even if they all decided to gang up on him, that would be better than watching their flesh melt into puddles.

Once he was outside, he turned his eyes to the overcast sky, searching for a burst of golden fire. A faint outline, growing quickly. Distracted, Urramach's blade swiped across his back, cutting a long, thin line across his shoulder blades. Pain radiated from Izkander's torn skin in streaks. Izkander whipped around and caught a second strike before the blade sliced into his torso.

They exchanged quick swipes, drawing in and pushing out, fixed in place on the cobbled path that led into the palace. Urramach came in with a series of tight slashes—left, right, down, over. Izkander caught an overhanded swing and held it.

Another bright cry from Fajar.

The crowd gasped. Heat like sunshine warmed his skin and the bottoms of his bare feet.

He looked into Urramach's eyes, flickering with tiny golden flames. "Last chance."

Urramach grimaced, eyes darting between Izkander and Fajar. His sword drooped by his side, and he gave a stiff bow. "If I die, you die too."

He sprang forward, blade aimed at Izkander's heart with all the fury of a man who had committed to his demise.

A suicide strike.

Izkander narrowly smacked the blade to one side. Urramach fumbled his sword but kept coming. The force of his body fell against him, knocking Izkander flat on his back. He dropped his sword. Urramach snatched a dagger from his belt and lunged for his throat. Izkander caught his wrist and twisted.

The ground under them rumbled and hissed with steam. Urramach's face contorted, hesitating. Izkander punched his nose. He wrapped his legs around his waist and rolled, coming down on top of him. The ground split with hairline fractures and red-hot lava sprung forth.

Urramach screamed in agony. Izkander drew back. He grabbed Urramach's shoulders and tried to pull him up, but his skin had adhered to the growing heat of the lava, like melted sugar. The cracks opened wider, consuming more skin. The color of the lava intensified, from dull red to bright orange until white-hot flames spurted up around the breaks.

Urramach's hair and clothes caught fire. A shriek tore from his throat, the scrape of metal on porcelain. Izkander scrambled back, teeth clenched. Throat parched. He watched as the flesh sloughed from Urramach's bones, fat dripping away in glistening rivers. Urramach screamed and thrashed. Bone showed under the flesh of his face.

The crack of lava broke open like a dam. A flow as wide as a river burst through, slopping up around what was left of Urramach's body.

The thick, viscous substance slowly swallowed what was left of the flaming body. The screaming finally stopped.

Izkander watched the place he had been, feet fixed while the ground beneath him shifted in gluey waves. He wiped his face and looked to the sky—to Fajar, to Mirri. The land split and liquified around him.

Shaking off his shock, Izkander brought two fingers to his lips and whistled for Squirt.

CHAPTER FORTY

Mirri

Mirri resisted the urge to stand on Fajar's back and laugh as the wind streamed through her hair. Her heart was pounding, electrified once more by the power of the Rukh surging in her veins. Maron would have loved it, too, and the thought lifted her heart just as much as the sacred bird whose sinewy muscles moved beneath her.

Fajar's massive wingspan made quick work of the distance between the mountains and Fyre's radiant castle, black obsidian catching the light of the moons as they traveled across the sky. She scanned the scene below. People poured out of the front gates, two figures in the lead with swords flashing.

Izkander.

She couldn't help the coy little smile that brushed her lips as she smelled him on her skin. The joy vanished as the face of the other person came into view.

Urramach.

Fajar saw them, too, for she let out an earth-trembling screech, not of fear or anger, but of pure joy and trust that Izkander would triumph. Mirri clung to that hope and let out a cry, releasing her fear and discontent and soaking up Fajar's faith. They swooped down with another screech, the Rukh plummeting in a tight spiral like a tornado of fire spinning toward the ground. The last of the people streaming from the castle burst into full sprints. The wind ran its greedy fingers through her clothes and strands of hair as Fajar leveled out, her wingtips brushing trees and the tops of homes that made up the city of Fyre.

Mirri closed her eyes.

She could easily feel the veins of the Flame pulsing underneath the valley, the main thoroughfare of its lava pouring from the center to the castle. She did stand, now, pulling strength from Fajar as she called to the Flame, the lifeblood of Fyre and the same blood that lived inside her.

The Flame responded with bubbling eagerness, the pulse of each channel waking within her own fingertips and in her limbs. Her feet nestled into Fajar's downy feathers. She raised her hand and scanned the ground once more. Urramach lunged at Izkander beneath the shadow of the Rukh. She inhaled sharply. With a quick pull of her fist, she yanked the waiting lava toward the surface.

A well of molten liquid, red and tacky, swelled through the cracks in the earth as Izkander caught Urramach and flipped him onto his back. Without the Flame rich in his veins, Urramach's body caught afire.

Mirri turned her head away, grateful that Fajar swooped swiftly past. She was glad to see the end of the man who had so haunted her with unwanted advances, but she still ached at the betrayal of his friendship. Incongruous. And wrong. And now gone. She turned her focus forward, calling up the fire beneath Fyre.

A jolt of Fajar's infinite love and belief in Izkander—in her—set Mirri's skin afire with little flickers of dancing blue flames. The earth split open below them, glistening orange streams wavy with the curl of heat. She felt the lifeblood of the Origin in the cracks and pushed the lava, farther and hotter until it reached the castle walls. The solid black blocks were built from the Flame, so they caught alight, too.

Every wall pulsed with little veins of red, webs of life and renewal that climbed the ramparts and lit every brick with a blinding brightness that cut through the snowstorm above. A cyclone of fire dusted the fields around the palace, heating but not burning, and picked up in a roaring flash that shot like a beacon into Qaf's dark sky.

A sign. A warning. To all the lands that drew life from the Origin that Fyre was blessed and right and protected by the Flame.

Mirri nudged Fajar toward the top of the glowing ramparts where she landed with the grinding crumple of crushed stone beneath her glorious talons. To Mirri's surprise, several soldiers waited for her on top. She hesitated, unsure of their loyalties.

Clasped fists hit their chests, and they bowed low before her. The peppered hair of General Riley emerged from the steps behind them, a limp in one leg and dried blood splattered across his jacket. She smiled at him, pouring such warmth into her eyes, the light of her gaze flickered across his skin.

"Ah-nis Na Righ." He nodded solemnly.

"General," she nodded back, brushing by him as he took up his place at her back.

One of Fajar's emanating *caws* shook the stone beneath her feet. The great Rukh ruffled her feathers in a burst of light, and the remaining soldiers on the ramparts stumbled back.

Mirri took courage. There could be no better symbol to her people that she and Izkander were the right than the Flame's Wisdom declaring it from the rooftops, daring anyone to challenge.

"Give me the keys to the dungeon," she clipped and held out her hand.

General Riley stuttered a few times but dutifully complied.

She sent him to gather what troops he could—loyal or not—to the throne room, along with the councilmen and citizens. She wanted them near the frothing fountain of Fyre's blood that bubbled in the center.

Mirri walked the winding steps to face the Fa Chomhair Righ, and though her heart skipped a few beats, her feet didn't falter.

She slapped open the door to the dungeon and marched in, squaring herself in front of her father's cell.

The old righ started when he saw her, then snarled and jumped to his feet.

Mirri didn't wait for him to answer. In one swift movement, she unlocked the door and reached inside. She grabbed her towering father by the front of his armor, her fist alight with the red tendrils of the Flame. The infinite heat singed his beard and lit fear in his eyes. She yanked him out of the cell and dragged him toward the throne room. He stumbled behind her but kept his mouth shut; every misstep or grunt he made only caused her fist to burn brighter.

When she reached the throne room, she kicked the doors open and strode inside, throwing her father to the ground at her feet. He stumbled and fell to his knees at the edge of the roiling pool of lava. Eyes widening, the Fa Chomhair scurried back.

Mirri walked the steps up to the quartz thrones that gleamed in bright fractals of red and orange, casting sparkles along the walls around the room. Izkander burst through the main entrance and jogged into the crowded hall. When his eyes found hers, they both smiled. She slipped her hand into his when he joined her on the steps, then tilted her chin up and addressed her muttering citizens who had gathered uneasily around the fountain in the middle of the tile floor.

She raised her voice and crisped her words so there would be no mistaking her message. "The Flame has blessed the people of Fyre today. It has called Izkander Green Eyes, Gaol Aig an Righ, and true descendant of The Wisdom's chosen people to us and blessed the valley with the cry of the Rukh."

Izkander squeezed her hand, and her own river of warmth spread across her chest. She raised their wrists high.

"Our Union has been sealed and blessed by The Flame as The Heart spoke of in the legends of our people. Today marks the end of the Marduks and the start of something greater. We will no longer be separate pieces of one, discontent and pretending we are not, The Wisdom and The Flame devoid of Heart. The people of Fyre and the people of The Wisdom's Fajar are one, reunited."

Mirri turned to look at Izkander, allowing a tiny crinkle in her nose despite the ogling eyes of her subject. "We need a name," she whispered. "We just did away with my family's, and I'm not sure naming the new line of righ and this people 'ibn Bakr' would be good for your father's ego."

He stared at her with eyes wider than she had ever seen them, his lips pressed into a hard line. He blinked, and the very edges of a laugh escaped through his nostrils. "No. No, it would not."

"So?" She bumped him lightly with her shoulder. "Your Wisdom, and everyone's watching."

He cleared his throat. "Okay. I'm feeling a little put on the spot here, but..." Biting the tip of his tongue, he looked up at the ceiling. He didn't move for an excruciatingly long moment. Then, a smile filled his face, and he rolled his shoulders. "The Mirri. Obviously."

A laugh brushed her throat before she softened it and turned back to her people. "The Gaol Aig an Righ has spoken. Anyone who wishes to express their discontent with the reign of the Mirri may step forward and do so now. Be warned, anyone who chooses to do so through violence will join the traitor Urramach in nourishing the Flame with their blood."

To emphasize her point, she gave the pool of lava of tug so it churned and frothed, but it proved unnecessary. Not a single soul stepped forward to challenge her or Izkander. Her father, the defunct Fa Chomhair Righ remained face down on the stone, and those who had remained loyal to her throughout the unrest took up a ringing cheer.

Mirri breathed a sigh of relief and giggled as Izkander twirled her into his arms. "You were magnificent, Green Eyes."

He stared at her with an open-mouthed smile and shook his head slowly. "You are a fire goddess."

"Oh yeah?" She pressed a hand to his cheek and indulged in a lingering kiss. "Then why am I so nervous?"

"Nervous?" he scoffed. "Are you crazy? We could take over the world. Not that I'm saying we should, but we *could*. I mean, *you* could. Really, I'd just be along for the ride."

Mirri looped her fingers into his collar and pulled him closer. "I seem to recollect being along for the ride not too long ago while you took over my world. And there are far harder things to conquer than Qaf."

He chuckled and bit his lip. "Do you have your sights set on the heavens?" He glanced up at the ceiling. "I hear stars are pretty tough, but I'm here for it."

"Just the clouds." She smiled sweetly. "One specific cloud in Ard. And the mama drakonte who lives on it that happens to have a token of approval I'm determined to get."

He dipped his head to one side, then wrapped some fabric over his hand and reached into his pocket. "I forgot to mention that she gave me this, didn't I?" he said, holding the gold coin out to her.

A wide smile broke across her face. "A little bit, Gaol Aig an Righ."

"Yeah. I think Umi kind of likes you, in spite of herself..." He bit his lip. "And I also begged."

"It was mostly the begging, wasn't it?" She raised a brow with a pucker of her lips.

"How could a fire goddess be scared of my mother?" He tapped the tip of her nose. "That is not going to do anything good for *her* ego."

"I guess I'll just have to consign myself to my inevitable fate."

He wrinkled his nose. "That doesn't sound good."

"I'd say it's better than good. Maybe even awesome." She wrapped her arms around his waist and pulled herself closer, savoring the smell of fire and spring. "Because for the first time in my entire life, I'm actually content."

Thank you for joining us on this escape! Please hop online and leave a review on Amazon and Goodreads. A star review is better than no review, a paragraph review is better than that, and a review with a paragraph AND your picture with the book is the best! Five stars means you liked the book and you're excited to read the next one!

ANY review helps the authors keep bringing you new adventures in Qaf! We're releasing new and exclusive content on www.eightmoonspublishing.com ALL THE TIME! Join us at the Community Fire!

GLOSSARY OF TERMS

Fyran Gaelic

Ah-nis na righ: The Now Ruler

Astar Nathair: Swift Snake, a breed of drakonte in Fyre that is known for its agility and speed.

Athair: Father

Bana-Phrionnsa : Princess

Beannaichidh Marduk thu: Marduk bless you

Bheil thu toilichte: Are you content?

Bòidheach: Beautiful

Boireannach grànda: Ugly woman

Cuidich mi: Save me

Daingead: Damn it

Fa Chomhair Righ: The Old Ruler

Fa Chomhair Subsidiary Ban-Righ: Subsidiary Ruler

Fad-Turas Astar Nathair: Long-Journey Swift Snakes. A breed of drakonte in Fyre that is specially trained for long journeys at a break-neck pace. They can travel across Qaf in 2 days without stopping, but then require a week to recuperate before doing so again.

Gaol aig An Righ: Love of the Righ

Gealach foghair: Harvest moon

Gu forneartach: Violently

Mac-cèile ùr: New son in law

Marduk beannaich e: Marduk, bless him

Marduk beannaich i: Marduk, bless her

Marduk sàbhail i: Marduk, save me

Marduk thoir maitheanas dhomh: Marduk, forgive me

Miltean: Thousands (of unit of measurement for distance)

Mìorbhuileach: Wonderful

Moladh Marduk: Praise Marduk

No breugach dìleas: Faithless liar

O, lasair shìorraidh mhòr: Oh great Eternal Flame

Peacach: Outcast sinner

Prionnsa: Prince

Ri Tichd: Future

Susbaint ann an cadal: Be content in sleep

Tha mi a 'tabhann ìobairt: I offer a sacrifice

Thig dheth: Get off!

Thoir matheanas dhi, Marduk: Marduk, please forgive her

Thug Marduk mathanas dhut: Marduk, forgive me

Qafian Arabic

Abn akhti: My nephew

Abnataya: Daughter in law

Agha: Nobleman

Al'ama: Blindness (damn)

Aleamat: Aunt

Aleamu: Uncle

Alhadhar: En guarde

Alkalba: Bitch

Bihaqi aljahima: What the hell?

Dajaj: Chicken

Eami: My uncle

Eayan almuhit: Precious baby boy

Farw alqaqim: Ermine

Habibi: My love

Ibn el sharmouta: Son of a whore

Khara, alqarf: Shit

Radfan: Butt

Rahimahullah: May God have mercy on him

Tahanina: Congratulations

Thuebani: My snake

Waqiha: Slut

Spanish

Mijo: My son

No hablo: I don't speak (Spanish)

Que demonios: What demons! (My goodness!)

Sí, por supuesto: Yes, of course

Turkish

Tebrikler: Congratulations

QAFIAN TIME AND THE EIGHT MOONS

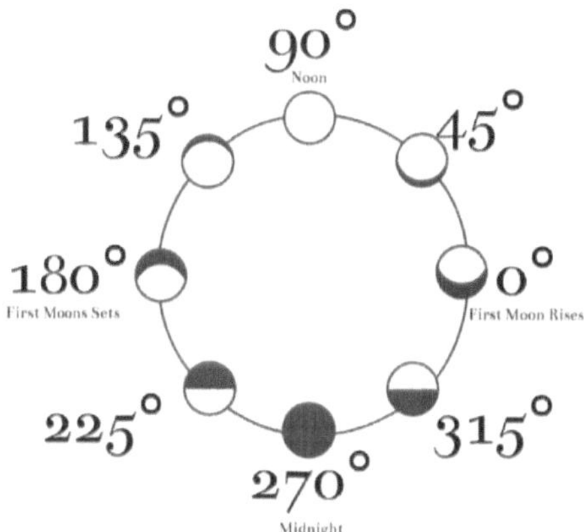

Time is measured in degrees based on the orbit of the First Moon. One degree is equal to roughly four minutes.

The First Moon:

A rough, rusty sphere of copper. The First Moon is the largest and brightest of the eight, taking up a full eighth of the sky when it is full. The path of the First Moon is the Qafian equivalent of 'daylight' and it is their main means of telling time. It comes up in the sharq and sets over the Bahamut Sea.

The Second Moon:

Quick-moving silver moon that passes through the sky about ten and half times every 360 degrees. This moon follows the first moon, rising sharq and setting bahamut.

The Third Moon:

Pale pink, this moon crosses the sky perpendicular to the first moon, bouncing back and forth as it chases the swish of the Bahamut's tail. It rises janu'ub/gharb to shamaal. It is common lore that the Bahamut's former lover lives on this celestial body, pulling and yearning for its true love and creating the Qafian tides. The position of the third moon is preferred for telling time because it is always visible except for when it dips behind each horizon.

The Fourth Moon (Lover's Moon):

A dim yellow, this moon is nearly impossible to see when the First Moon is out and is sometimes called the "night moon". It only shines brightly during Qaf's *night*. It is often referred to when saying people are up to no good because only criminals, ne'er do wells, and lovers stay up late enough to see the Fourth Moon.

This moon passes twice for every single pass of the First Moon, once during Qaf's day unseen, then once through Qaf's night when visible. This moon rises sharq/shamaal to bahamut/shamaal.

The Fifth Moon (Witch's Moon):

The witch's moon of soft green that passes through the sky five times, following the Five Winds and crossing the sky 3 hours (or Qaf's equivalent of 45 degrees) at a time (with 3 hours to pass over to the other side beneath Qaf). It starts sharq and crosses to bahamut, then rises in janu'ub and sets shamaal, then rises gharb and sets sharq, then inverts and rises bahamut and sets janu'ub, then rises shamaal and sets gharb, then rises sharq and sets bahamut like it started. This follows a 27 hour (405 degree)/27 day pentagon cycle and is difficult to track. It is the fortune teller's moon as they track its erratic behavior through the heavens and is often associated with Saqueia and the 5 Winds.

The Sixth Moon:

A soft-white moon that crosses the sky three times, two hours after the rise of the First Moon, four hours after midday, and at midnight. It travels from janu'ub to shamaal on each pass. It is the easiest moon to tell time by, has a medium heat, and most resembles Ard's moon.

The Seventh Moon (Shadow Moon):

This moon appears in odd years as a black circle in the sky that blots out the stars but does not give off any of its own light or heat. It takes an entire year to pass over the sky, and then is gone for an entire year. The measurement of Qaf's year and the seasons are determined by the movements of this moon.

It rises sharq/shamaal and sets gharb, dividing the upper and lower continents. It separates them but also forces them to look toward each other whenever they look at it and reminds them they share Qaf. Wars take place more often in the year this moon is hidden. It is also believed by some that it gives off no heat or light because it is the servant of a celestial that is dead or away or because the celestial they serve is.

The Eighth Moon:

A rare bright blue moon that only rises once every thirteen years—The Festival of the Eighth Moon. It rises janu'ub and sets bahamut/shamaal, rising directly behind Fyre. Every 130 years the appearance of the eighth moon will coincide with every other moon being visible in the sky. This is the "Festival of the Eight Moons," Qaf's most important holiday as it only comes once in most djinn's lifetimes.

It is the warmest moon, and Fyrans believe it serves the Origin, gaining its power from beneath Qaf like lava and only appearing rarely as a reminder to Qaf that the Origin is equal in power to the Bahamut, Celestials, and other minor deities.

The Moonless Night:

Every fourteen cycles of the First Moon comes The Moonless Night, when all of the Eight Moons of Qaf are hidden beyond the horizon at once and the Seventh Moon is in a shadow year. During this time, all heat is sucked from the land and the stars shine their brightest. It does not last the whole night.

GUIDE TO DJINN EYE COLORS

Humans read facial expressions; djinn read emotions in one another's eyes. In moments of high emotion, djinn's eyes flash with regular and predictable colors.

Black: Fear. Mist swirling in the eyes

Blue: Hope, Anticipation

Green: Jealousy, Envy

Purple: Sadness, Grief, Despair

Gold: Happiness, Jo

Pink: Anxiety, Nervousness

Red: Lust. Glows in pupils

Silver: Compassion, Commiseration

White: Shock, Surprise. Lines like lightning

Yellow: Disgust, Disdain, Loathing

Orange: Embarrassment, Humiliation

Copper: Confidence, Bravery, Pride

Brown: Malice

Gray: Awe, Amazement

Eyes are Clear: Honesty, Forthrightness

Eyes flash with bright light: Anger

Colors do not match what is being said: Deceit

About the Authors

Kyro Dean has written over 20 novels. She loves plants and people and spends an inordinate amount of time talking to both. Her works can be found on Kindle Vella, the writing blog VanillaGrass.com, and through Eight Moons Publishing. She lives in Lehi, Utah with her four children.

Laya V Smith's debut novel "The Lumbermill", published by Black Rose Writing, won the 2021 Maxy Award for Best Thriller and was a finalist for 2021 IAN Award for Best Debut Novel. She is the co-founder and co-editor of Eight Moons Publishing, a new boutique press specializing in upmarket romantic fantasy. When she isn't writing or reading, you can usually find her daydreaming, cooking, laughing at stand-up comedy, or playing with her children.